DANI CAPELLO
SHADOWS OF MEN

M.S. IZBICKI

A Highland Entertainment Publication

HIGHLAND ENTERTAINMENT EDITION, 2022

Copyright © 2022 Melissa Izbicki

All rights reserved. No part of this publication may be reproduced, distributed, or transmitted in any form or by any means, including photocopying, recording, or other electronic or mechanical methods, without the prior written permission of the publisher, except in the case of brief quotations embodied in critical reviews and certain other noncommercial uses permitted by copyright law.

ISBN: 979-8-9861786-0-8 (Paperback)
ISBN: 979-8-9861786-1-5 (eBook)

Any references to historical events, real people, or real places are used fictitiously. Names, characters, and places are products of the author's imagination.

Front cover photo by Chris Verde
Back cover photo by Andreas Fickl
Front and back cover design by Melissa Izbicki

www.melissaizbicki.com
www.danicapello.com

Printed in the United States.

To Arian for painstakingly reading every unfinished, way too long, and typo-ridden draft... this book would suck without you.

CONTENT WARNING

Dani Capello Shadows of Men is a gritty coming-of-age story. While much of the book focuses on the budding romance between Dani and Emma, the story does contain content that may be troubling to some readers. Scenes including sexual assault, violence, references to child abuse/pedophilia, drug/alcohol use, racism, homophobia, and depictions/references to death are present in this novel. Readers with sensitivities to these subjects, please take note.

DANI CAPELLO
SHADOWS OF MEN

1
THE PARTY

I was hiding in my room again. Aunt Olivia was on a freaking terror. It was the night of her big fundraising party—guests would be here in an hour—and she was having a total meltdown.

"Drake! Luca!" my aunt shouted for my brother and cousin. I heard a muffled exchange through the door, and my stomach churned. She was giving them shit about something wardrobe related. Pants? Shoes? Socks? I couldn't make out the details… but I knew it was only a matter of time until she worked her way down the hall and unleashed that anxious energy on me.

In a moment of panic (and self-preservation), I grabbed a book, slipped on my black hoodie, and scurried towards the balcony. My bedroom was conveniently located next to a huge oak tree with a sturdy branch perched over the railing, making sneaking out a cinch. I'd been using this mode of escape for years, and this was just the type of occasion where escape was an absolute necessity. If she couldn't find me, she couldn't force me to go to the party. I'd just stroll in once the thing was over, pretending I'd been there the whole evening—a foolproof plan. Obviously.

I gently opened the glass door, slung my foot over the balcony's edge, and began to shimmy my way onto the oversized tree branch.

"Shit." My hoodie was stuck.

"Daniella!"

Fuck.

I could hear her footsteps just down the hall. It was now or never. I gulped and tugged at my sleeve. It was caught on a sharp edge of the wrought iron railing. I struggled with it a few more moments and eventually freed myself with one final tug, causing a small tear in the cuff of the jacket.

"Daniella! For Pete's sake. What are you doing?" she said as she flung open the door.

Trying to get away from you... obviously. I looked up and smiled meekly. "Uhm. Just... hanging out."

She furrowed her brow and crossed her arms. "Well, get down from there. People will be here any minute."

I let out a defeated sigh and allowed my aunt to corral me back into the bedroom. She plucked a dress from my closet—one that I'd definitely never seen before, but this wasn't entirely surprising. My aunt had an annoying habit of constantly shopping on my behalf; attempting to reinvent my wardrobe was basically her life's mission.

"Here, put this on."

I raised an eyebrow, gawking at the outfit. "You can't be serious."

"What?"

I gestured back at the dress as if the mere sight of it should explain everything. "No. Freaking. Way."

"Well, you have to wear something."

"I am wearing something."

Olivia raised an eyebrow. "You know I can't let you dress like that."

"Why not?"

"Because it's a nice party, and nice parties require nice clothes." She grabbed my hoodie and examined the brand-new hole in the cuff. "There are holes in it! What would people think if I let you wear that?"

"That I don't shop at Whores-R-Us?"

"Daniella!"

"What?" I let out an exhausted sigh. We both knew I was exaggerating. The dress wasn't exactly whorish; just red, and frilly, and feminine. *Really* feminine. Which was so not my jam.

"I don't know how you can run your mouth like that when you spent the entire morning in church."

"Because Jesus forgives, and I've really taken that lesson to heart," I smirked.

"I've got half a mind to ground you."

"Do you really want to go on record grounding me for saying *Jesus forgives*? Because I have to say, Olivia, that feels a little blasphemous." I grinned triumphantly.

She folded her arms, obviously displeased. My charming sense of humor was apparently lost on her. "Please, Daniella. Just put on the dress."

"No way!"

"The Maltas will be here any minute. There're still a million things to do. I don't have time to argue with you about this."

"Wait. The Maltas are coming?"

"Apparently." My aunt sighed, letting me know in a glance that she'd only recently found out herself.

"Huh." I mulled over the revelation. Pino Malta is like… my uncle's business partner or something. He's kind of a big deal. He owns like half the real estate in Manhattan. And the fact that he was making the trip all the way out here to our house in Jersey for some lame-o fundraising event… well… that was a big deal. No wonder my aunt was acting more looney than usual.

"So, can we just skip the fight this one time?"

"Fine." I sighed.

"Thank you." My aunt squeezed my shoulder, then promptly left the room.

I put on the dress, but in a final act of defiance, I slipped on a pair of chucks and topped off the ensemble with my black hoodie. Pino Malta or not… I needed to maintain some sense of dignity.

I ambled down the stairs and scanned the foyer below, somewhat amazed at the turnout; there must have been at least a hundred people strolling around our elaborate home. Caterers dressed in crisp white uniforms wandered through the halls, offering hors d'oeuvres and drinks to the guests. I spotted Gino standing in the far corner of the living room. Gino is Uncle Tony's best friend. He's basically an Italian Santa Clause—round, friendly, drunk.

"Hey kid," Gino said as he gave me an affectionate pat on the shoulder.

"Hey," I said with a slight groan.

"What's eatin' you?"

I gestured to the party around us. "This."

"Ah, right…" Gino let out a heavy chuckle and sipped a half-empty glass of whiskey. He ran his hands through his greasy black hair and adjusted a cigar that dangled from the edge of his pursed lips. "What's this one for again?"

I shrugged. "Raising money for the church I think?"

"Right. Well... least it's for a good cause..." Gino took another sip of whiskey and casually peered out the window. After a long moment, he pulled the cigar from his lips and narrowed his eyes.

"What is it?" I asked, suddenly noticing the shift in Gino's formerly jolly behavior. He stepped aside, making room for me next to the sill. I brushed back the white curtain and glanced outside. There were gaudy vehicles lining every inch of the street... which wasn't so unusual given that my aunt had invited nearly every socialite in Newark. But then I saw what Gino was looking at—a pudgy man weaving in and out of the sea of cars. He was taking photos of the license plates and jotting down notes with a pad of paper and a ballpoint pen.

"Pigs," Gino said with an unmistakable tone of disgust.

"What are the feds doing here?" I feigned surprise, but I wasn't really. I knew what they were doing; they were trying to score dirt on Uncle Tony. Stuff like this had been happening for as long as I could remember. I barely noticed it anymore.

"Got no fuckin' respect. Just showin' up here to cause a scene." Gino exhaled a cloud of gray smoke.

"Daniella! What are you wearing?"

My train of thought was suddenly interrupted by my aunt's voice. I turned around and smirked. "The dress. Like you asked."

"I meant this." She grabbed the sleeve of my black zip-up hoodie. "And the shoes. Go back upstairs and change."

"No way!"

"We had a deal."

"You're right, we did. And you only said I had to wear the dress. You didn't say anything about how I accessorized." I grinned. "Be more specific next time."

"You have the insidious mind of a lawyer."

Before I could retaliate, Carlo freakin' Gatti injected himself into the conversation. "Liv, you've outdone yourself. The party is unbelievable," he said with a wide grin; his odious fake smile resembled that of a campaigning politician.

"Carlo!" My aunt smiled wide as she embraced Mr. Gatti with an affectionate hug; her anger with me instantly dissipated at the sight of him. "So glad you could make it."

Fuck.

I shouldn't have been surprised he was here. Carlo was always around. Or at least that's how it felt, ever since I moved in. See, Carlo works with Uncle Tony. He's like a family friend or whatever; Olivia and Tony love the guy. I guess he really "stepped up" after my parents died. My aunt always used to tell me how nice it was that he'd taken a profound interest in me and my brother. But those were my aunt's words, not mine, because really, I think he'd just taken a *profound interest* in me. At least when I was a kid, anyway.

"Wouldn't miss it," Carlo said as he planted a kiss on each of her cheeks.

"Is Cheryl here?" my aunt asked eagerly.

"She's around somewhere. Enzo too." Carlo looked around the room, attempting to spot his wife and son in the sea of guests.

"Little warm for a jacket?" Carlo asked as he placed his hand on my shoulder, where he left it just a little too long. My stomach churned.

"She was just about to change." My aunt furrowed her brow.

"Yeah… I'm going to go do that… or something." I wasn't actually going to change my clothes… but I was relieved to have an excuse to leave the conversation. I felt the blood rush from my cheeks. I doubt if there was an ounce of color left in my complexion. And I suddenly felt incredibly hot.

I walked into the kitchen and spotted an unsupervised tray of champagne flutes; in a desperate attempt to calm my nerves, I chugged an entire glass.

"Dani!" I heard a soft voice call.

I half jumped out of my skin, worried that I was about to be busted for swiping the booze. The last time my aunt caught me drinking, she completely lost it. I was grounded for two months, and she threatened to ship me off to some sort of nunnery.

I turned slowly and let out a sigh of relief when I saw Katie, Gino's six-year-old daughter, standing in the far end of the kitchen.

"What're you doing in here?" I asked with a warm smile as I picked her up and hugged her. I normally hated kids, but it wasn't like that with Katie. She was the closest thing I had to a sister, and I took it upon myself to keep an eye out for her ever since her mom died three years ago from cancer.

"I need a cup," Katie said as she pointed to a shelf that was just out of reach. I laughed and handed her one.

"What do you have there?" I asked, noticing she had something hidden inside the curled-up palm of her hand.

"A snail," she said as she opened her palm and placed the little creature inside of the cup, making a sort of cage for it.

"A snail?" I could hardly contain my laughter. If my aunt saw that insect crawling around her good china, she'd probably have a heart attack.

"Where'd you find a snail?"

"Outside. Duh." She giggled. "Do you know where my dad's at?" Katie asked with wide saucer eyes. "I wanna show him Sebastian. That's his name."

I peered back through the doorway into the foyer. Gino and Carlo were still talking to my aunt. I watched as Carlo handed Gino another tumbler filled to the brim with whiskey. Gino exhaled a cloud of gray smoke and took an impressively large swig from the glass. I couldn't fathom why anyone would willingly pour Gino another drink. It was only 6:00 p.m., and the man's cheeks were already flushed.

"He looks a little busy." And by *busy* I actually meant *drunk*. "Why don't we go outside? I think there're some other kids out there, and I bet they'd like to meet Sebastian."

She agreed, so I picked her up, slung her around my shoulders, and sauntered over to the backyard. I dropped her off, and within a matter of seconds, her new pet creature had made her the most popular kid in the group.

"Nice dress..." A voice suddenly burst into laughter from behind me. I turned around to find my brother, Drake, and our cousin, Luca.

"Shut up." I rolled my eyes. *This* was exactly why I didn't want to wear this stupid thing.

"You look like a girl." Drake paused and glanced down at my shoes. "Sort of."

"I am a girl, Drake."

"Here," Luca said as he tossed a small brown flask towards me.

I unscrewed the top and took a whiff of the liquid contents. The smell of whiskey permeated my lungs. "Thank God," I said as I helped myself to a quick swig.

"You see Becca in there?" Luca asked as he tilted his head, motioning back towards the party.

"Becca Mancini? Mikey's sister?"

"Yeah. She really, you know, *grew up* over the summer," Luca said with a wide grin as he mimed imaginary breasts with his hands. "You guys are friends, right? I'll let you keep the flask if you put in a good word for me."

I rolled my eyes. "No way."

"Ah, c'mon! Why not?"

"Because you're a creep. And I'm not going to lie to her so you can score a date." I paused and looked down at the flask. "But I am going to keep the flask because you're an ass and I hate champagne."

"No way!" he said as he tried to swipe it back.

"Take it, and I'll tell Becca you wet the bed until you were eleven."

"That's not even true!"

"It's how I remember it."

Luca looked at Drake for support. Drake shrugged. "Bro, a good word from Dani wouldn't do shit for you, anyway."

"What? Why not?"

"Because you act like a fucking jerkoff." Drake chuckled and shoved Luca. "Plus, I already called it."

"Fuck off. She wouldn't touch you with a ten-foot pole."

"You wanna put money on that?"

"Deal. Hundred for a blow-job. Two if you fuck."

"God. Stop! I'm right here," I snapped, completely annoyed by their machismo exchange.

"So?" Drake scoffed.

"So? I'm a *girl*. And Becca's my friend. I don't want to hear this."

"You're not a *real* girl. You're my sister."

I rolled my eyes.

"And *my* cousin," Luca chimed in. "You don't count."

"Whatever," I grumbled under my breath as Drake slipped past me and reentered the party.

"Where are you going?" Luca hollered after him.

"To win a bet, dickhole."

"Damnit. Wait up," Luca barked as he followed my brother back into the party.

I wandered inside, grabbed a can of soda, and spotted Uncle Tony in the far corner of the living room. He was surrounded by a small group of men, undoubtedly talking *business*. Work seemed to follow my uncle wherever he went. So did a small entourage. My uncle was rarely, if ever, alone. It was obvious, even when I was a kid, that my uncle wasn't like other people. He was important; a force of nature; everyone knew him; everyone respected him.

"Hey, Dani."

I turned around to find Michael, Becca's older brother. He brushed his shaggy brown hair to the side and adjusted a skinny blue tie.

"Hey, Mikey," I said with a half grunt as I looked back over his shoulder, curiously watching Tony and his entourage.

"So, I heard a vicious rumor that you've got the fun-flask."

"Maybe. What's it worth to you?" I asked, turning my attention to Mikey.

"My gratitude. In perpetuity."

"Not worth it," I said with a smile, noticing suddenly that Mikey was taller than I remembered, like he'd grown three or four inches over the summer. He'd also bulked up and was starting to grow a little stubble on his chin. I hardly recognized him.

"C'mon…" he said in a cheerful whine as he slung his arm around my shoulder.

"Fine." I rolled my eyes playfully and splashed a little booze into his cup.

He took a sip, then looked at me and smiled. "You look nice."

"Uh, thanks." I raised an eyebrow. I couldn't tell if that was sincere flattery or some sort of joke. "I sort of feel like a hooker."

He laughed and glanced down at my feet. "I don't know a lot of hookers that wear chucks."

"How many hookers do you actually know?"

"Three," he said with a sarcastic smirk.

"I sort of wish that was actually true."

"Why's that? You in the market for a streetwalker?"

I laughed. "No, but friends like that would make you infinitely more interesting."

"Ouch." He smiled.

I pulled the flask out from my jacket pocket and unscrewed the lid; it was almost empty. "Here. You can have the last swig. If you want it."

"Hold that thought," Michael said with a wide grin as he sauntered off towards Drake, Luca, and his sister.

I turned around to find Robert, my oldest cousin, staring at me with a big stupid grin.

Robert had spent the two years at a state college but recently dropped out to work for my uncle full time. It was a major point of contention with my aunt, but I was selfishly glad to have him back home. He was nothing like Drake and Luca. He was the sort of older brother-type that you could always depend on for advice, a favor, or to tease you relentlessly about your love life.

"What?" I raised a defensive eyebrow.

"That's an interesting development..." Robert smirked casually as he ran his hands through his thick head of brown hair. He grinned wide, forming two profound dimples on each of his cheeks.

"What's that supposed to mean?"

"You and the frog-boy."

"The frog incident was like two years ago," I said with a slight eye roll.

"Uh-huh." Robert took a sip from his beer. "So what? He's like your boyfriend or something?"

"No. We're just friends."

Robert raised an eyebrow. "Does *he* know that?"

"Of course, he knows that." I glanced over towards the other side of the room; Michael was staring at me with a sort of stupid grin. He waved, and I awkwardly waved back.

Robert burst into laughter.

"Shut up," I groaned as I watched Michael from a distance. By now, he had corralled Drake and Luca towards the bar, and the three of them were working in concert to distract the bartender. I crossed my arms and turned towards Robert. "Shouldn't you be like—off sucking face with Anna or something?"

"She's running late."

"Good luck explaining that to Olivia."

"She's late because she was *volunteering*. At the children's hospital."

"Seriously?"

Robert shrugged. "She's like a psychotic overachiever or something."

"Pretty, charitable, and smart? What's she doing with you?"

Robert half smiled and rolled his eyes. "Hysterical."

"I thought so." I glanced back over at the boys. After a few minutes of highly choreographed work, Luca had successfully stolen several bottles of liquor. When the group had reached a safe distance, Michael smiled and waved in my direction, signaling for me to follow them towards the garage.

"You better go. You don't want to keep your *friend* waiting," Robert said with a chuckle.

"Very funny," I groaned, turned my back to Robert, and followed Michael, Drake, Becca, and Luca out of the living room and into the garage.

We shut the door behind us, and Luca tossed one of the bottles to Becca. She twisted open the cap, took a swig, and passed it to Mikey.

"Anyone got a lighter?" my brother asked as he retrieved a joint from his back pocket.

I raised an eyebrow. "Who'd you swipe that from?"

"E gave it to me."

"E? Like Enzo? Gatti?"

"Yeah," Drake said as Mikey held a lighter to the end of the joint.

"God. I hate that guy. He's such a fucking creep."

"You just think that because you hate his dad." Drake passed the joint to Luca, then slung his arm around Becca, who smiled affectionately. Luca took a hit from the joint and rolled his eyes, knowing full well that he was positioned to lose the bet. "Why do you hate Carlo, anyway?"

My cheeks burned. "Because he's an asshole."

Drake rolled his eyes. "He's not an asshole."

"Whatever. Can we just—like talk about something else?" I snapped.

"Jesus. It was just a question. Chill," Drake snapped back, obviously confused by my harsh tone.

"Dani, you had Mrs. Walsh last year, right? For freshman lit?" Becca asked with a warm smile, attempting to steer the conversation into safer territory.

"Yeah."

"How'd you manage to keep up with the reading? It's insane. We're only like two weeks in, and I'm way behind."

"Yeah, she was kind of tough." I took a sip from the communal bottle and shrugged. "I think I still have my notes from last year. You can borrow them if you want."

"That'd be amazing. Thanks."

"Here," Luca said as he handed me the joint.

I placed it to my lips, sucked in the smoky air, and blew it out. I shrugged and handed it back to him. "I don't see what the big deal is. I don't feel anything."

"That's because you didn't do it right," Drake snapped. "You gotta *inhale.* Suck it down and hold it in your lungs for a long ass fuckin' time. Like this." Drake grabbed the joint from Luca, sucked in the air, and held it inside his lungs for a five-count before releasing the smoke from deep within the cavity of his lungs. "See."

All at once, he burst into a coughing fit. I raised an eyebrow. "You're not exactly making it look appealing, Drake."

Suddenly, the door flew open. Drake stashed the booze behind our uncle's pitch-black SUV, while Becca promptly extinguished the joint.

Tony looked at my brother, then at the poorly hidden bottle of whiskey. He knew exactly what was going on but clearly didn't have the time or the patience to deal with it.

"Hey!" my uncle barked at the lot of us. "Any of you seen Robert?"

"He was just inside." I shrugged.

"Well, he ain't now."

"Maybe he's with Anna…" Luca made a cylindrical shape with his fingers, brought his hand to his mouth, and made an obscene gesture.

"Ah, for Christ's sake!" my uncle half yelled. "Go find him, would you? Pino wants to meet him."

"Who's Pino?" Becca asked curiously.

"Pino Malta. He's like this big-wig business guy type."

"That's the understatement of the year," Drake scoffed. "The guy's infamous. And a total gangster."

"Drake, he's like 300 years old." I rolled my eyes.

"So?"

"So—it's kind of hard to run around doing gangster stuff when you can barely walk."

"You don't know shit, Dani. He's got like a literal army of goons to do his dirty work!" My brother turned towards Becca. "He's a total badass. C'mon. I'll introduce you."

"Cool!" Becca's eyes widened with anticipation.

I rolled my eyes as the group sauntered out of the garage to find Robert and the infamous Pino Malta.

I turned towards Mikey. "You know my brother's trying to fuck your sister. Right?"

He took a swig of whiskey and laughed. "I know."

"And you're ok with that?"

He shrugged. "It's her life. If she likes him, whatever. It's not really any of my business."

"Well, he's a jerk-faced moron. You should make it your business."

Mikey laughed. "I know he's your brother and so you're obligated to think he's a *jerk-faced moron*, but he's not really."

I rolled my eyes.

"Just last week—he helped me on our pre-calc quiz. I got a ninety-three."

"What do you mean *helped*?" I raised a skeptical eyebrow.

Mikey shrugged. "Cut me a deal. Only charged me fifty bucks for the answers."

"You got scammed." I laughed and took a sip of whiskey.

"What? Why?"

"Cuz he got the answers from me for thirty."

"What?!"

I laughed.

"Alright, then. What if you help me on the next one?" He smiled.

"Sure. But it'll cost you forty. Drake gets the family discount."

"Counteroffer." He moved closer. "What if I didn't cheat… and you tutored me?"

I furrowed my brow. "Going straight?"

"Just trying to avoid being a jerk-faced moron." He smiled. "How about it? Friday. We'll study for an hour or two, then grab a bite or something after. My treat. You know, as a thank you."

"Sure," I said skeptically. I meant it as a statement, but I think it sounded more like a question. I was completely caught off guard. Did he just ask me out?

I took a sip of the whiskey and noticed Mikey's arm gracefully float behind me, landing finally on the hood of the car. I felt my body freeze. My eyes locked with his. He leaned towards me. He smiled, moved closer, and…

"So, you goin' to share or what?" he asked as he reached out his hand, gesturing to the glass jug.

Right. Obviously. The whiskey.

"Here." I handed him the bottle. My hands slipped against the glass surface, and I realized, suddenly, that my palms were sweating profusely.

"You alright?"

"Fine." I replied with all the poise I could muster. Though I didn't mean it. I thought seriously that I might be losing my mind.

"Good," he said as he casually placed his hand around my shoulder and turned towards me.

What the hell was going on?

I looked up at him. His eyes locked with mine, and he took a small step towards me. He moved in closer, leaned in and—

"Hand me the joint!" Luca shouted as he reentered the garage with Becca and Drake.

"Keep it down, idiot," Drake barked back at Luca.

I half leaped across the car, as if I'd been caught in the act of something far more scandalous than an almost-maybe-not-even-really-half-kiss.

"What's the deal with you two?" Drake asked, obviously picking up on the weird vibe.

"Nothing," I insisted as I took a gargantuan swig of whiskey.

"Damn, Dani," Luca muttered under his breath. "Save some for the rest of us."

I wanted to come back with some snide remark, but when I opened my mouth, I had to stop myself from gagging. I wiped the remnants of whiskey from the corners of my lips and realized almost instantly that I had made a huge mistake. "I'll be right back." I barely managed to say. My head was spinning. I thought I was going to retch right then and there.

"Dani?" Mikey hollered. "Are you ok?"

I couldn't muster the strength to answer. I made a beeline out the back door, then collapsed over the side of a bush and hurled my guts out.

"Goddamn," I heard a voice say. I looked up to find a tall brute man staring at me, casually smoking a cigarette a few feet away.

I wanted to tell him to fuck off. To go away. But I couldn't muster the strength. I bent over and hurled again into the pathetic little bush.

The man chuckled.

"You don't have to laugh." I stumbled slightly and locked eyes with the strange man. Despite the warm August heat, he was dressed in a long, dark coat. His weathered face was tattered with several deep scars around the base of his chin, and his frightening old eyes were the palest shade of blue I'd ever seen.

"Sorry." He smirked.

I wiped the corners of my mouth and half gagged. The sour taste of vomit was overwhelming. "Can I bum one?" I asked suddenly. I didn't smoke, but I'd give anything to get the taste out of my mouth, and a cigarette seemed like it would do the trick.

He shrugged, held out a box of Marlboros, and I placed one to my lips. He flicked the end of a zippo and lit the tip.

"You some kind of friend of my uncle's?" I asked, already knowing the answer. He had that sort of look about him.

"Who's yer uncle?"

"Tony," I finally said, somewhat taken aback. *Everybody* knew my uncle. And everybody knew *me* by proxy. Even if we'd never met before.

"So yer Tony's niece?"

"Yeah."

"How old are you, Tony's Niece?"

I thought about lying for a minute but figured there wasn't any point. The Man with the Marlboros struck me as the kind of person who could sniff out a lie a mile away. "Sixteen."

"Huh," he said with a grunt. "You look older."

"Well, I'm not."

"That's too bad."

"Why's that?"

"Because now I've got to explain to Tony fuckin' Capello why I offered his sixteen-year-old niece a cigarette."

"Or you could, you know, *not* tell him."

The mysterious man raised an eyebrow.

"I can keep a secret, you know."

"Maybe," the Man with the Marlboros said with a casual shrug as he threw his cigarette to the ground. "But I can't. Not from Tony, anyway. 'Scuse me." He turned and walked back towards the house.

Fuck. I was dead. I knew I had to get back inside and clean up before this weirdo ratted me out. If I brushed my teeth and didn't smell like booze, vomit, and cigarettes, I might be able to lie my way out of the whole thing.

I snuck back upstairs, carefully approached my bedroom, and swung open the door.

"JESUS! Drake!" I yelped. Drake and Becca were sprawled out on top of my bed; their partially clothed bodies were completely intertwined.

"You couldn't knock?" Drake pulled his lips away from Becca's neck and turned around.

"Drake, it's *my* bedroom! I didn't think I had to."

"Well, sorry, but we're sort of in the middle of something here… so if you could, ya know, *leave* that would be great."

I rolled my eyes. "You couldn't do this in your own bedroom?"

"No. Gino's in there."

"So? It's your room. Kick him out."

"He's passed out drunk on the bed. Liv sent him in there to sleep it off."

"God. Again?" I groaned. "Where's Katie? Is she alright?"

"How should I know? Before you interrupted, I was kind of busy."

"Busy adulterating the sanctity of my bedroom..." I mumbled.

"Sorry, Dani." Becca slipped her body out from under Drake's. Her cheeks were a light shade of pink. "C'mon, Drake. We should probably leave..."

"No, we shouldn't." Drake pulled Becca back into bed beside him. She laughed, visibly charmed—for God knows why—by my obnoxious brother.

"Don't worry about it, Becca. It's fine." I rolled my eyes as the pair engaged in an obscene display of affection. "Just promise me if you, ya know, do anything gross, you'll wash the sheets."

"Fine."

I sighed, rolled my eyes, and shut the door behind me. I walked down the hall towards the other bathroom. I swung open the door and...

"What the fuck?" I snapped as a whirlwind of over-protective anger flooded my body.

Carlo and Katie were in the bathroom. Alone. Totally unsupervised.

"There was a little accident downstairs with some *juice*," Carlo said with that horrible odious fake grin. "I'm just helping her clean up."

"Are *you* really the best person to help her with that?"

"Your aunt's got her hands full downstairs, so she asked me—"

"We both know that's not what I meant."

"Excuse me?"

"Just get away from her." I gently grabbed Katie's hand and led her away from Carlo, out of the bathroom and into the hallway. I softened my voice and kneeled next to her. "Are you ok?" She looked up at me with wide, doe eyes and nodded with a sort of shrug. I stood up and locked my gaze with Carlo's. "Why don't I take it from here?"

"Are you drunk?" Carlo scoffed, catching a whiff of the unique blend of whiskey, vomit, and cigarette smoke that perfumed my breath.

"No! Of course not," I defensively snapped.

"Why don't you go get some water." He placed his hand on my shoulder.

"Don't touch me." I jerked my arm away from Carlo's grasp, and Luca's brown flask fell to the floor with a slight thud.

Fuck.

I looked at the flask and then up at Carlo.

"Katie," I said with a defeated sigh. "Why don't you go back downstairs with the other kids, ok?"

"Ok," she murmured as she sauntered down the hall.

Carlo locked his eyes with mine and slowly opened the small container. He gently tapped the lid, taunting me with a casual arrogance. "Why don't you just clean yourself up and sleep it off? I don't see why anyone needs to know about this. Agreed?"

"Fuck you." I spit in his face. The thick liquid landed on the side of his cheek. And just like that, he snapped.

"Listen here, you little shit—" He grabbed the collar of my sweatshirt, half choking me with the force of his grip. "I'm quickly losing patience with you. You got that?"

I swallowed hard. "Is that some kind of a threat?"

"Take it how you want." He released me from his grasp, slamming my body back against the wall. I stumbled, fell forward, and collided into an end table.

I looked down. There were small splotches of blood on my dress and broken ceramic pieces from what used to be a vase scattered along the floor.

I cringed as I examined my palms. Shards of the broken vase pierced my skin.

When I looked up, Carlo was nowhere to be found. I wrapped my palms in the sleeve of my black sweater and forced as much pressure onto the wound as I could muster. I staggered into the bathroom.

I turned the knob on the sink, ran my hands under the ice-cold water, and wrapped my wounds in a clean, white cloth.

"You've been drinking? Again?!" my aunt yelled as she entered the room, grabbed me by the back of my neck, and dragged me out into the hallway.

"I barely had anything."

"You're sixteen for Christ's sake. Any amount is too much."

"Everyone else was drinking."

"Well, everyone else didn't spit in Carlo freakin' Gatti's face. I can't believe you, Daniella. How could you do something so stupid while the

Maltas are here! Do you have any idea what—"

"Olivia! The guy pushed me! I fell straight back into the end table. I could have broken my neck!"

"He's a grown adult. The last thing on Earth that man is going to do is pick a fight with a sixteen-year-old girl," my aunt said with an enraged eye roll.

"I swear on my life, Olivia!"

"Daniella, you can barely walk straight. You're drunk. How stupid do you think I am?"

"Oliva. Will you just like—listen to me? For one second?"

She sighed and looked me in the eye.

"He was..." I paused for emphasis. "*With Katie.*"

"Ok?"

"*Alone.*"

"What do you mean, alone?"

"Like *alone*, alone! Together. In the bathroom!"

"So?"

"So?! Don't you think that's a little inappropriate?"

"I'm the one who asked him to help her clean up. So, no, Daniella. I don't think there was anything inappropriate about it."

"He lied. He said she spilled juice on her dress, but it was obviously whiskey. She reeked of alcohol."

"How can you tell? *Your* breath's as ripe as a sailor's."

"Olivia. Listen to me!"

"Keep it down, Daniella. The Maltas will hear you."

"I don't care! Let the fuckin' Maltas hear it. It's bullshit, Olivia. I hate that guy. I really fucking hate him."

"Seriously, Daniella. I'm warning you. Keep your voice down. One more—"

"Fuck you."

SMACK.

The blunt side of her palm collided with the side of my face. I rolled my eyes and rubbed my cheek.

"This family is cracked," I said as I stormed off.

* * *

It had been nearly two weeks since the "incident" at my aunt's fundraising party. I sat curled up in the tufted leather armchair in the far corner of the library. I normally loved this room. The books. The leather chairs. The fancy chessboard. It always gave me a weird sense of comfort on nights when I couldn't sleep. But tonight, it just felt lonely.

It was 3:00 a.m., nearly four hours until I'd be leaving.

I hadn't spoken to my aunt since she'd given me the news. She had it all figured out. Everything was arranged. She talked to the school. She talked to my teachers. Hell, she even talked to the freakin' Catholic church.

I pressed my fingers against my tear ducts and sighed as I aimlessly maneuvered a pawn across the chessboard.

I heard a gentle creak from the front door and knew immediately that my uncle was returning from a late-night of "work," whatever the hell that even meant.

The soles of his shoes tapped quietly against the wooden floors. I sunk back into the chair and held my breath, hoping to avoid any semblance of a confrontation.

The footsteps stopped.

"You should be in bed."

I turned around to find Tony standing in the doorway. I sighed, knowing I'd lost any hope of enjoying my last few hours of freedom in peace.

"Couldn't sleep," I said reluctantly as my uncle entered the room and took a seat at the opposite end of the table. We were probably a full three feet away, but even so, I could smell the rank odor of whiskey and cheap perfume stained to the fabric of his clothes.

"You all packed then?"

"It's 3:00 a.m. the night before my train. You really think Olivia would let me pack in the morning?" I folded my arms in an expressive display of defiance.

"You'd be wise to watch the attitude."

"Whatever."

"I mean it, kid. It's a good opportunity."

"Tony, that's a load of shit, and you know it. She's shipping me halfway across the country. Away from my friends. Away from my *family*. Away from everything."

"Yeah, well, maybe that's not such a bad thing."

"It is, Tony. It's completely horrible!" My eyes were red and puffy; my voice was starting to crack. "Please don't make me go."

I stared down at the chessboard and picked up one of the marble pawns. I fidgeted with it for a long moment, avoiding anything that remotely resembled eye contact. My uncle watched me closely, then suddenly broke the silence.

"It's a nice set, huh?"

I shrugged. "Yeah, I guess."

"The board's mahogany with a gold-plated inlay. Carved by hand. It's a real prize."

"It's nice, Tony."

"It belonged to your dad."

"What?" I looked up at my uncle curiously, surprised that in the ten years I'd lived under this roof, he'd never bothered to mention that before.

"See, when me and your dad were growing up, we didn't have much money. Your grandma barely had enough cash to put food on the table; let alone keep us entertained. But, we moved one summer and found a little chess set in the closet of our new apartment. It wasn't fancy, not like this one here. Our little set was a piece of garbage; made out of cardboard and plastic. But it's what we had. So, we played. It was fun for a while, but your dad, he got real good, real fast. He was a friggin' savant. I swear the guy could beat me with his eyes closed."

I raised an eyebrow. "Really?"

"Yeah. And let me tell you, I was a sore loser. I'd make a big stink about it. So finally, he has enough and he sits me down. And he says to me, 'Tony, you want to know why you always lose?' I told him to fuck off… because I was a hard-headed little shit… but, he kept on, and he says, 'The thing about chess is, you've always got to think two moves ahead. You've got to anticipate what your opponent's going to do, then plan your next moves accordingly. If you want to win, you need to do that.'"

"So what?"

"So, I think you could do with the same advice. You're making your moves in the moment. You're not thinking ahead."

"Tony, I don't even play chess."

"I ain't talkin' about the game, kid." He looked me straight in the eye. "You're getting to that age where you gotta start thinking ahead. You know, about life and the future?"

I shrugged.

"You're a smart kid. I know that. Your aunt knows it too. And this new school, it may not seem like it now, but it's a good thing. You'll see. You need to make a real go of it. Don't go mouthin' off or gettin' yourself into trouble. You understand?"

My uncle looked at me with a long excruciating stare. "It's what your folks would have wanted."

"I'm going to bed," I said as I tossed the little chess piece onto the board, got up, and left the room.

2
WILLARD ACADEMY

The train left at 8:00 a.m.

Aunt Olivia barked at Tony to bring around the car. She was especially irritable that morning, which was a load of shit given that I was the one being forced from my home. And it stung. The fact that I was leaving. Things weren't perfect, not by a long shot. But this was the closest thing to home I'd ever known, I mean, since my parents had died. And even though we didn't always get along, my aunt was the closest thing I had to a mother. I never thought she'd actually kick me out.

I swung my brown duffle bag over my shoulder and walked down the stairs, eventually making my way towards the car that was parked on the circular driveway.

"Hey!" Robert said as he stumbled out of the house in a pair of sweatpants and a white undershirt. "What kind of jackass leaves without sayin' goodbye?"

I turned around and sighed. "Didn't want to wake you…" I half-mumbled. I was actually just too busy feeling sorry for myself to muster the strength for any sort of formal goodbye.

Robert smiled and pulled me in for a hug. "I was thinkin' maybe I'd come up and visit you in a few weeks. Maybe even bust you out if it's real bad?"

"Sure. I guess." I smiled reluctantly.

"Dani! Come on!" I heard Oliva shout from the driver's side of her pitch-black Mercedes.

Robert grabbed my bag and tossed it into the back seat. My aunt flipped a pair of black Chanel sunglasses over her eyes, started the car, and pulled out of the driveway. I wouldn't be back home again until Thanksgiving break, almost three months from now.

We got to the station, and Olivia escorted me to my train.

"Well, this is it," my aunt said reluctantly.

I could tell she didn't know exactly what to say. The truth is, I didn't either. I wanted so badly for her to change her mind. But I'd already tried my hand at convincing her she was wrong, and I'd come to the unfortunate realization that this wasn't a battle I was going to win.

Suddenly, something in my aunt's harsh exterior softened. She took a deep breath and leaned in to hug me. Reluctantly, I hugged her back. I knew she meant well. I hated that my aunt was forcing me to leave, but I didn't actually hate my aunt.

"It's for the best. You'll see," she said in a soft voice, barely above a whisper.

* * *

It took nearly three hours by train to get to the academy. I sat helplessly, curled up in the plush red seat. I pressed my nose against the glass window and watched the greenery flash by. Everything felt so unfamiliar.

Eventually, I arrived. I stepped off the train and followed the sea of travelers away from the platform. After a short walk, I reached a loading zone and tossed my bag onto the ground beside me. My eyes scanned the parking lot, eventually landing on a white van with the words "Willard Academy" printed on the side panel. I sighed, picked up my bag, and walked towards the van.

I closed my fist and tapped my finger lightly against the glass. The startled nun inside the vehicle leaned across the passenger's seat and rolled down the window with an old hand crank.

"Sister Helen?" I asked meekly.

The woman smiled. "You must be Daniella! Get in! Get in!" she said as she unlocked the door and motioned for me to climb inside. I tossed my bag into the back and took a seat up front beside her. She shifted the car into drive, and moments later, we were off.

Sister Helen had a long pointy nose and wrinkles that lined almost every inch of her face. And yet, despite her age, she seemed as lively as anyone I'd ever met. She wasn't dressed the way I expected her to be. She looked nothing like the nuns you see in movies or television. Instead of a black robe and veil, she wore a long blue skirt, a white button-up, and a cream-colored sweater.

We pulled into the parking lot, and she shifted the van to a halt. I stared wide-eyed at the picturesque school before me. The campus was incredible. The grounds were perfectly manicured, like a picture from a brochure or something. And the place was massive. Fifty acres at least.

Sister Helen walked at a brisk pace, and I shuffled along the stone pathway as we approached a large, Romanesque building. I took a deep breath, walked up the stone steps, and entered what was apparently the administration office.

Sister Helen led me down a long hallway and eventually reached a waiting area.

"I'll let the headmaster know you're here," Sister Helen said, and just like that, I was alone.

I tossed my bag onto the ground, slouched into one of the wooden chairs, and pulled a book out of my bag. I flipped it open, making a pathetic attempt to read before I angrily tossed it to the side. I couldn't concentrate.

I tilted my head back and stared mindlessly at the ceiling. I contemplated walking out, then came to the unfortunate realization that even if I managed to make it off the grounds, I had nowhere to go.

"Tommy James?" I heard a voice say, interrupting my train of thought.

When I looked down from the ceiling, my eyes landed on a button-nosed, blue-eyed girl who was now sitting across from me. Her hair was blonde, shoulder-length, and sort of messy; but not the kind of messy like you've just gotten out of bed, the kind where it probably took ten pounds of product and two hours in front of the mirror to properly construct the perfect *I-just-don't-care* look. In sharp contrast to her spunky hair, she was dressed from head to toe in what I assumed was the school uniform: a plaid skirt, white knee socks, and a blue sweater.

"What?" I finally responded.

"The book," she said with a tilt of her head, motioning to the paperback sitting beside me.

"Oh." I looked down, remembering the book suddenly. I was reading Tommy James's biography… which was basically *Goodfellas* meets the music industry.

"It's crazy, right? To think that the Mafia is responsible for some of Billboard's biggest hits."

"You've read it?"

"Twice. I've got a soft spot for oldies. And the mob." She smiled. "Not exactly the same, but I'm reading the *Heroin Diaries* now. Totally nuts. In a good way. You can borrow it if you haven't read it yet."

I raised an eyebrow.

"What?" she asked with a coy smile.

"Sorry, you just—I don't know—you don't look like the type of girl who'd be into Mötley Crüe."

"And what kind of girl do I look like, exactly?"

I shrugged. "I dunno. Preppy. Rich. Boarding school material?"

She raised a curious eyebrow and looked at me closely.

"Sorry." I scrambled, realizing how bad that probably sounded and that I'd probably offended her. "I didn't mean it the way it came out."

"It's ok. I get it." She smiled. "So, I take it you don't fancy yourself the preppy boarding school type?"

I raised an eyebrow and gestured to my wardrobe; I was wearing ripped jeans, a V-neck, and a dirty black hoodie.

"Point taken." She looked me up and down before letting a smirk etch its way across her lips. "But it's just your first day. There's still time to convert. You could be as preppy as the rest of us by next term."

I laughed. "Doubtful."

Suddenly, the headmaster's door flew open, and Sister Helen re-entered the little waiting area. She looked at the spunky blonde girl and rolled her eyes.

"Ms. Bolton, what is it this time?"

"I just thought you might be lonely up here in the high tower, Sister," she said sarcastically as she handed the old woman a note that outlined whatever offense had landed her in the headmaster's office. Sister Helen sighed deeply.

"I'll deal with you in a minute, Emma." Sister Helen looked at me. "Daniella, you can go ahead. The headmaster will see you now."

After a stodgy fifteen-minute lecture on the school's "impressive" history, the headmaster directed me to his secretary, where I received my schedule and room assignment. The whole process was painstakingly tedious.

I was relieved when it was over. I grabbed my belongings, and Sister Helen escorted me towards my dorm.

We wandered down a long stone pathway, and the sun beamed as I made my way to the opposite end of the campus. Along the way, Sister Helen pointed out important sights and buildings around the campus. "Faculty housing is over there." She pointed to a building on the far corner of the lawn. "And this here is the infirmary... the chapel... the arts building... the gym... And here we are. Gellar Hall."

Sister Helen led me towards my room. She opened the door and handed me the key.

"At Willard, you will be treated as a young adult. As such, you will be expected to follow your schedule, show up to classes, participate in required activities and duties, and honor study hours and bedtime. Morning prayer begins at 8:00 a.m., and you will report to your first class at 9:00 a.m., prompt. And when I say *prompt*, I mean *prompt*. Arriving early is considered on time. Arriving on time is considered late. And late is simply unacceptable."

"Noted," I said with a raised brow as she handed me a pile of blue and white skirts, shirts, and sweaters: the school uniform. I felt like I was getting indoctrinated into some type of cult.

"Right, well then. Any questions, Ms. Capello?"

"Uh, no. Not right now. Thanks." And with that, she left. I threw my bag onto the empty desk next to the door and climbed into the adjacent bed. I stared around the room, noticing how painfully bare it felt. There were no pictures or photographs on the wall. No personal touches or belongings that I could see. The second bed on the other side of the room was empty—like it hadn't ever been slept in. Apparently, they'd placed me in an housing asignment alone. A perk, I guess, of starting the semester nearly three weeks late.

I stared at the ceiling until, eventually, I drifted to sleep. This place was depressing as hell.

* * *

I woke up the next morning at six-thirty, pulled myself out of bed, and staggered towards the dresser. I opened the top drawer and stared at the plaid blue uniform Sister Helen had given me the day before. I cringed at the thought of having to wear this stupid outfit for the next two and a half years of my life.

When morning prayer was over, I went to my first class, European History. Next was Religious Studies. Then Chemistry. Then Pre-Calculous.

In Pre-Calc, I sat next to a girl named Lauren. After class, she insisted I sit with her and her friends at lunch. I was glad I didn't have to sit alone, but none of us really had anything in common as far as I could tell. Their taste in music sucked, and they mostly talked about television shows and celebrities that I didn't like or had never heard of.

After dinner, we were "permitted" a few hours of free time before curfew and lights out. It worked like this: at 9:00 p.m. sharp, you were expected to be in your room and accounted for. Sister Helen would walk around the dorms, check each room individually, and check off your name on the master list. At 10:00 p.m., the night monitor would patrol the halls, ensuring that all of the lights were turned off, and the students were observing the mandatory "bedtime" of 10:30 p.m.

It seriously sucked. I was living in a glorified teenage prison.

3
EMMA, WHITNEY, AND MADELINE

It was nearly six o'clock on Friday night. I'd made it through my first week at Willard, and big freakin' surprise... I hated every minute of it.

I sat back in bed, stared at the ceiling, and sighed. I was starting to get restless. And desperate for something to do.

I wandered down the hall towards the common room. When I got there, Lauren and the other girls from my math class were watching some odious teen drama, so I decided not to stay. I didn't want to go back to my room, so I wandered towards a stairwell, figuring I'd explore the building.

I pushed open the heavy wooden door and looked up. It looked like the stairs led to the roof, so I made my way to the top.

Eventually, I reached a thick metal door and turned the knob, half expecting it to be locked. It wasn't. Intrigued, I pushed it open and walked outside onto the roof of Gellar Hall. I stared wide-eyed at the view; the tops of the campus buildings faded into a sea of green trees. I watched the sun dip casually behind a cloud in the distance and thought about home. I couldn't help but wonder how my brother and cousins were spending their Friday night. And I couldn't help but feel sorry for myself that I was stuck here, away from my friends, away from my family, away from everything.

I rubbed my eyes and took a deep breath, attempting to repress any semblance of emotion when suddenly, I heard a voice groan from behind me.

"Fuckin' A."

I turned around and saw three girls smoking in a circle. I realized almost instantly that the voice belonged to the shortest of the three. She had short brunette hair, a pointy nose, and thin eyebrows that made her look perpetually annoyed. To her right was a tall, thin girl with long curly brown hair. To my surprise, I recognized the third member of the group; it was Emma, the spunky blonde-haired girl I'd met my first day in the headmaster's office.

"Sorry. I didn't know anyone was up here," I said with a weak groan as I turned back towards the stairs.

"Wait," I heard Emma say. "You don't need to go."

"What the fuck are you doing?" The short-haired brunette snapped in an intentionally-audible whisper.

"Acting like a normal, friendly, human being." Emma turned and waved me towards the group with a bright smile. "Come here!"

I shoved my hands into my pockets and reluctantly ambled towards the group.

"I remember you. Daniella, right?" She took a drag from her cigarette.

I nodded.

"How long's it been? A week?"

"About that."

"What do you think of Willard so far?"

"It blows."

"You got that right," said the tall, curly-haired girl on the right. She took a puff from her cigarette and chuckled.

"Eventually you get used to it. This place feels like a prison at first, but it'll become more home than anywhere. You'll see." Emma said, reassuringly.

"It's true." The tall curly-haired girl held out her hand to introduce herself. "I'm Whitney, by the way."

"Dani." I shook her hand.

The short brunette shifted her gaze off towards the distance, deliberately ignoring the exchange. Suddenly, Whitney playfully tapped her friend on the arm. "Don't act like a jerk. Introduce yourself."

"If she doesn't know my name, she can't snitch."

"Jesus, Maddie. She's not going to snitch," Emma protested.

"How many times do I have to tell you to stop calling me that?"

Emma rolled her eyes. "Sorry—*Madeline.*"

"Well, fuck. The cat's out of the bag now," the brunette barked back, annoyed that Emma had revealed her precious name.

"If it helps, I don't know your last name. So, even if I was a snitch, there's not much I could do about it." I shrugged.

"She's got a point." Whitney laughed.

"You smoke?" Emma held out her cigarette, offering me a drag. I shrugged and took the light. The thick smoke eddied down my throat as I inhaled.

"I haven't seen you in class. What year are you?" Whitney asked.

"Sophomore." I exhaled slowly, and the pungent smoke escaped my lips, disseminating into the cool air.

"Huh," Emma said. "I would have pegged you for a junior at least. You look older."

I shrugged. "What about you guys?"

"We're seniors."

"You doing anything tonight?" Emma asked.

"Not really, no." I shrugged, not entirely sure what she meant. Lights out was at 10:00 p.m. on Friday and Saturday; so outside of staring at the ceiling, there wasn't much else I could have planned.

"Why don't you come out with us?"

"I didn't know babysitting was on tonight's agenda," Madeline grumbled under her breath.

What the fuck was this girl's problem? I snapped my head towards Madeline and narrowed my eyes. "I'm sorry—did I do something to offend you?"

"Ignore her. She's this pleasant around everyone. It's not just you."

"I kind of don't believe you." I raised an eyebrow at Madeline, who responded with an impassioned eye roll.

"You should; acting like a cunt is kind of her thing." Whitney laughed as she playfully poked her friend in the side.

"All three of you can go fuck yourselves." Madeline threw her cigarette on the ground and stomped it out in a huff.

"See," Emma said with a friendly smile.

"Uhhh… Yeah—I guess."

"What's your room number?" Emma tossed her cigarette to the ground.

"106."

"Perfect, first floor." Emma smiled wide. "I'll swing by after rounds."

I reluctantly agreed and followed the group down the stairwell. I went to my room at lights out and waited, not entirely sure what I was getting myself into.

At around eleven, there was a light tap on my window. I looked up and saw Emma waving from the other side of the glass. I slid off my bed and carefully opened the window.

"You ready?" she whispered.

"Yeah, I guess so…" I grabbed my black hoodie and climbed out the window. "Where are we going… exactly?"

"The Pit," Emma said matter-of-factly as she grabbed me by the hand and led me stealthily down a dirt path behind a row of bushes.

"The Pit? What is that?"

"It's kind of hard to explain." She smiled brightly. "You'll see when we get there."

After a short trek, we reached a large iron gate at the far end of campus, where we found Madeline and Whitney waiting for us.

"It's about time," Madeline said, and without a second thought, she grabbed the iron railing and hoisted herself up and over the barricade.

"We're leaving campus?" I asked, curiously.

"You can go back. You know, if you have a problem breaking the rules or whatever." Madeline smirked.

"Uh—no. It's cool. I don't mind."

"Good." Whitney smiled and hopped the fence after Madeline. "Because curfew makes having a life kind of impossible. So, if you actually want to do something fun, you've gotta sneak out."

I shrugged, grabbed the iron railings, and thrust my body up and over the barrier. It was dark, and most of the area was covered by thick woods, but the three of them seemed to know their way around, like they'd done this a million times before. After about a ten-minute trek, we entered a small clearing that kind of looked like a campsite, complete with a makeshift fire pit in the center of the glade.

Whitney grabbed a beer from a dusty cooler and took a seat on a log adjacent to the fire pit. Meanwhile, Emma lit a match, bent over, and placed it against some kindle in the pit.

"So, what's your deal, *Corn Bait?*" Madeline asked with a smirk.

"Jesus. Madeline. Don't call her that." Emma rolled her eyes.

"Why not? She looks like one."

I raised an eyebrow. "I get that this is some kind of an insult or whatever… but what exactly is a Corn Bait?"

"It's short for unicorn bait." Whitney tossed a sympathetic smile in my direction. "It's like… slang for a virgin… it means she thinks you're a prude."

I raised a skeptical eyebrow. "Oh."

"So, are you?" Madeline smirked.

"Am I what?"

"A virgin?"

"Don't ask her that." Whitney rolled her eyes and whacked Madeline on the forearm.

"What? She's a Sophomore, which makes her a baby. And that means, more than likely, Corn Bait is a fitting nickname."

"I seriously doubt it. But either way, it's rude."

"God. Fine." Madeline groaned. "*D-a-n-i-e-l-l-a.*"

"It's Dani, actually." I paused. "I mean, that's what I go by. No one really calls me by my full name."

"Oh, my God," Madeline groaned.

Whitney shot a friendly grin in my direction, deliberately ignoring Madeline. "Where are you from, Dani?"

"Jersey."

"What part?" Emma asked as she carefully flicked the ash from the end of her cigarette.

"Newark."

"Cool. You spend a lot of time in the city?"

I shrugged. "Yeah, I guess. On weekends sometimes."

"I love the city." Emma smiled as if reflecting on some pleasant memory from her last visit.

"So, what'd you do to piss off your folks? Why'd they ship you off to Willard?" Madeline inquired.

"What makes you think I *did* something?"

Madeline folded her arms and stared at me like I was from another planet.

Emma let out a sheepish chuckle. "Basically, there are two types of kids at Willard. The preppy scholarship bunch, and the ones who're sent here as some sort of punishment."

"And you look like the latter." Madeline raised an eyebrow.

"So, you think I'm rebellious enough to get kicked out, but not rebellious enough to have sex?"

Madeline shrugged. "I just call it like I see it."

"You know, I sort of resent that stereotype. I'm not a nerd, and I wasn't exactly sent here as a punishment," Whitney chimed in.

"Yeah?"

"Yeah. My odious stepmother shipped me off so she could have my father all to herself."

I raised an eyebrow. "That's lousy."

"Tell me about it. My stepmother's the worst."

"Oh, God. Here we go," Madeline moaned. "Can you get off this Cinderella shit already?"

"It's the truth. I can't help it if it sounds like the fable. You know, minus that whole prince charming thing..."

"Ugh. Gag me," Madeline scoffed.

Whitney playfully tossed an empty beer can towards Madeline. "You don't have to be a bitch about it."

"What about you guys?" I asked.

"My parents found a pregnancy test in the garbage and thought sending me away to an all-girls school would stop me from, and I quote, *whoring around*." Madeline grinned. "You'd think they'd have known the Catholic schoolgirl thing is a fetish."

"Jesus, Madeline," Emma chuckled.

"What? My stats went up twofold after sporting the Willard uniform. I should be thanking them."

"Ew. Madeline!" Whitney chirped.

"What? You're not exactly a prude, Whit."

"Maybe not. But I don't really want to think about your sex life and your ever-increasing scoreboard."

I looked at Emma. "What about you?"

She took a puff from her cigarette, then shrugged. "My parents want me to go to some Ivy League school, and I don't know... I guess they thought I was too *distracted* at home."

"Distracted? By what?"

Emma shrugged.

"Alright, so spill. What's your deal?" Madeline insisted.

I thought for a moment, wondering how to explain my situation without divulging any real information. "I don't really get along with my aunt."

"Your aunt? Why's she matter?"

"She's like my guardian."

"Your parents addicts or something?"

"No."

"So? What then? Wormfood?"

"Oh my God, Madeline." Emma interrupted, obviously appalled by her lack of tact.

"What? She just said her parents weren't around which means they're either unfit or dead in a ditch somewhere," Madeline protested. "I'm not wrong. Am I?"

"I guess not. It's the latter." I paused. "I mean, minus the ditch part."

Emma handed me her cigarette, and I took a puff.

"Sorry," she said as she locked her piercing blue eyes with mine. I took a deep breath, then averted my eyes, locking my gaze with the moist dirt beneath my feet. I took another puff from her cigarette and handed it back to her.

"It's fine. I was just a kid when it happened."

Emma shrugged. "Still sucks."

Suddenly, I heard the faint crackle of twigs against the leaf encumbered dirt. I turned around and saw two young men, about the same age as us, walking towards the makeshift campsite. The guy on the left was thin and wore a pair of ripped jeans with a faded flannel shirt. His dusty brown hair was coiled into loose curls tamed by undue gobs of hair gel. He carried a twelve-pack and a bag of ice and eagerly tossed both down beside the cooler. The guy on the right was wearing a mustard yellow sweatshirt. He had dark, moppy hair that was parted in the middle. He carried a bottle of tequila in one hand and casually smoked a half-burnt cigarette in the other.

"Sup," the guy in the yellow sweatshirt said and smiled a wide, boyish grin.

"Thank God. I freakin' hate beer." Madeline got up to greet the two newcomers. Without a second thought, she snatched the tequila from the dark-haired guy and took a swig straight from the bottle.

"Miss me?" He pulled her in close and planted a passionate kiss on her lips.

"No, just your fake ID." She smiled and engaged in another long, intense display of affection. Eventually, the one with dark hair turned and looked at me curiously.

"Who's the new chick?"

Madeline turned around. "Dani, Colin; Colin, Dani."

"What about me?" the other one whined.

"And that jackass is Dave," Madeline snapped as she pulled Colin towards the group.

Dave rolled his eyes and plopped down beside Emma. "Fuck you too, Madeline," he mumbled under his breath as he lit a cigarette and placed his arm around Emma, who recoiled ever-so-slightly from his touch.

"What took you guys so long?" Emma asked.

"Stephen's trying to bang Kim. So, we graciously lent him our services." Colin laughed smugly.

"Your *services*?" Whitney raised a skeptical eyebrow.

"We told him what to say while he was texting her."

"Like you two are so freakin' smooth?" Madeline scoffed.

"Suck a dick. It worked."

Emma rolled her eyes. "Well, aren't you a regular Cyrano de Bergerac."

"What?" Dave furrowed his brow, visibly confused.

"Never mind."

I laughed. "I'm not sure he's got the nose for it."

Emma smiled. "You're right, he doesn't." She paused. "You've read it?"

"This isn't my first prep school. Just my first boarding school."

Emma chuckled under her breath. "Right. I forget everyone had a life before Willard."

Madeline handed me a thin light, and I placed it to my lips without thinking. As I inhaled, my eyes suddenly grew wide as I felt a strong burning sensation from deep within my lungs. I burst into a coughing fit as I pulled what I now realized was a joint away from my lips.

"That—" Cough. "Wasn't—" Cough. "A cigarette—" Cough.

Madeline erupted into a barrage of laughter while Whitney, Emma, and the guys chuckled under their breath.

"That was mean, Madeline," Emma sniggered as she reached into the cooler, grabbed a bottle of water, and tossed it to me. "Here, this'll help."

"Thanks," I croaked as I tried and completely failed to suppress the cough.

"What's wrong Corn Bait? They don't have weed in Jersey?" Madeline cackled with a devious smile.

"We've got weed," I snapped, still struggling to hold back the cough to no avail. "It just helps to know you're smoking it first."

"Well, go on. Don't waste it."

I rolled my eyes and obliged, pulling the cloudy green smoke into my lungs before handing the joint back to her.

Dave's phone vibrated. He pulled it out and smiled wide. "Ay-oooh! Get it, bro!" He held out his phone and showed the group a picture of a young woman's naked body.

"Damn, Kim's stacked."

"Kind of weird nipples, though."

"God, Dave." Emma lightly punched him on the chest. "Put it away."

"What?"

"Does she even know you have that picture?"

He shrugged. "Don't know. Don't care."

She rolled her eyes. "Well, maybe you should."

"How's it my fault if she's slutty enough to let him take the picture?"

"Anyone can find a nude photo on the internet. It may not even be her. You can't even see her face," Whitney said with a casual shrug.

"And, if by the off chance that *is* Kim, Stephen getting laid had nothing to do with whatever you two said—it's because he's gorgeous, captain of the football team, and totally packin'."

All at once, my head grew heavy. I felt my body sway unsteadily, and my eyes grew wide. I looked at a tree in the distance; the bark seemed to pulse ever so slightly. My body jolted backward, as if it were somehow separated from my mind and surprised, all on its own, by the subtle movements of the tree.

Emma glanced in my direction and stifled a laugh. "You ok, Dani?"

I slowly leaned towards her and whispered. "I think so. Yes." I moved my head back slowly and chuckled, for no apparent reason.

She laughed at the absurdity of my behavior. "C'mon, there's a Burger Stop down the street. You'll probably want to eat." She held out her hand and helped me up. I stumbled as I got up and grabbed her shoulder for support. "You guys want anything?" she asked as she turned towards the rest of the group.

"No, I'm good, babe," Dave said as he got up and pulled Emma in for a quick peck.

"We'll be back." Emma linked her arm with mine to help me walk as we made our way down a dirt path into town. After about ten minutes, we arrived at the small fast-food joint. We opened the door and walked inside.

"You've never smoked before, have you?"

"Not successfully, no."

Emma laughed.

"What—" I blinked, "—gave it away?"

"Nothing specifically. I just sort of had a feeling." We both looked over the menu. "What do you want?"

"Milkshake. A chocolate one." I paused and thought for a painfully long moment. "And fries."

We placed our orders with the woman behind the counter, and I pulled out my wallet to pay, but Emma stopped me. "Don't worry about it. I've got it."

"Really? Thanks."

She smiled. "Yeah. Consider it an apology for Madeline's existence."

I laughed. "She is kind of a bitch."

"Yeah, she is." Emma smiled. "But she's not so bad once you get used to her."

"Yeah well... I don't think I'm ever going to get used to her calling me Corn Bait."

Emma laughed. "Don't worry. She's just being obnoxious. She'll get over it once she realizes it's not true."

I stared down at my feet. I could feel my cheeks turning pink.

"Wait—you aren't—are you?" Emma asked, curiously.

I shrugged.

"Huh," she said with a breathy chuckle.

"It's funny?"

"Sorry. I'm not laughing at you. I'm just surprised, that's all." She paused. "If you want, I can lie about it for you. Ya know, to get Madeline to shut up."

I shrugged. "Don't bother."

"Alright," she said as the woman behind the counter called our number, and we grabbed our food. "C'mon, we should get back."

4
HOMECOMING

Dave and Colin went to the local co-ed public high school, Pine Hills, which was only about fifteen minutes away from Willard. Apparently, this Friday night was their school's homecoming, so we made plans to meet up with the guys at a party after the game.

Light's out was always at 10:00 p.m., and the night monitor would finish rounds at around 10:30. So, we met up at the edge of campus around eleven that night.

After walking about three blocks, we arrived at a large, two-story suburban home. We opened the door and entered a murky haze of cigarette and marijuana smoke. I don't know how many people were there. Maybe thirty or forty. Maybe more. It was hard to tell because the house was so big.

Madeline guided us through the throngs of people, leading our little group into the living room and then into the kitchen. There was a keg next to the fridge and a handful of hard liquor bottles scattered around the tiled countertop.

Emma yelled in my direction, trying to be heard over the noise from the party.

"Dani, what do you want? To drink?" she asked and leaned in close, accidentally brushing her lips against my ear.

"Beer?"

She smiled, grabbed a red cup, and pulled the keg's tap.

Before I could take a sip, Madeline grabbed Emma by the arm and tugged her out of the kitchen. "Stop fucking around. Let's find the guys."

"Sorry," Emma mouthed with a shrug as she looked back in my direction.

With Madeline and Emma presumably occupied by their male suitors, Whitney and I wandered into the lifeblood of the party.

We took a seat on an oversized L-shaped couch with a few of Whitney's friends. There were two girls, Kim Schwartz and Kate Hillier, who were a grade above me at Willard. They were thin and pretty, and both seemed to be vying for the attention of Stephen, who sat snugly with his arms around both of them. Stephen had brown shaggy hair and a muscular build that was veiled by an oversized football jersey. He was strikingly good-looking, with that sort of classic, boy-next-door chiseled chin, and large, brown doe-eyes.

"Hey, guys," Whitney said with a friendly smile. "I heard the game tonight was intense."

Stephen smiled and high-fived some guy sitting to my right. "Fuck yeah, it was. Best game of my life."

"He was amazing. Really," Kate said as she gently played with Stephen's moppy hair.

"Not a big deal or anything, but there was a recruiter from Duke there… so, you know, Coach said I had to step it up."

"Duke?" Whitney's eyes suddenly lit up. "That's a great school. Especially for sports. I hope you get in."

"—and with an athletic scholarship." Kim wrapped her arm around his bicep.

I leaned towards Whitney and lowered my voice. "Is that like *Stephen*, Stephen?"

Whitney nodded. "And the girl on the right is—"

"Oh. Geez. The girl from the photo?" I asked stupidly.

"Allegedly," Whitney laughed.

"So, did you catch the game?" Stephen asked, his eyes suddenly focused on me as if he'd just discovered my existence.

"No." I shrugged and took a sip of beer.

"Too bad. It was epic. A total massacre."

"Let's hope the guys at Duke agree."

"You'll have to catch the next one."

"But I already missed the best game of your life, so the next one will probably disappoint."

"What was your name again?" Kim interrupted, visibly annoyed that

Stephen was attempting to talk to anyone that wasn't her.

"Dani."

"Isn't that a boy's name?" Kim inquired with a sharp cackle, not unlike a laughing hyena.

I rolled my eyes and took a sip of beer.

"It's short for Daniella," Whitney chimed in, attempting to be helpful.

"Weird," Kim said with a slight eye roll. "Why didn't your parents just go with something normal, like Danielle?"

"I don't know. Why'd your parents name you after a Korean dictator?"

"What?" Kim stared at me like I was crazy.

"You're named after some Korean dude?" Stephen asked Kim as he burst into laughter. "Epic!"

"No! I'm not! I don't even know what this freak's talking about."

"I'll bet you don't." I rolled my eyes.

"Anyways..." Whitney attempted to change the subject, noticing Kim and I were definitely not going to be BFFs.

"You into football, Dani?" Stephen asked suddenly, eager to divert the conversation back to sports and, more than likely, himself.

"A bunch of sweaty dudes tackling and slapping each other on the ass in a homo-erotic display of masculinity? What's not to love?" I said with a sarcastic monotone that Stephen either didn't acknowledge or couldn't comprehend.

"Homo-er-what?"

"Sports are great," I lied, not wanting to explain the comment any further. "Where's the bathroom?"

Kim pointed behind me. "Down the hall and up the stairs. Byeeee."

"Thanks. I think."

I awkwardly pushed through the crowd and eventually made my way up the stairs. There was a line outside the bathroom, so I leaned against a wall and waited. Suddenly, I heard a familiar voice from one of the bedrooms.

"Can you just—like—give me a minute?" I recognized the voice almost immediately as Emma's.

"Jesus. Fuck. I don't know why you're flipping out," I heard another voice say through the door.

"Well, maybe if you'd actually listen—"

"I've been listening for like a freakin' hour!"

"We've only been here for twenty minutes, Dave."

"Same difference."

"Can't we just go back to the party?"

"I don't want to."

"Well, I do."

"Fuck. Then go."

I didn't mean to overhear the fight, but I was still in line, and there really wasn't anywhere for me to go. The door swung open, and Emma let out a slight yelp when she saw me in the hallway.

"Fuck, you scared me."

"Sorry." I pointed to the door behind me. "Waiting for the bathroom."

"No, it's fine." She took a few steps down the hall, stopped, then turned to face me. "How much of that did you hear?"

"Not much." I paused. We both knew that wasn't the truth. "Sorry. I wasn't trying to eavesdrop."

"I know. Don't worry about it," she said with a shrug as she turned back around and walked down the hallway.

"You going or what?" some guy waiting in line behind me suddenly said, interrupting my train of thought.

"Huh?"

"The bathroom."

"Right. Yeah. Sorry." I shut the door, then took a seat on the not-so-royal throne. And then everything went dark.

"The fuck?" I mumbled as I scrambled to finish my piss. I was literally sitting on the toilet when the house blew a fuse. I pulled up my pants and hit my head on a slightly ajar cupboard on the way up.

"Fuck." I rubbed my temple.

I walked awkwardly through the now pitch-black living room, and my eyes scanned the crowd for a friendly face—Whitney, Madeline, Emma—anyone I actually recognized; but everywhere I looked, I saw strange oversexed teenagers sucking face in the shadows of the party.

After a few minutes, I gave up and decided to leave. I wasn't interested in finding a warm body to spend the evening with, so I reasoned that I could probably figure out how to get back to campus by myself. We hadn't walked far.

I gently shut the front door, walked down the cement steps, and stared at my shoes.

"Hey," I heard a voice say from behind me. I turned around to find Emma, smoking in the dark, empty street. The tungsten glow of the streetlights left an orange bloom on her skin as she took a puff from the end of a cigarette.

"Hey," I said, turning to face her. She pulled out a box of Camels and offered me one. I took it and placed it between my lips, as she held out a lighter. I took a deep breath, letting the smoky air penetrate my lungs.

I heard the faint vibrations of Emma's cellphone. She pulled it out of her blue pea coat pocket, then shoved it back inside after checking the caller ID. "It's Dave."

"I can go. If you need to talk."

She shook her head and gently kicked my shoe. "No, stay. He can wait."

I stared at my shoes and flicked the filtered tip of my cigarette. "Why do you even like that guy? He's kind of a jerk."

"Wow," she said, sort of laughing at my bluntness.

"Sorry. It's probably none of my business." My cheeks suddenly flushed red as I realized I was probably overstepping my boundaries.

"No, it's ok." She thought for a moment. "He's not so bad. Tonight was just—I don't know—an off night."

"Right," I said with a sarcastic chuckle. "Because normally he's a real charmer?"

She smiled and thumbed the filtered tip of her cigarette, visibly mulling over her next words carefully. "Sometimes—I don't know—I sort of just think we mutually use each other for the company or something."

"And to think I mistook you for a romantic."

A coy smile crept in between her cheeks. "You think I'm acting like some stupid girl, huh?"

"I wouldn't call you stupid." I shrugged. "I mean, I would if you thought that was the type of relationship you deserved. But I have a feeling you already know you're settling." I looked up at her. She averted her eyes and took another puff from her cigarette.

"Maybe." She looked down at the street and kicked a small rock with her shoe. She tilted her head up and met my gaze. "But when you're seventeen, sometimes I think there's only a small distinction between romance and a warm body."

I shrugged and took a long drag from my light.

"You're not what I thought you'd be like," Emma said suddenly as she took a puff from her cigarette. "You know, when I first met you in the headmaster's office."

"You're not disappointed, are you?"

"No, pleasantly surprised." She smiled. "C'mon, let's get back to campus. Whitney and Madeline can find their way back without us."

5
SKINNY DIPPING

"What's going on there?" I asked Madeline as my eyes wandered towards Emma and Dave in the distance. I couldn't tell what they were talking about, but their sweeping arm gestures made it look like they were fighting.

"Emma's breaking up with him," Madeline said casually.

"Really?"

"Yeah." Madeline turned a page in some type of teen-Vogue magazine. "She just woke up this morning and decided she was going to do it."

"I think she's being kind of stupid. We're at an all-girls school. It's not like the place is crawling with men." Whitney sipped a mocha frappuccino. "Plus, he's pretty cute."

"And dumb as a fuckin' rock," Madeline said without so much as glancing up from her magazine.

"So what? There's nothing wrong with a woman having a little arm candy."

I shrugged. They were both sort of right.

"Is that going to be weird? You know, because you're dating Colin? And they're like best friends?" I asked Madeline. She just about spit her coffee straight out of her mouth.

"I am NOT dating Colin."

"You're not?" I was totally confused. Not more than a day ago, I had seen them together.

"They have an *arrangement*," Whitney burst into a barrage of girlish giggles.

"What do mean—*arrangement*?"

"Fuck buddies." Madeline rolled her eyes.

I raised a skeptical eyebrow.

"Jesus, do I have to spell it out for you?" Madeline finally looked up, visibly annoyed.

"I'm not dumb, I know what it means. I'm just surprised. You just seem like, I don't know, you really like each other."

"Gag me," Madeline scoffed.

Whitney motioned for the two of us to look up at Emma and Dave. The argument had clearly escalated. Finally, Dave stormed away, flipping her the bird as he left. I watched as she rolled her eyes and walked towards the three of us.

"So, it looks like he took it well," Madeline said sarcastically.

"Yeah, well, Dave's always been the pinnacle of maturity." Emma folded her arms and slouched down into the chair beside me.

"Are you ok?" I asked, noticing her eyes were a little red and puffy.

"I'll be fine," she said with an exhausted sigh.

* * *

"You ready?" Emma chirped. It was almost five o'clock, and Emma was waiting for me to walk over to the dining hall to grab dinner.

"Hold on a sec." I barely looked up to acknowledge her. I was knee-deep in an article from the New York Times and couldn't quite tear myself away. After a long moment, I suddenly felt Emma's presence hovering above me. I slowly looked up from the tattered paper. "What?"

"You've been glued to that paper for an hour." Emma grabbed the paper from my grasp and studied the front page. "What's the deal? You got a report coming up or something?"

"No."

She raised an eyebrow. "Well?" She flipped through the pages as if to examine if there was something hidden inside.

"Well, what?"

"Oh, come on, Dani. You can't expect me to believe that you think this is *leisurely* reading."

"You know I like to read, Em."

"Yeah, about ex-rockstars with a penchant for angel dust... but the business section of the *New York Times*? Not so much."

I smiled. "Well, maybe I've got a hidden passion for the market. Blue chips and arbitrage could really be my thing."

"Maybe." Emma laughed. "But I seriously doubt it." She flopped down beside me, and I moved over, making room for her on the bed. She leaned her head against my shoulder to get a better look at the article. "Who's the old guy?"

I raised an eyebrow and stared at her like she was from another planet. "You're serious?"

"Not all the time, but right now, yes."

"Pino Malta. You know… as in the Malta family?"

"Pino—what?"

"I don't seriously believe you've never heard of the Maltas. They're like infamous."

"Not to me, they aren't," she said with a furrowed brow as she studied the paper.

"He's like—a big wig businessman sort of guy."

"So? What's the big deal?"

"The big deal is that he owns this company. Tecraid. It's like this gasoline distributor. And there were all these shell companies under it. I guess they were moving the gasoline from one shell company to the next to avoid taxes or something."

"Old rich dudes avoiding taxes? That's not so interesting."

"Em, it's a billion-dollar scandal."

"And?"

"What do you mean, and? It's a *big* deal. There are like two senators involved. They're saying everyone is going to be indicted."

"So, that's what's got you so going all *Wolf of Wall Street*? Some old dude who might go to jail?"

"Yeah, that… and… I know him. Sort of."

"You know that guy?"

"I mean, not well. I've only met him a few times. He's like—" I paused and thought for a moment; trying to find the right words, "—a client or something. Of my uncle's."

"Really?" Emma asked, grabbing the newspaper back curiously. She studied the article for a moment. "Huh. Says here there are other allegations…

labor racketeering… drug trafficking… prostitution. Says it's a *slam dunk RICO case*…" Emma smiled wide. "What is this dude, some kind of Mafioso?"

"No." I smiled. "He's like a feeble old man."

"So was Carlo Gambino," Emma smirked. "So, what kind of business does your uncle do with this guy, anyway?"

I shrugged. "I don't know exactly."

"You said your uncle's in construction or something, right?"

"Uh—sort of. His company distributes concrete and like… building materials."

"Huh," she said as she read the article for a few more moments. "Sounds like your uncle's going to need a new client. This guy's going to jail for sure." She tossed the paper onto my desk, grabbed my hand, and pulled me out of bed. "C'mon. We're late. And I'm starved."

"Fine." I grabbed my black hoodie from the floor and slipped it on.

We walked down the hall and entered the cafeteria. My tray hit the wooden table with a clank, and I gently slid a chair out from underneath the long dining hall table. The food was never particularly exciting, but today there were French fries, which was a pleasant surprise. I took a modest handful of the slender fried potatoes and dipped them into a small ramekin of mayonnaise.

"That's disgusting," Madeline said as I took a bite from the handful of potatoey goodness.

"What?" My mouth was still half full.

"Why can't you dip your fries in ketchup like a normal person?"

I shrugged and swallowed my food.

"I think they eat it that way in France. So, it depends on who's definition of normal we're talking about." Whitney smiled triumphantly. Somehow, she always had the perfect retort for Madeline's obnoxious observations.

"So, I'm not *disgusting*. I'm *refined*. Like the French." I smirked.

"The French also don't wear deodorant or shave their armpits," Madeline scoffed.

"I don't think that's true." Emma reached across the table and dipped her own fries into my mayonnaise. She took a bite. "It's not bad. It's like aioli."

"Heathens," Madeline grumbled.

"So, what do you guys want to do tonight?" Emma asked.

Madeline looked at Whitney suspiciously, then focused her gaze back up at Emma. "I've got a thing… with Colin."

"What about you guys?"

"I'm good with whatever." I shrugged.

Whitney was silent. Suddenly, I felt a scuffle under the table.

"Ow!" Whitney yelped in pain. "Jesus, Madeline. You didn't have to do that."

Madeline rolled her eyes. "Whitney's got a date."

"Oh, cool," Emma said with an indifferent shrug. "With who?"

Whitney was silent for a long moment. She stared intently at her plate, unwilling to make eye contact with anyone at the table.

"This is awkward." Madeline smiled wide as she leaned back in her seat, obviously enjoying the drama.

Whitney looked up at Emma; her cheeks were a light shade of pink. "I wanted to ask you about it first…" Whitney narrowed her eyes at Madeline. "In private."

"Oh," Emma said as she started to understand the situation. "You're going out with Dave?"

"Not if you're not ok with it." Whitney smiled sheepishly. "You know, hoes before bros or whatever."

"It's just kind of—I don't know—random." Emma poked at the food on her plate. "Since when do you even like Dave?"

"Since fucking forever," Madeline retorted. "She's had a thing for him since like the ninth grade."

"Madeline!" Whitney half shrieked, visibly embarrassed by Madeleine's crass revelation.

"What? It's true. Everyone knows it."

"I didn't!" Emma looked at Whitney, stunned that this was the first time she was hearing about the crush.

Whitney's cheeks turned a bright shade of pink, and she locked her eyes on the table, visibly mortified.

"So, c'mon. Will you just tell her it's ok so we can all move on with our lives already?" Madeline pressed.

Emma bit her lip and sighed. "Uhm. Yeah, I mean. Of course. It's fine, Whit."

"See. I told you she wouldn't care." Madeline took a sip from her soda. "Now that this is all out in the open, *we're* going to the movies at six… but you guys could meet up with us later tonight at the Pit."

I just sat there silently, playing with my food. I didn't mind meeting up with them later, but the whole thing seemed painfully awkward.

"Great." Emma poked her food.

"Great." Madeline smiled.

"Great." Whitney slunk into her chair.

Nothing about this actually seemed all that *great* to me.

* * *

It was almost eleven o'clock when Emma and I made our way to the edge of campus that evening. I hoisted my body up and over the fence, while Emma trailed behind me.

"Why'd you agree to go?" I asked as I hopped down into the grass on the other side.

"Madeline didn't give me much of a choice…" She leaped from the top of the fence and landed beside me. She tripped for a moment and grabbed my shoulder for support.

"Yeah, well… if I were you, I wouldn't want to hang out with them. I mean, given the circumstances and all. Whitney's kind of being a jerk."

Emma shrugged. "Maybe. But I also feel kind of like a jerk. I had no idea she liked Dave. I never would have gone out with him in the first place if I'd known."

"Yeah. I guess." But it still bothered me.

"Thanks, though."

"For what?"

"For caring." She smiled, placed her hands on the small of my back, and pushed me up the hill to quicken my pace.

After about a fifteen-minute trek, we found Madeline and Whitney sitting around a small fire with Dave and Colin. Emma took a deep breath, then joined the four of them. She was as pleasant and bubbly as I'd ever seen her.

"How was the movie?" Emma asked the group, cheerfully.

"Don't know," Madeline answered with a smug grin.

Emma rolled her eyes, but I was naive enough to inquire further. "How could you not know if the movie was good or not?"

"Because they weren't watching the movie…" Emma explained sympathetically as she tossed me a beer from the cooler.

"Jesus, Corn Bait, it's not rocket science. We were hooking up," Madeline made a lewd gesture with her fingers.

Whitney narrowed her eyes at Madeline. "Would you cut that out? You don't need to call her that."

"What? I don't mean anything by it. It's like a term of endearment for my young, virgin friend."

"So why haven't you done *it* yet?" Colin suddenly asked.

Simultaneously, we all snapped our heads towards him, stunned that he chose to join the conversation with that particular inquiry.

"What? It's a fair question." He shrugged. "If I were a girl, I'd like—fuck dudes all the time."

"I bet you would, faggot," Dave cackled.

"That's not what I fuckin' meant, dickhead." Colin punched Dave on the arm, hard.

"He's got a point. Your cumbucket's not empty cuz of your face. What's the deal?" Madeline raised a curious eyebrow.

"What does that even mean?"

"In Madeline's boorish mind, that was a compliment." Emma smiled. "The translation being—you're pretty. Guys like you."

"Ergo… you could be getting laid."

"—if you wanted to."

"Oh," I said as I took a sip of beer. "Uhm. Thanks. I guess."

"Well?" Madeline pressed on.

"I don't know. I never thought about it before."

"You've never thought about *sex* before?" Madeline narrowed her eyes. "What are you, some sort of asexual or something?"

"Jesus. Madeline. Stop." Whitney rolled her eyes.

"What?"

"That's obviously not what she meant."

"Well? What then?" Madeline locked her gaze with mine, pressing me for an answer.

"I don't know. I guess I'm just waiting. For the right person or something."

"That's adorable." Madeline laughed hysterically and pinched my cheek like I was some sort of child.

"What?" I asked bitterly as I shooed her hands away from my face. "None of you guys lost your virginity to someone you cared about?"

"Lost mine in a threesome in Mexico," Colin said, proudly.

"Don't be an ass, Colin. You and Dave paid a discount hooker to fuck you both," Madeline said with a scoff. "And while that technically counts as a threesome, it's not the kind you brag about."

Colin shrugged. "It's not like our dicks touched."

"Whatever helps you sleep at night."

I looked at Emma and Whitney for support. They both shrugged.

"Lost mine two summers ago at a college party to some frat guy," Whitney said with surprisingly sincere nonchalance. "He was cute, and I just wanted to get it over with."

I looked at Emma.

"Back seat of a senior's car my freshman year. We were technically dating, but it wasn't serious." Emma shrugged.

"You even seen a dick, Corn Bait?" Madeline cackled, utterly amused by her own odious sense of humor.

Emma handed me a spliff. "Don't answer that; it won't go well for you no matter what you say."

I smiled, took a puff, and inhaled deeply, hoping to avoid the question by concentrating solely on the cloudy green smoke inside my lungs.

Madeline smiled deviously. "I have an idea."

"Oh, God." Whitney groaned. "What?"

"Skinny dipping. Who's in?"

"Me," Colin said immediately.

"Me too," Dave agreed, already pulling off his shirt.

"Of course you two are," Madeline scoffed. "Fucking Eskimo sisters."

Whitney and Emma reluctantly agreed. No one waited for me to answer. The five of them just got up and walked away from the fire while I sat there uncomfortably. I really didn't want to go.

Emma stopped and turned around. "You aren't seriously going to make me go skinny dipping alone with my ex-boyfriend and Whitney, are you?" She smiled, attempting to pass it off as a joke, but I could tell she was mostly sort of serious, so I got up and walked towards her.

"I guess not," I groaned and dragged my feet along the dirt.

Emma grabbed my hand and pulled me towards the group. "Besides, if you don't do this, Madeline will never let you hear the end of it. It's really a small price to pay if you think about it."

After a short trek, we arrived at a small lake where we found Madeline, Colin, Dave, and Whitney already swimming freely in the nude.

I dipped my toes into the water, and a chill shot through my spine. It was freezing. Emma threw her shirt onto the muddy ground and turned towards me.

"You coming?" She smirked, removed her bra, and playfully tossed it in my direction.

I awkwardly slipped off my shirt, knowing full well that I just needed to get this over with. I walked towards the water. The wind felt cold against my skin as I submerged my upper half in the freezing cold liquid.

"If you swim around a little bit, you'll warm up faster." Whitney popped up from behind me then dunked her head under the water.

My face stung as the wind swirled over my wet skin, and my mind drifted back to the warm fire back at the campsite. I wondered how long I'd have to stay in the lake to avoid being the butt of Madeline's obnoxious sense of humor.

Suddenly, I felt a wave of icy water clip the back of my neck. I turned around to find Emma treading water nearby. "Don't tell me you already want to get out?"

"No, of course not." I smiled. "Catching a small dose of hypothermia was exactly how I wanted to spend my Saturday night."

"Lucky for you, my dad's a doctor, so I'll score you a deal on the medical bills." She chuckled and swam away.

With a few kicks, I glided towards the center of the lake. Whitney was right; the more I moved around, the less I seemed to notice the cold. After a few minutes, the water actually felt nice. I tilted my head upwards and stared at the sky.

Suddenly, I felt a slight tug on my shoulder. I turned around to find Emma, who tilted her head slightly, motioning for me to look in the other direction. I turned and saw Whitney and Dave making out in the distance.

"Wanna get out of here?" she asked with a touch of despondence in her voice.

I nodded, and we swam back to the shore.

When we got out of the water, we threw on our clothes and ran back towards the warmth of the makeshift campsite. When we arrived, Emma grabbed a couple of towels and tossed one my way.

I opened a beer, and we sat huddled up next to the warm fire, bundled up inside the fluffy towels. "You ok?"

"Fine," she said as she finished rolling a joint. I grabbed a lighter and held it underneath the tip. She breathed in deeply, inhaling the smokey air.

"I don't really care, you know? It's just a little weird. That's all."

"Yeah." We sat silently for a long moment, with nothing but the faint echo of wind clattering from the woods surrounding us.

"I think it's nice," she said, suddenly interrupting the quiet.

"What? Whitney and Dave?"

"No." She laughed. "That you want to wait. You know, until you find the right person."

"Oh."

"You don't want to be like Madeline... I love her, but the girl's a mental case."

I laughed. "What about you?"

"What do you mean?"

"You didn't wait. You regret it?"

She thought for a moment as she took another puff from her joint. "I'm not sure regret is a very productive emotion when you can't change the past."

"—that was a clever way to avoid answering a question."

"—or a clever way of saying it's complicated."

I shrugged.

Emma offered me a hit, and I took a long puff from the end of the joint. "You ever been kissed?" she asked.

I thought about lying for a moment but changed my mind. "No," I answered honestly.

Emma shifted her body and turned towards me. As if it were the most normal thing in the world, she leaned in close and kissed me softly on the lips. She slowly pulled away and left her forehead gently resting against mine. "Now you have." She raised her eyebrows with a flirtatious smirk.

I laughed. "I can only imagine what Madeline would say if she found out my first kiss was with a girl."

"You'd never hear the end of it." Emma laughed. "But it'd probably earn you a nickname other than Corn Bait."

"I think you're right about that."

"Sorry, I guess that was kind of selfish. I've just always wanted to be someone's first kiss."

I smiled. "I'm not sure how I feel about being just another check on your bucket list, Emma."

"How about flattered?" Emma smirked and linked her arm with mine.

"Cheap and used feels more appropriate." I grinned and took a sip from my beer.

"Well, now I feel bad." She laughed and took a long drag from the end of her joint. "If you want, we can walk over to the Burger Stop and I'll buy you dinner. You know, so you don't feel like such a tramp."

"Sounds romantic." I playfully rolled my eyes. "But I am kind of hungry."

Emma smiled. "Me too, c'mon let's go."

6

A STREET CALLED MONTGOMERY

"Dani. Come on. We're late." Emma tugged at the end of my comforter. I rubbed the crusted rheum that had formed along my eyelids and looked up groggily. Emma was freshly showered, dressed, and ready to go.

"Fuck," I groaned from underneath my pillow. It was Sunday morning, and the very unfortunate side-effect of attending a private Catholic boarding school was that the students were required to attend Sunday morning mass. Every week. No matter what. It was worked into the education. You couldn't graduate if you didn't go. And it was a serious pain because we were usually hungover from whatever we'd done the Saturday night before. And today was no exception. My head ached. I was dizzy. And my stomach felt like Jell-o.

I stumbled out of bed and grabbed my uniform from the floor.

"Dani, no."

"What?" I groaned as I slipped on the skirt and realized almost instantly that the hangover had had some completely horrible effect on my balance. I stumbled back onto the bed, sat down, and decided to focus on putting on my socks, a much safer activity.

"Sister Helen is going to kill you if you wear that."

"Em, it's the uniform. You're literally wearing the same thing."

Emma playfully rolled her eyes. "I meant that it's dirty. And wrinkled. And looks like you just pulled it up off the floor."

"Well, that's probably because I *did* just pull it up off the floor."

"Can't you like, iron it or something?"

"No."

"Why not?"

"Aside from the fact that I don't want to, I don't exactly own an iron."

Emma raised her eyebrow and looked at me like I was from another planet. "You're serious?"

"Well, if I had an iron, people might actually expect me to iron things," I half groaned. I normally liked that Emma was basically my polar opposite when it came to this sort of thing; like the yin to my yang, but I really wasn't in the mood for a lecture about my cleanliness. Or my wardrobe. Or my lack of owning an iron. I was too busy feeling awful. And hungover. And trying desperately not to vomit.

"Here," she said as she undid the top button of her blouse, revealing a green lace bra underneath.

"What are you doing?" I asked with a raised brow as she continued to undress. She reached the last button and slipped her arms through the sleeves then tossed the shirt in my direction.

"Taking your shirt. And giving you mine." She grabbed my shirt and slipped it on. "This way only your skirt's wrinkled, and this whole disheveled, hungover, mess thing you have going on will be less noticeable."

"It's not that bad, is it?"

"You look like shit, Dani."

"Thanks, Em," I said with a sarcastic smirk as I slipped on her crisp, clean white shirt. I took a deep breath, and the fresh lavender scent of Emma's perfume-covered blouse penetrated my lungs.

"Don't thank me yet." She smirked. "It comes at a price."

I raised an eyebrow. "Which is?"

"An extra-large cappuccino. After mass. On you." She smiled. "And it'll be one every day this week if Sister Helen reams *me* for wearing *your* wrinkled shirt."

"Deal."

We ran out of Gellar Hall towards the church on the far end of campus. I looked at my watch; it was 8:01 a.m. I sighed in relief. We were late, but not as late as I thought we were going to be, and one measly minute probably wasn't enough to warrant any type of *real* punishment.

When we pushed open the doors, Madeline and Whitney waived for us to come sit by them. They had saved us both seats in the back pew. We scurried down the aisle right as Father Michaels and his attendants processed to the altar. Sister Helen shot us a death stare from the front pew as we shuffled to our seats, attempting, and completely failing, not to disrupt the service.

"About time," Madeline grumbled under her breath as we all grabbed our hymn books.

"Glory to God in the highest." The congregation began to recite The Gloria and their voices echoed tumultuously against the stone-walled church.

I tried to ignore it. To just go along with the hymn, like everyone else. But as my eyes trailed the blurry words in the book, I could feel my legs numb and my knees begin to buckle.

"We praise you. We bless you. We adore you…" Emma chanted along with the congregation.

"I need water or something," I half-mumbled to Emma. "I feel like sh—"

"Shh—" Whitney nervously pleaded from the other end of the pew, not wanting to draw any further attention from Sister Helen.

I took another deep breath and caressed my stomach. It felt like an army of ants was slowly crawling up my esophagus.

"We glorify You. We give You thanks for Your great glory."

My heart violently thumped in my chest, and my hands were shaking.

"Lord Jesus Christ, Only Begotten Son, Lord God, Lamb of God, Son of the Father…"

I tried to swallow, but it felt like someone had lodged a sock in my throat and was trying to shove it down with their bare hands.

Fuck.

I couldn't take it anymore.

"Dani? Are you ok?"

No. No, I'm not ok. I'm dying. I'm literally dying. I felt the sour taste rise from my gut like a volcano.

FUCK. My hands shot over my mouth, and I barely managed to contain the vomit. I ran out of the pew and made a beeline for the back door. I scurried around the corner and collapsed beside a group of bushes and retched, right there, on the House of God.

After a few moments, I felt Emma's hand gently pull back my hair as I hurled one final time. The tips of her fingers swirled against my back, gently luring my body to return to normalcy. I finally pulled myself up off the ground, and she handed me a paper cup filled with water.

"Thanks."

"Dani, are you ok?" She was biting her lip, attempting and completely failing to hold back laughter.

"Better now. Thanks." I took a sip from the little paper cup.

"Good." She barely let the word slip off her tongue before she completely cracked. She burst into a frenzy of laughter. And she'd really lost it. I seriously thought that she was going to piss herself from laughing so hard.

I sat down on the bench outside of the church and took a deep breath. I wiped the vomit off the corner of my lips with my sleeve.

"Remind me never to let you borrow my clothes again." Emma smiled a wide sarcastic grin.

"Sorry." I smiled sheepishly.

"Here. Drink more water." Emma held out the cup.

After a couple of minutes, we'd both regained some semblance of composure and went back inside. When the service was over, Emma grabbed me by the hand and pulled me out through the crowd before Sister Helen could get a good look at me. She'd been suspiciously eyeing us during the service and had definitely seen the entire incident unfold.

We scurried off campus and headed straight to the Deerfield Café in town.

"A deal's, a deal. Pony up." Emma smiled wide, as we entered the shop.

I laughed and turned towards the lady at the cash register. "An extra-large cappuccino and a black coffee, please."

"Really? You take your coffee black?" Emma laughed and took a seat at one of the small tables.

"What's wrong with black coffee?" I plopped down beside her. "It tastes fine…"

"Sure, it tastes fine. But a cappuccino tastes ten times better," she said as she held out her drink, offering me a sip.

I playfully rolled my eyes and took a sip. "It's alright."

Madeline and Whitney entered the café and walked towards us.

"We covered for you guys," Whitney said with a chuckle as she took a seat beside us.

"Yeah. I told Sister Helen it was just a touch of morning sickness." Madeline smirked.

"You… what?" My eyes widened.

Whitney rolled her eyes at Madeline. "*I* told Sister Helen that Dani had the flu. And that Em was just checking on her."

"Thanks," Emma said with a soft chuckle as she visibly replayed the incident over in her mind's eye.

"You're lucky Sister Helen didn't ream you, Puke-a-tron," Madeline croaked.

"Well, I *was* sick. Technically. She can't ream me for that, can she?"

"Sick or not—vomiting in Mass has got to be like—some sort of blasphemy. You're probably going to hell."

"It's not that big of a deal."

"Are you dense?" Madeline barked back at me. "It's a *Catholic school*. Religion is like the one thing you don't fuck around with here. I've seen Sister Helen go ape shit on girls for sneezing by the holy water."

"Come off it, Madeline. That's not true." I looked over at Emma and Whitney, attempting to decipher the exact extent of Madeline's exaggeration.

"Sister Helen *is* really strict about Mass. She's probably just cutting you slack because you're new."

"I would have been ok with a couple extra hours of sleep. I'm just—I don't know—not exactly a morning person."

"That's the understatement of the year." Emma laughed as she took a sip from her cappuccino.

"You can go without me next time. If you're worried you're going to get in trouble for being late."

"It's ok. You let me crash in your room the last couple of weekends. So, waking you up when you're pulling a total exorcist is a small price to pay." Emma smiled and poked me in the side.

"Ha-ha."

"Trouble in paradise?" Madeline asked Emma.

"Erin's just—I don't know—been on my case lately." Emma took another sip of coffee. "She's convinced I'm, like, implicating her or something when I go out past curfew."

I furrowed my brow, pondering Emma's predicament. I'd half-forgotten Emma had a roommate. She didn't talk about her much, and I rarely ever went over to Emma's room. Since Madeline and Whitney were roommates, we usually just hung out over there.

"She said she's going to rat if I keep it up. Hence, I've been crashing at Dani's."

"Tell Erin to fuck off," Madeline said.

"Last time we had a confrontation about it, she flushed my cigarettes down the toilet."

"Cunt, much?"

"Yeah, well, she thinks she's doing me some kind of favor. Speaking of which—" Emma looked at me. "I bought a joint from Colin last night. It's stashed in your desk. You mind keeping it there?"

"Depends. You sharing?"

"Obviously," she said with a smile as she linked her arm with mine.

We left the café, and the four of us walked through the quad. I was craving a cigarette, so I opened my bag and dug inside for my pack of Marlboros.

Madeline stopped suddenly. "Who's the guy?"

"Dunno." Whitney shrugged.

"...I think he's waving at us." Emma raised an eyebrow, puzzled by the stranger's friendliness.

"Do either of you guys know him?" Whitney asked.

"No, but I'd like to," Madeline said with a salacious grin.

"He is pretty cute."

"That's the understatement of the year. He's fuckin' hot," Madeline barked with a raised eyebrow.

"He's alright. I guess." Emma shrugged.

"Are you two blind? Corn Bait. Weigh in here."

"Huh?" I half grunted as I flipped the pack of cigarettes over and packed it against my left palm. I didn't really care who or what they were looking at.

"Boy-toy. Twelve o'clock," Madeline said.

Emma tapped me on the arm to get my attention. I looked up, and my eyes widened when I registered who, exactly, it was they were looking at. It was Robert. He was leaning casually against his gray Buick and waved in my direction.

"Oh, my God!" I smiled wide. "Robert!" I immediately dropped the pack of cigarettes back into my bag and ran off in his direction.

"Nice uniform," he said when I'd reached the parking lot. He barely contained his laughter as he pulled me in for a hug. "You look ridiculous."

"I'm going to let that slide because I'm happy to see you." I pulled away from his embrace and looked him up and down. There was something completely unreal about him being at Willard. Like my two worlds were colliding.

"I told you I was going to visit, didn't I?"

"Yeah." I shrugged. "But I sort of thought you'd give me a heads up first."

"And ruin the surprise?"

"It is sort of a great surprise." I pulled him in for another hug.

"You smell like shit." He pulled away, obviously picking up on the vomity stench that permeated my wardrobe.

"She vommed in Mass," I suddenly heard Madeline croak from behind me.

"Seriously?" Robert asked with a chuckle.

"Well, you know how I feel about religion…" I joked, struggling to hide my embarrassment. I turned around and narrowed my eyes at Madeline.

Emma and Whitney jogged over to the group, and Madeline rolled her eyes impatiently. "So, are you going to introduce us or what?" She crossed her arms, visibly annoyed.

"Right. Sorry." I turned to the group. "Robert, this is Madeline, Whitney, and Emma."

"Nice to meet you guys," Robert said with a half-wave as he slung his arm around my shoulder.

"Dani, you never told us you had a *guy* back home." Whitney playfully tapped me on the arm.

"He's my *cousin*," I said quickly, eager to clear up the misunderstanding.

"Oh, cool." Emma casually turned to face Robert. "It's nice to put a face to the name. Dani talks about you all the time."

"But she failed to mention how incredibly attractive you were…" Madeline said with a smirk, visibly undressing Robert with her eyes. "Way to drop the ball, Dani."

"Jesus. Madeline." I rolled my eyes. "We're going to go," I said as I shoved Robert towards the headmaster's office.

Olivia had called ahead, so there wasn't an issue when Robert signed me out to leave campus for the day. We grabbed a burger at a diner in town.

"So…" I said as I slurped my soda. "Spill. What's going on back home? What am I missing?"

Robert shrugged. "Drake flunked a math test or something, and Dad went fuckin' nuts. Made him and Luca get jobs at Gino's to *teach em' discipline* or some shit."

"That's mildly hysterical." I chuckled.

"Oh. And he and Becca are officially *a thing*, which is driving Luca off the wall. Which is pretty fuckin' funny too."

"Yeah?" I said with a scoff and a slight eye roll. Becca and I weren't the best of friends, but we were friendly, and it sort of drove me a little nuts to think that their whole relationship was based on a crude bet.

We finished our food, and Robert pulled out a wad of cash. I watched as he counted the bills slyly under the table; he was carrying an unbelievably large load, mostly hundreds. He left a few twenties on the table, and we left.

We got back to the car, and Robert reached around and grabbed a box from the back seat.

"Here."

"What is it?"

"Care package. From Mom."

I rolled my eyes.

"Guess someone's still pissed…"

"Ya think?" I scoffed sarcastically.

"She's not happy about any of this either. Just so you know."

"That's a load of shit."

"I mean it. She misses you. A lot."

"Yeah, well. I have a solution for that…"

"Just take it. Ok?"

"Why?"

"For one, she'll be pissed if I come home with it. And for two, there's a strategically placed bottle of Jack tucked away between the socks, the ramen, and the fabric softener."

"Really?" I laughed as I shifted some of the items around in the care package, attempting to find the hidden bottle of booze.

"Yeah, really. But don't go poking around too much. I spent like twenty minutes tucking it in just right to keep it from clanking around. And don't go getting busted with it either. Alright?"

I laughed. "I won't. Thanks."

"You're welcome."

Robert put the car into drive and pulled out of the little parking lot.

"We don't have to go back yet, do we?"

"Sorry."

"What? Why?"

"I've got shit to do. In Warren."

"Take me with you."

"Fat chance."

"Please? It's only been like an hour. And you're the first person I've seen from home in nearly a month."

"Hey! Don't pull that guilt shit on me." He furrowed his brow and sighed.

"Seriously. I won't get in the way. I swear."

"No way." Robert rolled his eyes. "I can't."

"Sure you can. I'll just wait in the car while you do, you know, whatever it is that you do. Besides, it's a long drive to Warren. You'll want company." I smiled. "And, you know, I can be useful. Keep an eye out for cops or thugs or narcs or whatever."

Robert raised a skeptical eyebrow. "You'll keep your mouth shut?"

I nodded.

"I'm serious. You can't go blabbing to Mom or Dad or anyone. Ok?"

"I won't. I swear."

"Fine."

We drove for nearly an hour. I knew we were going somewhere around Warren County, but where, specifically, I wasn't sure, and I knew better than to ask. Robert had that sort of mysterious air about him like he wasn't keen on answering questions.

After an hour or so, Robert pulled off the highway and eventually pulled into an alley along a street called Montgomery. Overgrown weeds protruded from cracks in the asphalt, and there was this sort of dilapidated chain link fence with a metal No Trespassing sign stitched across the rusted surface.

Robert shut the driver's side door hard, and it completely spooked me. My palms were sweaty, and my heart was beating hard. I tapped my fingers against my thighs nervously. I wasn't sure exactly what I'd gotten myself into, and I suddenly regretted begging Robert to let me tag along.

"You coming?" Robert turned around, noticing I was still sitting in the car.

"You want me to come in?"

"Kind of a shit neighborhood." Robert shrugged. "Probably not safe sittin' around the alley alone."

I swallowed hard. He had a point. I reluctantly got out of the car and followed Robert as we approached one of the derelict buildings.

"Fuck!" I shrieked as a German Shepherd came running up from behind the rusted chain-link fence. It was barking and snarling its teeth, ready to rip us to shreds.

"Hurry up," Robert said as he held open a heavy metal door. I took a deep breath and followed him into the warehouse.

The inside of the place was completely bizarre. I don't know what I was expecting, but this definitely wasn't it. Fluorescent lights flickered from the ceiling, illuminating a large expanse of shelves that were piled high with electronics, but not new shiny electronics fresh out of the box; these were old, crappy, electronics that would best be described as total junk.

"What is this place?" I whispered to Robert, mesmerized by the seemingly endless supply of electronic garbage.

"Vito's," Robert said casually as if that somehow explained everything.

As we made our way through the winding rows of crap, we eventually found a counter on the other side of the warehouse. Sitting behind the counter was an old man. The few strands of hair he had left on his head were combed over, and he wore large wire-rimmed glasses that looked like they belonged to a computer nerd from the 80's.

"Is that Vito?" I asked Robert, just a notch above a whisper.

"Nah, it's Henry."

I raised an eyebrow. I was totally confused.

Henry looked at Robert, and without saying a word, he pressed a button under the table. A loud sort of buzz rang through the building, and a latch clicked on the door behind the counter. Robert walked behind the counter, pushed through the door, and entered a dark room. I couldn't make out what or who was behind the door.

I wasn't sure if Robert expected me to follow him into the back room, and I also wasn't sure if I even wanted to know what was going on back there, so I just stood in the main warehouse lobby, awkwardly watching this Henry fellow. He held a magnifying piece over his eye as he used a soldering iron on one of the dilapidated electronic pieces.

"So, uh, what're you making?" I asked casually.

"What's it look like I'm makin'?" he scoffed and simultaneously spit a wad of chewing tobacco into a little can.

"Dunno."

"A bomb."

My eyes widened as a wicked shot of adrenaline rushed through my veins. "You serious?"

"No." The man let out a sort of breathy release that I think was some sort of chuckle or a laugh or a cough. I don't know, really. It was hard to tell. But I could tell by the twinkle in his eye that he thought he'd said something really clever. I raised my eyebrow.

Suddenly, the back door swung open.

"Dani! Get in here, Vito wants to meet ya," Robert said as he waved me over.

"Shit. Sorry. It was nice to meet you, er, Henry." I hurried back behind the counter as Robert opened the door and pushed me inside.

"Hey! Vito!" Robert shouted as we walked into some sort of office. The lights were mostly off, except for a lamp sitting on the desk at the far corner of the room.

Suddenly, a greasy man with slicked-back hair opened another door and walked into the room.

"Vito, Dani. Dani, Vito," Robert said as he casually introduced me to the greasy man.

"Well, I'll be damned. Cristof's kid?"

Robert nodded, and I stared at my feet. It was weird hearing my father's name like that. Especially from a total stranger.

"It's like lookin' at a picture 'er somethin'. Got the same nose n' everything." He leaned in real close and studied me like I was a Picasso in a museum or something. "Christof fuckin' Capello. Man. Yer dad was really something, kid."

"How'd you know my dad?"

"Known him since we were kids. Grew up on the same street."

"Huh," I said, mulling over the revelation.

Robert's phone went off. He glanced down, checked the number, then looked up at Vito. "Clocks tickin'. Can we get on with it?"

"Right. Sorry," Vito said as he walked over to a dark utility closet and gracelessly shoved boxes of trinkets or God knows what around. After a few long moments, he came back with a tiny little box that he placed on the table.

"Dani, you mind?" Robert tilted his head, motioning for me to step outside, back into the other room.

"Oh. Yeah. Sorry." I meekly made my way back into the main warehouse. Henry was still hard at work on whatever weird electronic device he was making. He wasn't really paying attention, so I intentionally left the door slightly ajar.

"We good?" I heard Vito ask.

"Yeah. We're good." Robert nodded.

"Well, pony up. This ain't no charity."

I glanced through the crack in the door and watched Robert place a stack of hundreds on the table. Vito carefully counted the bills, twice actually, and once he'd determined the appropriate amount of cash was in hand, he gave Robert the little brown box. And without another word, Robert took the box, tucked it into his jacket pocket, and we left.

"What's in the box?" I asked as soon as we'd pulled out of the alleyway.

"Nothin'."

"You paid like six grand for it."

"So?"

"So, it's obviously not nothing."

"Part of the deal with you tagging along was that you wouldn't ask questions."

"No, it wasn't."

"Said you were going to keep your mouth shut, didn't you?"

"Yeah? So?"

"Well, you can't keep your mouth shut if you're asking questions."

"Whatever." I rolled my eyes and placed my hand out the window, letting the cool breeze flow through my fingertips. I was insatiably curious about the little box, but I knew, at this point, any further questions about the matter wouldn't be tolerated. "What does Anna think you do? Like, for money?" I blurted out suddenly.

"She thinks I work with Dad at GCF... because I do."

"I know but, like, what does she think your job is?"

"She thinks I'm a Materials Transit Consultant. Because I am."

"What's a materials transit consultant even do?"

"What it sounds like, stupid. I consult on matters involving the transit and distribution of construction materials."

"And that means?"

"You know, I work with the unions. Tell them how to get product from point A to point B."

"And by product… you mean… drugs?"

"I mean fucking concrete and shit. What kind of fuckin' question is that? I'm not a goddamn mule."

I shrugged.

Robert furrowed his brow. "What's the matter with you?"

"I don't know… just wondering, I guess."

Suddenly, I heard the light vibration of Robert's phone. He glanced down at the little black device, checked the number, and rolled his eyes.

"Who's that?"

"Dad. Again."

"What's he want?"

"Fuck if I know." He sighed and shoved the phone back into his pocket. "He's been ridin' my ass lately."

"Drake mentioned he was in a mood…"

"A mood? That's a joke. The guy's a fuckin' nut. He's completely lost it. Can't get a minute of fuckin' peace."

"Because of the Tecraid thing?"

"What do you know about Tecraid?"

"Just what they're saying in the news. And, you know, that the Maltas might be indicted."

"It's horse shit."

"So they're not going to be indicted?"

"No one's going to be indicted. Not over some fucking gas station tax bullshit."

"The Times said it's a slam dunk RICO case. And that it's not just the tax thing…"

"They just print whatever's going to sell papers. It's nonsense. Believe me."

"You don't need to lie to me. I grew up in the same house you did. I'm not stupid."

"I didn't say you were stupid."

"Anna's not stupid either."

"I don't know what the hell you're getting at, but would you quit it with the third degree? I've got enough to deal with as it is; I don't need to take shit from a sixteen-year-old."

"You don't need to yell at me. I was just wondering," I said with a huff as I crossed my arms in an expressive display of defiance.

"Well, quit wondering about everything, ok?"

"Whatever."

I flipped on the radio and stared out the window.

Robert sighed and ran his hands through his hair. "C'mon. Can't we talk about something else? How's school?"

"Fine."

"Your friends seemed, you know, nice. I guess."

"Whatever."

"Dani, c'mon. Don't be like that."

"I'm not being like anything. I just—" I thought for a long moment. "I just want to know what the hell is going on. That's all."

"Look. The Maltas have got like half the state of New York working the case."

"That doesn't mean anything."

"It means they aren't going to jail. You understand?"

"I'm not worried about *them* going to jail."

"So? What then?"

"He's one of GCF's biggest *clients*. There's no way Tony's not involved."

"We've got no ties to the gas station bullshit. Tony made sure of that."

"Yeah, but the Times said it's not just the gas shit."

"We have nothing to worry about. Trust me, Dani. It's under control."

"Ok."

"You believe me?"

"Yeah. I guess so."

"And you don't need to worry about Anna." He looked over in my direction. "She gets it."

"Gets what exactly?"

"You know, everything."

"And she's ok with it?"

"No, not really, but we have an understanding." Robert sighed. "Besides, this shit is all just temporary."

"What do you mean?"

"Workin' for Dad. I don't want to do this shit forever."

I raised an eyebrow. "Does Tony know that?"

"No. And you're not going to tell him." There was a long moment of silence. "Can I show you something?"

I shrugged. "Ok."

"You gotta promise not to rat to Mom and Dad. Alright?"

"Fine. Whatever."

Robert pulled the little brown box out from his jacket pocket and handed it to me. "Open it."

I carefully flipped open the box. "Holy shit," I said as my eyes scanned the glittering jewels attached to the white gold ring in front of me. The light from the sun permeated the smooth surface of the brilliant not-so-little gem, creating a rainbow of colors that reflected onto the dashboard.

"So?" Robert stared at me impatiently, as if the glittering jewels should explain everything.

"So what? You going to sell it or something?"

"Fuck no! It's for Anna."

"Huh?"

"It's an engagement ring, dummy."

"Holy shit. Really?"

"Yeah. Really."

"When are you going to do it?"

"Christmas. Anna got into med-school in California." Robert smiled and looked in my direction. "I'm goin' out there with her next year."

7
NEVER HAVE I EVER

Colin's parents were out of town, so Madeline convinced him to have an impromptu party. We snuck off the grounds and made our way to his house. When we walked inside, it was sort of surreal. The whole place felt like it was frozen in time like nothing had changed since the seventies. Every room was covered in a sort of mustard yellow wallpaper, and the floor was carpeted with a long brown shag.

"Drinks are in the kitchen," Colin said as he casually shepherded us into his home.

Emma and I wandered into the kitchen and found Dave and Stephen huddled in the corner of the room, unintentionally blocking our path to the liquor. I hadn't seen Stephen, the football-obsessed man-boy, since the homecoming party when Whitney introduced me to him and Kim Shultz.

"You mind?" Emma grunted with a not-so-subtle eye roll. Dave mumbled something profane and moved out of the way.

Emma's formerly bubbly nonchalance about the Whitney-Dave situation seemed to be rapidly disintegrating. And it wasn't one-sided. Dave made it pretty clear that he wanted nothing to do with her either. The vibe was awkward, to say the least.

"Hey, Dani."

"Uh, hey…" I said as I turned around and saw Stephen flashing a pearly white smile in my direction.

"You two know each other?" Emma asked as her gaze shifted between the two of us.

Stephen nodded and slung his arm around my shoulder in a friendly embrace that seemed to imply that we were much *friendlier* than we actually were.

"We met at the homecoming party. Whitney introduced us," I said with a shrug and simultaneously removed my body from his grasp.

"Oh." Emma furrowed her brow, glanced in my direction, then suddenly locked her eyes on the liquor bottles placed on the countertop. "Makes sense, I guess."

"GET IN HERE FUCKERS!" Madeline shouted from the other room. I grabbed a beer, and the four of us filed out of the kitchen.

Now, at this point, it was still early in the night. There were only seven of us, and things hadn't really gotten started, so Madeline made us play some stupid drinking game before the others arrived.

"Alright, Whit. You start."

"Never have I ever… been to Mexico," Whitney said, grinning wide at Colin and Dave as they both took a sip from their drinks.

I looked over at Emma, visibly confused.

"You take a drink if you've done it." She smiled, obviously amused by my innocence.

"And if I haven't?"

Emma shrugged. "You just sort of sit there and wait." Emma paused and looked around the room. "Ok. Never have I ever done cocaine."

Madeline and Whitney drank. So did Colin.

"Ok, here's a good one." Madeline smirked. "Never have I ever… had sex in a movie theater." She locked her eyes on Whitney and Dave, who both grinned salaciously as they proudly sipped their beverages.

"Jesus," Emma mumbled with a not-so-subtle scoff. "I could have lived without knowing that…"

"If you've got something to say, why don't you speak up, Emma?" Dave boomed with narrow eyes.

The mood was suddenly very tense, and I half thought the two of them were going to leap onto the table and strangle each other.

Emma locked her eyes with Dave's and raised her voice, just a notch above her former mumble. "I said, *I could have lived without knowing that.*"

"Suck it," Dave barked from the other end of the table. "Oh, wait. You already have."

"Can we just play the game?" Madeline protested, deliberately not giving Emma a chance to retaliate.

"Yeah, go on, Stephen. Your turn," Whitney said, attempting to change the subject. She gently grabbed Dave's hand in a sort of half-assed attempt to "ask" him to back off. She obviously didn't want the two of them fighting, but she also, obviously, didn't want to get involved in the dispute.

"Never have I ever… kissed someone in this room." Stephen smiled as he looked around the room, wondering who would take a sip.

I looked down at my drink and then up at Emma; she smirked and stifled a laugh. We both knew that, technically, I had kissed someone in the room—her. But I assumed that didn't count. And even if it did, I wasn't exactly going to volunteer that information to Madeline.

I placed my drink down on the table. Everyone in the room—except me and Stephen—had taken a sip.

"Jesus, Corn Bait, I don't think you're ever going to get to play." Madeline let out a shrill laugh as she threw a bottle cap in my direction. "Hey, Stephen, maybe you should give Dani a big peck on the lips so she can actually drink."

He smiled, leaned over, and kissed me.

"That counts. Drink." Whitney smiled wide.

I rolled my eyes and took a sip. I know a lot of girls would have killed to be on the receiving end of a kiss from Stephen, the "hunky" quarterback, but the whole thing was really unsettling; like, his lips were too big for mine, and they were slippery and wet, which reminded me of kissing some sort of reptile.

"Never have I ever… seen a dead body." Colin looked around the room, hoping someone would take a sip.

A warm, uneasy wave of adrenaline rose from my gut, gradually oozing its way through my limbs. I rubbed my temple, trying to clear my mind, trying desperately to erase the uneasy sensation with nothing more than sheer will-power.

"Anyone?" Madeline asked suddenly, interrupting my train of thought.

I looked down at my drink. My face was tingling and hot. And my mouth was dry. I really wanted a fucking drink. But I didn't take a sip. Not for that.

"You alright?" Emma whispered, deliberately trying not to attract the attention of the others. I shrugged and gave a half nod.

"Yeah, that's what I thought. Way to waste your turn, Colin." Madeline rolled her eyes. Colin shrugged.

"Where's the bathroom at?" I asked suddenly.

Colin pointed down the hall, but Madeline and Whitney insisted that Stephen show me where it was. I got up from my seat and borderline chugged my beer as we walked away from the group. And then things got weird.

Stephen didn't just show me where the damn thing was. The guy followed me right inside. I thought it was all some kind of joke, but then he shut the door and cornered me up against the wall; and I swear to fucking God, he spit out some cornball line like, "There must be something wrong with my eyes... because I can't take them off of *you*."

I almost spit my drink in his face, the whole thing was so ridiculous. I mean, the guy *was* really good-looking, enough so that he probably didn't get turned down a lot—regardless of the stupid shit that came out of his mouth. But seriously. Who the fuck did he think he was? And who the fuck talks like that?

"Look, uh, Stephen..." I stammered. "I'm not kidding. I really do have to use the bathroom."

He laughed, like I was playing hard to get or something, and then moved in to kiss my neck.

"Seriously," I said as I slid out from under his arms. "You're obviously—uh—attractive—and you seem like a nice guy—I guess—but I'm on my period—and, well—I really need to change my tampon." That wasn't the truth, but I knew enough about men to know that you mention your period and they go running for the hills. And this was no exception.

His face sort of scrunched up with repulsion, and he immediately shuffled out of the room. "Uhg. Too much information..." he mumbled, and I locked the door as he left.

I sat down on the toilet and took in a huge sigh of relief. Who knew it was this fucking difficult to take a piss?

When I opened the bathroom door, I saw Stephen standing there waiting. He sort of slung his arm around me, got in real close to my face, and said, "We don't have to go back, you know..."

"Huh, well, that's true. But, I finished my drink, and could sort of use another one." I pointed to my now-empty bottle of beer.

"Nice. A party girl. I like that." He nodded as we walked back to the group.

I sat back down next to Emma, who looked pissed as hell, presumably because of Dave. Eventually, Stephen came back with my beer, and we played a few more rounds of the game. By this point, Madeline and Whitney were annoyingly drunk, and they kept making stupid comments about me and Stephen; and I was silently plotting ways to kill them both. It was bad enough that I had to tolerate the guy to begin with; the last thing I needed was for them to convince him I was actually interested.

I took a gargantuan swig of beer, then looked up and saw Dave kissing Whitney at the far end of the table. She was playfully pushing him to the side, like she wanted to kiss him back but wasn't sure if a full-fledged public display of affection would upset Emma.

"Dave… c'mon…" she giggled as she jokingly slapped his hand away.

He just sort of laughed and kept going. He wouldn't lay off. He just got more aggressive and she didn't seem to mind. It was nauseating.

"I'm going to grab a smoke," Emma suddenly announced as she walked out of the room and borderline slammed the door on the way out.

I could tell she was pissed, so I got up to check on her.

"Where you goin'?" Stephen asked with a Joey Tribiani nod as he stood up and blocked my path.

"To check on Em. You mind?" I raised an eyebrow and motioned for him to get out of the way.

"Good." Madeline rolled her eyes. "Tell her to chill the fuck out."

I pushed open the sliding glass door and saw Emma sitting beside a large pool in the backyard. Ripples emanated from the slow movement of her feet as she gently dangled her toes in the water.

"You ok?" I asked as I took a seat next to her.

"All good." She took a drag from her cigarette.

"That's convincing." I chuckled and looked down at my hands, suddenly remembering I was holding both our drinks. I handed the red cup to her. "Here. You left your drink inside."

"Thanks," she said as she took a sip. "I just thought I'd grab some fresh air. That's all."

"We can leave if you want. If it's weird. You know, being here. With them."

"It's fine." Emma shrugged. "I think Dave's a creep. But if Whitney likes him, then that's her problem."

"Alright."

"You can go back inside if you want. I'm fine. Really."

"I'd rather be out here. I mean, unless you want to be alone."

Emma smiled and handed me a light. I slipped off my shoes, rolled up my jeans, and dipped my feet into the water.

"You were lying in there," Emma said after a long moment, finally breaking the silence.

"What? You mean about kissing someone?"

"No." She chuckled and took a drag from her cigarette. "I mean, yeah. I guess that too, technically. But I meant about the other thing."

I was silent for a moment.

"When'd you see a dead body?" Emma asked. She locked her eyes on mine with an intense stare, and I shifted my gaze immediately.

My mind drifted for a moment, then I blinked, suddenly snapping myself out of a sort of abstraction. "I thought open caskets were a Catholic thing. I would have thought everyone at this crummy school had seen a dead body at some point in their lives."

She looked at me again, as if she could see through me. Like she knew I had just told only half the truth.

"Your parents had an open casket?" Emma asked curiously.

I shrugged. "I think so."

"You think?"

"My grandmother wouldn't let us see." I took a sip from my beer. "Thought it'd be like—traumatic or something."

"No shit it would be traumatic." Emma laughed lightly as she took another puff from her cigarette. "You miss 'em?"

"I guess. Occasionally." I shrugged and thought for a long moment. I took a slow drag from the cigarette and exhaled slowly. "Can I tell you something fucked up?"

"Sure."

"Sometimes I forget what they look like." We were both silent, and I ran my free hand through the water, attempting to distract myself from the gravity of what I'd just said.

"I don't think that's fucked up."

"No?"

"You were only six, right? When it happened?"

I nodded.

"It makes sense if you think about it. They've been dead most of your life. What do you really have to remember?" Emma took another puff from her cigarette.

She was right. There wasn't much to remember. And the memories I did have grew fainter with every passing day. I took a deep breath and locked my gaze on the cool blue surface of the pool.

"Sorry—I didn't mean—" Emma stammered. "I think that came out wrong."

"No, it's ok. You're right. There isn't much to remember."

"No—I just meant that, you know, you shouldn't feel guilty about it. You're only human. That's all."

"Yeah, I guess." I shrugged and continued to fix my gaze on my beer. "Why'd you think I was lying?"

"I dunno," she said, taking another drag from her cigarette. "I guess you looked all glassy-eyed. Like you were thinking about something you wished you could forget."

"It's weird, the things you remember," I said with a shrug as we sat silently for a long moment.

"They're crystal clear, you know, the bad things. The fucked-up shit that tears you apart. But the little things, the pleasant details that remind you life's worth living, they're always the first things you forget," Emma said as she took a drag from her cigarette.

I swallowed hard and stared intently at the still surface of the pool. As I shifted my gaze back to Emma, my eyes spotted a deep scar across her upper thigh. "What happened there?" I asked, assuming it was the result of some sort of childhood mishap. I had a few similar scars across both my knees from climbing trees and subsequently falling out of them when I was a kid.

Almost instinctively, she pulled away, covering up the scar with the seam of her dress. She took a long drag from her cigarette, then looked up at me, locking her gaze with mine. "It's stupid, really. I tripped and cut it against the sharp edge of a metal bedpost." She showed me the scar again. "It's old. Happened when I was sixteen. Right before my parents sent me to Willard."

"Looks like it hurt." I shrugged.

"Probably did."

"What do you mean, *probably*?"

"I don't really remember." She looked up and smiled sheepishly. "A bottle of vodka and one too many Vicodin might have played a small role in the incident."

"Oh," I said, suddenly realizing the weight of the conversation I had unintentionally stumbled into. "Were you, uhm…"

"Trying to hurt myself?"

I nodded.

"No." Emma shrugged. "It was just a stupid mistake. I didn't know what I was doing. That's all."

I shrugged and took a sip from my beer.

"You believe me?"

"Yeah." I locked my gaze with hers. "Why wouldn't I?"

Emma shrugged. "Nobody else does. That's why they sent me to this crummy school. My parents are idiots."

"Maybe… but I'm glad they did," I said with a smile. "Because otherwise, I'd be stuck alone with Whitney, Madeline, and Stephen."

"Speaking of which…" Emma grinned. "I've got to know. How do I compare to Stephen the oh-so-*hunky* quarterback?"

"What?" I laughed, taken aback by the question.

She gently bumped me with her elbow and smirked. "On a scale of one to ten, who's the better kisser?"

I rolled my eyes and tried my best to feign nonchalance, but I could feel the heat creeping into my cheeks. "Em, you know a lady's not supposed to kiss and tell…"

"Oh! Come on!" She poked me playfully in the side. "Inquiring minds want to know."

"I have a feeling the only right answer to this question is *you*."

"Only if that's the truth." She smiled. "But I've had a fair amount of practice, so I'm feeling pretty good about my odds."

I laughed. "You're almost as arrogant as he is."

"He *is* kind of a tool." She paused. "I mean, no offense. If you like him."

"None taken. I don't."

"Huh," she said, mulling over the revelation. "I thought you might."

"No. I think he's a jerk."

"Whitney said he couldn't stop talking about you after the homecoming game..."

"Stop. She did not." I rolled my eyes and laughed.

"Did too. Apparently, you made quite the impression. What'd you do? Give him a blow job in the bathroom or something?" She raised her eyebrows salaciously.

"Oh, my God. You sound like Madeline."

Emma laughed. "That's a horrifying thought."

"It is. And no. I didn't."

Emma smiled. "Well, she wants to set you guys up."

"Grrrreat. We can talk about biceps, beer, and football."

"What? That's not your idea of a dream date?" She smiled playfully.

"No. Not really." I smiled back.

"Well, I guess I shouldn't be surprised."

"Why's that?"

"Well, I mean, since I was your first kiss, your expectations are just too high now. I've ruined you. Everyone else is going to seem subpar."

I smiled. "You're full of it."

"What?" She laughed hard and leaned back on the pool-side cement, staring up at the stars. "I really think I owe you an apology."

I slouched down beside her. She affectionately wrapped her arm around mine and laid her head against my shoulder.

"Em, why'd you break up with Dave?" The words suddenly spilled out of my mouth; I wasn't even sure why I was asking.

"Why are you changing the subject?"

"Why are you dodging my question?"

"Because you dodged mine."

I smiled. "Touché."

"Well?" She raised her eyebrows triumphantly.

"You're a better kisser than Stephen the hunky quarterback," I said with a reluctant grin.

"I knew it!" She smiled wide.

"But don't get too excited. I don't think that's saying much."

"You don't need to downplay it, Dani." She smiled and winked playfully. "It was good for me, too."

"Ok, I take it back. You ARE as arrogant as Stephen."

She smiled. "I broke up with Dave because of you."

"What?"

"I'm answering your question. I broke up with him because of what you said. The other night."

"Oh." My face turned a warm shade of pink. "I'm sorry. For saying all that stuff. It probably wasn't any of my business."

"Don't be. You were right. About all of it." Emma glanced back inside; a few more kids from Pine Hills had arrived. "We should probably get back. To the party, I mean."

"Alright." We sat up, grabbed our drinks, and joined the rest of the group back inside.

8
FUZZY GREEN TENNIS BALLS

"Hey, wait up," I heard a voice say as I exited the classroom. I turned around and saw Whitney waving in my direction.

"How was class?" she asked as she jogged in my direction.

"Good, I guess." I stopped in the hall, giving her a moment to catch up. "Mr. Akerman is kind of a bore."

"Yeah, I had him last year for AP Chem. He's the worst."

I noticed Whitney fidgeting awkwardly with a tennis ball in one hand and a tennis racquet in the other. "You on your way to practice or something?"

"Oh, yeah. Ever think about going out for the team?" She casually tossed the fuzzy green ball in my direction.

I caught it and shook my head. "Not really. I sort of hate sports."

"Right. Madeline too, actually. Her parents made her join. You know, to get an extracurricular on her college applications," Whitney said with a sort of shy smile. "The big schools care about that kind of thing. They want, like, well-rounded students or whatever."

"Makes sense, I guess."

"Hey—uh—" Whitney stammered as if her next words were on the tip of her tongue but she was struggling to get them out. "Have you—uhm—talked to Emma lately?" She stared at her feet, and her cheeks flushed a light shade of pink.

I thought that was a weird question. The four of us had eaten breakfast together that morning. "I dunno, I mean, not since this morning."

"Oh."

"Is something wrong?"

"I don't know. I feel like things have been kind of weird between me and her lately." She took a deep breath. "You know, ever since I started dating Dave?"

"Oh." I didn't really want to be talking about this. "Don't you think you should talk to *her* about this?"

"I've tried. But you know how she is."

"I guess," I shrugged, but I didn't actually know what she meant.

"Will you talk to her for me?"

I sighed. "I don't know."

"Please?" she begged. "She won't talk to me, and if Madeline talks to her, it'll end in disaster. Besides, you guys are so close. You're the only person I think she'll really listen to." She stared at me with wide, pleading eyes. "I really like Dave, and I don't want to break up with him. But I will if it means things are going to be weird between me and Em…"

"Ok," I said reluctantly.

"Thank you." She pulled me in for a hug. "Seriously, I owe you."

* * *

I sat up in bed and stared at the wall as I ran my fingers across the neon fuzz of the small green tennis ball. Steam from the shower was slowly leaking from under the bathroom door. Emma was crashing in my room again to avoid her roommate.

I heard the squeal of the shower knob, and all at once, the water stopped. Moments later, the door eased open, and Emma poked her head through the small crack.

"Do you have any lotion?"

"Under the sink."

"Found it! Thanks."

Moments later, Emma exited the bathroom with her body wrapped tightly in a fluffy yellow towel. She hoisted her leg onto the chair adjacent to my desk and began lathering her legs in the milky white cream.

I tossed the ball up towards the ceiling as I mulled over my next words carefully. "So, uh, Em…"

"Yeah?"

"Can I ask you about something?" My eyes were still intently focused on the fuzzy green tennis ball.

"Uh, yeah? Shoot."

"Is everything, like, I don't know... ok?"

She looked at me like I was crazy. "Uh, yeah? Why? What do you mean?"

I sighed and took a deep breath. "You know, like, between you and Whitney?"

"Seriously?" Emma groaned with a not-so-subtle eye roll. "This is the third time today I've had this conversation. Twice with Whitney. Now with you."

"Look, I know that. I didn't even want to bring it up."

"Then why did you?"

I sighed. "I just kind of promised Whitney that I'd talk to you about it. That's all."

"Ok? So, what do you want to talk about?" She paused and crossed her arms. "I'm sorry, I mean, what does *she* want us to talk about?"

"You don't have to be like that."

"I'm not being like anything." She sighed. "Why don't you just tell me what she said?"

"She was just all freaked out about everything. She thinks you're—I don't know—upset with her or something."

Emma groaned, visibly annoyed. "She's free to do what she wants. I don't know how many times I have to say it... I really don't care."

"Well, it seems like you do."

"What's that supposed to mean?" she asked with an ambiguous tone. I couldn't tell if she was annoyed or sincerely curious.

"It means—I don't know—you have been acting a little weird lately." I paused, mulling over my next words carefully. "Not like you're mad, necessarily. But, I don't know. It's like you have a lot on your mind. Whitney was probably just picking up on that."

Emma shrugged, turned around, dropped her towel, and slipped on a pair of pajamas. I stared up at the ceiling, averting my eyes while she dressed.

"Have you?" I asked.

"Have I what?"

"Have you had a lot on your mind?"

"I don't know. Maybe."

"You know you can talk to me. I wouldn't tell her. Or anyone. If you didn't want me to." I threw the small green ball back up in the air.

"I know that." Her expression softened a little.

"So? Are you ok with everything? You know... with Whitney and Dave?" I asked as I scooted my body to the right, making room on the bed for her to lay beside me. She placed her head on the pillow, and we both stared up at the ceiling for a few moments.

"The situation is weird. I don't love it, but really, I'm not mad at her, Dani," Emma said, lost in thought, still staring blankly at the ceiling. Her voice was suddenly calm; her breath was slow and deliberate. "I want her to be happy. It's the truth. Really."

I looked at her for a long moment. "Are you still into him?"

"Dani—"

"What?"

"We both know you were right. With Dave, I always knew I was settling." She thought for a moment. "I don't want to be with someone like that. I want to be with someone that I have a connection with, not just physically, but, like, intellectually. Wasting time with a warm body doesn't make much sense when you could be spending your time with someone who actually cares about you, like, as a person."

"Ok. But you didn't answer my question."

"What?"

"Are you still into him?

"Does it matter?"

"Yeah, it matters."

"Why?"

My chest tightened. My mouth was dry.

"Well?" she pressed.

"I don't know. Because it does." I felt my cheeks turn a cool shade of pink.

"Because we're *friends*?" She looked at me for a moment, as if studying my body language. "And you care about me?"

"Yeah." I tried to inhale, but my lungs were already filled. "Because I care about you."

She smiled and placed her head on my chest, curling up beside me in a painfully equivocal embrace. After a long moment, she placed her hand flat across my chest and left it there, feeling my heartbeat.

"Dani, your heart's pounding," she finally said, locking her gaze with mine.

"Is it?" I asked, my mind completely drawing a blank as a warm sensation flushed over my body. She nodded, and all at once, I felt the hair on the back of my neck stand, as if a cold breeze had gently blown through; and somehow, despite everything, despite the waves of emotion crashing tumultuously through my body, I was frozen.

"Am I making you nervous?" she asked with a smirk, obviously charmed by the obscure brand of innocent anxiety flushing through my body. I shifted my hips, locking my gaze with hers. I could feel the weight of her body pressed against mine, the delicate gravity of her lips deliberately sucking me in.

"No," I finally said in a sort of loud whisper as her hand gracefully slid down my mid-section, landing finally on my waist. "I'm not nervous."

She pressed her forehead against mine. The centimeters between us felt like miles. She moved in closer. Then closer again. The centimeters became millimeters. And then, all at once, I felt her pull away, as if rethinking the whole thing. She turned onto her back and stared at the ceiling. The distance was excruciating. We were miles apart.

"Do you want me to go?" The words shot out of her mouth in some sort of anxious reflex.

I locked my gaze on her thin frame as she lay flat on her back, staring at the ceiling. The pace of her breath was quick.

Inhale.

Exhale.

Inhale.

Exhale.

There wasn't enough air in the room to fully recover.

"No," I finally said.

"Ok." Her eyes were still laser-focused on the ceiling above us. "Good."

I bit my lip and watched her curiously. There was a lump in my throat. I tried to swallow, but I couldn't.

She turned her head, and her blue eyes shifted from the ceiling to meet my gaze. I saw myself reflected in their glassy surface. It was hypnotic. And all at once, I felt myself move closer as if my mind had been separated from my body. I felt my hand delicately graze her cheek, finally cradling her head in my arms. I felt my lips move closer and closer until finally there was nothing between us.

* * *

When other girls would talk about some guy they had a crush on, I saw what they saw. The good hair, the nice face, the muscular build. But I never felt much of anything: the butterflies, the fireworks, the feeling of being totally and completely swept up off your feet. Nothing.

And honestly, I didn't give it much thought. I thought that all those feelings were some sort of bullshit fantasy; something made up to make movies and TV shows more interesting, or to help Hallmark sell a few extra greeting cards around Valentine's Day. It never occurred to me that the real reason, the reason I was so apathetic about the opposite sex, was that I might not be attracted to the opposite sex… like… at all.

The clock clicked 6:45 a.m., and the sun beamed through the blinds as my eyes gently fluttered awake. I looked down to find Emma asleep, her head gently resting on my chest. I smiled as the warm sun rays reflected on her skin. I wrapped my arms around her and kissed her forehead.

She gently drifted awake and looked up at me. "Hi," she said. Her voice was pleasant and sleepy.

"Hi," I smiled. We were both dead tired. Last night's tryst didn't go any further than kissing, but even so, we didn't get much sleep; the adrenaline kept me awake.

"It's almost seven," I said just above a whisper. "We'll miss breakfast."

"Are you hungry?"

"No… But we're supposed to meet Whitney and Madeline. They'll wonder where we are."

"Let them wonder." Emma gently rolled on top of me and lifted my hand to her lips.

I smiled and pulled her in close, smothering her in my embrace. "Trust me, I could stay here all day."

"Then why don't we?" She grinned.

"Because we both have class. And I could use some coffee."

She looked up at me with a playful pout. "Fine. But you should know that you're annoyingly practical."

I laughed as she begrudgingly tossed the sheets to the side and pulled me out of bed.

We walked down the hall to the cafeteria, just as we had done a million times before. Everything was the same, except, somehow, it wasn't. Every smile, every touch, every word had taken on some new hidden meaning.

When we got to the cafeteria, Madeline and Whitney were already sitting at our regular table. I grabbed a cup of coffee and a bowl of cereal and took a seat next to them. Emma did the same.

Madeline studied us both curiously. "You guys look like shit."

I took a sip of coffee, desperately trying to avoid eye contact. My eyes wandered towards Emma. She was staring intently at her bowl, shifting the frosted cereal bits around the milk with her spoon.

"Your eyes are all bloodshot," Madeline exclaimed as she moved her face uncomfortably close to mine. "What happened to you?"

I swallowed hard. Reality suddenly kicked in, and it felt like I'd just been sucker-punched in the gut. My stomach churned as I realized what could happen if anyone found out about last night—about me and Emma. And that pleasant airiness, the feeling like I was floating, the butterflies in my stomach—it all melted into tiny pools of anxiety, fear, and guilt.

I took a sip of coffee and wiped my palms against my skirt. I was sweating profusely.

Silence.

"Hello?" Madeline continued.

"What?" I finally looked up, attempting to feign obliviousness.

"What. The. Hell. Is. Going. On. With. You. Two?" Madeline croaked in an annoyed monotone.

"Nothing," I lied. "We're just tired."

"Tired?" Madeline asked as she raised a curious eyebrow. "Why? What'd you guys do last night?"

Silence.
A sip of coffee.
Silence.
A bite of cereal.
Silence.
Sip.
Silence.
Swallow.

Silence.

"Hellooooo?" Madeline was getting annoyed. "Are you guys even listening to me?"

"We were watching TV and lost track of time," Emma finally said. "Hence, we're *tired*."

I nodded in agreement, relieved that Emma and I were on the same page, that we needed to lie.

"What'd you watch?" Whitney asked, attempting to join the conversation with a friendly question. Another warm wave flushed through my cheeks; my hands were clammy and shaky; my breath was shallow.

"A movie," I lied.

"What movie?" Madeline asked, still suspicious.

"Uh—" I stammered.

"Pulp Fiction," Emma lied.

Thank God, I'd seen it. I took a deep breath.

"Ew. The guy with the foot fetish?" Whitney scrunched up her face in repulsion.

"Uh. Yeah. Tarantino," I mumbled as I took a sip of coffee.

Madeline studied us again, eying us up and down. "I swear to God if you guys are on drugs, you better fucking share."

* * *

The coffee lasted maybe an hour or two before the weight of sleep deprivation fully kicked in. My body felt heavy, like a pound of bricks was dangling gently from my eyes, softly teasing the lids with the prospect of sleep.

Tick. Tick. Tick.

The clock on the wall was hypnotic. My eyes drifted slowly. My head fell downward, obeying the seductive temptation. At last, I could rest.

WACK.

I awoke to the sound of an oversized Bible colliding with the surface of my desk. My eyes bolted open, and I could hear the sound of my classmates sniggering as I looked up to find Sister Helen towering above me.

"So," she said calmly. "The Good Book isn't stimulating enough to keep you awake, Ms. Capello?"

"No—" I stopped to correct myself. "I mean yes, it's uh—stimulating." I took a deep breath. The class laughed even louder. "I'm just tired."

"I see that," she said as she removed the huge book from my desk and handed me a detention slip.

I sighed and took the slip reluctantly.

* * *

After serving two hours of detention that afternoon, I was eventually excused. I picked up my books, left the room, and found Emma relaxing on a bench in the adjoining hall. When I opened the door, she sat up and handed me what must have been the largest cup of coffee I'd ever seen.

"Word on the street is you fell asleep in Sister Helen's class." She playfully shook her head and kicked my shoe. "Rookie mistake."

"I'll remember that next time." I smiled and took a sip of coffee. As we walked down the empty hallway, I was hyper-aware of the space between us. I was self-conscious and nervous that I might accidentally bump into her or brush my hand against hers. And despite my best efforts to maintain distance, it happened over and over again, like there was some sort of gravitational pull between us. "You aren't tired?"

"Skipped third and fourth period to take a nap." She smiled as her shoulder brushed against mine. Her lavender perfume penetrated my lungs. "Said I had *womanly* problems."

"I wish I'd thought to do that," I groaned.

"Plus, I'm on my third round of coffee."

"So where is everyone?"

Emma laughed. "Madeline is on a terror because she's convinced we took shrooms without her."

"What? Really?"

"Yeah. So, her, Whitney, Dave, and Colin drove up to Syracuse to buy some."

"What's in Syracuse?"

Emma shrugged. "Colin's brother. He goes to school there, and I guess he's like—I don't know—the resident dealer for his dorm."

I laughed. "Why does she think we did shrooms?"

"I may have told her that." Emma stared down at her feet. "She wouldn't let up about this morning. She kept talking about how weird we were acting. And how bloodshot your eyes were. And, uh, so that's what I said. You know, to get her to shut up." She looked up and locked her unmistakably shy gaze with mine. "Is that ok?"

I nodded.

"Cuz, I mean. We hadn't really talked about it. And I didn't know if—"

"Of course it's ok," I interrupted.

"Ok," she said awkwardly. "Good. I guess."

9
STEPHEN LIKES CATS

"I'm sorry, what are we supposed to do again?" I asked Madeline as we sat in a circle in Colin's living room; his parents had gone to Albany and wouldn't be back until late that night.

"You just sit there and make sure we don't throw ourselves off the side of a building or something," Madeline snapped back.

"People do that on shrooms?" Whitney stared down at the small mushroom piece in her hand with wide eyes.

"Not if they're smart enough to have a trip sitter. And we've got two." She paused and looked me up and down. "Eh, more like one and a half."

"If you're insinuating that, somehow, I'm a bad trip sitter, then I'm going to be forced to prove you right and let you fling yourself off the side of a building later tonight."

"Do it and my ghost will fucking haunt your ass."

"Don't worry about it." Emma placed her hand on Whitney's shoulder, completely ignoring mine and Madeline's contentious exchange. "It'll be fine."

"So we're clear then?" Madeline barked.

"Yup," Colin said as he popped the entire mushroom in his mouth. Dave did too.

"Were you just supposed to take the whole thing at once like that?" I asked with a raised brow. The guys shrugged.

"Dunno," Colin said with a blank stare.

"Whit, if you're nervous about it, we can cut it up and boil it into tea. That's supposed to make the effects less intense."

Whitney nodded, and Emma took the little shroom from her hand.

"Want me to make you some too, Madeline?" Madeline nodded and I got up to help Emma with the tea.

"I don't feel anything," Colin said, studying his hands as if expecting them to melt away.

"Me neither," Dave chimed in.

Emma and I entered the kitchen. I hoisted myself up on the counter while Emma wandered around the room, opening cupboards and drawers, searching for whatever tools she needed to make the tea.

"How do you know how to do this?"

"When I lived back home, my brother and his friends used to do stuff like this all the time." Emma shrugged.

"I didn't know you had a brother. Where's he at?"

"He's in Humboldt County. He's, like, really into the earth and lives on a commune or something." Emma smiled. "What about you? What's your brother like?"

"Kind of a dick."

"C'mon, he can't be that bad."

I shrugged. "Maybe you'll get to meet him one day, and you can decide for yourself."

Emma laughed. "You're already going to take me home to meet the family?"

I felt my face turn red.

"I'm just teasing." She laughed. "It's sort of funny."

"What?"

"You're hard as a rock with just about everybody, but I can always manage to make you blush."

"I'm not blushing." The words spilled out of my mouth in some sort of defensive reflex.

Emma laughed and placed a pot of water on the stove. "Sorry. I didn't mean anything by it."

There was a light vibration from my jacket pocket, so I reached inside and removed my cell phone.

"Who's that?" Emma asked as I glanced at the notification on the front screen of the phone.

"Stephen." I shrugged and put the phone back into my pocket.

"Stephen? Like *Stephen* the quarterback Stephen?"

"Yeah."

"Oh," Emma said with a certain sort of inflection; her formerly playful mood shifted to something more… I don't know… dejected. "So what? You guys—like—talk?"

I shrugged. "Not really. He sends me pictures and stuff sometimes."

"He sends you pictures? Like what? Dick pics?" She tried to play it off like a joke, but I could tell she was mostly serious.

"No." I rolled my eyes and laughed. "Like—of cats."

"Cats?"

"Yeah, cats."

"You're serious?"

"Yeah. He likes cats. A lot. Apparently."

Emma was silent.

"What?"

"Nothing. I just think it's weird—that's all."

"Yeah. I guess. But cat people usually are pretty weird, so relatively speaking, it's kind of normal."

"That's not what I meant."

"What'd you mean then?"

Silence.

Her eyes were laser-focused on the cutting board in front of her, an obvious effort to avoid eye contact. I raised my brow and studied Emma closely, wondering why she cared about Stephen's stupid text.

And then it suddenly dawned on me.

Oh my God. She thinks I like Stephen.

"Wait—Em—"

Colin suddenly entered the room and made a beeline towards the fridge. I half groaned, totally annoyed that he had barged in before I could clear up the misunderstanding.

"So, what's the deal with this shit anyway? How long's it take to kick in?" Colin asked casually.

"Not long," Emma said with a curt tone. Her headspace was obviously still back on our conversation, and she didn't seem thrilled about the sudden interruption.

"So what? Like twenty minutes?"

"Depends on the quality. Sometimes. Sometimes longer."

"Cool," Colin said as he opened the fridge and pulled out a container of tapioca pudding. "Mmmmmm." Colin smiled wide and took a bite. "Tapioca is like—the best flavor—you know—of all the puddings."

"Uhm. Yeah. It's good… I guess," I said with a shrug. I wasn't really paying attention; mostly, I was trying to figure out how I could get him to leave.

"What'dya mean you guess? It's SO friggin' good." Colin took another bite, and then suddenly, his eyes grew wide, like he was looking at something spectacular. "Woah." He walked over to a lamp and put his face up real close to it. He turned it on, then off, and then glided his index finger around the base… as if to make sure it was actually there. "Did you see that?"

"See what?" I raised a skeptical eyebrow.

"The lamp—it like—I dunno—it kind of like—moved." He wiggled his arms around, presumably imitating whatever movement he thought the lamp had made.

"It didn't move. You're just starting to feel it." Emma looked at him skeptically. "I think."

"Really?" Colin stared at his palms like he suddenly discovered he had stigmata or something. Then he furrowed his brow. "Bro. This is weird."

Emma rolled her eyes and pushed Colin back into the other room. "Just go back over there and like—I don't know—think happy thoughts. Ok? We'll be right out."

"What kind of happy thoughts?"

"Puppies."

"Cool. Puppies are dope." Colin wandered out of the room and rejoined the others.

I watched the door carefully and waited until Colin was definitely out of earshot.

"Em, I don't like Stephen," I blurted out, eager to get back to the original conversation and get this whole thing sorted out.

Emma sighed. "Ok. But if you did. You know, I'd get it."

"What?"

"I just mean—I don't know—you're your own person—and if you wanted to pretend last night never happened, that would be ok. I wouldn't care."

"You wouldn't?" I felt like I'd just been sucker-punched in the gut. After Emma and I had, you know, gotten together, my biggest concern was that someone might find out; it never occurred to me that we might not be on the same page, that the feelings weren't mutual. I swallowed hard, attempting to expunge any semblance of emotion.

Her shoulders slumped, and her expression softened. "Dani, I'm sorry. I think that came out wrong."

"No, it's fine. Really." I took a deep breath and bit my lip, trying my best to conceal any semblance of emotion. "I get it. You don't care."

"Dani. No. Of course, I care… I just meant…" She thought for a long moment. She opened her mouth to speak, but before she could get the words out, Whitney barged into the room.

"Guys. Colin's acting really weird."

Emma sighed a long hard sigh. "He's just feeling it, Whit. He's fine."

"Are you sure? Because he's rubbing his face on the couch and like—I don't know—mumbling something about a Corgi? Is that normal?"

Emma shrugged. "For mushrooms… kind of… yeah."

"Holy shit!" Madeline bounded into the room, laughing hysterically. "Whit. You gotta see this. Dave's doing it too."

"Seriously? Dave! Are you ok?" Whitney's voice brimmed with anxiety as Madeline pulled her out of the kitchen back into the main living room.

"He's fine, Whit, you don't need to worry—" Emma hollered after her, but I don't think she heard.

I shoved my hands into my pockets and started to walk towards the door. "I should probably go—trip sit—or whatever it is we're supposed to be doing."

"Dani, wait." Emma grabbed my hand and turned me back towards her.

"Yeah?" I locked my eyes with Emma's and waited for her to say something. Anything.

Silence.

I stared at my shoes.

Silence.

I took a deep breath.

Silence.

"Can you hand me that?" she finally said as she pointed to a knife on the other side of the room. I walked over and grabbed it for her.

I handed her the knife and bit my lip, trying to formulate the right words to say. "Em, I don't like Stephen," I finally blurted out, trying to break the silence.

"You've said that."

"I think he's a jerk."

"Ok."

"You believe me, don't you?"

"Yes, Dani. I believe you." Emma stopped chopping the little mushroom pieces and locked her eyes with mine. "But I still don't know how you feel about me."

I was frozen.

I didn't know how to answer that. Because the truth was, I didn't fully understand how I felt. I knew that when we were together, I felt an itchy sort of feeling in my chest that made my heart flip flop in a way that was amazing and also terrifying all at the same time, and I knew that the thought of her being with someone else would drive me insane. But I also knew that all of these feelings made me anxious and confused and also sort of guilty in a way that I didn't fully comprehend and wasn't sure I ever really would.

There was a long moment of silence.

My heart was thumping in my chest.

My palms were sweating.

I thought about lying for a moment. Or changing the subject. But then, suddenly, I felt the words come out of my mouth. Before I could stop them. "I don't want to pretend last night didn't happen."

"Yeah?"

"Yeah." I swallowed hard. "I'm glad it did."

Emma smiled. "Me too."

There was another painfully long moment of silence.

"Here." I finally said as I handed Emma my cell phone, flipping it open to Stephen's texts. "Read it. It's totally harmless. And I hardly ever respond. I swear."

"I don't need to read it, Dani."

"I want you to."

Emma laughed and took the phone reluctantly.

"You like me," I teased, smiling wider than I probably ever have in my entire life.

"Shut up." Emma smiled and kicked my shoe. "You like me too."

"Hey!" Madeline suddenly barged into the room. "What the hell is taking so long?"

Emma half-rolled her eyes. "Nothing. It's ready." She handed Madeline a cup of tea, and the two of them walked out of the room. I smiled a big goofy smile and followed after.

"Here," she said as she handed the cup to Whitney.

Whitney and Madeline sort of eyed each other, like they were playing a game of chicken, waiting for the other person to take a sip. Colin and Dave, meanwhile, had lost interest in rubbing their faces on the couch and were now sitting cross-legged in front of the wall, rubbing their fingers genially across the wallpaper.

"Well, come on. This was your idea, Madeline," Whitney croaked.

"Fine," Madeline said as she took a sip. She scrunched up her face with repulsion. "God. That tastes like cat urine."

10
THANKSGIVING BREAK

I grabbed my duffle bag and tossed it onto the bed. I reached into my drawers, pulled out a few miscellaneous clothing items, and stuffed them into the bag.

"You're terrible at packing," Emma said as she leaned back in my chair, kicking her heels up on the desk in front of her.

I shrugged. "Well, I'm good at so many other things. Something had to give."

"You're awfully self-assured, *Daniella*." Emma smiled deviously.

I smiled and rolled my eyes. "I hate when you call me that."

"What? Why? It's your name!"

"My name's Dani. And I'll respond to Danielle in a pinch."

"That's not fair. You call me by my full name."

"That's because Emma's a normal name."

"Daniella's totally normal." Emma chuckled softly under her breath.

"You can't even say it with a straight face."

"Not because of the name. It's because you look like you're going to pop a vein in your forehead every time I do."

"So, you just enjoy torturing me?"

"A little. Yes."

"That seems cruel."

"Or incredibly amusing, depending on whose side you're on."

"Whatever, *Bolton*."

Emma shrugged. "You can call me that if you want, but it's not going to bother me, *Capello*."

"What's your middle name?"

"Dana."

"Huh… Emma Dana Bolton." I paused, mulling over her first, middle, and last names. "That's the most normal, white-girl name I've ever heard."

"And *Daniella* is the most adorable, Italian-girl name *I've* ever heard."

"I hate you," I said with a meek smile. I threw a pile of clothes into my duffle bag and then zipped it up. Emma sat up from the chair and walked over to me.

"I can't believe I'm going to be away from you for a week," she said, wrapping her arms around my waist and pulling my body close to hers.

"I know, it's kind of weird. Right?" I smiled as the warm weight of her breath clipped my neck.

"You'll call me and stuff?"

"God, you're such a girl," I teased with a facetious grin.

"Yeah, I am," Emma said, matter-of-factly. "And so are you."

"I'll call you every day." I paused. "Unless that's too much."

"It's not." Emma smiled. "I'm going to miss you, Dani."

"I'm going to miss you too, Emma Dana Bolton." I smiled, leaned in, and kissed her.

* * *

My eyes slowly fluttered awake. I glanced at the clock; it was nearly 10:30 a.m. I couldn't believe Olivia had let me sleep in so late. Before I was exiled to Willard, I can't remember a single time she'd ever let me sleep past 8:00 a.m. By the time I'd showered and dressed, the Thanksgiving festivities had already started downstairs.

Olivia and her sister, Sofi, were working away in the kitchen, delicately putting the final touches on the turkey by dousing the 30-pound poultry giant in globs of butter.

I made a beeline for the coffee maker, poured a cup, and leaned lazily against the peninsula. "Morning," I said groggily.

"Dani! Happy Thanksgiving!" Sofi gleamed with a wide smile. Her brunette bobbed hair shimmied in the light as she turned around to greet me. Her lips were stained with a purplish hue, most likely from the glass of wine sitting on the countertop.

I gave her a sort of half-assed hug.

"Look at you! Yer so tall… and *grown-up*," she said with a sort of inflection that seemed to imply that she was talking more about my womanly parts than my age. "How long's it been since I've seen you, kiddo?"

I shrugged. "A year, maybe?"

"Oh, come on, now. It can't have been a year."

I shrugged. It had definitely been a year.

"Sleep well?" my aunt asked with a bizarrely chipper grin.

"Guess so." I took a gargantuan swig of coffee.

"Then you won't mind making yourself useful." My aunt handed me a peeler and a bag of potatoes. I rolled my eyes, wandered towards the sink, and began the arduous task of veggie peeling.

"You want any cream? For the coffee?" Sofi asked as I placed a freshly peeled potato on the counter. Before I could answer, she sauntered over to me, placed her fingers to her lips in a shushing motion, and simultaneously topped off my coffee with a splash of cream liqueur.

I looked at Olivia with wide eyes, like a deer caught in the headlights. This was definitely some form of entrapment, and I didn't trust Sofi—at least, not enough to take the bait.

"Sofi!" My aunt playfully slapped her sister on the arm.

"What? If you're going to put her to work, the least you can do is let her have a little fun!" She smiled wide. "Right, Dani-girl?"

"I'm not complaining," I smirked.

My aunt smiled and rolled her eyes. "Just this once, ok?"

I smiled wide and took a sip.

"Need any help, ladies?" a voice suddenly called from the living room. I turned around to find a woman with thick, red lips, bright purple eyeshadow, and huge hoop earrings standing in the doorway. "I'm happy to lend a hand. I make a helluva sous chef."

"We're good, Samantha, thanks," my aunt said with an odious fake smile as she shooed the woman back towards the living room.

"You sure? I feel like such a jerk just sittin' around while you girls do all the work without me!"

"Don't be silly! You're our guest." Olivia let a half-smile escape her lips.

"Alright, well. You let me know if you change your mind," the woman responded with a sort of pout as she shimmied back into the other room.

"Who's that?"

"Samantha Moretti," my aunt groaned.

"Also known as the South Side Floozy."

"Stop that," my aunt said with a sort of playful laugh that seemed to imply that she didn't entirely disagree. "She's Gino's new girlfriend."

"Oh." I finished peeling another potato. "What's Katie think of her?"

"Oh, who knows? I doubt they've even met."

"Really? Why not?"

"The girl's been staying with her grandmother. In Maine."

"Staying? Like on a visit?"

"I don't know, Dani. Indefinitely, maybe? It's not really any of our business, is it?"

"No." I vigorously peeled another potato. "I guess not."

"So, tell me about this new school of yours? Liv says it's some kind of hoity-toity place?"

"Something like that." I took a sip of coffee and pointed my pinky finger outwards, in an over-the-top display of hoity-toityness.

"What're yer classes like?"

"Same as Mountain Grove. Except, you know, some of them are taught by decrepit nuns."

Sofi furrowed her brow. "Nuns? Really?"

"It's a Catholic school."

"That's a drag."

"—and if by drag you mean it's one of the best schools in the country, with the highest acceptance rate into the Ivy Leagues, then yeah, it's a real drag," my aunt bragged.

Sofi looked at me. "You got your sights set on an Ivy League education?"

I shrugged. "Dunno. Maybe."

"Makes sense, I guess. Yer mom and dad were sort of brainiacs," Sofi said as she took a sip of wine.

"Robert mentioned he'd met a couple of your friends a few weeks back?" Olivia chimed in.

"Yeah. Some of them."

"Any boys?" Sofi asked with a salacious grin, attempting to engage in some form of girl-talk.

"It's an all-girls school."

"Christ. Really?"

"Yeah." I shrugged.

"It's so they can focus on their schoolwork. In class. You know, minimize distractions?"

"...and a social life," Sofi scoffed.

"Nonsense. The woman in charge of admissions assured me they do social events year-round with the local schools. Right, Dani?"

"Yeah. I guess." I shrugged. "I've met a few guys from Pine Hills."

Sofi smiled wide. "You like any of them?"

"They're ok."

"Speaking of boys… the admissions woman also mentioned some sort of winter formal. That should be right around the corner, huh? You think you'll go?"

"Probably not."

"Why not?"

I rolled my eyes. "I hate dances."

"How can you be so sure? You've never actually been to one."

"Because the music sucks, and I hate dancing."

"You know, you can take anyone you want. It doesn't have to be a boy from… what'd you say that school was called?"

"Pine Hills?"

My aunt smiled wide. "You could ask that Mancini boy to go with you."

"Mikey?"

"Yeah. He asks about you nearly every time I've seen him. I'm sure he'd love to go."

My cheeks burned as I vigorously peeled the last potato. I needed to get out of the kitchen. I needed this conversation to be over. "That's the last one. Can I, you know, be excused?"

"Dani, we've barely gotten started!"

"Please?"

My aunt furrowed her brow. "Ok. Fine. Go on."

"Thanks!" I took my coffee and scuttled away from the uncomfortable conversation.

When I entered the living room, I found Tony and Gino glued to the television, reclining like kings in our oversized La-Z-Boy style sofa. They were sipping glasses of scotch and watching the game. Benny, Gino's man-child nephew, was slouched over, sitting on the floor and stuffing his face full of a family-sized bag of potato chips. Samantha, Gino's apparently brand-new girlfriend, was staring at the television with wide eyes, like she was watching someone solve a complex physics equation or something.

I took a seat on the other side of the couch and grabbed a soda.

Luca and Drake suddenly stumbled into the living room from out back. They had a sort of mischievous look about them like they'd just finished doing something terrible, like torturing a small child or blowing up someone's mailbox.

"Where's Robert?" I asked, suddenly noticing he was nowhere to be found.

"Don't ask," Drake mumbled under his breath, simultaneously shaking his head like I'd committed some type of heinous offense.

"What? Why?"

"Sore subject," Gino groaned as he took a gargantuan swig of scotch.

Tony was silent.

"Well?" I looked around the room, waiting for someone to spill the beans.

"He's at the little Asian girl's house," Benny finally said, breaking the awkward silence.

"You mean his *girlfriend*? Anna?"

"Yeah. Her."

"So?"

"Whadya mean so? It's Thanksgiving. He should be with his family," Tony roared from the other side of the room.

"Yeah. Not some chick he's banging one out with," Luca chimed in like a grade-A kiss-ass.

"They've been together for over a year." I rolled my eyes.

"So?"

"So, don't you think by now it's a little more serious than that?"

"It's never more serious than that." Drake shrugged and grabbed the bag of potato chips from Benny.

"Do they even celebrate Thanksgiving?" Luca suddenly asked with such sincere curiosity it made me want to hurl.

"Yes, Luca. Asian-Americans celebrate Thanksgiving. Especially ones born and raised on the outskirts of Jersey."

"Yeah, but like, what do they eat?"

"What kind of question is that?"

"Yeah, stupid. They eat dog," Drake chimed in, laughing his ass off.

"Drake. Jesus. Stop. That's incredibly offensive."

"And incredibly hilarious."

"No! It's not." I looked around the room like I was trapped in an insane asylum. "You can't say things like that."

"I wish Robert would get back together with Andrea Ricci. I really liked that girl," Olivia said as she dropped off a tray of meats and cheeses.

"Why? She was a total bitch."

"Language," Tony barked.

The irony of Tony getting pissed about my "foul" language while the entire family literally acted like bigoted assholes was not lost on me. "It's the truth. She was awful."

"She is not awful. Her mother and I are on the PTA together. Andrea's a wonderful girl. And pretty too."

"There are better things to be than pretty," I scoffed. "You know, like a good, decent, human being."

"The Riccis are great people, Daniella. They're Catholics. We see them at church every Sunday."

"I'm not sure what that has to do with anything."

"Liv's right. Andrea's the better catch. Way hotter," Drake said with an amused chuckle.

"You think?" Luca asked as he squinted his eyes, trying to visualize a side-by-side comparison.

"Bigger rack," Drake smirked. "Anna's got a major case of pancake titties."

"Drake!" my aunt barked.

"What? It's true."

Tony and Gino stifled a laugh; they obviously thought it was funny but didn't want to evoke the wrath of my aunt.

I rolled my eyes, completely annoyed by everyone in the room.

"Anna's a great person. She's really nice. And smart. Like REALLY smart. She's going to med school next year."

"An Asian going to med school? Big whoop."

"Oh my God." My face had to be a million different shades of red at this point. I was totally fuming.

"Dani, he's just teasing to get a rise out of you. Calm down, would you?"

"No! Prejudice isn't something you can just *tease* someone about. It's a big fucking deal."

"God. What's your problem?"

"My problem is that Robert should be allowed to date anyone he wants. It shouldn't matter if she's Asian, or Black, or White or Italian or whatever. If they're happy—and they love each other—then that's all that should matter. Ok? Like, it's none of your business who he dates. Or whether you approve of it or not. It's just like—it's his life, ok?"

"Ok. Ok." My aunt threw her hands up in surrender. "You're right. We get it. Robert can date anyone he wants."

Drake smirked. "Unless it's a dude. Cuz that's just fuckin' gross."

I rolled my eyes and stormed out of the living room into the backyard. I pulled out my phone and began typing.

My family is seriously the worst.

Mine too, Emma wrote back almost instantly. *What happened?*

***

It was Saturday afternoon, my last day home for Thanksgiving break. I guess all that talk on Thanksgiving about dances and boys really got my aunt worked up because she took it upon herself to arrange some type of double date with me, Mikey, Drake, and Becca. The three of them were all waiting for me downstairs, and in some type of major fight or flight moment, I took it upon myself to escape.

I swung my hips over the balcony, grabbed a thick branch with my right arm, and thrust my weight onto the wooden limb. Gently, I lowered my body down the tree trunk, eventually hitting the ground with a light thud.

As I brushed the grass from my jeans, I looked up to find Robert and his girlfriend, Anna, staring at me from a few feet away. I slowly tilted my head up, locking my eyes with their startled gazes.

"Sorry," I said with a meek smile, realizing suddenly that I had interrupted some sort of romantic encounter.

"You know this place has a front door, Dani," Robert said with a subtle eye roll as he peeled his body away from Anna's.

"Yeah, well, I was desperate." I shoved my hands inside my jacket pockets and walked towards them.

"Mom giving you shit again?" he asked with a lilt of sympathy.

"She ambushed me with some sort of blind date with Michael Mancini."

Robert laughed. "That's mildly hilarious."

"No, it's not," I whined. "It's completely horrible."

"I thought you liked Frog-boy?"

"No," I grunted. "We're just friends. And barely even that. We haven't talked since I left for Willard."

Anna took a few steps towards the kitchen window and peered inside, catching a peek of Michael, who was chatting up a storm with my aunt. Drake sat on the kitchen counter beside them, his arm slung around Becca, Michael's younger sister.

"He doesn't look so bad," Anna said with an indifferent shrug.

"It's not his looks I have a problem with."

"Then what is it? His taste in appetizers?" Robert burst into laughter.

"I don't get it." Anna looked at Robert like he was crazy.

I rolled my eyes. "In 8th-grade biology, we were dissecting frogs, and Drake bet him twenty bucks to eat a piece of the intestine."

"You're joking," Anna said incredulously as she looked back through the window, eyeing Michael with disgust.

"All the guys in my class thought it was hilarious, so they chipped in an extra hundred to get him to flush it down with the liver and an eyeball."

"Hence the incredibly accurate nickname, Frog-boy." Robert laughed hard, obviously visualizing Michael eating the innards of a halfway dissected biology frog.

"That's disgusting. And really dangerous. They douse those things in formaldehyde." Anna furrowed her brow, then looked over at me sympathetically. "Maybe you should just lie and tell your aunt you're dating someone else so she'll leave you alone."

"Don't you think she'd get curious about who, specifically, I'm dating?" I asked with a bleak half-smile, unamused at the irony of the suggestion. It wouldn't actually be a lie. I *was* dating someone. I just couldn't tell anyone about it.

Anna shrugged. "You're like four hours away at that fancy school most of the year, aren't you? Just say you met some guy there."

"Maybe." I locked my eyes with the ground, kicking a small rock into the nearby grass.

"Alright, we're heading out," Robert said nonchalantly as he grabbed Anna by the hand and led her down the walkway in the opposite direction. "Good luck with your date."

"Wait. Where are you going?" I asked as I trailed after them.

"Work," Anna said with a friendly smile as she followed Robert towards the backyard's gate. "I've got a shift at the hospital."

"What about you?" I looked over at Robert.

He shrugged. "Probably grab a bite or something after I drop her off."

"Daniella!" I heard my aunt holler from inside the house. My eyes widened with fear.

"Take me with you," I pleaded and simultaneously ran after Robert and Anna.

Robert laughed. "Not a chance."

"I won't bug you. I swear. You can just drop me off somewhere."

"DANIELLA!" My aunt's voice grew louder.

"Come on. I can't go back in there."

"No way. Mom'll freak."

"Seriously, Robert. Olivia is like three seconds away from forking up the down payment for a summer wedding."

"Aw, Robert. Look at how panicked she is," Anna said, with a sympathetic grin.

My aunt suddenly burst out the back door. "There you are. Are you almost ready? Everyone's waiting on you."

I looked up at Robert with pleading eyes and mouthed the word, *please*.

Robert sighed. "Wait. Mom," he finally said. "Dani can't go."

Thank God. I let out a sigh of relief.

"What do you mean she can't go?" Olivia asked.

"*Remember...*" He nudged his head, indicating that I should play along with the ruse. "She's helping Anna at the hospital today."

Olivia raised a suspicious brow. "What? Why on Earth would she do that?"

"College credit." Robert shrugged casually.

"Oh. Yeah." I smiled wide, thankful for Robert's quick wit. "They really hound you on the value of volunteer work at Willard… one teacher was saying we'd need at least forty hours to be competitive on college applications."

"Oh," Aunt Olivia said with a frown. "Well, I guess if it's for school…"

"It is." I smiled wide and followed Robert and Anna out of the backyard towards the car.

* * *

We dropped Anna off at the hospital, then drove a few blocks to a local pizzeria.

"Thanks for, you know, saving me from Olivia," I said as I slid into a corner booth.

"You're welcome," he said, placing a huge pepperoni pizza on the table. "But you owe me. Big time."

I smiled, grabbed a slice of pizza, and pulled my phone out from my pocket, attempting to check for any missed calls or text messages. "Damnit," I said as I shoved my phone into my jacket pocket.

"What?"

"It died." I held up my phone and sighed.

Robert laughed. "Worried yer gonna miss a call from the Frog-boy?"

"Uhg." I rolled my eyes.

"What's the deal with you two anyway? You had a thing and like… broke up?"

"We didn't have a thing." My cheeks burned. My voice cracked.

"That's convincing." He laughed.

"It's true!"

"Then what's the big deal about going to a movie? You guys used to hang out all the time."

"Yeah, well, it's different now. I don't want him to like… get the wrong idea."

"I know I give you shit, but Mikey's not such a bad guy."

"I know that."

"So maybe you should cut him a break. He obviously likes you."

"Yeah, well, I don't like him back."

He looked at me for a long moment. "Why? You got some other squeeze back at that fancy school?"

Silence.

Robert smiled wide at my lack of a response. We both knew I'd been found out. So, he pressed on. "Alright. Who is he?"

The question looped like a melody in my head, crescendoing at the all-important word: *he*.

Silence.

"Yo—Earth to Dani." Robert playfully waved his hands in front of me.

"It's nothing. I mean, no one," I finally responded.

"C'mon, you can tell me."

"Seriously. It's nothing," I insisted, knowing full well that nothing about my tone or mannerisms was even remotely convincing. My stomach churned.

"Dani, you're like a hundred different shades of red."

"I am not."

"If you don't want to tell me, you don't have to," Robert said as he took a bite of pizza. "But, just so you know, I wouldn't tell Mom. Or Dad. If that's what you're worried about."

I raised a curious eyebrow.

"As someone who gets shit from them nearly every day about Anna, I get why you wouldn't want them to know."

Silence.

I twirled my straw around in my soda and stared down at the table.

"Can I ask you a question?" I finally asked.

"Shoot."

"How do you deal with it?"

"What?"

"I don't know… that Liv and Tony sort of… don't approve of Anna… and you know… wish you'd date someone else."

Robert shrugged. "I don't know. I just figure that it's my life. And if they don't like it, that's their problem. Not mine."

"Yeah, ok. But isn't it kind of hard? To listen to their shit? Day after day?"

He shrugged. "I guess. But the alternative would be worse."

"What do you mean?"

"I don't know. Dating someone you don't love. Just to make your parents happy. Sounds kind of miserable." Robert looked at me closely. "Why? You worried they won't like your mystery boo back at school?"

I shrugged. "Something like that…"

"Well, fuck em'. You don't need their permission to be happy."

I laughed. "Thanks."

11
CHEMISTRY

I tapped my pencil against my desk as I finished reading an incredibly dull chapter from my chemistry book. I had a test next week and wasn't feeling particularly prepared. As I mumbled chemistry problems under my breath, Emma relaxed casually on my bed a few feet away, nonchalantly flipping through the pages of a magazine.

I sighed and put down my book.

"What is it?" Emma asked, peering up at me from beneath the veil of a glossy Teen Vogue.

"I don't suppose you know the molecular formula of an organic compound with the empirical formula CHO and a molecular mass of 232?"

Emma smiled and hopped out of bed. She took my pencil and started writing next to the problem. "So, you have carbon plus hydrogen plus oxygen… which gives you," she paused for a moment and glanced at the periodic table in the back of the book. "Right. So, you've got 12 + 1 + 16… which is 29." She continued scribbling furiously next to the problem. "So, now you just need to solve 232 divided by 29." She mumbled a few nonsensical chemistry terms under her breath and finally tossed the pencil down triumphantly. "The answer's C sub 8 H sub 8 O sub 8."

I stared back at her, dumbfounded at the simplicity with which she just solved the problem.

"What?" She smirked. "Just because I'm pretty doesn't mean I'm stupid."

"And humble." I teased.

She grabbed my textbook and playfully flipped the cover shut. "Come on, take a break with me. You've been studying for hours."

"And I still haven't made any progress."

"How about you take a break now, watch a movie with me, and I'll help you study when it's over." She smiled. "I aced AP Chem when I took it two years ago. Plus, I'm a great tutor. So, I can promise you're in good hands, Capello."

"Fine," I said as I reluctantly let her pull me into bed beside her.

I flopped onto the pile of pillows as Emma teed up the movie and pressed play. She leaned back beside me, entangling her body in my own. Within a matter of moments, the encounter inevitably took a turn for something slightly more… well, physical. We were hardly watching the movie at all.

"Have you done this before?" The words haphazardly slipped out of my mouth, and I felt the sharp sting of embarrassment; I instantly regretted asking the question.

"Uh, yeah, Dani." Emma laughed. "I've made out during a movie before. And so have you, for the record." She leaned in and resumed kissing my neck.

"That's not what I meant."

"What'd you mean?"

"Forget it."

"C'mon. Don't be like that." She tilted my head upwards. "What'd you mean?"

"Well, like… this. Have you been with someone who's…" I gestured between the two of us, "you know—not a guy."

"Oh," she said as she raised her eyebrows, suddenly understanding the nature of my question. She opened her mouth to respond, but I jumped in before she could formulate the words.

"I wouldn't care if you had. Or hadn't. I was just wondering. That's all." I didn't look her in the eye. I just stared off at the corner of the room.

"No. I haven't." She placed her head against my chest, and for a few moments, we actually watched the movie.

"Emma," I finally broke the silence. "You ever worry that this, I don't know, might get complicated at some point?"

"What do you mean?"

"You know, if things didn't work out and you changed your mind or something."

"What makes you think I'd be the one who has a change of heart?"

I shrugged. "I don't know. I just wouldn't want to do anything that would make things weird."

We were silent for a long moment.

"I'd be lying if I said the thought hadn't crossed my mind." She thought for a moment. "Losing you romantically would be hard. But losing you as a friend would be even harder."

I looked down at my feet again, unsure of what to say.

* * *

Mr. Ackerman called on me to answer a question; I hadn't quite made out the details. It was something about a first-order reaction.

"What?" I looked up slowly. I hadn't paid an iota of attention to the lecture. I was torn between embarrassment and guilt. My grade wasn't great, and I knew that, of all my classes, Chemistry was the one subject I *should* be paying attention to, but the more I fell behind, the more I hated the subject, and the more I hated the subject, the less I wanted to do the work.

Mr. Ackerman smiled when I asked him to repeat the question. I was annoyed because he had that sort of smug look on his face—you know, the one that every teacher gets when they catch a student in the middle of a daydream.

"Explain how the data on chart thirteen is consistent with a first-order reaction."

Fuck.

I flipped the book open to the appropriate page. I traced the diagram with my index finger as I read the words under my breath. *Catalyzed isomerization... butene... trans... two... butene...* I was fucked.

Before I could formulate an answer, the door swung open, and a freshman girl brought a note to Mr. Ackerman. He read it under his breath, then looked in my direction.

"Lucky break." He handed me the note and told me to grab my things. Apparently, I was to report to Sister Helen's office immediately.

The class erupted into a barrage of giggles and *ooohs*, the kinds of childish noises your schoolmates tout with delight when they assume that you're in some sort of trouble. I rolled my eyes, dumped my books into my bag, and walked out of the room.

The halls were empty. My shoes clanked against the marble floor, and each step echoed softly down the hall. I slipped my bag over my shoulder and wondered what I was about to be punished for. There were a handful of possible offenses. Drinking and sneaking out past curfew had become such a regular occurrence that I half forgot it was off-limits. There was also the contraband: I had a bottle of whiskey and two joints stored back in my dorm.

And then it hit me.

Emma.

What if someone had found out?

Fuck.

Someone must have seen us… but who? The night monitor? A janitor? A teacher? Or worse yet… a student?

My heart thumped in my chest.

My hands were shaking.

We'd be kicked out of school. I knew that much. Student relationships were strictly "prohibited" per the honor code; it was grounds for expulsion for sure. But more so than that, I knew I'd be dead back home. Uncle Tony and Aunt Olivia weren't exactly open-minded when it came to this sort of thing.

I sat, nervously, outside Sister Helen's office for a few minutes, staring mindlessly at the ceiling. I swallowed hard and tapped my foot anxiously against the tiled floor.

Suddenly, Sister Helen emerged from her office. She waved me inside, so I picked up my bag and followed her through the door. She looked at me funny, like she couldn't quite meet my gaze.

I took a seat and stared at my shoes. The silence was deafening. I felt like my insides had been completely twisted. The anticipation was making me nauseous. I wiped my palms against my uniform. I thought seriously that I might keel over and faint from sheer panic at any moment.

Finally, she broke the silence.

"Dani, I'm so sorry," she said with a half stutter as she proceeded to tell me the terrible news.

"Excuse me?" I stammered, completely dumbfounded. I thought I had misheard her. She repeated the story again—this time, slower.

"Your cousin, Robert. He's been shot." Her words were hushed like she was trying to give me some semblance of privacy, even though we were the only two souls in the room. "He's in critical condition."

I instantly felt foolish and consumed with guilt. This wasn't about me and Emma. It was bigger than that.

Once she had finished the arduous task of explaining the very few details she'd been given, she offered to escort me back to my dorm. I needed to pack. I'd be gone for the rest of the week. My aunt had asked that I come home for at least that long.

I grabbed my bag from under my bed and tossed a few things inside. Sister Helen picked up my black sweater from the floor, handed it to me, and I stuffed it into my bag. I didn't really want help packing, but it was too late to refuse the gesture.

"Don't worry about your schoolwork," Sister Helen said as she gently placed her hand on my shoulder. "I'll let your teachers know you've got an extension."

"Thanks," I said as I walked into the bathroom and packed my toiletries. I looked in the mirror. My eyes were red and puffy. I pressed my fingers against my tear ducts, attempting to suppress any sign of emotion.

There was a car waiting for me in the lot.

It took nearly three hours to get to Saint Joseph's. I arrived at 2:57 p.m. that afternoon. But Robert had passed at 2:35 p.m. I'd missed his last breath by a mere 22 minutes.

A nurse escorted me into the waiting area in the ER.

Anna was sitting next to her mom and dad. Her eyes were bloodshot, and her arms were curled up around her body as if forming some sort of protective cocoon. Tears trickled from her mother's cheeks, half because the news was tragic and half because she obviously couldn't bear to see her daughter in so much emotional distress.

Luca and Drake sat in the other corner of the room. Drake stared at his shoes, and Luca wiped his eyes, trying desperately to hold back any semblance of tears.

And then I saw Olivia. I barely recognized her. Her usual rosy complexion had faded to a dusty pale sort of yellow. She looked sick, like she might retch at any moment.

My uncle wasn't there.

The men had supposedly left to take care of the arrangements. But I had a feeling that *taking care of the arrangements* actually meant something more akin to *revenge*. There was no way Tony was going to let Robert's death go unchecked. Whoever did this was going to pay.

I took a seat beside Aunt Olivia and grabbed her hand. We didn't speak a word. There was nothing to say.

The funeral was two days later.

My uncle insisted on an open casket. The bullet wounds had left most of Robert's chest disfigured, but his face was just the same.

I sat in the front pew next to Olivia, while the men brought the casket in from the back of the church. I stared at my shoes and held her hand while she silently cried. Once the casket was in position, Tony, Gino, Drake, and Luca took a seat beside Oliva and me. The service was basically the same as any other I'd attended before. There was a viewing of the body, several readings from the Bible, and a handful of eulogies—one from Gino, one from Tony, and one from Robert's college roommate, Jake.

I don't remember what they said, really. The service was a blur. Before I knew it, we were attempting and failing at an orderly exit from the church towards the cemetary. When we arrived, the pallbearers brought the casket to the gravesite and placed it on top of a stand. The priest said a few final words and then, just like that, the casket was lowered into the ground. We piled back into the limousine and were quickly whisked away, leading the procession towards the memorial service. It took us nearly an hour to get to Gino's restaurant. That's where the memorial service was being held.

When we arrived, Olivia meticulously examined the buffet, ensuring everything was in order: the silver was polished, the chafing dishes were positioned just right, the plates and silverware were clean and orderly.

I don't know how to describe the vibe of the thing, except to say that it was strange. It wasn't exactly lively, but it wasn't exactly solemn either. Everyone had divided into little groups. I could hear them whispering amongst themselves. Speculating about what happened.

"How does a twenty-two-year-old end up shot? Dead?"

"He must have been in trouble…"

"He must have had enemies…"

"Who could have done such a thing?"

A part of me was annoyed by their whispers. The speculation. But another part of me understood. Because I was just as confused. How *does* something like this happen? Who would have done it? And why?

It all makes no sense.

And I want to cry. But I can't.

I'm numb.

It doesn't even feel reel. The fact that he's gone. That I'll never see him again. That he'll never get to tease me about who I'm dating or not dating… or give me advice… or make me laugh when what I really want to do is cry…

And then. Shit. The ring. The engagement. He was supposed to propose. He was so excited. He loved Anna so much. He wanted to move to California. To quit the family business. He wanted a family of his own. He wanted kids. I can't wrap my head around it.

I need to get out of here.

I need to think.

I walked out the front door and wandered down the cement steps into the parking lot. I pulled out a pack of cigarettes from my jacket pocket and pressed the filtered tip against my lips when I felt a drop of moisture hit my cheek. I looked around; it was starting to rain. I sighed, scurried over to the overhang outside the entryway, and took shelter under the ivy-draped awning.

I shivered as a cold breeze brushed my cheeks. I held the lighter against the end of the cigarette and struggled to hold down the fuel lever with my quivering thumb. The flame lit but only for a second, and my eyes narrowed as I struggled with the switch, trying my best to focus.

Suddenly, my trembling hand gave way, and the lighter slipped from my fingers, falling to the ground with a delicate clank. I bent over to pick it up.

"Here," I heard a scratchy voice say as I slowly tilted my head upwards.

I took a deep breath as my eyes locked on the haggard man standing in front of me. I recognized the weathered face immediately. It was the Man with the Marlboros from Olivia's fundraiser. He pulled out a small pack of matches from his back pocket, struck one, and gently held it out while his callused hand guarded the flame against the wind. "Sorry. About Robert."

"Thanks," I said reluctantly as I dipped my cigarette into the flame. "You knew him?"

"Met him once 'er twice." The Man with the Marlboros lit a cigarette of his own, then exhaled a thick cloud of gray smoke. "Seemed like a nice kid."

"He was." I took a long drag from the cigarette. We stood there in silence for a long moment. Eventually, the Man with the Marlboros tossed his cigarette to the ground and walked back towards the restaurant.

"Hey," I said suddenly, calling after him. He'd reached the door and turned around, locking his cold blue stare on me. "What's your name?"

He took a deep breath and swallowed hard, as if contemplating whether or not to answer the question. "Lou. Collins."

12
THE PAST AND PRESENT TENSE

I'm having trouble with the past and present tense.
Was…
Is…
Was…
Is…
Dead.
Whatever.

I can't wait to get out of here. To get back to Willard. Being home is beyond depressing. And there's no privacy. Our house is full of people. Constantly. Gino, Carlo, Lou, Benny, and others.

They shuffle in and out of my uncle's office; day in and day out; God knows what they're actually doing in there. But I know something's up. They're full of electricity. Full of fury. They're wired like an army bracing for war, waiting for a declaration from the all-knowing general.

Tony emerges from the office only occasionally. When he does, I can tell that he's different.

He's harder than usual.
Pensive.
Musing.

Olivia hasn't left her room since we got home from the service. Her sister, Sofi, is staying with us to "help take care of Liv," which mostly translates to helping her self-medicate with antidepressants, muscle relaxers, and booze.

Luca has adopted some sort of escapist mentality. He's nearly catatonic, hunkered down in front of the television, eating loads of junk food, watching too much TV.

As for Drake, I don't know where he is.

I'm alone in my room. My phone blinks.

Dani?
You ok?
Where are you?
I'm worried.
What's going on?
Are you alright?
Hello?

Countless missed calls and text messages are piling up on my phone. Mostly from Emma. And the few I got from Whitney and Madeline were no doubt orchestrated in some capacity by Emma. I felt bad for being unresponsive. But everything had happened so suddenly. I didn't get a chance to tell anyone where I'd gone or why. And right now, I couldn't stomach the strength to call anyone, much less explain what had happened.

Sorry for being AWOL. Phone died. Be back Tuesday.

I wrote the text and sent it to Emma before I could change my mind. My phone wasn't dead. But saying that was easier than explaining Robert was. I just—I just didn't know what to say.

I stared at the ceiling. My eyes burned. I can't remember the last time I'd slept. But it's nearly impossible to sleep right now. It's too quiet. I closed my eyes. My mind was racing, buzzing with images, thoughts, questions; electrified with sadness, anger, and disappointment.

"Coffee?" Robert asked with groggy, bloodshot eyes.

"No. I'll grab some on the road."

That was our last exchange, our last conversation. The morning I caught the train back to Willard after Thanksgiving break. Why was I in such a hurry? Why didn't I have coffee with him? Why didn't I extend the few precious moments we had left?

Because I was in a hurry.

Because I wanted to get back to Willard.

Because I was wrapped up in my own stupid shit.

And there it was again, that heavy feeling in my gut. I try to push it out, but I can't stop it: the pain, the regret, the horrible sinking feeling like my insides are collapsing on themselves.

I don't know how to deal with any of this.

My phone buzzed again.

I already knew who it was.

I didn't need to check.

Fuck.

I'm such a fucking asshole.

I barely had time to pull myself out of bed. I jerked the sheets off my body and ran towards the bathroom with my hands covering my mouth. I collapsed on the cool tile floor, lifted the lid to the toilet, and threw up. I hadn't eaten in nearly twenty-four hours, so there wasn't much more than greenish-yellow bile to expunge.

A prickly feeling enveloped my limbs as I let my body slink away from the toilet and onto the floor.

I can't do this.

I can't sleep.

I need to shut off my brain.

I pressed my cheeks against the cold tile floor for a few minutes and eventually mustered the strength to push myself up and off the ground. I wandered out of my bedroom, down the hall towards the kitchen. The house was quiet. The only light around was the reflection of the moon pouring in through the oversized windows around the house.

I opened the fridge and found a six-pack of beer. I swiped one, then grabbed a pack of cigarettes and stumbled out the backdoor onto the patio. I stared up at the sky. There wasn't a cloud in sight, but light pollution kept the stars mostly hidden.

My phone buzzed. Again.

Sorry for calling/texting incessantly. Just wanted to make sure you were alright.

I sighed and started to type back when I suddenly heard a voice from behind me.

"Since when do you smoke?"

I turned around and saw Drake standing in the doorway. I scowled in his direction and instinctively shoved my phone in my pocket. "You don't have anything better to do than give me shit?"

"Fuck. I didn't mean anything by it. I was just surprised."

"Where've you been, anyway?"

He doesn't respond. He doesn't explain. Instead, he changes the subject. "Can I bum one?"

"Whatever." I handed him a light.

"Thanks," he said as he slung a little backpack over his shoulder and wandered out into the yard. He opened the back gate, and I hollered after him.

"Where are you going?"

"Away."

"No shit." I rolled my eyes.

"You can come. If you want."

I shrugged, looked around, and then scurried after him. Anything was better than being trapped in our life-suckingly morbid house.

We walked a few blocks in silence and eventually made our way to a park on Clement's Street. The park was sort of spooky at night. The place was really only lit by the moon and a single streetlamp that spilled a murky orange glow onto the playground.

"I haven't been here since we were kids," I said casually as we approached the old, rusted jungle gym. It was surrounded by a huge, rectangular sandbox, the contents of which had hardened into a semi-solid crust from years of weather. I ran my fingertips against the playground spring riders. They were shaped in a bizarre assortment of animals: a dinosaur, a horse, an elephant, a cat. Olivia used to take us here when we were kids, and I remembered how shiny and new everything used to look back then. Now, the entire park looked sort of rusted and old.

Nothing was the way I remembered it. Everything had changed.

We took a seat on a little cement picnic table. Drake pulled a sports drink out of his little backpack and a small, plastic zip-lock bag from his pocket.

"What's that?" I asked stupidly, staring at the little glittering white rocks inside the baggy.

Drake just looked at me like I was a complete idiot. He didn't bother dignifying my question with a response. Instead, he dumped the little crystals onto the tabletop and went to work.

I lit another cigarette as Drake removed a few "tools" from his bag and diligently crushed the little rocks with the underside of a blue sports drink, eventually creating a fine powder. When he was done, he separated the pile of drugs into portions with the help of his student ID.

He pulled out a twenty-dollar bill from his wallet and wrapped it into a tight little cylinder, placed one end in his nose, and leaned over the sparkly white powder. With a determined snort, he inhaled the drugs and tilted his head way back, like he was staring straight into the heavens.

"Shit," Drake said as he wiped his nose with the corner of his sleeve. He blinked a couple of times then opened his eyes wide like he was seeing the world for the very first time. "Gimme that." He motioned to the sports drink. I handed it to him. He took a long swig and wiped the bright blue dribbles from his lips. "You want in on this?"

I took a deep breath and watched Drake closely, searching for some sort of visible sign of distress. Everything I'd ever been told about drugs, *real* drugs I mean, made me expect the worst. Like, at any moment he might keel over and writhe in some sort of uncontrollable drug-induced seizure.

But that didn't happen.

He was totally fine.

Better than fine even.

His wide eyes glittered in the moonlight. And he was sort of calm, and happy, lit up by something mysterious and fiery and eternal. Watching him was like watching someone uncover a secret—a wild, exciting, and infinitely intriguing secret. And I knew, suddenly, that I wanted to know exactly what that secret was all about.

"Ok," I said as he passed me the rolled-up bill. "What do I do?"

"Lean over and breathe in, really hard. Ok? If you breathe out, you're going to blow the shit everywhere. Don't fucking waste it. Alright?"

"Ok," I said as I took a deep breath. I was suddenly nervous. Really nervous. I didn't want to do it wrong, and I also didn't want to die. I didn't even know where the drugs came from. What if they were laced with like… rat poison or something? I tried to think of something else. But I was totally freaked.

"Like this?" I asked wearily, trying my best to feign confidence, but my voice cracked, which was a dead give-away that I was having second thoughts.

"You aren't going to puss out, are you?"

"No," I insisted. "But what if I take too much and like—overdose or something?"

Drake burst into laughter.

"Drake! Don't laugh. I'm serious!"

"You're not going to OD," he said as he carefully made a line and took another hit from the little pile of powder. "Look. I'm fine. No big deal."

I don't know why, but that was evidence enough to convince me. I leaned over and...

"Oh my fucking God!" I gasped for air as the powder flooded my nose and struck the back of my throat like a goddamn fucking fireball. My heart was pounding in my chest. I felt like I'd just swallowed battery acid.

"Drink," I barked as I reached for the sports drink and took a long swig; attempting to soothe my seared throat.

It didn't take long for me to feel *it*.

And *it* was amazing.

I don't know how to explain it exactly, except to say that I felt like I was fucking invincible. And all the bad things, the bad thoughts and feelings that clouded my mind, they melted into tiny pools of nothingness.

"Where'd you even... you know... get this?"

"Enzo hooked it up."

"Right," I scoffed. Enzo was Carlo's son, and everyone knew he was a dealer. I don't know why I was surprised. Of course, he sold it to Drake.

Drake raised a curious eyebrow. "Pitch in some cash, I'll swing by his place and get another load."

"I'll think about it." As soon as the words slipped off my lips, I understood how people got addicted the first time they used. Getting the drugs was easy. Feeling high was easy. Everything was easy.

But you know what isn't easy? Coming down. The next morning, I felt awful. My head throbbed. My body ached. My eyes were red and sore. As I helplessly struggled to pull my aching body out of bed and into the shower, I made a deal with myself. I swore I wouldn't get more. No matter what.

13
BACK AT WILLARD

"Hey," Emma said with an uneasy smile as I took a seat beside her in the dining hall. Whitney and Madeline were sitting opposite us.

"Hey," I said back, trying to force myself to be as pleasant as possible. I felt like shit. I hadn't slept in what felt like a lifetime. I poked at the bowl of cereal in front of me. I wasn't hungry.

"How're you feeling?"

"Fine." I took a sip of coffee.

"I picked up your homework from Sister Helen for you," Emma said meekly.

I shrugged.

"She said you missed some sort of test or something."

"Fuck." I rubbed my head and rolled my eyes. "Chemistry."

"It's ok. She said you could make it up," Emma tried, in vain, to reassure me. "I'll help you study if you want."

"No, thanks," I half grumbled. I appreciated the offer, but at that particular moment, I couldn't wrap my head around studying for anything, let alone a stupid Chemistry exam.

"Where've you been? You were gone for, like, a freakin' week." Madeline took a bite of cereal.

"Home."

"Really? They let you go home?" Whitney asked curiously.

I shrugged. "I was sick."

"What kind of sick?" Madeline asked, raising an eyebrow.

"What do you mean *what kind of sick*?"

"Well… you were gone for a long time."

"Your point?"

"They don't normally send kids home when they're just like—shitting bricks with a fever. You're not like… dying, are you?"

"I had the flu. I went home to see the family doctor. My aunt insisted," I lied.

"You aren't contagious, are you?" Whitney asked with wide saucer eyes.

"No."

"Because we've got this big choir competition coming up and—"

"I said I wasn't contagious. Ok?" I snapped back with a flash of anger that I rarely ever exposed.

"Wow, Jesus. Calm down," Madeline chimed in, attempting to come to the defense of Whitney, who was totally taken aback by my seemingly random outburst.

I could feel Emma watching me, studying my body language.

"Jesus. What are you? On the rag or something?" Madeline mumbled under her breath.

"Maddie. Stop," Emma chimed in, like a mother hen protecting her young.

"Don't call me that," Madeline barked, visibly annoyed.

"Fine. But quit it, ok? You're acting like a jerk."

"I'm acting like a jerk?" Madeline slammed her cup onto the table. "She's running around with a ferocious stick up her pussy, and somehow, I'm the one acting like a jerk?"

"Just let it go."

"Oh, here we go."

"What?"

"You're doing it *again*."

"I'm not doing anything, Madeline."

"Yeah, you are. You're babying her. Like she's a freakin' infant."

"I'm right here." I narrowed my eyes. "In case you forgot."

"Yeah, well. Whatever. It's the truth."

I took a sip of coffee and then put it back down on the table. "I'm going to go."

"Dani, wait," Emma called after me in a sort of desperate plea.

"Where are you going to go? Morning prayer's not for, like, another hour?" Whitney asked, sincerely confused by my sudden departure.

I shrugged, slid out from my chair, got up, and walked away.

I stormed back to my room, slammed the door, and hurled my body onto the bed in an angry sort of huff. I buried my head under the pillow and fought the urge to scream.

A few minutes passed, and the pillow fell to the floor. I looked up from the sheets, and my eyes scanned the bedroom; the blinds were closed, and the orange morning glow peaked in through the vertical slits, painting an oblique shadowy pattern against the wall like a scene from a noir.

I grabbed the tennis ball from the corner of my desk and tossed it up towards the ceiling, replaying the morning's events in my head.

Fuck Madeline.

Fuck this place.

Fuck everything.

I reached into my desk drawer. My hand swatted the contents back and forth until finally, I found the little pack of Marlboros that was hiding in the back corner. I pulled out a cigarette and placed it against my lips while my free hand sifted through the drawer for a lighter. Eventually, I found it.

I fumbled with the lighter for a moment. My hands were shaking. My finger furiously slid against the spark wheel, but nothing happened.

Fuck.

The damn thing was out of fluid.

I threw the useless plastic container against the wall.

I still wanted a fucking cigarette. Or a drink. Or anything really.

My mind was racing.

Robert.

Dead.

Funeral.

Memorial.

Home.

Drake.

Drugs.

"Fuck it."

* * *

I bought a ticket to Union that morning. The bus left at 7:45 a.m., and by some fluke, I made it to the station just in time. After I paid the teller, I ran to the stop. I nearly missed it.

The ride felt quick, and I slept for maybe an hour or two before we'd reached the destination. It was nearly a quarter till ten when the bus pulled in.

After a short walk from the station, I found myself at a small, rundown shack of a place. The white paint had mostly chipped through, revealing the rotten wood underneath. The remaining scraps of paint had faded to a grayish-yellow.

I pushed open the chain-link fence, and the metal gate let out a shrill creek. The dried vegetation crackled against my sneakers, and I wandered nervously up towards the door. I placed my hand against the wooden surface, took a deep breath, and knocked.

"Go away!" a voice bellowed from inside the house.

"C'mon, E. It's me, Dani. Open up!"

"Dani who?"

I rolled my eyes. I knew he was messing with me; I'd known Enzo since we were kids. "Oh, my God. Cut the crap, will you? Let me in!"

The door swung open, and Enzo burst into laughter as he shepherded me inside the little shack. "Jesus, you gotta lighten up. I'm just fuckin' with you."

"Sorry," I grumbled. But I wasn't really. I hated this guy. And I sort of hated myself for coming all this way here… to see him… to buy crank.

Enzo "E" Gatti was Carlo's son. He was older than me—nineteen or twenty I think—and he was basically the spitting image of a Jersey wise-guy-wanna-be. He had greasy, slicked-back hair, a thin chiseled face, and concave cheeks like some kind of male model on crack. He almost always wore a gold chain, loose track pants, and a white tee that was strategically a size too small so he could show off his intensely muscular build; the guy seriously looked like he hit the gym three times a day.

I took a seat on an oversized La-Z-Boy style sofa in the living room and nervously fiddled with my hands. I couldn't shake the feeling that coming here was a mistake.

"Yo! Tits!" Enzo shouted down the hall, to someone presumably in the other room. "We got company."

"Who?" a man shouted back as if the quality of the guest would determine whether or not he'd deign to greet me.

"Capello's sister."

"Tony's kid?"

"Yeah, ya fuck. Get out here." And within a few moments, the man whose name I assumed was Tits staggered into the living room.

Tito "Tits" Scordelli had to be in his twenties, but he didn't look young exactly. Mostly because he was huge and by "huge" I don't mean tall. I mean, he *was* really tall, at least six foot four. But what I really meant was that he was big in the belly. Like, *really* big. He looked like some sort of Italian sumo wrestler.

"Sup," Tits said as he plopped down on the couch next to me. Within a matter of seconds, a tiny Chihuahua bounded into the room and leaped onto the sofa. The little animal had a pink collar with silver spikes. It curled up next to Tits, who simultaneously grabbed a bong from the coffee table.

"Shouldn't you—like—be in school 'er something?" Tits asked as he took a massive hit from the bong.

"Ditched."

"Ya shouldn't—" cough. "—cut class," he said as he put the bong back on the coffee table in the center of the room.

"I don't... normally," I said awkwardly as my eyes scanned the room and landed on a fly buzzing around a pile of old Chinese take-out boxes.

"You want a hit?" Enzo asked as he plopped down on the couch next to me and handed me the bong.

"Thanks," I said with a shrug as I took the bong, placed my mouth against the piece, and held the clutch. Tits leaned over and lit the bowl, and I took a deep breath, pulling the smoke into my lungs. After a long moment, I exhaled and released the smokey air.

"So, what's yer deal?" Enzo finally said, interrupting the quiet. "You come here for somethin' in particular? Or just dropping by the neighborhood?"

"I'm looking for crank," I said suddenly. I didn't know if I was supposed to be more subtle than that. I'd never taken part in a drug deal before. I had no idea how this was supposed to go.

"Can't help you."

"What? Why?"

"You're Tony's kid niece. No fuckin' way."

"You sold it to Drake."

"He's a dude."

"So?"

"Waddya mean, *so*? It's different."

"Are you serious? That's totally sexist. You know that, right? Like you can't just not sell to me because I'm a girl."

"She's got a point, bro," Tits suddenly chimed in as he took another hit from the bong. "Equality n' shit. Don't be part of the problem. Be the solution."

"I'm not going to tell Tony. I'm not an idiot. And besides… if I don't get it from you, I'll just get it somewhere else." I crossed my arms. "But I want to get it from you. Drake said your shit was good. That it was safe. And I know other people, well, they lace their stuff with like bleach and rat poison. And I don't want to get fucked over like that, you know?"

"Kid's got a point. Better she gets it from you than some shithead off Madison." Tits blew out another cloud of smoke. "Those jerk-offs are always pushin' wack shit. Especially to kids who don't know any better."

Enzo raised a skeptical eyebrow. "How much you need?"

"I don't know. Not much?"

"You got cash?"

"Yeah." I opened my backpack and dug deep inside for my wallet. "Is this enough?" I shoved the cash into his palm.

Enzo didn't say anything. He just took the money, got up, and walked into the other room. After a couple of minutes, he reentered the room with a small brown paper bag. "Here," he said as he tossed it in my direction.

I looked inside, making sure everything was in order. There was a small plastic baggie filled with maybe a teaspoon of powder. I didn't know if that was the right amount, if he was giving me a deal or screwing me over. But I nodded like everything looked good, then got the hell out of his place.

* * *

It was nearly 5 p.m. when I got back to town. I didn't feel like heading back to campus. I didn't want to see anyone. I didn't want to deal with all that.

I wandered off the main road, trekking up an overgrown dirt path that zig-zagged up a hill. My bag was heavy, but the illicit contents tucked away inside weighed more on my mind than my body. I was completely consumed with an internal debate as to whether or not I should actually do the drugs.

I slouched under a shady tree, lit a cigarette, and stared out at the view. I could see the main road, the diner, and Willard off in the distance. After a long moment, I let my body fall back onto grassy earth and stared up at the sky. A cloud floated by. Then another.

Do it.

What if it's rat poison?

It's not.

Enzo's a dirtbag. You can't trust that guy.

Drake took them. Drake's fine.

What if I get addicted?

You won't.

I don't know.

Do it.

I don't know.

Do it.

I don't know.

For Christ's sake, just do it.

"Hey." I suddenly heard Emma's voice from behind me, interrupting my train of thought.

I sat up and reluctantly allowed a smile to form between my cheeks. "How'd you know I was here?" I motioned for her to take a seat on the ground beside me. I pulled the cigarette from my lips and watched the smoke disseminate into the cool air.

"Honestly?" She paused, mulling over the question. "I wish I could say it was because I just knew you well enough and had a feeling about it. But the truth is, I spent the last two hours looking for you. Everywhere. Around campus. Around town. Pine Hills. I was about to give up when I haphazardly decided to check the pizza place off Mill and only by chance caught you sitting up here out of the corner of my eye." She pulled a stray hair back behind my ear. "Are you alright?"

"I guess." I shrugged. "I'm sorry you spent the day looking for me."

"It's ok." She smiled shyly. "But maybe next time you get the urge to ditch class, you'll give me a heads up. You're not the only rebellious soul at Willard, Dani. I would have come with you."

"I know that." I sighed.

She locked her eyes on the ground, unable to meet my gaze. "You didn't answer when I called."

"I left my phone in my room."

"I sort of thought you were ignoring me."

"I wouldn't ignore you." I let a half-smile etch its way across my cheeks.

"Ok, good." She paused for a moment. "I got your homework from Sister Helen for you. Again."

I shrugged. "Thanks."

"Dani," Emma took a deep breath. "I know you weren't sick. I mean, at least, I know that's not why you were gone last week."

I exhaled a cloud of gray smoke. "What?"

"Sister Helen told me about your cousin." She placed her hand on mine. "I'm really sorry. You must be feeling awful."

"Oh," I said as I looked up at her.

Emma looked back at me with pleading eyes. "I didn't ask or anything. She just volunteered the information. Like, she thought maybe you already mentioned it to me or something. And that's why I was picking up your homework." She looked up at me, a tinge of dejection twinkling lightly in her eyes. "I assume you didn't tell me for a reason, so we don't have to talk about it or anything. If you don't want to. I just—I don't know—figured I should tell you that I knew. Because, otherwise, I would have felt like I was lying to you or something."

I was silent for a long moment.

"Do you want me to go?"

I shook my head. "No. Stay."

"Ok. Good." She paused for a long moment. "You know, if you did want to talk about it, I'm here. And I don't just mean that figuratively. I'm like right here. Right next to you," she said with a warm smile as she wrapped her arm around me, emphasizing our literal closeness. "So, if you need a shoulder to cry on, I'm prepared to take the challenge."

"I'm ok." I stared down at the grassy earth.

"You don't have to be like that all the time. Not with me, anyway."

"Like what?"

"Stoic. Like you don't have a sentimental bone in your body."

I shrugged.

She held my hand tightly and locked her gaze with mine. "You know,

Dani, the strongest stone erodes over time from something as unsuspecting as a little water. People aren't so different. Even the strongest soul becomes fragile in the right weather. And it's nothing to be ashamed about. A little water and weather have created some of the most beautiful landscapes in the world."

She gently kicked my shoe, urging me to meet her gaze. I looked up.

"But don't take my word for it. You can go to the Grand Canyon one day yourself and tell me what you think. Unless you've already been."

I smiled. "I haven't."

"Well, I have. And it's probably the most picturesque sight I've ever seen. It hardly looks real. Like you're looking at a painting or something." I shrugged, and she grabbed my hand. "C'mon. We should get back. We'll miss dinner."

I smiled, got up, and walked with Emma back to campus. After dinner, I went back to my room and flushed the drugs down the toilet.

14

FATHER MICHAELS

It was Sunday morning, and Father Michaels had given a painfully long sermon about *the difficult decisions facing today's youth* or something totally dense like that. I started to nod off halfway through the service when Emma gently nudged me to wake me up.

"Thanks," I whispered groggily. While it wasn't formally written in the code of conduct, I assumed falling asleep in Mass warranted some type of major punishment.

"You ok?" she whispered back.

I forced a smile and nodded, but the truth was, I wasn't ok. I was exhausted. I hadn't had a full night's sleep in God knows how long. At night, my mind was constantly buzzing with images of Robert... memories from the past... speculation about who could have killed him. I couldn't turn it off.

When the service finally ended, I followed Emma, Madeline, and Whitney out of the pew, towards the door. They were serving a late breakfast in the cafeteria, and I was dying for a cup of coffee.

"Daniella!" I heard a voice call from behind me. I stopped and turned around to find Sister Helen standing beside Father Michaels; they were both waving in my direction. "Ms. Capello, a word?"

Madeline, Whitney, and Emma stared at me, obviously wondering what exactly I had done to summon the attention of the two individuals most frequently involved in major matters of punishment.

"Crap," I mumbled under my breath. "You don't think they saw me sleeping, do you?"

Emma shrugged. "Dunno."

Sister Helen waved again. "Daniella! Come here, please!"

"I'll catch up with you guys later."

"Good luck," Madeline said with surprisingly genuine sympathy.

"Thanks." I shrugged reluctantly and wandered over to the front of the church.

Sister Helen and Father Michaels shepherded me into their office, which was located in the basement under the church. There was a musty sort of smell lingering in the room like a water leak decades-old had caused a mold infestation that was never properly expunged.

I took a seat and immediately went on the offensive. "Did I do something wrong? Am I in trouble?"

"Of course not, Daniella." Father Michaels chuckled with an overly friendly tone as he pulled up a chair beside me.

"Uhm. Ok. Then, why exactly am I here?"

"You and I haven't really gotten a chance to get to know each other very well, have we?"

I shrugged. "No, I guess not."

"I suppose I owe you an apology for that. I try to get to know all the students here on a personal level."

"I've only been here a few months. I've barely had time to make friends, let alone get *personal* with the faculty." I know it's terrible, but I had to fight back the urge to crack about a million zingers; something about a priest getting personal with underaged students was, well, too easy.

"And how's that been going?"

"What?"

"Making friends? Adjusting to a new school? I know it can't be easy. It's difficult for even the most outgoing people—entering an unfamiliar place, trying to fit in."

I raised an eyebrow. "I've got friends."

"I've noticed you spend a lot of time with some of the seniors: Emma Bolton, Madeline Gallagher, and Whitney Chambers?" Sister Helen asked for confirmation.

"Yeah. We're friends."

"Quite the vivacious bunch," Father Michaels chuckled. "I can't emphasize enough how important the relationships are that you cultivate here. It's astounding how a shared bond like this—the experiences you share here—the ups and the downs—how it brings people together. Like family."

I shrugged. "Uhm. Ok. I'll keep that in mind."

"Speaking of ups and downs… I understand that your family recently experienced a serious loss."

My chest burned.

My gut ached.

Silence.

"The death of a loved one is never easy. I can only imagine how you must be feeling."

I'm feeling like I want to get the hell out of your office.

Silence.

"The growth and development of our students here at Willard is of the utmost importance, and I don't just mean academically. I mean personally."

I raised an eyebrow. *Just cut to the fucking chase already.*

"And being young presents a myriad of challenges in and of itself; I know you girls have a lot on your mind… boys, hormones, and, you know, bodily changes…"

Oh my God. I wanted to hurl. The last thing on Earth I wanted to do was discuss *boys, hormones, and bodily changes* with Father freakin' Michaels.

"And, of course, starting a new school is difficult. And the workload here is rigorous. It's a lot to ask of a person. Keeping up with classes. Meeting new people. Trying to fit in. And now you're dealing with very serious grief; you must be feeling a lot of pressure."

"I'm not going to fling myself off the side of a building or whatever. If that's what you're getting at."

"That's not what I meant, exactly." Father Michaels chuckled. "But good to know, nonetheless."

"I'm alright. Really."

"I admire your fortitude." Father Michaels looked at me sternly. "But I want you to know that I'm here for you. If you ever want to chat. We can talk about school. Your life. Or anything that might be troubling you."

"Uhm. Thanks. I guess."

"I think you'll find that talking about these things will be helpful," Sister Helen chimed in.

"Ok. I'll keep that in mind." I sighed. There was a long, awkward silence. I stared at my shoes and bit my lip. "Can I, uhm, go now? I don't want to miss breakfast."

"Of course, dear." Sister Helen said and I got up and left the dingy office.

* * *

I set my cafeteria tray down on the table beside Emma.

"Coffee for breakfast?" Emma asked, noticing that the only item on my tray was a colossal cup of black coffee.

"Wasn't hungry."

"Dani, you need to eat."

I shrugged. "Where is everyone?" I looked around the cafeteria, suddenly noticing Madeline and Whitney were nowhere to be found.

"Madeline's sucking face with Colin, and Whitney's got choir practice or something."

"On Sunday?"

Emma shrugged. "They're prepping for some sort of competition. Whitney's all freaked out about it. She went straight to Keller Hall for practice after Mass." She took a bite of cereal. "Speaking of which... what happened with Sister Hellen and Father Michaels?"

"What do you mean?"

"You know... when they summoned you to their lair?"

I rolled my eyes. "They're like, I don't know. Worried about me or something."

"Worried?"

"Because of... you know... my family or whatever."

"Oh. You mean your cousin?"

I shrugged.

"Father Michaels wants me to... I don't know... check in with him and talk about my feelings or something." I groaned.

"Huh," Emma said with a certain sort of tone; I don't know how to explain it, but there was something very loaded about the inflection—like she was holding back, like she wanted to say something else.

"What?"

"Nothing."

"Emma." I furrowed my brow and narrowed my eyes. "Just spit it out, would you?"

"I don't know. I just—maybe you should give it a chance. Maybe it's not such a bad idea."

"Are you kidding? It's a terrible idea. Like, literally the worst. I don't want to be trapped in a small room with a priest, being forced against my will to partake in asinine conversations about my feelings."

"Ok. I mean, I get why you'd be reluctant."

"Reluctant is an understatement. I've got better things to do than subject myself to pseudo-therapy served with a side of woo-woo Catholic bullshit."

"I get that. But I just mean, like, I don't know. It couldn't hurt. Having someone to talk to. And I know you're not huge on religion or whatever, but priests deal with these sorts of things all the time, you know, loss and grief, the healing process. And you don't seem to want to talk to me—or anyone else for that matter—so I don't know, I guess I just think that it might be helpful. That's all."

"Emma. I'm fine. And I haven't talked to you because there's nothing to talk about. I'm good. Really."

"You can't actually expect me to believe that."

"What's that supposed to mean?"

"Dani, you haven't slept through the night in nearly a week. And that's just the week you've been back at Willard. Who knows if you got any sleep while you were at home? You're running on caffeine and fumes. And you're not eating."

I sighed.

"And nobody but me even knows that anything's wrong. Madeline and Whitney are still operating under the lie that you were out sick last week. They think you have the flu or something. Whitney washed her hands like ten times this morning because she's paranoid she's going to catch your fictitious illness before her big competition next week."

"So?"

"So, Dani. They're your friends. They care about you. I care about you. And we want to help. We want to be there for you, but we can't. Not if you don't let us."

"I appreciate the concern… but you don't need to worry about me, Em. I'm fine. I mean it." I stuck a spoon in Emma's cereal and took a bite. "See? I'm eating."

Emma smiled reluctantly. "Dani."

I sighed. "Really. And if it bothers you, ya know, that Madeline and

Whitney don't know. Then you could tell them if you wanted. I wouldn't be mad."

"Are you sure you wouldn't rather tell them yourself?"

"Yes." I sighed. "But not because I, like, have a problem or whatever—I just don't feel like dealing with whatever boorish remark Madeline will inevitably make."

"She means well. Most of the time."

"Yeah, well. Still."

"I get it. I'll talk to them. As long as you're sure you won't be mad."

"I won't be."

* * *

I swung by Emma's room the next day.

"Come in…" she shouted from the other side, and I turned the knob and poked my head inside.

"Hey…"

"Hey yourself…" Emma said, barely looking up from her textbook. I'd obviously caught her in the middle of an intense study session, but I couldn't tell if she was being curt or just genuinely focused on what she was doing.

"Is Erin around?" I asked, scanning the room, looking for a sign that Emma's roommate might be around.

"No, she's at softball practice or something…" Emma flipped a page in the book, still intently focused on her work.

"Good." I smiled and shut the door behind me and walked over to her desk. "I got this for you," I said with a half-smile as I pulled a book out from my bag. It was the Carrie Brownstein memoir, and I knew Em was dying to read it.

She furrowed her brow, pleased but also puzzled by the gesture. "Thanks. What's this for?"

"An apology for being kind of—I don't know—grouchy at you about the whole Father Michaels thing."

She smiled.

"I'm sorry. You know, for acting like a jerk."

"It's ok. I know you've got a lot going on. I just want to help."

"I know. And that's why I kind of thought maybe you could help me take my mind off of things…"

"Intrigue." She smirked. "What'd you have in mind, Capello?"

"Dinner?"

"What? You mean like tonight? At the cafeteria?"

"No." I smiled and laughed. "I meant like this weekend. Away from Willard. At a non-cafeteria type place."

"You mean, like, on a date?"

"Yeah. I guess so."

Emma laughed. "Wow. That was unexpectedly sweet. Maybe you should get crabby more often."

"Is that a yes?"

"Well, obviously, Dani."

* * *

I grabbed the check and placed my debit card in the small black faux leather folder, then slyly handed it back to the waiter before Emma could protest. She smiled and tapped me lightly on the arm.

"Dani, you don't have to pay. We can go Dutch."

"I asked you out, remember? If you want to pay, then you'll have to ask me next time."

She smiled. "Deal."

We exited the restaurant and started the trek back to Willard. I suddenly heard the soft vibrations of her cell phone. She reached into her jacket pocket, looked at the caller ID, and let out an exhausted sigh as she placed the phone back into her bag.

"You're not going to get it?"

"No," she groaned. "It's my mother."

"Ah," I raised my eyebrows, knowingly.

"What?"

"Nothing."

She smiled sheepishly and tapped me playfully on the arm. "Go on, Dani. You can say whatever it is you're thinking. I can see a faint judgmental glow in your eyes."

"I'm not judging… really."

"It's just so annoying. You'd think after the tenth time I ignored her call, she'd get the hint." Emma sighed and kicked a rock on the pavement.

"Ten times? You're exaggerating."

"I'm not." She held out her phone and scrolled through the missed calls. My eyes widened. She wasn't exaggerating—her mom really did call ten times today. "Em, maybe you should answer. What if it's an emergency?"

"It's not an emergency. It's the deadline for Brown's early admission."

"Oh."

"And like—it's just so infuriating. I've told her nearly a thousand times that I want to take a year off. But she doesn't care." Emma sighed. "I just wish for once in her life she'd actually listen to me."

"Can I ask you something, though? Without you getting mad?"

She shrugged, so I pressed on.

"Why don't you want to go to college next year?"

"I've already told you. I just want to take a year off. It's not permanent."

"Yeah, ok. I get that. But a lot of people never go back to school after a hiatus. Not that I think you'd be one of them, necessarily, but I get why your parents would be wigged. It's not the most logical decision in the world."

"That's probably half the appeal."

"But you also love school. You're really smart. Probably the smartest person I know."

She laughed. "I'm flattered, but I'm also a year and half your senior. I've just had more school than you, hence the convincing illusion of superior intelligence."

"Em, you're the only person I've ever met who considers 19th-century Russian literature to be leisurely reading."

"When you say it like that, I sound like a nerd."

"You are." I smirked. "But in a good way."

She laughed. "Thanks... I think."

I stared at my feet for a moment and fiddled with the seam of my shirt. "I also might have heard a vicious rumor that you're graduating at the top of your class."

"Who told you that?"

"I overheard Sister Helen lecturing you when you had detention last week. I wasn't trying to eavesdrop or anything... I was just sitting outside the classroom waiting for you." I looked her in the eye. "So, it's true?"

"Yeah. Maybe." She shrugged.

"Well, congrats."

"Thanks. I guess. It's not official yet." She shrugged. "I still have next term to screw it up."

"But we both know you won't." I smiled. "So, what do you want to do exactly? For a whole year? If you aren't going to school?"

"Work. Travel." She shrugged.

"Where do you want to go?"

"Everywhere."

"How about Prague?" I smiled. "I've always wanted to go there."

"You're going to come with me?"

"If you'll let me." I smiled.

"What about school?"

"I don't know if you've heard, but there's this amazing thing they call winter break. Rumor has it, they've got one in the spring too."

"Oh yeah. That." She laughed. "So how about Prague in the winter and Barcelona in the spring?"

"Deal."

15
MORNING PEOPLE AND THE MALL

It was Saturday morning. I laid on my back pleasantly with Emma entangled in my arms. My eyes were heavy, and I knew the alarm would go off at any moment, but I wanted to linger in bed until the last possible second.

Suddenly, there was a loud BANG on the door, and Madeline's voice pierced through the walls as she rattled the locked doorknob.

"WAKE UP, SLUTS!"

"Yeah! Open up!" Whitney's giggly voice trailed behind Madeline's.

Surprised by the unexpected visitors, Emma shot up and out of bed, lost her balance, and stumbled onto the floor. As she fell, she hit her head on the side of my desk with a heavy thud.

"Ow." Emma rubbed her forehead as she lay flat on her face.

"Oh, my God. Emma, are you ok?" I tried to hold back laughter to no avail.

"Yes," she said as she slowly peeled her body up off the floor. She sat in a scrunched-up ball and rubbed her head. "Are you laughing at me?"

I bit my lip and lied, "No."

"Yeah, you are!" She let out a slight laugh, too. "I could really be hurt, you know."

"I know. I'm sorry. It's not funny."

"Liar." She smiled back, letting me know she wasn't actually mad.

"WHAT ARE YOU DOING IN THERE?!" Madeline screamed as she relentlessly beat the door.

"Crap," Emma muttered under her breath, still recovering from her fall.

"Do you need ice?" I leaned over to help her up off the ground.

"OPEN THE DOOR!" Madeline screamed again.

"YEAH!" Whitney giggled. "LET US IN!"

"CHRIST! WE'RE COMING." I looked at Emma, this time with sincere concern. She waved me off with a slight flick of her hand and motioned for me to get the door. I twisted the lock, and within seconds, Madeline and Whitney came bounding into the room.

"JESUS. What took you guys so long?" Madeline asked.

"Just recovering from a slight accident," Emma said, rubbing her head.

"Accident?" Whitney asked curiously.

"She fell out of bed," I responded without thinking.

Madeline looked at the perfectly made bed on the other side of the room and the pile of sheets on the floor next to my bed. "Did you guys—like—sleep together or something?"

"What? No." A warm wave of adrenaline flushed over me; my stomach churned. "Why would you think that?"

Madeline raised an eyebrow. "Because *she* fell out of bed, and *your* sheets are on the floor."

Emma looked at me, bit her lip, then took a deep breath. "I woke up before Dani and thought it'd be funny to jump on her to wake her up."

I nodded in agreement, amazed at the ease with which Emma formulated the lie.

"And then, I don't know, I just sort of slipped and hit my head." She pointed to her forehead.

"Ouch," Whitney said sympathetically. "Do you want an ibuprofen or something?"

"No. It's ok. I'll be fine."

"Oook," Madeline said, raising an eyebrow, still visibly suspicious.

"So, what's the big emergency, Madeline?" I chimed in, eager to change the subject.

"We're going to the mall."

"Uhm ok. Have fun?" I grunted, annoyed that they'd woken me up for that particular announcement.

"I meant *we're*—as in all four of us."

"What? No!" I whined.

"The van leaves in ten minutes. And I already signed us all out."

Emma rubbed her head and sighed. "What's at the mall?"

"We need dresses for winter formal." Whitney smiled cheerfully.

"And that means we have to come because?" I half scoffed.

"Because I said so," Madeline snapped.

"And also because I'll need a second and third opinion when Madeline tries to make me buy the sluttiest dress she can find." Whitney tugged at Emma's arm. "C'mon, you promised."

Emma looked at me apologetically and shrugged, letting me know in a glance that she did actually promise Whitney she'd go. "I'm going to need coffee…"

"We'll get some at the mall," Whitney said, dragging Madeline out of the room. "Why don't you two get dressed and then meet us in the quad?"

"Fine. Whatever." I slumped my shoulders, defeated. Whitney shut the door on her way out. I walked over, clicked the lock, and let my back rest against the door, relieved that they were finally gone.

"Jesus, Dani. That was close." Emma sighed.

"I know. I'm so sorry. It's my fault. I didn't think."

"It's not your fault. It was bound to happen eventually. Honestly, do you think they'd even care?"

"What?"

"If we told them. Is it really that big of a deal? You know they won't tell anyone."

"I don't know," I said with obvious discomfort. We were friends and all, but I definitely didn't want Madeline or Whitney to be *in the know* about me and Emma.

Emma took a deep breath, visibly disappointed. "Ok."

"I'm sorry."

"I know." Emma sighed. "It's fine."

"You sure?"

She took a deep breath. "Yeah, Dani. I'm sure."

"Ok," I said meekly.

Emma smiled and pulled me into her arms. "Really, it's fine. Now get dressed before Madeline comes banging on the door again."

* * *

"I'm sorry—why do we need to shop for underwear again?" I asked the group as we strolled through the lingerie section of a department store.

"Is that a serious question?" Madeline scoffed.

"Kind of."

"They need sex underwear." Emma laughed.

I raised an eyebrow. "Is that some sort of joke? Because I can't tell."

"It's not a joke, Dani," Emma said with a smile, chuckling at my innocence.

"Why do you need new underwear for sex? Isn't that like, one of the few activities in life that doesn't actually require underwear?"

"If you ever want me to call you by your real name, you're going to need to stop giving me reasons to call you *Corn Bait*."

"What do you guys think about this one?" Whitney held up a purple bra.

"Ew. No. Try this. And this." Madeline shoved a handful of unmentionables into Whitney's arms.

I shoved my hands into my pockets and slowly wandered away, trying my best to casually distance myself from the sex-underwear-buying experience.

Emma walked towards me, raised an eyebrow, and laughed. "Having a good time?"

"What do you think?" I picked up a lacy pink thong, held it out, and raised an eyebrow.

"I think blue's more your color." Emma smirked and tossed a blue garment in my direction.

"Ha-ha."

"You didn't hang out with a lot of women at home, did you?"

I shrugged. "I grew up with four boys. What do you think?"

"So, what'd you do for fun? Run around in the mud and play basketball?"

I laughed. "Exchange basketball for the shooting range, and you basically described my childhood."

Emma furrowed her brow. "The shooting range? What do you mean? Like skeet?"

"—and the occasional handgun."

Emma's eyes widened like two big saucers. "You shoot guns back home?"

I shrugged. "My uncle's been taking us to the range since I was a kid."

"Wait. They let *kids* shoot *handguns*?"

I smiled. "They do when they're accompanied by a legal guardian."

She furrowed her brow. "And this is why I'm a huge advocate for gun control…"

"Really?" I chuckled.

"Yes, really."

"You've never actually shot a gun before, have you?"

"No, of course not," she said with a furrowed brow. "But I don't see what that has to do with anything."

I laughed. "Well, how about I take you some time?"

"Dani, no. I don't want to do that. It sounds awful."

"More awful than you dragging me out to go shopping for Madeline's sex underwear?"

"You win." She smiled.

* * *

I made a beeline for the coffee kiosk in the mall's food court. "You want something?" I asked Emma, as I pulled out my wallet.

"Cappuccino. Thanks." She smiled.

I turned towards the lady at the cash register. "Two extra-large cappuccinos, please."

"Woah. *Two* cappuccinos?" Emma poked me in the side. "I thought you only drank your coffee black."

"I did…" I laughed and shooed her hands away. "But then some crazy blonde girl showed me the light."

"Hey! I resent that. I'm not crazy. I just have good taste."

I playfully rolled my eyes. "Something like that…"

Emma and I sipped our coffees and took a seat beside Madeline and Whitney, who both had large bags resting beside them, filled to the brim with various forms of lingerie and formal attire.

"Hey, is that Stephen?" Whitney asked, looking up towards the other side of the food court.

Emma shrugged. "Yeah, I think so." She glanced in my direction and smiled deviously. "Maybe he's going to the pet store to look for some *cats*."

"Cats?" Whitney asked, taking a bite of food. "Why would Stephen want to look at cats?"

"Because he's a weirdo cat person… apparently." I rolled my eyes.

Madeline perked up immediately. "How do you know that?"

"What?"

"That Stephen likes cats?"

Emma's cheeks suddenly flushed pink, realizing she'd made a mistake. We both knew that sharing even small tidbits of information with Madeline could be… well… dangerous.

"Hold the phone. *Dani* and *Stephen*? You guys, like, talk?" Madeline's eyes lit up like a Christmas tree.

"Sorry." Emma looked at me and half cringed, bracing herself for whatever Madeline was about to say.

"HEY! STEPHEN!" Madeline shouted at the top of her lungs, waving him down from the other side of the food court.

"Jesus, Madeline. He's coming." I sunk deep into my chair and groaned.

"Uh, yeah. That was kind of the point."

"I don't want to talk to him."

"You sure about that? Because you're like fifty shades of red right now, which only further convinces me that you have a boner for him."

"Why don't you drop it? I was just messing around… they don't talk," Emma insisted.

"No way, this is hysterical. Dani's got a crush."

"No, I don't. I think he's an arrogant tool."

"Hey, Stephen," Madeline said, ignoring me as he approached the table.

"Hey, ladies." He smiled wide, obviously loving the attention. "What're you doin' here?"

"Shopping for formal," Whitney said, gesturing to the bags beside her.

"Oh, yeah?"

"Yeah!" Whitney half squealed as she took a bite of her food. "It's going to be so fun. We're renting a limo and everything."

"Are you going?" Madeline asked Stephen.

"No one from Willard's asked me yet."

"Huh, that's interesting." Madeline smiled wide, like the Grinch who stole Christmas. "Dani doesn't have a date yet."

I just about spit my drink out of my mouth. "Madeline!" I shrieked as I kicked her from underneath the table.

"Ow! What the fuck was that for?" Madeline barked back at me.

"Uh, you ok?" Stephen asked Madeline, sincerely puzzled by the exchange. He was completely clueless.

"Yeah. I, uh, stubbed my toe." Madeline narrowed her eyes at me.

"Dani, there's a store on the other side of the mall I want to see." Emma grabbed me by the hand and pulled me up and out of my seat.

"Wait. What store? Should we come?" Whitney asked, totally confused.

"We'll be right back."

"Freaks," I heard Madeline mumble under her breath as we walked away.

I shoved my hands inside my jacket pockets and stared at my feet. "I'd say thank you for saving me, but since you're the reason I needed to be saved, I'm not sure if *thanks* are actually in order."

Emma linked her arm in mine. "Are you mad?"

"No. Not as long as you don't gloat."

"Gloat? What would I have to gloat about?"

"I don't know. You're the one who wanted to tell them about us. Stuff like this wouldn't happen if we did."

"While there's some truth to that, I wasn't trying to prove a point or anything."

I shrugged. "Yeah. I know."

"I wish this wasn't so complicated," Emma said as she stared down at her shoes.

I sighed. "Me too."

16
INTERVIEW AT BROWN

I got out of class a few minutes late, which may not sound like a big deal, but a few minutes can make a major difference when it comes to the length of the lunch line. When I finally made it to the cafeteria, the place was totally packed. Madeline, Whitney, and Emma were already sitting at our regular table, chowing down on their respective lunches.

"Fuck." I groaned under my breath. I was going to spend half the lunch period waiting in line. I sighed, grabbed a tray, and tapped it impatiently against my thigh.

"Stephen's not into you. Just so you know."

I turned around and saw Kate Hillier standing behind me. "Uhm. Ok. Thanks for the update." I scowled, unsure why Kate was even talking to me. I'd seen her and Kim around Willard after I first met them at the homecoming party, but it was pretty obvious that they didn't like me, and I didn't like them, so we mostly opted to stay out of each other's way.

"He's going to formal with Kim."

"Good for them." I gave her a sarcastic thumbs up and turned around. I poked my head up over the crowded line, trying to see what exactly was on the menu for today.

"She asked him yesterday. And he said yes."

"What are you? Her spokesperson?" I rolled my eyes.

"I just thought you should know that you should like… back off."

"Back off? What does that even mean?"

"That stunt you pulled at the mall. He told Kim all about it."

"It wasn't a stunt. I didn't even—"

"And like—texting him and stuff. You need to stop."

"I don't text him. He texts me. Why don't you get *him* to stop?"

"You wish."

"Whatever."

"Just like—don't do it again—ok?"

I rolled my eyes.

"I mean it."

"Right. Well, thanks for the warning," I said sarcastically as I grabbed my food and walked away.

I placed my tray on the table and plopped down beside Emma.

"What's going on there?" Emma asked as she took a bite of salad. She was watching Kim and Kate from the corner of her eye; they were throwing a smorgasbord of bitchy glances in my general direction.

"Apparently, Kim and Kate are going to kick my ass."

"What? Why?" Emma just about busted a rib from laughter. To be fair, it was completely ridiculous.

"They think I'm moving in on Stephen in some sort of orchestrated coup d'état to be his formal date and general life partner."

"That's mildly hilarious." Madeline laughed.

"Yeah. I'm totally bemused," I said sarcastically.

"Whatever. You could take them." Madeline glanced across the cafeteria and studied the two girls closely, like she was picking a winner for a boxing match. They looked over and saw her staring. Madeline waved and flipped them the bird. They looked away suddenly, like they'd been caught doing something far more scandalous than staring across the cafeteria.

"I've literally seen them shed tears over broken nails. There's no way they'd be able to take a right hook to the face."

"Or, I could, you know, ignore them. Because I don't like Stephen, and this entire thing is ridiculous and one-sided."

"Still. I fucking hate Kate Hillier. I've got your back. You know, if you need it."

"Uh. Thanks. I think."

"You want me to talk to them?" Whitney asked, attempting to be helpful. "Kim's on the tennis team with me. We're friends. I could tell her to lay off."

"No, thanks," I said as I took a bite of overcooked pasta. "I'm hoping this thing will all blow over after that stupid dance or whatever it is they're so worked up about."

* * *

"As always, my loving stepmother sent me…" Whitney paused for dramatic effect. "Nothing." She slammed the golden metal mailbox shut with a dour sigh. "You'd think my father could at least be bothered to send something. A postcard. A care package. A letter."

"The world's smallest violin…" Madeline slammed her own mailbox shut with a loud thud and chuckled, utterly amused by her own boorish sense of humor.

"Nothing again?" Emma asked from the other side of the mailroom as she opened her own box with a flick of the wrist.

"Nadda," Madeline confirmed. "What about you, *Corn Bait*?"

"Nothing really." I held up a single letter.

"Looks like something to me." Madeline snatched the white paper envelope from my hands.

"It's from my aunt." I swiped the letter back.

"Aren't you gonna open it?" Whitney asked.

"Wouldn't you rather ask Emma about the pile of mail in her arms?" I smirked, noticing Emma perusing a handful of envelopes.

At the sound of her name, she slowly looked up to find Madeline, Whitney, and me eyeing her like a pack of wolves.

"Way to throw me under the bus, Capello."

"Self-preservation, Bolton."

"C'mon. Give it here," Madeline barked as she snatched the stack of letters from Emma's hands.

"It's nothing good. Mostly junk."

"Hey, look at this!" Madeline pulled a single envelope out from the pile. "Our little Ivy Leaguer got a letter from Brown."

Emma rolled her eyes and snatched the letter back from Madeline's grasp. "Jesus, you're worse than my parents."

"Bite me," Madeline chirped as she stole the envelope back from Emma and proceeded to open it. "Dear Ms. Bolton. Thank you for your application to Brown University. We're pleased to invite you to interview with our admissions department on—"

"Can we just drop it?" Emma grabbed the letter from Madeline. "I'm not going."

"Why'd you even apply? I thought you wanted to take a year off."

"It's a requirement for graduation," Whitney chimed in. "The powers that be force every senior to apply to at least three universities."

Emma shrugged in agreement. "Plus, my parents are legacies. They would have sent the application in with or without my consent. You know, to ensure I follow in their oh-so-prestigious footsteps."

"Oh, come on. I'd kill to get invited to an interview at Brown," Whitney whined. "You have to go."

"I don't *have* to do anything."

"Your mom will flip if you blow it off." I shoved my hands into my jacket pocket and stared at the ground, bracing myself for Emma's reaction.

"Well, I guess she's going to flip."

"I think you're looking at this all wrong." Madeline smiled from ear to ear. "I say, you take the interview."

"Come off it, Madeline. I'm not doing it."

"Wait. Hear me out. Brown's like a four-hour drive. You'll need a car. And a hotel 'cause you'll want to stay the night. Maybe even two nights if you want to see the campus, you know, thoroughly."

"What's your point?"

"So, an interview seems like a small price to pay. You spend twenty minutes with the admissions department, and when you're done, *we'll* tear the place up. Find a frat party. Drink their booze. Smoke their weed." Madeline smiled wide. "It's going to be epic."

"I'm in!" Whitney eagerly agreed.

Emma looked at me, waiting for an opinion.

"I hate to admit it, but this is one of those rare occasions where Madeline actually makes a good point." I smiled sheepishly.

"Way to back me up, Dani."

"Sorry." I shrugged and kicked her shoe in a friendly surrender.

"So?" Madeline pressed on.

"My mom will never agree."

"But if she does?"

"Then fine. We'll all go. But I'm not saying she will. And I'm not saying I'm going to be happy about it."

Madeline and Whitney smiled wide at their victory.

* * *

"Yeah, we're on the road… mmmhmm… we've got the directions… yes, Mom, I know. Stephen Robert's Campus Center… yes, I wrote it down… yeah, I know… three o'clock… anything else?" Emma was silent for a long moment, while her mom jabbered into the other end of the phone. "Thanks, love you too… bye."

"Wow," I said with a smirk and a raised eyebrow. "That was probably the most pleasant conversation I've ever heard you and your mom have… like… ever." I know how that sounds, but I wasn't being sarcastic. I was sincerely impressed. Emma and her mom pretty much never got along, and most conversations ended with, well, a lot of yelling.

Emma shrugged. "She's really… I don't know… chilled out lately. It's like I can actually breathe for once in my life."

"I told you this trip was a great idea." Madeline smirked as she gracefully swerved around the vehicle in front of us.

"Yeah, well, I'm still sort of in shock that she's letting me go with you guys… it's like… so incredibly unlike her… I'm kind of half expecting her to be there at the hotel waiting for us…"

I shrugged. "I don't know, you are eighteen… and you're probably the most responsible person I know. Maybe she just trusts you."

"Maybe…" Emma said with a skeptical shrug.

"Or maybe she finally got a hold of some mood stabilizers," Madeline suggested with a smirk.

"That sounds more accurate…"

"Either way. Probably best not to question a good thing." I gently tugged at Emma's arm.

"Yeah, you're probably right." Emma leaned against the window and buried her head in a book entitled: *Ivy League College Admissions: Everything You Need to Know*.

* * *

Madeline stood in front of the mirror, putting the finishing touches on her eye shadow… or mascara… or whatever it is she does to her face.

Suddenly, the door clicked open. Emma shimmied her way into the hotel room, removed her blue suit jacket, and dumped a leather portfolio onto the bed.

"The prodigal child returns!" Madeline shouted with delight, eager to begin the wild and crazy evening.

"How'd it go?" I asked casually, trying to gauge Emma's mood.

"Yeah!" Madeline joined in. "You Ivy League material or what?"

"It was fine."

"Well, what was it like? What'd they ask? Did they like you?" Whitney discharged a series of rapid-fire questions.

"They talked. I talked. And that's about all I want to say about it."

"Oh, come on! You have to give us more than that!"

"Less talking. More drinking." Emma opened her purse, pulled out a bottle of tequila, and held it up proudly.

"My girl!" Madeline smiled wide, snatched the bottle, and poured a round into four tiny paper cups.

"I thought you hated tequila?" I asked with a raised brow.

Emma shrugged while Madeline distributed the booze-filled cups to each of us. "To a night we won't remember!"

We echoed the toast, took our shots, and slammed the tiny paper cups down onto the table.

"Whitney, what gives?" Madeline noticed a full shot sitting on the nightstand beside Whitney.

"I'm still doing my makeup." Whitney held a compact mirror to her face and applied a layer of foundation. "If I start drinking before it's done, I'm going to look like some kind of circus freak."

"More for me." Emma swooped in, grabbed the shot, and downed it. "Whit—can I borrow some lipstick?" she asked as she wiped a dribble of tequila from the corner of her lip.

"Sure." Whitney tossed a travel-sized make-up bag towards Emma.

"Speaking of getting ready..." Madeline looked in my direction. "What are we going to do about *this* situation?"

"What?" I scowled as Madeline grabbed the sleeve of my black hoodie and gestured up and down my body.

"You can't go to a frat party like that. I can't even see your tits."

I looked down at my T-shirt and jeans. "I didn't know tits were a requirement for entry."

"Are you dense? It's a *frat* party… of course they are!" Madeline snapped back.

I looked over at Whitney and Emma helplessly, hoping one of them would back me up.

"Sorry. We both planned on dressing… you know… not casual," Emma said with a sympathetic shrug.

"What do you want me to do? I didn't bring anything else."

"Here," Whitney said. "You can borrow something of mine. We're probably about the same size." I groaned as Whitney removed an array of dresses from her luggage.

Emma popped up behind me, smiled wide, and handed me a freshly poured shot of tequila. "Here. It'll be less horrible with a liquid blanket."

"Thanks. I guess." I sighed and reluctantly accepted the shot.

"Which one shows the most cleavage, Whit?" Madeline carefully examined the pile of dresses.

"This one…" Whitney cheerfully grabbed a red dress from the pile. "Oh! But these two are busty *aaaaand* leggy."

"What do you think?" Madeline held up the red dress to my body and studied it closely. "Now, before you answer. Bear in mind, we're on a mission."

"God. What mission?" I narrowed my eyes. I was not amused.

"Operation bow-chicka-bow-wow! Tomorrow morning—I don't want to be able to call you *Corn Bait*." Madeline shrieked with glee as she held up what had to be the most revealing dress I'd ever seen. "Perfecto! Am I right?" She looked at Emma and Whitney for approval.

"Madeline! There's, like, nothing to it!"

"That's the point. Duh."

"Yeah." Whitney smiled. "I've *bow-chicka-bow-wowed* like three times in that dress."

"Oh, my God."

Emma bit her lip with laughter. "Definitely a grade-A sex dress."

"I'm going to look like a hooker!"

"Which only further convinces me that I made the right choice! GO!"

"Oh! She'll need heels." Whitney roared with laughter. "Em—red or beige?"

"Beige."

"Gah!" I shrieked as Whitney tossed a four-inch pair of Steve Maddens my way.

Emma grabbed me by the hand, spun me around, and gleefully sang the lyrics to Roy Orbison's *Pretty Woman*. Whitney joined the chorus using her hairbrush as a faux microphone while Emma let out a playful whistle.

"This can't be happening…" I groaned, completely unamused by the group's antics.

"Stop fucking around. Get dressed!" Madeline shoved me towards the bathroom.

"Yeah, we still need to do your makeup!" Whitney erupted into a volcano of girlish giggles.

"And hair." Madeline smiled.

I reluctantly grabbed the dress, downed the shot of tequila, and walked into the bathroom to change. "I hate all of you right now."

I shimmied the dress up my body, twisted my torso, and searched for the zipper. It was just out of reach. "Can I get a little help?" I called to anyone who would listen. After a few moments, Emma appeared in the doorway. She looked at me with wide-saucer eyes, then suddenly burst into laughter.

I narrowed my eyes. "Thanks. My self-esteem is through the roof."

"Sorry." Emma gently brushed my hair to the side and slowly moved the zipper up my body. "I didn't mean to laugh. I've just never seen you like this before. You look great. I mean it."

"I don't believe you."

"Does it fit?" Whitney shouted from the other side of the room.

Emma pushed me out of the bathroom, then spun me around like a show dog on display. "It definitely fits."

"Damn, girl!" Madeline stared directly at my boobs and gave each of my *girls* an individual jiggle. "It's like tittie city up in here!"

"Oh, my God. Stop!" I slapped her hands away from my breasts.

* * *

Madeline sipped a small black flask as the four of us strolled down the narrow street, searching for the fraternity house. I shivered as the crisp air pierced my skin.

We turned the corner and entered a courtyard surrounded by a seemingly endless supply of brick buildings with Greek letters adorning their doorways. We followed the music and eventually found our destination.

Whitney pushed open the large wooden door, and I felt the formerly muffled sound of the party flush over me. There must have been at least a hundred people packed like sardines into the confines of the frat house.

"C'mon," Madeline shouted above the deafening music. "Let's grab a drink."

The four of us snaked our way in and out of the crowd, moving deeper into the party. Eventually, we found ourselves in the kitchen. There was a makeshift bar with seemingly every type of liquor imaginable and a young guy, probably a freshman, dressed in a bow-tie and vest, ready to make drinks on command.

"Shots, please!" Madeline barked at the bartending boy and pointed to the four of us.

"Ew," Whitney said with a scoff as Madeline handed her a small glass filled to the brim with tequila. "I'm not taking this."

"Suit yourself," Madeline said with a shrug as she downed both glasses with ease. "Peace out." Madeline dashed away from the group, like an excited dog who'd caught wind of a particularly intriguing scent.

"Where are you going?" Whitney yelped after her.

"To find something cute," Madeline squealed as she disappeared into the lifeblood of the party.

"I'm going to go supervise *that*." Whitney looked back at the two of us. "Will you guys be alright?"

"We're good." Emma smiled, took a shot, then accepted another from the bartending boy.

"Em. You hate shots. What're you doing?"

"Getting trashed, dude," she said with a faux accent, like a surf bum from California. "Isn't that what we're supposed to do this weekend? Wasn't that the big freakin' plan?"

"Yeah. I guess. But—"

"But nothing! Cheers!" she said as she downed the shot and waited patiently for me to take mine.

"How many drinks is that?"

"I don't know. Three? Four? Seven?" She smiled goofily. "Who's counting?"

"Apparently not you." I smiled. "What if—maybe—you cooled it on the tequila and had some water or something?"

"But we just got here… and I want to have *fuuuun*."

I smiled. "It's easier to have *fuuuun* when you're not puking your guts out."

"Fine," she said with a playful smirk as she reluctantly accepted a cup filled to the brim with plain old water. She narrowed her eyes and lowered her voice like she was telling me something top secret. "But only because I like you. And want to kiss you later. BOOP!" She poked my nose with her index finger and burst into laughter.

"Oh my God, you're drunk." I laughed hard; this had to be the first time I'd ever seen Emma truly and completely wasted.

I looked around, noticing a door that led outside into a large backyard. A handful of party-goers had formed a sub-party on the back porch. "C'mon, let's get some fresh air."

"But the drinks are in heeeeeere!" Emma whined.

"And they'll still be here in twenty minutes when we come back for more. Plus, I could use a smoke."

"Fine." She pouted playfully as I shepherded her outside.

The air was crisp, but it was a welcome change from the warm crowd inside. Emma pulled a pack of cigarettes out from her purse, placed one against my lips, held out a light, and I gently sucked in the smoky air.

"Sooo—Dani-Banani—" she hiccuped. "How're you enjoying yer first-ever collegiate party?"

"It's like—totally rad—dude," I said, mocking her earlier attempt at the surfer-bro dialect.

"You're miserable, aren't you?"

"Not miserable. Exactly."

"But?"

"But I wish I could wear my normal—nonslutty—regular clothes. I feel like everyone's staring at me or something."

"They aren't staring at *you*. They're staring at *your tits*," she said, bursting into a drunken fit of laughter.

"Oh, like that's so much better. Em, I look like a dime a dance."

"Stop. You look nice." She let a drunken hiccup escape her lips. "I mean it. You look really—" she stopped mid-sentence as her body was overcome by a dainty drunken belch. "Pretty."

I stared down at my body with a furrowed brow, visibly skeptical of Emma's flattery.

"Hey. Megan, right?"

Emma and I both turned suddenly to find a young guy, probably eighteen or so, standing casually with a red cup in one hand and a cigarette in the other. He was wearing a preppy bright green polo with the collar flipped up in the back. He leaned up against the railing, half to look casual, and half to keep steady; he was obviously pretty drunk.

"From Professor Rinker's class?" he continued, locking his gaze with Emma's.

"Uh, no," she said with a smile and breathy chuckle.

"Melody?"

"Nope."

"Marissa?"

Emma laughed. "Sorry. I think you've got me confused with someone else." She hiccupped.

The drunken man-boy furrowed his brow. "Really? So, you're not in my game theory class?"

"No, sorry."

"And you're sure about that?"

"I'm sure. We've definitely never met before."

He smiled wide. "Well, maybe we should. My name's Joe."

"Nice save." Emma chuckled and stuck out her hand for a shake. "Emma. And this is Dani."

"And this is my friend, Rod," Joe said with a wide smile as he turned around, grabbed his buddy, and shoved him into the conversation.

"Sup?" Rod said in a thick, bellowing voice.

"Sup?" I responded with a slight nod. Rod was probably six feet tall and built like a linebacker.

"So, Joe, what's yer major?" Emma asked as she took a drag from the cigarette.

"Econ, technically, but I'm thinking about switching to business. You?"

"Undecided." Emma took a drag from her cigarette.

"Cool. What about you?" Rod asked.

"Egyptology." I smirked.

"What the hell is that?"

Emma just about spit her drink out of her mouth. "Yes, Dani. Do tell."

"It's the study of ancient Egypt. You know, the history, the language, the culture..."

"That's a thing?" Joe asked, with a furrowed brow.

"Of course it's a thing." I feigned offense. "You know, I get that question all the time, and I'm actually starting to get pretty tired of it. People study ancient cultures all around the world. It's not so unusual. Especially at a prestigious university..."

"I guess." Rod scratched his head, still visibly confused.

"What do you even do with that type of degree?" Joe asked.

"I don't know what the other guys in my program have planned, but I was thinking about venturing out to Hamunaptra to find the Book of the Dead."

"Sounds like some Indiana Jones shit," Rod said, visibly bewildered by my fictitious plans.

"Close, but you've got the wrong franchise."

"Huh?"

"Never mind."

"I'm going to grab another drink," Emma said with a wide smile and a hiccup. "Nice meeting you guys."

"Maybe I'll see you around campus?"

"Maybe," Emma said as she wrapped her arms around my waist and pushed me back inside, grinning from cheek to cheek as we made our way back towards the bar. "Seriously, Dani? Egyptology?"

"What? You don't think that sounds like an interesting subject?" I smirked.

"I think you're lucky they didn't call you out on making it up."

"I didn't make it up. It's real."

"You're joking."

"I'm not." I smiled. "In fact, Brown has one of the best Egyptology programs in the country."

"Really? Why do you know that?"

"Because while you were busy with the admissions department, I got sick of watching Madeline cat-call the entire fraternity row, so I decided to catch up on some light reading. You know, about the many, many subject matters available for study here at this fine institution."

Emma smiled. "Oh, yeah?"

"Yeah." I took a sip from my frothy beer. "And I sort of thought that if you ever ended up going to Brown after your hiatus, that I should see what kinds of majors they offered. You know, so I can pick one for myself."

"You'd go with me to Brown?"

"Depends."

"On?"

"Whether or not you'd be ok with that." I smiled.

"You're sweet," Emma said with a shy smile as we finally approached the bar. "Hey. Look." Emma pointed to a shiny, brand-new bottle of Jack Daniels sitting on the countertop, completely unsupervised. The bartending boy was busy sucking face with some girl. Emma picked up the bottle and undid the plastic seal.

"Emma! What're you doing?"

She smiled wide. "Swiping the bottle."

"What? Why?"

"Because a wise man once said *never delay kissing a pretty girl or opening a bottle of whiskey*. And I intend to take that advice." She held out her hand, waiting for me to grab it.

"Leave it to you to quote Hemingway when you're totally smashed."

"You coming, or what?"

"Let's go." I smiled as Emma pulled me down a long hallway. Within a matter of moments, she swung open a bathroom door and playfully pulled me inside. For the first time during the trip, we were alone.

Emma shut the door and locked it behind us. She opened the whiskey, took a swig, then handed it to me. I took a sip then wiped the whiskey from the corner of my lips. Suddenly, I felt her move in; she pushed my body back against the door and pressed her lips against mine.

"Wow," I said as her hand ran delicately across my neck and she pulled me in close with careful force. "That was—unexpected." The words stammered off my lips as I struggled to catch my breath.

"In a good way?" she whispered as she slid her hand down my chest and across my stomach, finally resting her fingertips around my waist.

My chest tightened; my heart was pounding. "Yeah," I finally said. "In a good way."

"Dani, you're trembling."

"I'm ok."

"Should I stop?" she asked as she pulled her lips away from mine.

"No." I wrapped my arms around her shoulders, returning her affection. "I'm just a little cold. That's all."

She looked around the room, then locked her eyes with a blue and gold Greek-lettered sweatshirt that someone had seemingly forgotten. "Here," she said as she pulled the sweater from the counter, knocking a few plastic cups and beer cans into the sink. "Better?" she asked with a smile as she wrapped the sweater around my shoulders. She gently placed the hood over my head, and pulled me in close, tugging at the ends of the blue fabric.

"Yeah." I smiled. "Thanks."

"You're welcome." She gently pressed her body against mine, slowly pushing me back towards the wall. She cradled my neck in her hand, and I felt my body land against the cold tile. Her fingertips moved gently up my dress, but despite her best efforts, I felt my head awkwardly collide with the slick, white-tiled surface behind me.

"You ok?" she stammered as she moved her lips down my neck, towards my chest.

"Fine," I barely managed to say. The pace of my breath was quick.

Inhale.

Exhale.

Inhale.

Exhale.

I felt her hand glide slowly up my thighs, her fingers finally sliding beneath the fabric of the thin lace garment beneath my dress. Her lips worked their way back up from my neck. I took a deep breath and leaned back, biting my lip with anticipation.

CLANK.

Something somewhere had fallen and hit the side of the porcelain tub. A jolt of adrenaline rushed through my veins. My body tightened as I suddenly pulled my lips away from Emma's.

"Was that us?" I asked in a low whisper.

Emma shook her head. "No," she said with wide eyes as she bit her lip and looked around the room nervously.

We stared at each other for a moment with blind confusion, then Emma's gaze wandered slowly towards the bathtub. She peeled her body away from mine and cautiously approached the large porcelain vat. All at once, she pulled back the dark blue shower curtain, revealing a drunk fraternity pledge relaxing casually inside. He took a sip of beer and calmly adjusted a towel behind his head.

"Nice," he said, grinning from cheek to cheek. "*Lesbians*."

"Oh, my God." Emma grabbed my hand and pulled me out of the bathroom.

"You want a third?"

"NO!"

"Can I at least have my jacket back?"

"Fuck off, creep." I shoved him hard, pushing him back into the tub with a loud THUD.

"Are you ok?" Emma asked as we made our way back into the lifeblood of the party.

"Yeah." I smiled with a light chuckle. It was hard not to laugh at the absurdity of the situation. "You?"

She stumbled and grabbed my shoulder for support. No response.

"Em, you ok?"

She stared at the floor, breathing heavily.

Inhale.

Exhale.

Inhale.

Exhale.

"Earth to Em? You ok?"

"I think I'm going to be si—" Her hands shot over her mouth as she scurried out into the front yard. I ran after her and watched helplessly as she knelt over the patio railing and puked her guts into the spongy green grass below. I held her hair and rubbed her back as she excavated her insides for the next ten minutes.

"C'mon… Let's get some food in you." I helped her up. She stumbled to her feet, and we careened down the cement walkway.

* * *

"You feeling any better?" I asked as we strolled down the street, heading back towards our hotel.

"Physically, yes." Emma sipped a soda and took a bite from a handful of French fries. "But my pride's a little beyond repair." She stumbled, and I linked my arm with hers, offering my weight as support. "And also the ability to walk is still... elusive."

"Try to eat some more. The fries'll soak up whatever it is you drank."

She laughed, shoved her hand into the white paper bag and returned with another handful of fries. "Thanks for, you know, taking care of me back there. I feel like a jerk."

I shrugged. "It's ok, you know, to let loose every now and then. Really. Don't worry about it."

"I guess."

I felt a wave of frosty air chill my body as we walked down the sidewalk. "Em, can I ask you a question?" I asked, finally breaking the silence.

"Sure."

"Do you wish I'd dress like this all the time?"

"I think they'd suspend you from Willard if you showed up to class wearing Whitney's slutty-as-fuck party dress." Emma laughed.

"I know that you know that's not what I meant."

Emma stopped and looked me in the eye. "No, Dani. I don't." She paused for a moment and smiled. "I know I tease you about it, but I've kind of grown fond of the grubby sweater look."

I shrugged and kicked a rock.

"I mean, don't get me wrong, I like the way you look tonight, too. But if you think that's the reason I was moments away from jumping your bones back there, then you'd be wrong."

I stared at my feet. "It's just that you—I don't know—you've never done that before."

"I've also never drank, and subsequently thrown up, an entire pint of liquor."

"So what? You only want to hook up like that when you're drunk?"

"What? Dani, no. That's not what I meant."

"Then what'd you mean?"

"I don't know... I guess I meant that we were in a dirty fraternity house bathroom. There were beer cans on the sink and some guy hiding out in the bathtub. And, now I'm looking at you, and you're looking up at me like you're cold, uncomfortable, and a little self-conscious. And I don't want to make you feel that way."

I shrugged and shoved my hands into my pockets.

She wiped her eyes, attempting to hold back any glint of emotion. She stumbled on the cement, and I gently grabbed her arm for support. "Sorry, Dani. I really screwed things up tonight."

"Em—"

"No. Really. I'm way too drunk. I can barely walk. I feel so stupid. I was just frustrated. And feeling sorry for myself. And—God—I'm an idiot."

"You're not an idiot, or stupid, or any of those things."

"Yeah, Dani. I am."

There was a long moment of silence.

"You want to talk about it?"

"About what?"

"About whatever's got you feeling sorry for yourself, calling yourself stupid, and pounding shots of tequila?"

She was silent.

"If it's about the interview—I'm sorry. We shouldn't have pushed you into it. If you really didn't—"

"It's not that. Exactly. It's just..." She thought for a long moment. "It's Sheila."

"Your mom?"

"Yeah." She paused and thought for a long moment. "It's just like, totally and completely amazing how we can literally be separated by over a dozen states and yet somehow, she still finds a way to micromanage every aspect of my life."

"What happened?"

"She knew the freaking interviewer, Dani. At the admissions department. She knew her, and she didn't even tell me. Not a single heads up."

"Oh."

"Yeah. It was some kind of friend of a friend. From their country club or something. The woman already talked to my mom like three times on the phone. She didn't even ask me a single *real* question because my mother already told her, and I quote, *everything she needed to know*. I'm as good as in. The admission woman's words. Not mine."

"I don't know what to say."

"Well, I do. And it's a big fat fuck you, Mom and Dad." She pulled a cigarette out from her purse and placed it to her lips. "And you know what the worst part is? I was shocked when my mom agreed to let me do the interview by myself. It was so, SO, incredibly unlike her—to give up control—to not dictate what I say, what I wear, what I do, what I *think*. And so, I thought, maybe we were making progress or something, like she finally heard me, like she actually listened."

"I'm sorry, Em."

"Yeah, well. Me too." She sighed. "It's just—it's so messed up. They want me to be just like them—to have their life, to be their little clone—and I just—I just don't get it. They work sixty hours a week at jobs they hate. And as far as I can tell, they hate each other. What kind of life is that?"

She took a puff from her cigarette, kicked a rock with her shoe, and sighed. "My entire life, I've been taught to be a certain way. To wear certain clothes, to read certain books, to date certain people. And I just—I don't want to do that anymore. I don't want to live that life. I don't want to hide in the shadows of somebody else's expectations."

"That's why you didn't want to do the interview? Why you want to take a year off?"

"Basically. Yes." She sighed. "And like, I get it. I'm not stupid. I know I'm going to have to go back to school eventually. And that's ok. I love school. I love learning. It's part of who I am. I know that. But right now, I just want a break from it all."

"You couldn't, you know, pick a different school? Study something you like?"

"Not if Mommy and Daddy are footing the bill."

"Oh."

"And, I'm just not ready to do it. Not yet, anyway."

I thought for a long moment, then suddenly broke the silence. "I'm really sorry that your parents kind of suck. And I'm really sorry that they've planned a life for you. You know, one that you don't really want. But mostly, I'm sorry that some part of you actually believes that somehow you don't have a choice, that their crummy life is the inevitable consequence of being born the daughter of Sheila and Ted Bolton."

Emma shrugged.

"Go to Brown or don't go to Brown. Take a year off, or don't. It doesn't matter. Because you aren't like them, Emma. You're different. You're the kindest, most selfless person I've ever met. And whatever it is you're afraid of, you know, about their life or the life they want for you… it's just not in the cards. I promise."

"Thanks, Dani."

"You're welcome," I said as I tucked a stray hair back behind her ear and wiped a tear from her eye.

We were both quiet, slowly soaking in the night.

"Hey, Dani," Emma said, softly as she placed her head on my shoulder.

"Yeah?"

Emma paused for a long moment. "I love you."

Before I could say anything, she moved in and kissed me. I took a deep breath as she pulled her lips away from mine. She locked her gaze with mine and waited…

Silence.

My heart thumped in my chest as a warm swell rose inside me. My hands trembled. My mind was cloudy. I couldn't think. I couldn't speak. I was frozen.

Inhale.

Exhale.

Inhale.

Exhale.

"You don't have to say it back," she said finally, just above a whisper. "I just thought you should know."

* * *

I put the small plastic key card into the thin metal door slot. The light suddenly blinked green, and I pushed the door open carefully, trying not to make too much noise. As the door creaked open, I saw the glow of the television in the corner of the room.

"Hey," Whitney said. Her voice was soft and sleepy.

"Hey," we said simultaneously; I quietly shut the door behind us.

"Don't worry, you're not going to wake her up," Whitney said matter-of-factly, pointing to Madeline, who was sprawled out on the bed beside her. Half of Madeline's body was dangling onto the floor, and she was snoring like some type of wildebeest.

"Jesus, how long has she been like that?" Emma asked as she slipped off her dress and threw on a T-shirt and pajama bottoms.

"I dunno. About an hour." Whitney shrugged.

I pulled a pair of sweats and a shirt from my bag and changed in the corner.

"You should have seen her earlier," Whitney said, laughing a little. "I couldn't get her to shut up. She kept singing the Spice Girls. The room next door called security, so she tried to dropkick the concierge because—and I quote—*it's what Scary Spice would do.*"

"Please tell me you got this on video?" I asked as I climbed into bed next to Emma.

"No," Whitney smiled. "But the concierge said he'd give me the security footage if we promised not to stay an extra night."

"That seems perfectly reasonable." Emma snuggled her head into her pillow.

I put my head down beside hers and pulled the short metal cord attached to the lamp. The room suddenly went dim except for the glow of the television.

I closed my eyes and tried to let myself fall asleep, but I couldn't do it. I was totally and completely distracted—distracted by the warmth of Emma's body beside me, the tips of her blonde hair tickling my forehead, the smell of her lavender perfume. I wanted more than anything to wrap her in my arms, to pull her in close, to act just like we always did when we were alone. But I knew we couldn't. Not with Madeline and Whitney no more than a few feet away.

Emma must have been thinking the same thing. She rolled over, grabbed my hand under the covers, and gave it a gentle squeeze as if acknowledging how weird this was.

Why was this so hard?

"Hey guys," Whitney suddenly interrupted my train of thought.

"Yeah, Whit?" Emma asked.

"I think I'm pregnant."

17
THE CLINIC

Colin let us borrow his car. Emma made up some sort of excuse to explain why we needed it; I don't know what she said exactly, something about Madeline and Whitney having a tennis tournament. He didn't ask questions. Which was good, because Whitney didn't want Dave to know about the whole thing. She went back and forth on that decision for a while—whether or not to tell him about the pregnancy—but there was a lot of anecdotal evidence that seemed to favor not telling him.

Madeline told us about one of her friends back home who was dating this guy for a little while. She wanted to use a condom, but the guy nagged her so incessantly that she gave in. When she told him about the "mistake" and asked him to pitch in for the abortion, he called her a slut, told her the baby wasn't his, and never spoke to her again.

"You really think Dave would do that?" Whitney asked with wide-saucer eyes as Madeline recounted the story.

We all shrugged like we didn't know, but I think on some level, all of us knew it was a real possibility.

There was also a lot of concern that she might tell him about the pregnancy and then he'd want to keep it. Or his parents would find out and make him keep it. They were nutty religious, apparently.

"Well, that's not an option," Whitney said as we hashed out the pros and cons. And she was right. It wasn't an option. Not if Whitney wanted to stay in school, anyway.

Apparently, last year, a girl named Britney got pregnant at Willard and decided to keep the baby. "It was a big scandal because she was immediately expelled for breaking the honor code," Emma explained. "It was really sad because she was crazy smart, and she'd already been accepted to like her dream school—Yale or something—but she had to give up her slot since she wouldn't be finishing high school on time."

I don't know how Dave actually would have reacted if Whitney had told him, if he'd be a jerk, want to keep it, or be cool and supportive. But I can see why Whitney decided not to tell him. It was just too much of a gamble.

I don't know how long we had been waiting in the clinic. Maybe an hour. Maybe more. But I was feeling really restless. I tapped my fingers against the uncomfortable wooden chair. Emma was reading a book, and Madeline flipped through a few pages in a magazine. I had an essay due the next day, and I tried to jot down a few lines in my notebook, but I couldn't concentrate. I looked around the room. There were pamphlets and flyers everywhere. About family planning. About birth control. About your "options" when you're pregnant.

I looked at the door—the one that separated the waiting room from the other area—you know, where they do checkups and perform the procedures. And I wondered what Whitney was doing, what she was thinking, how she was feeling.

I bet she was scared.

And probably sad.

And maybe lonely.

It was all so fucked.

It wasn't fair that she had to be scared and sad and lonely while Dave got to run around town in ignorant bliss, completely unaware of the colossal emotional undertaking Whitney was enduring to afford him the luxury of that ignorance.

I picked up one of the little abortion pamphlets from a wall of "educational" materials. I skimmed the flyer, then stumbled upon a particularly alarming statistic. *Women under the age of twenty are six times more likely to attempt suicide after an abortion.*

I swallowed hard and rubbed my sweaty palms against my jeans, "Fuck," I mumbled under my breath as I awkwardly got up and stumbled towards the door. "I'll be right back."

I pushed open the glass door and stood outside. The air was heavy and cold. I gently rubbed my hands together to warm them up. I exhaled deeply and watched my frosty breath float into the air. I reached into my jacket and pulled out a cigarette.

My hands were shaking, partly from the cold and partly from my nerves. It was hard to light the cigarette with the tremor, but eventually, I managed to get it. I pulled the smoky air deep into my lungs.

"You alright?" I heard a voice say from behind me. I turned around to find Madeline.

"Yeah, fine," I lied. "You?"

"I don't really know how I feel." Madeline shrugged.

"It's a weird vibe in there. Very… sterile."

"Uh, yeah. And depressing as fuck."

"Yeah. That too." I laughed at her bluntness. "Emma still inside?"

"Yeah. Probably won't move an inch until the doctors let Whitney go. Not even to go to the bathroom." Madeline chuckled. "That girl's like a golden retriever. Loyal as fuck."

I laughed. She wasn't wrong.

"So, you going to offer me a light or what?"

"Sure—sorry—" I pulled a pack of cigarettes out from my coat pocket.

After a few long moments, Madeline finally broke the silence. "You know, Whitney was the first person I met at Willard."

"Yeah?"

"Yeah." Madeline smiled. "We were freshmen, and she was late to class. I don't even think it was her fault. She just got lost because she was new, and it was the first day of school. But they're strict about that sort of thing here. So, Mr. Keller gave her detention, and you should have seen the look on her face. She was petrified. Like she'd just received a life sentence or something."

"I'm kind of not surprised." I laughed. "She sort of crumbles under the pressure of authority."

Madeline laughed. "Yeah, well. I felt bad for her. She had that deer caught in the headlights sort of vibe. Like at any moment she might burst into tears. So, I thought it'd be funny to distract Mr. Keller, you know? So maybe he'd cut Whitney a break."

"What'd you do?"

Madeline smirked, recalling the details of the encounter. "I asked him a lot of inappropriate questions about his love life."

I raised an eyebrow. "—like what?"

"Like if teaching at a Catholic school made him prefer missionary more or less over something non-traditional... like doggy style."

"You didn't." I laughed.

"I also offered to let him borrow my uniform. You know, in case he and his wife wanted to try something new."

I laughed. "Jesus. I'm surprised you weren't suspended."

Madeline shrugged. "I may have insinuated that if he punished me, I'd tell everyone that borrowing my uniform for sex was his idea."

I laughed. "You're evil."

"I know." She smirked. "And it totally worked. He was so flustered that he completely forgot to write Whitney up. She never actually got detention." Madeline took a deep breath, her tone suddenly growing more serious. "We've been through everything together. First beers. First breakups. First smokes. She's my best friend. I'd do anything for her. But right now—with this—" She took a long drag from her cigarette and gestured back towards the clinic. "I can't help her with this one."

I shrugged. "You're here now. It may not feel like it, but I bet it means a lot to Whit."

"I guess... I dunno... it just... sucks." Madeline took a deep breath and looked away—like her eyes were watering but she didn't want me to see.

"She'll be alright."

"Yeah," Madeline said as she exhaled a cloud of gray smoke and tossed her cigarette onto the ground. "C'mon, let's get back inside."

18
CHRISTMAS

At Willard, dealing with everything was made easier by the routine of it all. There was a schedule to stick to, homework to think about, friends to distract me with unbridled rule-breaking, but the schedule and routine that I'd grown to depend on—to ground me, to shield me from everything I was working diligently to ignore—was inevitably interrupted by the holidays, a "special" break from routine that refused to be ignored. I wasn't interested in celebrating Christmas. I also wasn't interested in coming home. The irony of it all was that up until a month ago, I was itching for a break—to get away from my self-proclaimed prison, to go home, to sleep in my familiar bed, to see my family, to see my old friends. But not now. Home was no longer a place I wanted to be. Home wasn't home without Robert.

Olivia's sister, Sofi, picked me up from the train station that afternoon. I didn't bother asking where Tony or Oliva were or why they hadn't bothered to pick me up. It was just the same to me.

I tossed my bag into the back and flopped into the passenger's seat. Powdery white snow danced against the windshield as we drove through the city. Winter had embalmed the buildings in white sheets of ice, and strings of glittering lights twinkled from nearly every building surrounding us.

"How're you feelin', kiddo?" Sofi asked with a sort of forced pleasantness. "Good to be back home?"

Hell no. It's terrible. It's seriously, ridiculously terrible to be back home.

"Yeah. Good," I said with a shrug as I pressed my nose against the window, gazing at the sloshy puddles of mud and ice that decorated the streets.

"We've missed you. All of us, of course. But your aunt especially. She talks about you all the time."

I didn't know what to say, so I didn't say anything at all.

Eventually, Sofi flipped on the radio, and we suffered through a marathon of painfully spirited Christmas carols for the remaining twenty-minute ride home.

As we pulled into the driveway, Sofi clicked the remote to open the garage door. "Your aunt's been shopping all day, made like three trips to the grocery store. She was hoping we'd all sit down for a nice dinner tonight. You know, to celebrate your coming home and all. How's that sound?"

"Fine." I shrugged. "Is Tony home?" I asked, already knowing the answer.

"He's been—you know—busy. With work."

"Right," I said as I grabbed my duffle bag from the back seat and shut the car door.

She looked at me for a long moment. "Hey, Dani?"

"Yeah?"

"Your aunt's still taking everything pretty hard. Be strong for her, will you?"

"Ok." I swallowed hard, unsure of exactly what that meant. Or what I should say. Or how exactly I should feel about it.

As soon as I got to my room, I tossed my bag beside my bed, pulled out a joint, and lit the tip. I tried to be discreet about the whole thing. I stood by the window and fanned out the smoke to prevent it from trailing down the halls, but it obviously didn't work because almost immediately, Drake wandered into my room like a curious puppy.

"Yo, give it here," he said with a wide smile like he couldn't believe his luck. I rolled my eyes and reluctantly shared.

"Quality shit," Drake said, apparently impressed by my score. "Where'd you get it?"

"Guy at school." I shrugged and took another puff. "His brother goes to Syracuse. Apparently, they smuggle it in from Canada."

"Fuck yeah. Canadian weed," Drake said as he took another hit. "That fucking doll is creepy AF," Drake suddenly said as he stared at a porcelain doll my aunt had given me for my ninth birthday.

"I know." I looked at the doll and shrugged. It was positioned on top of my dresser in a little metal stand. I'd always hated the thing. It looked like it came straight from the set of a horror movie or something because it had this deathly white skin and absurdly dark brown eyes that seemed to follow you around the room. "I've tried stashing it away like a million times. But Liv always finds it and puts it back."

"You sure it's Liv doin' that?"

"What's that supposed to mean? Of course, it's Liv."

"But like—have you seen her do it?"

"No?"

"See!"

"See what, Drake?"

"That fucked up doll is like the bride of Chucky or something. Comin' to life and shit. Watchin' you in your sleep. Waiting for the perfect moment to—"

"Fuck off," I chucked a pillow at Drake, who burst into laughter.

"What?" Drake erupted into a high-pitched, grade-A stoner laugh. "That doll is seriously creepy."

"And you're seriously baked." I took another hit and held the joint away from Drake, just out of reach. "I'm cutting you off. I don't want Liv to catch on."

"Ah, come on! She's not going to notice," Drake whined. "She's all hopped up on booze and happy pills."

"Still. I don't want to get busted."

Eventually, we heard Sofi calling us from downstairs, and instinctively, I stashed what was left of the joint in my dresser. Drake and I sprayed the room with some air freshener, and the two of us staggered out towards the kitchen.

Sofi and my aunt had cooked a small feast. They'd assembled an epic Caesar salad, garlic bread, and a larger-than-life ziti. The whole thing was sort of nauseatingly sweet, mostly because my aunt made a big fuss about it being *my special dinner*.

"I ran into Mrs. Giorgi at the grocery store this morning," my aunt said pleasantly as she took a sip of wine.

"Manny's mom?" I asked and took a bite of pasta, trying desperately to put on my best sober act.

Olivia nodded. "I guess Manny's some sort of superstar athlete. Said he went to the state championships for cross country last month."

"Big whoop." Drake rolled his eyes.

"It is a big whoop." Sofi smiled. "Colleges like that sort of thing, you know."

"Mmmhmmm." Olivia took another sip of wine. "His mom's through the roof. Talkin' athletic scholarships. The whole nine yards."

Drake stuffed his face full of ziti and twirled his finger in a sarcastic woop-die-doo motion.

"What about you, Dani?" Sofi asked as she topped off her glass of wine.

"What about me?"

"Don't they make you girls play a sport or get involved in some kind of extracurricular at that school of yours?"

I shrugged. "I got out of it this term because I was new."

She nodded. "So, next term?"

"The powers that be will probably force my hand and make me do… something."

"What about you boys?" My aunt looked over at Luca and Drake. "You both ought to go out for a team. It'll look great on college applications."

"I don't play a sport," Luca grumbled with his mouth half full.

"You don't have to play a sport to be on a team. You can do something simple, like track or cross country."

Drake smirked. "Yeah, Luca. I bet Manny'd *loooove* to help you train."

"Fuck off." Luca punched Drake in the arm hard.

"Luca!" my aunt shrieked, appalled by his seemingly random outburst. "Cut it out. Not at the table."

"Yeah. You don't have to get defensive. I just think Manny would really like to see you in those short little track shorts." Drake burst into laughter.

"What's so funny?" My aunt looked at me as if somehow I could decode whatever the fuck was going on. I shrugged.

"He's a fag, mom," Luca explained matter-of-factly.

"Fag? What do you mean *fag*?"

"You know—he fucks dudes."

"Drake! Jesus. What's gotten into you? Don't say that."

"What? It's true."

"It is not. Stop that."

"He beat off Jack Plumber after junior prom last year."

"For Christ's sake!" My aunt was completely aghast.

"What? Stacy Peters saw them."

"Well, I don't believe it. We see the Giorgis every Sunday at church.

There's no way Manny could be like that. He doesn't even look gay!"

"And what's a gay person look like, exactly?" I snapped, but then immediately bit my tongue and instantly regretted joining the conversation. I took a sip of water and resigned to shut my mouth thereafter.

My aunt shook her head. "Oh, you know what I mean... He just doesn't look *that way*. He looks normal. Like any of us."

The irony of that comment was not lost on me. My stomach did a little somersault, and a warm wave erupted from my insides like a volcano. I shifted the remaining bits of pasta around my plate while my aunt continued to pester my brother and Luca about extracurriculars.

"It wouldn't kill you to put in a little effort. Lord knows, your grades aren't going to get you any sort of special treatment from the college admission boards."

"I don't even want to go to college," Luca said, much to the dismay of my aunt.

"What do you mean you're not going to college? Of course, you're going. You have to."

"Whatever," Luca mumbled as he took another bite.

"Yo, can I get a little help here?" Drake motioned for my aunt to place another helping onto his plate.

"Anyone else?" my aunt asked with a sigh as she plopped the cheesy pasta dish onto my brother's plate.

"Can I be excused?" I asked suddenly as I dropped my fork.

"You all done?" my aunt asked with obvious surprise.

"Yeah. Stuffed."

"You feelin' alright, hon?" Sofi placed her hand against my forehead, feeling my temperature. "You don't look so great."

"Fine." I shooed her hand away from my head. "I'm just tired. That's all."

"Ok." My aunt sighed with a hint of disappointment. "You can leave your plate here. I'll clean it up when we're done."

"Thanks," I said as I got up from my seat and left the kitchen. I went to my room, pulled the joint out from my dresser, and took a few long puffs before collapsing onto my bed.

I gazed at the ceiling, waiting to feel like myself, to feel the heavy weight in my chest release, to feel normal, whatever the hell that even meant. But the feeling never came.

* * *

I knew coming home was going to be some unbearable combination of depressing, weird, and all-around uncomfortable, but I don't think I was entirely prepared for the experience. Robert's absence was heavy in the house. My aunt had left his room just the same. And now that he was gone, it just sort of felt like an empty shell—a dark cave of depression, scattered with reminders, memories, and precious relics of the person he once was. I avoided the room at all costs, though I occasionally found my aunt milling about, staring longingly at his old belongings.

Despite her best efforts to conceal it, Olivia's grief was palpable. When she wasn't asleep, or crying, or drunk, she was shifting through tumultuous waves of phony positivity, manically pretending everything was "just fine." She'd grit her teeth and smile these wide, unnerving grins, and she kept robotically repeating phrases that I assumed she'd picked up from some type of grief counseling handbook.

"Everything happens for a reason."

"God makes no mistakes."

"Robert would want us to be strong."

"He'd want us to move on."

Blah.

Blah.

Freaking.

Blah.

In one manic episode of determined positivity, Olivia decided that we *simply MUST* go to the mall to polish off whatever shopping was left on the Christmas to-do list (even though Sofi had offered to do it nearly a million times). I stupidly agreed to tag along, half because of Sofi's *be strong for her* guilt trip, and half because I knew there was this book store, Harold's, on the first floor of the mall, and I desperately needed to buy Emma a Christmas present before I saw her at Whitney's New Year's party next week.

When we got to the mall, Olivia dragged me to one of those big-box department stores, claiming that she wanted to buy Tony a coat or something.

"You tricked me!" I whined after Olivia shoved me into a dressing room with a stack of dresses I already knew I hated. Apparently, nothing in my wardrobe was "appropriate for Christmas Mass," or any other type of occasion where people would be forced to look at me.

"I didn't trick you." She spun me around in a circle like I was some sort of show animal and studied my current outfit carefully. It was a floral blue sheath dress that made me feel like Southern Baptist Barbie. All I was missing was a pearl necklace and a colossal mound of bobbed hair, teased and sprayed to perfection.

After Olivia hand-selected a brand new, society-approved wardrobe for me, we made our way to the bookstore. I was relieved because I'd been racking my brain for the perfect Christmas present for Emma, and I knew Harold's would have what I was looking for. See, this place isn't your run-of-the-mill kind of bookstore; everything they sell is really unique—special editions and one-of-a-kinds. They've got classic volumes, plated in gold, some of which are worth a small fortune. And the place didn't disappoint. I found exactly what I was looking for.

When we got home that evening, I made a beeline to my bedroom and safely tucked away Emma's present in my duffle bag.

That night, Sofi had whipped up dinner for the six of us. We waited an hour or so for Tony to show, but he never came.

Around midnight, I found Olivia sitting at the dining room table alone. The food was exactly as we'd left it, and my Uncle's plate was still positioned at the head of the table as if he'd be home any minute. She sipped a glass of wine and just stared out the window, watching the snowfall.

"Any word from Tony?"

My aunt didn't answer. I could tell I'd just snapped her out of some sort of abstraction because she looked up at me with wide, startled eyes.

"I'm sure he's fine. Just working or something," I continued. "You don't need to worry."

"Thanks," she said as she casually took a sip of wine. "Can I get you anything else to eat? There's plenty left over."

"No," I said as I watched her walk towards the sink and begin to wash a few dishes.

Tony didn't come home that night.

* * *

The morning of Christmas Eve, Tony bustled in through the front door, his arms piled high with brown paper bags full of groceries.

"Hey! A little help!" he barked at Drake and Luca, who were sprawled out on the couch like a couple of bums. They grumbled under their breath and reluctantly peeled their bodies up off the comfortable surface.

We all followed Tony into the kitchen as he tossed the groceries onto the counter and began to hustle around the room, pulling a variety of cooking utensils, pots and pans, and knives out of the various cupboards.

"What's going on?" Luca asked as he rubbed his groggy, bloodshot eyes.

"We're preppin' dinner," Tony barked as he tossed a bag of potatoes and a peeler towards Luca.

"I don't cook," Drake groaned as Tony shoved him in front of a cutting board.

"You do now." Tony slapped Drake upside the head and handed him an onion and a knife. "Start cuttin'."

Drake let out an exhausted sigh.

For the next hour or so, it was total chaos in that little kitchen. None of us really knew what we were doing. Outside of boxed mac and cheese and oven pizza, I'd never really cooked before, so the idea of preparing a reasonable Christmas dinner seemed like a colossal undertaking.

But it wasn't long before the whole place began to smell like familiar holiday foods. The scent must have drifted upstairs because Olivia eventually staggered into the kitchen curiously. She'd obviously just woken up. Her hair was disheveled, and her silky pajamas were veiled by a thick, wrinkled robe.

"What's going on?" she asked with a smile, her eyes half filled with happy tears, obviously pleased at the sight of all of us cooperating in the kitchen.

Tony didn't answer. He just popped open a bottle of wine, poured Olivia a glass, and clicked on the radio. He grabbed her by the hand, twirled her around the room, and shook his butt to the chorus of *What Christmas Means to Me*.

"What's gotten into you?" my aunt asked Tony with a wide smile. It was the first time she looked genuinely happy since I'd come home.

"Just gettin' into the Christmas spirit," Tony said as he kissed her on the cheek and passed her off to Luca, who must have been stoned, because he danced along without putting up much of a fight.

The song changed to *Rockin' Around the Christmas Tree*, and by this point, Uncle Tony was really getting into it. He was belting out the lyrics like he was some kind of rock star. His voice was terrible, scratchy, and off-pitch, but his lack of skill coupled with his enthusiasm was endearing. He grabbed a potato masher from the drawer and placed it under his lips like it was a microphone. He pulled me next to him placed the faux mic to my chin, and before I knew it, I was singing along with him like we were Sonny and Cher.

Sometimes I forgot how charming Tony could be. He really knew how to turn it on. And he really brought the house down that morning. We were having a ball—being silly, enjoying life and each other, acting like a regular, happy family. It was one of those rare occasions where everything was perfect and simple, and you just want to freeze time because in that brief, inexplicably wonderful moment, we could forget about it all. We could let go; we could all finally feel normal.

And then there was a knock at the door.

"I'll get it," I volunteered cheerfully. I walked down the hall and opened the door to find two plain-looking men in dark suits.

"Can I help you?" I asked with a raised eyebrow. I peered out the doorway behind the two men; there was an unmarked Crown Victoria parked in the driveway—the tell-tale sign of a detective.

"We're looking for Mr. Capello."

"You're going to need to be more specific," I smirked. "There's three Mr. Capellos in residence here."

They rolled their eyes. "Mr. *Anthony* Capello."

"One sec," I said as I shut the door in their faces. I walked back towards the kitchen. "Tony. There're some guys here to see you." I shrugged. "Suits."

"Ah, for Christ's sake." He half slammed his wine onto the counter and wandered out of the kitchen. I followed behind and watched curiously from the living room. I peered around the corner wall, attempting to eavesdrop while keeping my presence mostly hidden.

Tony swung open the front door. "Waddya want?" he barked at the men.

The balding man on the right reached inside his jacket and pulled out a black leather wallet. He flipped it open, revealing a shiny gold badge on the inside. "I'm Detective Farris, and this is my associate, Agent Haak."

Tony raised an eyebrow and smirked. "Agent Hack? Is that some kind of a joke?"

"It's not a joke, Anthony. We're with the NYPD Brooklyn South Task Force."

"Well, pleased to meet you, Mr. and Mrs. Hack, but if you ain't got a warrant and I ain't under arrest, then get the fuck off my property. It's Christmas for Christ's sake."

"We'd like to have a chat with you."

"Yeah, and I wanna Ferrari." Tony started to shut the door, but one of the men jammed it open with his foot.

"We have some questions about your involvement with Tecraid Industries."

Silence.

"We're throwing you a softball here, Mr. Capello. Don't make this any harder for yourself than it has to be."

Silence.

"It doesn't have to be today. But I trust you understand that your cooperation on this matter is imminent." They handed my uncle a white business card. "Have your lawyer call us with a date and time." The detective tucked his leather wallet back into his jacket. "But don't wait too long. We think you're going to be very interested in what we have to say."

They turned casually and walked back towards their car.

Tony shut the door. He held the little white business card in his hand and flicked the edge with his middle finger before placing it securely in his back pocket. "Fuckin' cock suckers," Tony mumbled under his breath as he wandered back down the hall.

"What was that about?" Olivia asked curiously, while Tony sipped a glass of wine as if nothing out of the ordinary had just happened.

"Nothin'." He took another gargantuan sip. "Just a couple o' Mormon boys canvassin' the neighborhood."

* * *

Later that evening, Olivia stood in my doorway with two garment bags in hand. She knocked on the door to get my attention, then held them both up high to display their full length.

"I got these pressed. You know, just in case you wanted to wear one," she said with forced cheer, but I noticed the bags under her eyes. I could tell she'd been crying. "You don't have to. But I just thought—"

"It's fine. I'll wear the blue one," I said as I removed the garment from her grasp. I was trying my best to be nice about the whole thing, even though we both knew I'd definitely prefer not to wear either of these stupid dresses. "Unless you'd rather I wore the green one."

"No, the blue's fine," my aunt said with a half-smile.

The Christmas service was packed. The entire place was decorated with wreaths, garlands, bows, and lights. Everyone was dressed up, beaming with holiday cheer. And we all looked the part: me in the blue-Southern-Barbie-Baptist dress, the boys in perfectly tailored suits, our hair shiny and sprayed and gelled to perfection, neat and perfectly presentable.

After the service, we went back home. Gino and Samantha, his new girlfriend, came over for dinner. Apparently, Katie, Gino's six-year-old daughter, was still staying at her grandmother's house in Maine. Olivia put the final touches on the colossal assortment of food that we'd all prepped that morning, and we all sat around the dining room table, eager to eat. Before Tony could say grace, Gino stood up from his chair.

"Hey, er, listen up." Gino tapped his glass with a spoon, signaling the room's attention. We all looked up at him, visibly annoyed that he was delaying the feast. I was seriously starving.

"I ain't that good at this kind o' thing. But Ton' and Liv, really, all of you guys, you know, you been like family to me. And well, I guess I'll just get right down to the point. See, we, er', well—you wanna tell em', hon?" He looked at Samantha, who smiled wide from cheek to cheek.

I raised an eyebrow and looked around the table, trying to gauge if anyone else knew what the hell was going on.

"We're pregnant! And gettin' married!" Samantha suddenly shrieked, barely able to contain her excitement. She waved her ring finger in the air proudly, displaying a fat diamond.

"Hey!" My uncle bounced up from his seat, shook Gino's hand, and pulled him in for a manly embrace. "Congratulations!"

"Does Katie know?" I asked with a raised eyebrow. I was happy for them… I guess… but this whole relationship and pending marriage happened within the span of a few months, most of which Katie hadn't been around for.

"She sure does! Gonna get her one of those cute little flower girl dresses and everything. I can't wait to have another girl around the house." Samantha smiled softly.

"She's coming home?"

Samantha nodded. "Next week."

19
NEW YEAR'S EVE

Whitney lives in this ritzy suburb in Maryland, about a three-hour drive from our house in Jersey. I'd only managed to convince Olivia to let me go to the party with the help of Sofi, the deal being that after dropping me off at Whitney's, my aunt and Sofi would drive East to Atlantic City for some *much needed R&R* (Sofi's words, not mine).

Emma and Madeline had both taken flights the day before and were already at Whitney's by the time I arrived. After saying goodbye to my aunt and Sofi, Whitney gave me a quick tour of her place and showed me to the guest bedroom that I was sharing with Emma.

Once Whitney left, I shut the door, tossed my bag to the side, and immediately wrapped my arms around Emma, smothering her in a week's worth of missed affection.

"It's nice—to see—you too," she barely managed to say in between breaths.

"I missed you, Em."

"I missed you too," she said with a cheeky grin as she pulled herself out of my embrace and flopped down on the bed behind us. She scooted back and motioned for me to join her.

"Where are Whitney's parents at?" I collapsed beside her and positioned a pillow comfortably under my head.

"Cabo. I think." Emma shrugged and burrowed comfortably into my chest. "Her dad and stepmom go every year during the holidays."

"So, they just leave her here? By herself?"

"No, that'd be reckless," Emma said with a lilt of sarcasm. "They pay a

Puerto Rican maid minimum wage to keep her company."

"Jeez."

"Yeah. It's kind of terrible. Whit's been really depressed lately. You know, after the abortion. She tried to convince her dad to stay home this year... but apparently her stepmom shut that down."

"That sucks."

"I know. Whitney can barely manage to get her dad on the phone... and now that she's finally home, he's not even here." Emma shrugged.

"What about her real mom?"

"She like, I don't know, lives in Paris or something."

"Really?"

"Yeah. I don't think Whitney's seen her since she was a kid."

"Yikes..."

"Yeah." Emma smiled meekly. "But thanks to her lousy parents, Whitney throws an epic New Year's Eve party every year, which means that you and I get to ring in the new year together."

I smiled. "Well, thank God for bad parenting, then."

"Thank God." Emma brushed a stray hair from my eyes. "So, how was your break?"

"Fine."

"And your family?"

"Annoying. No surprise."

Emma smiled sheepishly and tapped my arm. "I meant how are they *doing*? It must be hard. The first Christmas without your cousin."

I shrugged. "Tony was mostly absent. Olivia was hopped up on pills. And my brother and Luca were insufferable. So, all and all, it wasn't that different from any other Christmas at the Capello house."

"What about you?"

"What about me?"

"How are *you* feeling?"

I smiled. "Like it's New Year's Eve and my hands feel a little empty without a cocktail."

"Funny." Emma sighed and grabbed my hand. "You know, you can talk to me about this... your cousin... your family... or anything... right?"

"I know that." I shrugged and stared down at my feet.

Silence.

Inhale.

Silence.

Exhale.

Silence.

Emma sighed, obviously disappointed that I didn't have anything else to say.

"What'd you get for Christmas?" I asked suddenly, attempting to change the subject.

"Clothes, shoes, *this*…" She held out a brand-new iPhone and smiled.

"Nice."

"What about you? Anything good?"

I shrugged. "I guess that depends. Do you think a rolled-up wad of cash is good?"

Emma raised an eyebrow. "Your family just got you money?"

"It's supposedly for my *college fund*." I rolled my eyes. "But in reality, my uncle's just been really… I don't know… busy lately. Work stuff. I guess."

"What about your aunt?"

I groaned. "She got me like a million dresses and shoes to match. Plus a gift card to Sephora."

Emma burst into laughter. "You're joking."

"I'm not."

"Does she even know you?"

"Yeah, and I think that's the problem. My aunt's gifts are more like subtle hints that I should, you know, change everything about myself."

"Dani. Your aunt loves you. I'm sure she didn't mean it that way."

"Maybe." I shrugged, grabbed my duffle bag, and pulled out a medium-sized rectangular box. "Merry Christmas."

She smiled wide. "What is it?"

"That's not how presents work, Em. You've got to open it."

She smiled and carefully unwrapped the red paper, revealing a leather-bound copy of *Swann's Way*. She ran her fingers against the leather casing, then looked up at me. "Dani, this is amazing."

"Careful with the binding. It's an antique."

"It's beautiful." She paused and locked her gaze with mine. "How'd you know I wanted to read this? I know I've never mentioned it before."

"Lucky guess."

"Dani!" She playfully tapped me on the arm.

"Emma!" I mocked her phony outrage.

"Nobody just guesses about a present like this." She smiled and kicked my shoe.

"I just figured. I don't know. You're kind of a lit snob, and at some point or another, every lit snob gets around to reading the king of boring French authors. Right?"

She laughed as she ran her hands along the gold-plated pages, delicately flipping the book open.

"Alright, so come on. Where's my present?"

Emma reached into her bag and pulled out a small box, delicately wrapped in sparkly red paper.

"Ok. So, I know you're not really into jewelry or whatever… but I saw this and it looked very *you*."

I smiled, intrigued, as I took the small box and gently undid the wrapping paper. I opened the lid of a little white box, revealing a bracelet inside. The bracelet was made of black leather straps bound to a small silver plate, making a sort of infinity symbol where they attached. I ran my fingers along the smooth silver surface. There was an engraving on the underside of the plate.

"September eighteenth?" I read the engraving out loud, a little puzzled.

Emma smiled sheepishly. "It's the day we met."

"Really?" I beamed as I slid the bracelet on my wrist. "You remembered the date?"

"Of course." She said playfully as she poked in the side.

I ran my fingers along the bracelet's leather straps and smiled. I normally hated jewelry, but I really did love this. Not just because of the sentiment, but also because Emma was right—the bracelet really was very *me*. "I love it. Thank you," I said as I kissed her.

Emma smiled and rolled her body on top of mine. She ran her hands up my shirt, gently swirling her fingertips across my skin. Within a matter of moments, I had lost myself in the moment.

Suddenly, there was a knock at the door. A jolt of panic rushed through me, and I immediately jumped out of bed. I tripped on my bag and fell flat on my face. "FUCK."

Whitney opened the door. "What was that?"

"Just me. Practicing my idiot walk." I groaned as I pulled my body up off the floor.

"Huh?"

"Dani tripped. On her luggage." Emma sighed and pointed in my direction.

"Oh," Whitney said as she looked around the room. "You almost ready? The guys just got here, and we're kicking off the night with a round of shots."

"Yeah. We'll be right there," Emma said as Whitney wandered out of the room.

I clicked the lock and stumbled back towards the bed.

"You alright?" Emma asked as she brushed a stray hair from my eyes.

"Fine." I sighed. "That sort of killed the moment, huh?"

"Yeah. Kind of." Emma let a half-smile creep between her cheeks. "C'mon. They'll wonder where we are," she said as she pulled me up from the bed and dragged me out of the room.

* * *

Emma and I were tucked away in the corner, half watching the New Year's Eve special and half people watching. Colin, Dave, and Stephen drove down and had been taking turns on a beer bong all night, much to the chagrin of Whitney and Madeline, who—based on their outfits, hors d'oeuvres, and champagne flutes—were clearly expecting a more refined New Year's Eve celebration.

"Missed ya over break." Stephen suddenly slung his arm around my shoulder and mussed up my hair like I was some kind of puppy. His cheeks were flushed, his hair was disheveled, and he could hardly stand up straight.

"Uhm. Thanks. I think." I took a sip of beer and slipped my body away from his embrace.

"Hi, Stephen," Emma said as if to remind him of her existence.

"Yo, Em-dawg." Stephen smiled and attempted to give Emma a high five. He missed, half because he was drunk and half because there was no way in hell she was going to play along.

Emma raised an eyebrow. "Maybe you should, you know, drink some water or something?"

"Nah, water's for pussies." Stephen refocused his attention back on me.

"So, what'd ya get for Christmas, Dani?"

I shrugged. "Nothing good. Clothes mostly."

"I know how that feels..." He took a sip from his red cup. "I didn't get what I wanted either."

"Oh. Uh, yeah?" I said, trying my best to be polite, but I really wanted him to leave, and I could tell Emma was getting annoyed.

"Yeah! Cuz all I want for Christmas is… yoooooooooou," he belted out an off-key rendition of the Mariah Carey song and winked seductively like he was the most charming guy on the fucking planet.

Almost immediately, Emma tugged at my arm and pulled me away from him with a harsh shove. "Shouldn't you be worrying a little less about Dani, and a little more about your girlfriend—Kim," she said.

"We broke up." Stephen smiled a stupid drunken grin. "I'm sa-sa-sa-single!"

"Look out ladies…" Emma rolled her eyes.

"Right?" Stephen suddenly looked down at his crotch and furrowed his brow, as if coming to a sudden realization. "Gotta take a piss. BRB."

Emma raised an eyebrow and watched him walk away. "Did he seriously just use BRB in a sentence… like… while talking?"

"Sorry… I don't know why he's attached himself to me tonight."

"Yeah, well I do." Emma rolled her eyes. "He's sa-sa-sa-single. Remember?"

"You're mad?"

"I'm not mad, I'm just—I don't know. Annoyed."

"I get that… but the guy can't take a hint. What do you want me to do?"

"Nothing, I guess." Emma sighed. "I wish he'd just go away."

I looked back down the hall, realizing Stephen was bound to pop up again soon. "C'mon." I grabbed Emma by the hand and dragged her towards the front door.

"Where are we going?" Emma asked.

"For a walk." I smiled.

"A walk? Seriously?"

"Yeah. It's like twenty minutes till midnight and, you know, in addition to ditching Stephen, I'd like to make sure I'm somewhere where I can actually kiss you." I walked towards the door and plucked a bottle of champagne from a nearby ice bucket. "You coming, Bolton?"

Emma smiled reluctantly and followed me down the hall. "You realize it's like thirty degrees outside, right?" Emma teased as she slipped her arms through the sleeves of her blue pea coat and wrapped a gray scarf around her neck. "You aren't worried it's going to be kind of, like, cold?"

"Not if you keep me warm," I smirked.

Emma grinned and pushed me out through the front door by the small of my back. "Come on, Casanova."

I felt a wave of frosty air chill my body as we walked down the cement steps. I pushed my fingers against the cork, releasing the pressure with a sudden pop.

Emma playfully snatched the bottle from my hand and took a swig. "Nothing for you?"

"I sort of thought we could share."

"That's interesting, Dani, since I know you hate champagne." Emma chuckled and tilted her head like a curious puppy.

"Yeah, but you don't. And it doesn't taste so bad when I know it makes you happy. Or at least, happier than a bottle of whiskey would have."

"Thanks for making the big sacrifices. You know, for the good of our relationship."

"You're welcome." I smiled and took a sip from the bottle. "Besides, isn't champagne like the traditional drink of the evening?"

"Something like that," Emma said as she wrapped her arms around her body, trying to hold back the urge to shiver.

"You're cold."

"A little."

"Here." I slipped the white beanie from my head and placed it snuggly around hers. "Take my hat."

"Thanks, Dani," Emma said with a brittle smile, her eyes drifting back to the party behind us.

"You want to go back inside?"

"No, I want to be here. With you."

"You sure?" I asked with an unmistakable lilt of insecurity.

"Yeah, I'm sure."

I furrowed my brow and looked around. Whitney's garage was just a few feet away. "You think it's unlocked?" I asked, motioning towards the side door.

"Only one way to find out..." Emma smiled as we walked towards the detached garage.

I twisted the knob and... we were in luck. We walked inside, clicked the light on, and shut the door.

"Wow," Emma said, walking around the room. The place was basically a glorified man cave. There was a classic Chevy truck on the far end of the room, a bar top, and a couple of couches positioned against the wall.

"Score." I smiled wide as I opened a mini-fridge and found an assortment of beer. I popped the top and clinked the glass against Emma's bottle of champagne. "Cheers."

She smiled, took a sip, and walked towards the truck. She ran her hands along the powdery blue paint.

"Dani—" Emma said with a sigh as she locked her eyes on the vehicle.

"Yeah?"

Emma bit her lip and took a deep breath. "Do you ever get tired of the secrecy?"

"What do you mean?"

"Well, like, with us? And like, hiding in Whitney's dad's garage... you know... just so we can spend the evening together?" She turned around and looked me in the eye.

"Oh," I said, realizing the gravity of her question. "I don't know," was all I managed to say.

"It's a little weird sometimes, you know? Like, Madeline and Whitney are my best friends. You and I both see them every day. They're like sisters to me. You too, probably. And there's this huge part of our lives they don't know about."

I shrugged. "Yeah. I guess that's a little weird. When you put it that way."

"And like in there, with Stephen... I hate that I can't just tell him to back off..." She sighed. "It's just—it's really hard. Keeping everything bottled up. It feels like I'm two different people sometimes."

"So, what are you saying?"

"I'm saying that I just wish I could do things like hold your hand—or kiss you at midnight without wondering who's going to see and what they're going to say about it."

I stared down at my feet. "So, you want to tell them? About us?"

"Not like right now—this second—necessarily. But I guess I just want the conversation to be on the table."

I slouched down into the black leather couch and watched as her eyes glistened in the fluorescent light. I fiddled with the bracelet on my wrist and sighed. I knew full well that I couldn't bring myself to say what I knew she wanted to hear.

Silence.

"Are you worried what people will think?" She sat down beside me and gently tugged at my arm, urging me to meet her gaze.

"About us?"

She nodded.

I shrugged. "Getting caught up worrying about what other people think kind of seems like a waste."

Emma sighed. "I hate when you do that."

"Do what?"

"When I ask you a question and you carefully craft a response that sounds like an answer but isn't, actually."

"I'm not deliberately avoiding the question."

"Dani." She furrowed her brow.

"I'm sorry. I guess... I don't know... I don't know what to say."

"You could start with how you feel."

"Yeah, well... maybe I don't know how I feel..."

"That's not the truth, and we both know it. And look, Dani. It's fine if you don't want to bare your soul to just anyone, but we're in a relationship—and when you're in a relationship, you can't just ignore intimate or uncomfortable conversations. It's not fair. This has to go both ways."

"I don't ignore intimate conversations."

"Dani, you can't even tell me you love me."

"What?"

She stood up from the couch and walked back towards the truck. "It's been nearly four weeks. And you still haven't said it back."

"Oh." I thought for a moment, remembering the night at Brown when Emma had told me she loved me, and I said... nothing. I stood up from the couch, shoved my hands into my jacket pockets, and walked towards her. "I guess... I don't know... I just thought... you knew..."

She turned to face me. "Well, I don't. Not if you don't tell me."

Inhale.

Silence.

Exhale.

Silence.

"Seriously?" she said with an exhausted sigh as she wiped a single tear from her eye and turned towards the door.

"Em, wait. Stop." I grabbed her hand and turned her back towards me.

"Why?"

"Because. I don't want to fight. You're upset, and I want to—I don't know—fix this. Can't we talk?"

"That depends, Dani. Because I don't really want to talk if I'm the one who's going to be doing all of the talking."

"What do you mean? That's not fair."

"It's completely fair, Dani. I just—I feel like I tell you everything. About me. About my life. What I do. Where I go. How I *feel*. And it's always felt easy. But when it comes to you, I don't know, nothing's easy. You don't tell me anything. I feel like I'm constantly guessing how you feel about me—about us—how you're dealing with all this, if you're doing ok. And I really just don't get it."

Silence.

Inhale.

Silence.

Exhale.

Silence.

"I can be there for you. For the good. For the bad. You don't have to bear the weight of the world alone. But it feels like every time I take an inch and ask you how you feel, how you're doing, you shut me out. And that hurts, Dani. It really, really hurts."

"Em, I'm sorry. I didn't know I was doing that. I'm not trying to hurt you..."

"Well, you are, Dani. You do it all the time. And you're doing it now." Emma took a deep breath and locked her gaze with mine. "And look, it's fine. Ok? I'm not in the business of forcing these things. If you don't want to let me in—if you don't want to let me be part of you—if you don't love me—then I guess I just have to accept that." She turned to walk towards the door.

"Where are you going?" I asked, desperately.

"Back to the party. I need to—I don't know—I need to think."

"Think about what?"

"About this. About us. I want to be with you, Dani. But I can't be in this relationship if you're not in it with me."

"Em, stop." I grabbed her hand with gentle force, turning her body to face mine. "I love you."

"Don't do that."

"Do what?"

"Tell me you love me like that—here—now—like this. Words have meaning, Dani. You can't just throw them out in a haphazard attempt to end an argument. I won't let you manipulate me like that."

"I'm not manipulating you. I'm just—"

"You're just what, Dani?" She paused, her eyes welling into a sea of frustrated tears.

"I'm sorry. Ok? I'm so, so sorry. I don't know why I'm like this. I don't know why this is so hard for me." I felt the words pour out of my mouth; my breath was as turbulent as my mind. Emma turned around, her exhausted gaze met mine.

"Really, Em. There are a million things I want to tell you. All the time. And I try, really, I do. I run the conversations over in my head. It's like I'm crazy or something. And the words are there. Believe me, Emma. They're right fucking there. But they don't come out. No matter what I do. And I'm trying. I'm really, really trying. But half the time, it feels like there's a gun pressed to my lips, and any time I want to tell you something—something bigger than a joke or casual conversation—it's like someone pulls the hammer, and I'm just standing there. Frozen. I can't move. I can't think. I just—I just can't do it. And I swear, I would change in an instant if I could. If I could just snap my figures and be normal, like everybody else, I'd do it. But I can't, Emma. I just can't. But I'm doing the best I can.

"And you don't have to believe me. You don't have to believe how difficult this is for me. But you do have to believe me when I say that I love you. I love you more than anything. When I'm not with you, you're all I think about—every little thing reminds me of you. And I love that, Emma."

I took a deep breath and stepped closer. "I love that my sheets smell like your lavender perfume. I love that I'll never be able to drink black coffee again, simply because it's not a cappuccino. And I love that anytime we go anywhere, you make me wait a full sixty minutes while you intentionally muss your hair in a way that only you would ever notice."

I grabbed her hand and locked my eyes with hers. "I don't even know who I was before I met you. You're the best thing that's ever happened to me. And I'm sorry. I'm so sorry it took me so long to tell you that."

"Dani, I love you too." She took a step closer, wrapping her arms delicately around my neck, placing her forehead against my own. I felt her soften, her body melting into mine, as she ran her fingers up my spine, simultaneously pulling me in for a kiss. "Dani?"

"Yeah?"

She tilted my chin towards her, forcing our eyes to meet. "Are you afraid of telling people? About us?"

"Yeah, Em. Of course, I am." I took a deep breath as I inadvertently allowed my eyes to drift away from her gaze. "I'm not ready to deal with all that, with our friends, my family; I can't do it, not yet."

"Ok," she said as she pulled my chin back towards her, forcing our eyes to meet once again. "Then we won't tell them. Not until you want to."

"I'm sorry," I said as she kissed a stray tear snaking down my cheek.

"It's not something you have to apologize for. Or feel bad about. It's just the sort of thing I need you to tell me. That's all."

I nodded, and she kissed me gently, letting me know it was fine, that we were fine. I pulled her in with the weight of my body, our flesh delicately collapsed onto the couch behind us. Her head fell into the plush pillow as she slid my shirt up over my head. She arched her body as we kissed, my hands drifting up her ribs, my fingers swirling across her silky skin, eventually landing gently on the underside of her breast. She delicately bit my lip and pressed her hips against mine.

Her eyes closed, and my lips worked their way down from hers, my fingers simultaneously working their way up, slowly exploring her soft skin. I slipped my hand under her dress, carefully wrapping my fingers around a thin lace thong. I half expected her to pull away. She normally did when we got this far, but when she didn't, I felt a tremor race through my formerly steady hand. "Should I stop?"

"No." The words escaped her lips in a breathless whisper. My fumbling fingers pulled the lacy garment from her skin, down past her thighs. My breath was nervous and shallow. I carefully continued, working the delicate fabric down further, past her calves and over her ankles.

My fingertips wandered back upwards across her calves, up her thigh, exploring her flesh. Her body was soft and damp with sweat.

Her hand moved upward and grabbed the pillow. Her firm grip pierced the plush surface, clenching it tightly, as if any minute the earth beneath us might give way. "Jesus—Dani—" she mumbled senselessly into my ear, grazing my lobe with the tips of her teeth.

She shivered and pulsed as the tension left her body. My cheek fell against her shoulder, and she swirled her fingers up across my spine.

Emma tousled her hands through my messy hair as my head lay on her chest listening to her heartbeat. I traced my fingertips along her forearm, relishing the little details: the smell of her lavender perfume, the taste of champagne on her lips, the freckles on her skin.

"I love you, Em."

"I love you too, Dani."

20

BACK AT WILLARD II

Girls slowly arrived back at the dorms over the weekend. You'd know when a girl would show up because you'd suddenly hear a gaggle of their excited friends shriek and squeal at their return. And while the behavior would normally annoy the hell out of me, I was so relieved to be back at Willard that I only found it to be a minor nuisance. Everyone was teeming with a sort of refreshed energy, eager to start the new term off with a clean slate, and I was no exception. It was good to be back.

* * *

"Jesus, Em," I said, gawking at the pile of mail she'd received. "Is like every college in the country trying to recruit you?"

"Just the good ones." She flicked the gold flap of her mailbox shut, smirked, and tossed a pile of recruiting tri-folds into the garbage. "Too bad I'm not interested."

I gazed at the pile of mail she'd dumped into the trash. "So, when are you breaking the news to your parents?"

She shrugged as we exited the mailroom alongside Madeline and Whitney. "I haven't exactly worked out the details on that yet."

"Well, you already got early admission to Brown. Don't you think they're going to start putting pressure on you to commit?"

She shrugged. "Yeah, which is why I've started screening their calls."

"That's funny because when I screen my aunt's calls, you tell me I'm acting like a child."

"I never said I wasn't a hypocrite." She playfully stuck out her tongue and linked her arm with mine.

"If I were you, I'd just accept your spot and defer enrollment," Madeline said. "That way, you don't have to deal with your parents losing their shit, and you won't lose your spot when you change your mind."

"I'm not going to change my mind."

"Uh, yeah you will." Madeline rolled her eyes. "I guarantee it."

"At least you guys know what you're doing next year." Whitney slunk her shoulders and stared at the ground with an obvious pout. "I haven't heard from any of my top schools yet."

"Don't be stupid, Whit," Madeline snapped. "You're going to NYU with me. End of story."

"Yeah, well, I'll have to get accepted first. I'm getting majorly freaked out that I haven't heard back from anywhere yet."

"You've got nothing to worry about. Your grades are good. Your extracurriculars are off the chart. And it's still early. You'll hear back any day now. I'm sure of it." Emma smiled brightly.

"Yeah. It's going to be great. We'll be roommates. Explore the city. And fuck like every guy on fraternity row." Madeline grinned.

* * *

"So…" Whitney said casually as she took a bite from her salad. "I heard there's a Valentine's Day dance with Barston Academy this Friday."

I took a bite of my fries, completely disinterested. Barston Academy was our "brother" school. During my six-month stint at Willard, there'd been a handful of co-ed social events with Barston, but I'd never opted to go.

"Hard pass," Emma said without so much as looking up from her meal.

"Why?" Madeline raised a skeptical eyebrow.

"Because there are about a million other things I'd rather be doing than fighting off a half dozen banker boys trying to cop a feel."

"Banker boys?" I asked with a raised brow.

"Most of the guys from Barston are seriously loaded."

"Isn't everyone *here* seriously loaded?"

"Not like this. We're talking like—Rockefeller money."

"You say that like it's a bad thing." Madeline rolled her eyes.

"It *is* a bad thing. Those guys have spent their entire lives living in some kind of privileged bubble. They're completely vapid."

"Uhm. News flash. We all live in a privileged bubble."

Emma rolled her eyes. "Either way. That doesn't change anything."

"Well, that's too bad because I already signed us all up."

"What? No!" I protested. "I don't want to go to some stupid dance."

"Sucks to suck. You're going."

"No way. I'll just tell Sister Helen to take my name off the list."

"Look, I didn't want to bring it up this way, but you're not giving me a lot of options here." Madeline's tone suddenly shifted; she was more serious, like a parent punishing two misbehaved children.

"Bring what up?"

"Yeah, Madeline… bring *what* up?" Emma asked with a raised brow; she was some combination of curious and annoyed.

"Oh, Madeline. Don't do this now," Whitney groaned.

"What? Someone needs to say something. And fuck knows you don't have the balls to do it."

"Do what?" A twinge of panic rushed through my veins. I had an uncomfortable feeling about where this conversation was going.

"Look. We've tried to ignore it, but it's become painfully obvious what's been going on with the two of you. And it's messed up, ok?"

I swallowed hard.

My stomach churned.

Silence.

Emma's cheeks turned a light shade of pink. She wiped her sweaty palms against her skirt and locked eyes with Madeline. "And what exactly do you think is going on, Madeline?"

"A seriously major romantic dry spell. The two of you need to get fucked. And stat." Madeline crossed her arms and raised an eyebrow, waiting for our reaction.

Holy shit. I exhaled a deep sigh of relief. That is not where I thought this conversation was going—like—at all.

"Excuse me?" Emma clearly didn't share my relief; she looked like she was about ready to climb over the table and strangle Madeline with her bare hands.

"What Madeline *means* is that neither of you have really, you know, been seeing anyone. Or putting yourself out there. And we don't want you to spend the rest of the year, you know, alone. Because, like, that would suck. And, uhm, we want to help. You know, set you up? That's all," Whitney said, attempting to soften the blow.

"And it's like, I normally wouldn't care. You know, if the two of you wanted to be single cat ladies for the rest of your pathetic little lives, but we're less than three months away from prom. Meaning, you two need to start grooming potential suitors."

"If it means that much to you, Madeline, why don't you just auction us off to the highest bidder?" I scoffed.

"Don't think the thought hasn't crossed my mind."

"You don't have to worry about us." Emma rolled her eyes. "We can manage."

"Judging by your sexless little lives, I think not."

I could feel my face burn, my cheeks turning a bright shade of red. My relief was shifting to a series of other emotions—embarrassment, anger, confusion… guilt.

"Madeline, I don't even know if I'm going to go to prom." Emma narrowed her eyes.

"What do you mean you aren't going?" Whitney was completely aghast. "It's our senior year. You have to! You both do."

"Uhm—I think you're forgetting a key detail here," I interrupted. "I'm a sophomore. Prom's for juniors and seniors only. I couldn't go even if I wanted to."

"Not true. You can go if your date's a senior." Madeline smiled wide. "And lucky for you, Willard and Barston are co-hosting the prom, and I happen to be *well acquainted* with most of Barston's senior class."

I rolled my eyes and scoffed. "God. *Well acquainted*? I'm not going to prom with your sloppy seconds, Madeline."

Madeline thought for a moment, glanced down at her hands and wiggled her fingers, visibly performing some sort of mental calculation. "That only eliminates like five guys. There are still plenty of options."

I rolled my eyes. "Yeah, well, too bad. I hate dances."

Whitney looked totally confused. "What could you possibly have against dances?"

"The music sucks, and the whole ritual is just some archaic excuse to drink and fuck."

"And your point?" Madeline rolled her eyes.

"My point is that I don't need an excuse to drink and fuck."

"You sure? Because last time I checked, you were still a virgin." Madeline smiled wide and took a triumphant bite of meatloaf.

"Very funny, Madeline. But I'm still not going."

"Yes, you are. Whit and I already put a deposit on a limo for prom, and we need to meet a minimum headcount. Ergo, you two need to find dates."

I raised an eyebrow. "Not my problem."

"Yeah, well, I'll make it your problem if we have to get a town car."

21
PARENTS' WEEKEND

BROOKLYN, NEW YORK — Ten alleged members of the Malta crime family were killed Monday, ambushed by gunmen in their respective homes, apartments, vehicles, and regular points of gathering. The victims include Sonny Marino, Antoni Buratti, and Paolo Donati — who police allege were caporegimes, high-ranking captains within the Malta criminal organization.

Family members of the deceased are outraged and horrified by the brutality of the attacks. One of the victims, Tommy De Marco, was shot twice in the chest at point-blank range while others were stabbed, strangled, and/or mutilated.

"This is the most prolific instance of mob violence since the St. Valentine's Massacre," Mario Signorelli, a mafia historian and best-selling author, said about the attacks. "We haven't seen flagrant displays of violence of this magnitude since the 1920s."

The massacre came nearly two weeks after authorities released the formal indictment of Pino Malta amid the Techraid Industry scandal. Sonny Marino, Antoni Buratti, and Paolo Donati were among the ten victims. The killing of these three individuals is a significant turning point in the ongoing case against Pino Malta and Techraid Industries, as all three individuals were cooperating with the police and were expected to appear as key witnesses in the prosecution's case against Malta's organization.

Gerold Flint, the lead prosecutor in the case, declined to comment.

Police believe the attacks were orchestrated and conducted by more than one individual over the course of a twenty-four-hour period. "The killings," said detective Haak, were "executed with military-like precision," leaving police officials to believe that the murders were "premeditated" and conducted by "experienced *professionals." Officials confirmed that there are no suspects at this time.*

"It is very likely that these attacks were ordered by one or more rival organizations. Especially ones that might have been implicated by the testimony of the now-deceased caporegimes," said author Mario Signorelli. "If history is any indicator, this is the beginning of a significant regime change."

"Earth to Dani."

I gently lowered the newspaper beneath my eyes and looked up at Emma.

"Huh?"

The four of us were gathered around our regular dining hall table for breakfast. The cafeteria was bustling with activity; girls were gossiping, fixing their hair, quizzing one another for upcoming midterms, and I was glued to the pages of the New York Sun. I'd read the article five times already and couldn't put it down.

I knew I should have been focused on other things—studying, friends, etc.—but I was completely consumed by curiosity, fascination, and fear. Things had escalated with the Techraid scandal. People were dying. And I couldn't let it go. I couldn't shake the feeling that my uncle was involved. And I couldn't shake the feeling that he ordered the contract.

My stomach churned.

"I asked if your aunt and uncle were coming? You know, to parents' weekend?"

"Oh." I'd heard Sister Helen mention parents' weekend during the morning announcements, but I hadn't actually given it much thought or bothered to mention it to Olivia or Tony. "I don't know. Probably not."

"Really? I figured your aunt would want to come for sure."

"Yeah, well..." I took a bite of sausage. "I haven't exactly told her about it."

"Go figure." Emma laughed and swirled her spoon in a milky bowl of frosted Wheaties.

"What about you? I find it hard to believe you actually invited your parents."

"I didn't," Emma groaned. "They invited themselves. They're, like, subscribed to the parent's newsletter and read it religiously. It's seriously annoying."

"What about you guys?" I looked at Whitney and Madeline.

"Hell yeah, they're coming," Madeline said. "And they're bringing their platinum cards for some seriously well-deserved retail therapy."

Emma rolled her eyes. "Well deserved?"

"I studied my ass off for that stats midterm. It's only right that they reward my efforts with a pair of Choo's."

"What's a Choo?" I furrowed my bow.

Emma laughed. "She means Jimmy Choo's. They're like—a kind of shoe."

"Oh. My. God." Madeline rolled her eyes and threw her hands up in the air in a dramatic display of exasperation.

"God. Calm down. It's just a shoe."

"It's not just—" Madeline's mouth hung ajar in total exasperation. She locked her eyes on Emma and pointed in my direction. "Fix her."

Emma rolled her eyes and looked at me with a sort of sympathetic, all-knowing smile. "It's like a thing. I'll explain it to you later."

"Can't wait." I rolled my eyes.

"My dad's not coming—no surprise—but he's sending my stepmom in his place," Whitney groaned. "Apparently, it's going to be a—quote—*good bonding opportunity for us*."

"That sounds like literal hell," Madeline said.

"Tell me about it." Whitney sighed and bit her lip. Her eyes glistened like she was fighting the urge to cry.

The bell rang, and moments later, we all shuffled off to our respective first periods.

I thought that was the last I would hear about parents' weekend, but Emma brought it up later that night.

"Hey, uh, Dani?" Emma asked shyly.

"Yeah?"

"About parents' weekend." Emma looked down at her shoes. "It's not a big deal or anything, but my parents are probably going to want to, you know, meet you at some point while they're in town."

"Really? Why?"

"Uh, well, because I've told them about you. I mean, not everything, obviously. But they know we're close. And, uh—my mom mentioned it yesterday—"

"Oh."

"I was thinking we could all do dinner together or something?"

"Yeah, ok. I can do dinner. If you want."

"Really?"

"Yeah, I mean, it's not that big of a deal—is it?"

"Well, it's just, we're together, and meeting your significant other's family—it's kind of a thing, and I guess, I don't know, I wasn't sure if you'd be up for it."

I shrugged. "They don't know we're together. So, all in all, it's not really any different than if I were going out to dinner with Whitney or Madeline's family."

Emma looked up at me with a raised brow.

"That wasn't the right thing to say… was it?"

"Not really." Emma half-smiled. "But it's ok. I get it."

* * *

"What do you want me to wear?" I flopped onto my bed and stared at the ceiling.

"Wear whatever you want," Emma shouted from inside the bathroom. She was putting the finishing touches on her makeup or hair or something to that general effect.

"You don't mean that."

"Of course, I mean it, Dani. I want you to wear what makes you feel comfortable."

"Ok, well, I feel comfortable in a pair of ripped jeans and a Distillers tee." I rolled my eyes. "But I have a sneaking suspicion that Sheila and Ted Bolton might think that's a little inappropriate for a five-star restaurant."

"What do you care? You're just my *friend*. Like Madeline or Whitney. Remember?" Emma smiled a wide, cheeky grin.

I narrowed my eyes. "C'mon, Em. I'm serious." I sat up and scooched my body onto the edge of the bed. "I don't want your parents to like—hate me. What are they like? Are they going to expect me to, like, wear a dress or something?"

"The restaurant I picked is nice but casual. You'll be fine in jeans. Just make sure you wear a nice blouse or something with it."

I raised an eyebrow. "I don't think I own anything that would qualify as a *nice blouse*."

"You know what I mean. No death metal T-shirts."

"Em, at this point in our relationship, I really shouldn't have to explain to you that the Distillers aren't death metal."

"Whatever." Emma playfully rolled her eyes. "Just make sure it's ironed. And clean."

* * *

Emma's parents sent a town car to pick us up from Willard. They were staying at a nearby hotel, about a half-hour away from campus. The school must have made some kind of deal with this particular hotel because I recognized nearly every other person in the lobby as a fellow classmate.

Emma called her parents when we got to the lobby. I slouched into one of the oversized chairs and stared at my shoes while we waited.

"It's sort of cute that you're nervous," Emma said with a pleasant smile as she took a seat beside me on the chair's armrest.

"I'm not nervous," I lied and wiped my sweaty palms on my jeans.

"Ooook," she said, with obvious disbelief.

In a matter of moments, Emma's mom, Sheila, emerged from the elevator at the far end of the lobby. She waved cheerfully and walked casually to where we were sitting.

Mrs. Bolton had short blonde hair, blue eyes, and the smoothest skin I'd ever seen on someone over the age of forty-five. She was wearing a pearl necklace, a silky blue blouse, fitted white pants, and a pair of beige heels.

"You must be Dani!" Emma's mom pulled me in for an awkward hug.

"Where's Dad?" Emma asked curiously, noticing that she was missing one of her parents.

"On the phone. Work stuff." Sheila rolled her eyes, obviously annoyed that her husband wasn't joining them on time.

"He's going to meet us at the restaurant."

"Are you sure he doesn't want us to wait?"

"I'm sure, honey. Let's just go."

* * *

The waiter showed us to our seats, and Emma's mom ordered a bottle of wine and an appetizer. After about twenty or thirty minutes, Emma's dad arrived, and she flagged him down, waving him in our direction.

"Sorry, I'm late," he said as he took a seat next to Emma's mom. He had a full head of brown hair, peppered with a healthy smattering of grays, and a wide bright smile that made you feel instantly at ease. "Hope I haven't kept you waiting long."

Emma's mom held up her watch and impatiently tapped the timepiece with her index finger.

"Yikes. Already a quarter till nine? Must have lost track of time."

"It's ok, Dad. You're here now," Emma said, trying to ease the tension.

He perused the menu. "So, tell me, what have you ladies been talking about? What'd I miss?"

Emma's mom took a sip of wine. "Emma was just telling us about her calculus teacher. What did you say his name was?"

"Mr. Groningen."

"Oh, right." Ted nodded. "What's he like?"

"He's alright." She shrugged. "But I'm not feeling super confident this semester. The workload is getting to be… I don't know. A lot."

"Your grades aren't slipping, are they?"

"No, it's nothing like that. It's just—I don't know—really hard. That's all."

"Well, you'll just have to work a little harder. Put in a few extra hours. Meet with your teacher after class," Sheila said as she grabbed a piece of bread and began buttering it. "Right, hon?"

"I guess." Emma shrugged.

"How're you settling into Willard, Dani? Emma mentioned it was your first year?" Emma's dad asked as he poured himself a glass from the nearly empty bottle of wine.

"It's taken some getting used to… but, uhm, it's good. Overall. I guess." I took a sip of water.

"Different from your last school, I bet?"

I nodded. "Yeah, the workload is definitely… more intense."

Emma's mom smiled. "You'll be glad when it's all said and done. Believe me. You girls will have the pick of the litter when it comes time for college." Emma's mom took a bite from her plate. "Have you given any thought to where you might apply, Dani?"

Emma rolled her eyes. "Mooooom."

"What? It's a reasonable question."

"Not yet," I said as I fiddled with my napkin anxiously. "I should probably figure out what I want to study first. And, you know, start narrowing it down from there."

"Thought you had your heart set on Egyptology?" Emma smirked, and I just about choked on my water.

"Ancient Egypt, huh?" Ted mulled over the revelation. "Interesting. But not a very practical subject matter. Is it?"

"Uh—no, sir. I mean, I don't know if it is or isn't but—" I coughed hard, trying to clear my throat. "It was just a joke. I'm not actually interested in Egypt. I mean, it's interesting, I guess, but I'd never want to—you know—study it or whatever."

"Well, I don't blame you. I mean, what do you even do with a degree like that?" Emma's mom asked.

"Research at a University? Teach?" Emma shrugged.

"Well, that's not much of a profession, is it?"

"Oh my God. Mom," Emma groaned.

"What?"

"You can't say that."

"What? I can't say what?"

"That teaching isn't a real profession."

"That's not what I said, Emma."

"But it's what you meant."

"No, what I meant was that professors make terrible salaries."

"So what if they do? The value of a person's work isn't determined by what's written on their paycheck."

"Well, actually, economically speaking, it is."

"Teaching is a dignified profession. It's important. Without teachers—"

"Of course, of course, I know that, dear. I'm not disparaging teachers. It's a noble profession. We all know that. I just meant that if you have other options—if you're educated the way you two girls are—that there are just other more sensible choices. That's all."

"There's more to life than money, you know…"

"Of course, there is, sweetie. But it's nice to have both. That's all I'm saying."

Emma rolled her eyes. "Can we just talk about something else?"

"Ok, fine. But I don't see what the big deal is. I'm not offending anyone." Emma's mom took a sip of wine. "Dani's parents aren't teachers, are they?"

"Oh, uhm." I took a sip of water. "My uncle owns a business."

"An entrepreneur! How wonderful."

I didn't bother to mention that my mom was actually a teacher... you know, before she died.

"Right. Well, anyway..." Ted chimed in, deliberately paving the way for a new subject. He was obviously used to playing the referee in bouts between Emma and her mother. "So, if not Egyptology, what are you interested in studying, Dani?"

"I don't know. Uh, maybe pre-law?"

"Law! Now that's a wonderful career." Emma's mom took a sip of wine.

"So, you must be a good student, then?" Ted asked casually.

I nodded. "Not as good as Em, because she's—you know—valedictorian smart and all. But still good."

"Dani's being modest." Emma smiled. "She's probably the most well-read person I've ever met."

"Oh, yeah? What do you like to read, Dani?"

"A little of everything." I shrugged. "Emma's got me on *The Trial* right now."

"Wait—don't tell me—" Ted took a sip of wine and scratched his chin, obviously scanning the confines of his mind for the information. "Tolstoy?"

"Kafka."

"Ah, right." He took a bite of bread.

The waiter brought our food, and dinner was pleasant enough. But then it was time for dessert, and that's when things took a turn for the worse.

"That artist you like—what'd you say their name was? You know, the one who does the glass blowing?"

"Ginny Ruffner?"

"Yeah, her." Emma's mom smiled. "I heard she's going to have an exhibit not too far from here next month. I thought maybe I'd come out, and we could go together. How's that sound?"

"It sounds... really cool, mom," Emma said with a skeptical tone as she took a bite of cheesecake.

"You'd have to make sure your aunt and uncle don't mind, Dani. But you're welcome to come along, too, if you'd like."

"Sure." I looked at Emma. "Who's Ginny Ruffner?"

"She's this Seattle-based artist who makes these amazing glass sculptures. Back in the nineties, she got into this horrible car accident—the doctors thought she'd never walk again—and like, she never let it slow her down. Super inspiring."

"Sounds cool," I said as I took a bite of my dessert.

"Well, it's settled then. I'll have Natalia make the arrangements." Emma's mom smiled brightly. "It's on a Saturday, so I was thinking I'd fly into Albany, rent a car and we'd drive out to Providence Friday afternoon?"

"Wait—what?"

"We can even leave in the morning if it won't interfere with your coursework. I'm happy to sign you both out a little early so—"

"Mom." Emma folded her arms and narrowed her eyes angrily. "You can't be serious?"

"What?"

"The exhibit's in Providence? Rhode Island?"

"Yeah, so?"

"In what world is that not too far from here? It's like a five-hour drive!"

"I figured you wouldn't mind… since, you know, you seemed to really like this Ruffio person…"

"Ruffner. And I don't mind the drive. I mind the location. Providence. Rhode Island."

"Oh, Emma. Stop."

"Were you ever going to tell me that's the real reason we were going? Or were you just going to ambush me when we got there? Pull up to the Brown admissions department and sign my life away?"

"Jesus, Emma. You're overreacting."

"I'm not overreacting. You lied."

"I didn't lie about anything. It's just a coincidence. That's all."

"It's not a coincidence. You knew exactly what you were doing!"

"Yes! I was trying to spend some quality time with my daughter. So sue me."

"That's such bull, and you know it!"

"Oh, for Christ's sake." Sheila slammed her glass of wine on the table. "Will you just stop it already? Not everything I do is some big, fat, horrible plan to ruin your life."

"Sheila. Please."

"Don't *Sheila please*, me. Listen to her. Are you going to let her talk to me like that?"

"Can't we all just have a nice dinner together? For once," Ted pleaded.

"That's what I was trying to do until mom totally lied to me."

"Lied to you? I'm trying to do something nice for you."

"Oh, please. You've been asking me about Brown for weeks. There's no way you didn't think it through. It's not a coincidence. It's all just some sort of twisted ploy to get me to commit."

"And would that kill you? To just sign the papers already?"

Emma let out an audible groan. "Here it goes…"

"What? They're offering an incredible scholarship. It's a great school. A wonderful school!"

"I don't want to talk about it, Mom."

"You never want to talk about it."

"Because you never want to hear what I have to say!"

"Of course, I do! I want what's best for you. And somehow, in your mind, that makes me the wicked witch of the west!"

"Have you ever stopped to think for one second that maybe—just maybe—going to Brown isn't what I want?"

"Ok? So, what is, then? Yale? Columbia? MIT? Is that what this is about?"

Emma rolled her eyes. "I don't want to talk about it, Mom. Not right now."

"Well, I do."

"Fine." Emma half slammed her fork onto the table. "I want to take a year off."

"A year off from what?"

"From school."

"That's a joke, right?" Ted just about choked on his wine.

"It's not a joke. And I've already decided."

"Over my dead body, you have." Sheila turned to her husband and threw her hands up in exasperation. "Are you hearing this? Did you hear what she just said?"

"Yes, Sheila. I'm not deaf. I heard her loud and clear."

"Well, do something!"

"What do you want me to do?"

"The check. Please." Emma flagged down the waiter while her parents began to bicker with each other.

They were causing a real scene. You could tell half the restaurant was staring at us. And it was honestly really embarrassing. I slumped down into my seat and watched the sparring match continue, feeling sort of sorry for Emma and mostly just helpless since there wasn't really anything I could do about it.

"I'm not letting her throw away her future. She's not going to end up like Ben. I don't care if I have to drag her to that school kicking and screaming… she's going. End of story."

"Don't bring Ben into this."

"Yeah." Emma folded her arms. "It has nothing to do with Ben."

Sheila diverted her attention away from Ted towards Emma. "I know you love your brother—but he's a burnout, Emma. You don't want to—"

"He's not a burnout!"

"Oh, please. The boy's living in a crack den, for Christ's sake. Is that what you want?"

"Do you hear yourself? You're acting insane. It's not a crack den. It's a holistic community."

"Holistic community is hippie speak for crack den!"

Emma rolled her eyes.

"Is this about a boy?"

Emma's eyes widened in some combination of shock and anger. "What! No. Jesus. Mom. This is about me."

"The one you were dating a while back? Dan—Drew—Dev—whatever. He was bad news. I knew it. You have so much potential, Emma. Don't throw it all away for some local hick."

"Sheila, will you just drop it? We can talk about it later."

"I'm sorry, I'm just trying to salvage our daughter's future. God forbid you back me up on anything. Ever."

"Salvage my future? Mom, you're being completely ridiculous. Taking a year off isn't going to ruin—"

"Please. Lower your voices. Both of you," Ted said in a hushed tone as he threw a wad of cash onto the table. "The bill's paid. Let's leave."

"Leave? I'm not going anywhere. Not until we talk some—"

"Fine. *We'll* go. Thanks for dinner. It's been a real hoot." Emma grabbed her jacket and stormed out of the restaurant.

"Uhm. It was nice meeting you both," I said awkwardly and then ran after Emma. By the time I'd found her outside, she'd already hailed a cab.

22
WALD-A-MOHR

I've had a lot of time to think about things. But not in a good way. I've been lying in bed mostly, staring at the ceiling, wondering what life at Willard will be like next year when Emma, Whitney, and Madeline graduate.

It all started last Wednesday. It was the senior trip, so they all got to go to some sort of amusement park called Walda World or Wald-a-Mohr. I can't remember. But either way, the point is this—everyone was gone, having a good time, and I was left back at Willard, alone, with all the other non-seniors.

I'd sort of become friendly with a few girls outside of Whitney, Madeline, and Emma, but I didn't exactly have any close friends in my grade. This fact was especially obvious when it came time for lunch Wednesday afternoon. I looked around the cafeteria hopefully, only to realize that I didn't know anyone well enough to invite myself to sit at their table. So, I ended up just sitting alone in the back of the dining hall.

It wasn't being alone so much that bothered me; it was more that I felt like I was missing out on something. And the entire thing was made worse when Sister Helen stopped me in the hall that afternoon.

"Daniella, a word?"

I sighed and followed her down the hall, towards her classroom. Apparently, she noticed I was sitting alone at lunch, and took that to be some sort of sign of emotional distress.

"I think you ought to get involved in an extracurricular," she announced literally a split second after I'd taken a seat. "It's a great way to meet new people. And, of course, it'll look good on college applications."

"I have friends."

"I meant, *new* people in *your grade*."

"Oh." I raised an eyebrow. "What do you want me to do? Join a club or something?"

"It doesn't have to be a club. It could be a sport. Or an academic team. Whatever interests you."

"What's an academic team?"

"Like speech and debate. Or decathlon."

"Sounds like nerd city." I slumped into my chair and fought the urge to raise hell.

Sister Helen furrowed her brow, obviously debating whether or not to acknowledge my nerd city comment. "I'm sure you'll find something that suits you. Here." She handed me a pamphlet that listed all of the available activities. "I've circled the ones I think you'll find most interesting, but you certainly don't need to stick to my suggestions. I thought maybe you could take the week to think about it, and we'll connect next Monday with your decision?"

"I'm assuming this is mandatory?"

Sister Helen smiled. "It's not a punishment, Daniella. In fact, I think you might find whatever you choose to be quite rewarding."

I sighed. "Ok. Whatever."

* * *

I was reading in the library when Emma texted me that she was back from the trip. I shoved my books into my bag and headed back towards the dorm to meet her.

"How was Wald-a-Bore?" I asked with fake enthusiasm as I entered her room.

"Amazing," Emma said with a bright smile. "I mean, the place is kind of tacky as hell, but it was nice to get away from campus for the day."

"I'll bet," I said with an inadvertent eye roll as I flopped onto Emma's bed. It was hard not to be a little bit jealous. Being left alone at Willard was seriously depressing.

"And look." Emma smiled wide, reached into her purse, and pulled out a small, stuffed tiger. "I got this for you."

I let a half-smile creep in between my cheeks. "What is it?"

"The Wald-a-Mohr mascot. I've apparently got a hidden talent for ring toss carnival games."

"Thanks." I sighed and flicked the stuffed tiger's ears.

"Is something wrong?" Emma asked, noticing my unintentionally less-than-pleasant demeanor.

"No."

"Dani." She furrowed her brow.

"Today's just been—sort of—I don't know. Weird."

"Weird how?"

"For starters, Sister Helen is forcing me to join an extracurricular."

Emma raised a curious eyebrow. "Like a sport?"

I shrugged. "Apparently, I'm too much of a loser, and I need to make new friends."

"Dani, that's ridiculous. You have plenty of friends."

"Yeah, all of which are graduating this year."

"Oh." Emma sighed, suddenly understanding Sister Helen's concern. "What are you going to pick?"

"Dunno," I said with a shrug as I tossed the pamphlet onto Emma's desk.

"I can help you pick if you want." She grabbed the flyer and skimmed through the choices.

"Em, can I ask you something?"

"Sure," she said as she tossed the pamphlet onto her desk and flopped onto the bed beside me.

"What're we going to do next year? You know, when I'm at Willard, and you're… well… not?"

"What do you mean?"

"Like, are we going to break up?"

"What? Dani, no. Of course, not."

"Yeah, ok. But if you're off traveling or whatever it is you want to do next year… how are we even going to see each other?"

"I won't be traveling the whole time. I'll need to work."

"Yeah, ok. But then you'll also need a place to live. Apartments aren't cheap, and your parents live all the way out in New Mexico."

"I'll figure something out."

"Well, you're not going to want to get an apartment around here. This place is a wasteland."

She shrugged. "Pittsburgh's not so far."

"It's also not so cheap. And I know you sort of have your heart set on going abroad."

"Dani, where is this coming from?"

"I don't know." I shrugged. "I guess I just had a lot of free time today, you know, with you and everyone being gone for the trip. And this thing with Sister Helen got me thinking…"

"Dani, you don't need to worry. I'm going to make this work. I promise."

"Yeah, ok, but—"

"But what?"

"I wish we had a plan."

"What do you mean?"

"Like, at least if you went to Brown, I'd know I could take the train up every other weekend or something to visit."

"Oh."

"I don't know where you're going to be. Or what you're going to be doing. And that's fine, because, you know, it's your life—and I don't want to get in the way of you doing whatever it is that you want to do—but I guess I just don't like not knowing what's going to happen. That's all."

Emma picked up the extracurricular pamphlet from the desk and skimmed through the options again. "Can I ask you something?"

I shrugged. "Yeah?"

"How hell-bent is your aunt on you staying at Willard?"

I raised an eyebrow. "Liv was pretty eager to ship me off, Em."

"I don't mean go home. I meant, would they be open to a different boarding school?"

I shrugged. "I don't know, why?"

"I've been reading about these sort of convent places in Europe. They've got these situations where you work for room and board, and I was sort of toying with the idea of doing that."

"What's that got to do with me?"

Emma smiled. "There's a lot of stellar boarding schools abroad. They're more or less the same cost as Willard, aside from the airfare, but comparatively, that's pretty nominal, so price shouldn't be an issue."

"Really?"

"Yeah. We could look a couple up. You could transfer to a different school. I could scam some free room and board from some local farmers, and we won't have to worry about not seeing each other."

"I don't know if Liv'll go for it."

Emma smiled. "I'll do some research and pick out some potential schools. Once we've got a plan, we'll make your aunt an offer she can't refuse." Emma lowered her chin and scratched an imaginary beard a la the Godfather.

I rolled my eyes. "Your Marlon Brando sucks, but I like where your head's at."

23
NYU AND THE PARTY AT COLIN'S

"You sure you don't want to come with us?" Madeline teased Whitney, whose concentration was laser-focused on an intimidatingly thick statistics textbook. Madeline twirled and danced around Whitney and took a swig from a personal-sized bottle of tequila. Madeline was sporting a purple NYU sweatshirt, celebrating the fact that her parents had paid her tuition deposit that morning, so her admission acceptance was officially official.

"I want to come with you. But I also don't want to fail stats." Whitney sighed, her voice was brimming with anxiety. "I'm already three chapters behind. If I don't catch up, I'm seriously going to bomb the midterm next week."

"Haven't you heard of a little thing called senioritis? The year is more than halfway over. Grades don't matter."

"That's easy for you to say. You're already set on NYU. I haven't heard from any of my top schools yet."

"But you will. Any day now. The letters are definitely on the way."

Whitney sighed. "Yeah, well, until then…" She held up her statistics textbook, "I don't have much of a say in the matter."

"Fine. Get good grades. Whatever." Madeline rolled her eyes and took another aggressive swig from the bottle.

Emma laughed and snatched the booze from Madeline. "As much as I would love to hold your hair later tonight while you puke, why don't you cool it on the tequila for a bit? At least until Sister Helen finishes rounds."

Madeline groaned. "Whatever. Mom."

"LIGHTS OUT!" a voice shouted from down the hall.

"Alright. I'm heading back to my room." Emma walked towards the door. "Meet by the gate at a quarter to eleven?"

Madeline and I nodded in agreement.

* * *

Despite the fact that I'd been to Colin's house nearly a million times before, I hardly recognized it tonight. The lights were dim, and there were party-goers seemingly everywhere. You could barely move, let alone see three feet in front of you.

We made our way back towards the kitchen where a gamut of liquor bottles was situated. We hadn't been there for more than a few moments when Stephen made a beeline in our direction.

"La-la-laaaaadies." He slung his arms around both me and Emma. Madeline, meanwhile, had disappeared somewhere, presumably to suck face with Colin.

"Careful, I think you're making someone jealous," Emma said with a faint chuckle as she motioned her head towards Kim on the other side of the room. Kim was staring at Stephen, and now me. Emma shot a faux-friendly wave in her direction. I rolled my eyes and casually slipped away from his embrace.

"Psh—Kim is—" Hiccup. "Really—" Hiccup. "Mean," Stephen stammered in a drunken slur. Emma raised her eyebrow curiously, and Stephen drunkenly stumbled into her arms. "You're not mean." He looked up at Emma like a sad puppy, and I swear to God, I thought he was going to kiss her.

"Woah there, tiger." Emma tried to back away, but he was resting his weight against her in a way that made them both wildly unstable. I swooped in, grabbed his elbow, and peeled him up and off of her.

"She was always—" Hiccup. "Telling me—" Hiccup. "What to do n' stuff." He swayed from side to side and inadvertently tugged at my jacket as I gently plopped him down in a chair at the nearby kitchen table.

"Right well. That sounds like Kim," Emma said sympathetically.

"This is—" Hiccup. "Soft." He rubbed his face against my black zip-up hoodie, which I slid off of my body to get away from him.

"Can we get you some water or something?" I asked with a raised brow. Stephen smiled wide. "Nahhhhh." Hiccup. "I don't need—" Hiccup.

"Water."

"We'll get you some anyway... you know... just in case..."

Stephen smiled goofily, slumped back into the chair, and snuggled my jacket like a stuffed animal.

We walked into the kitchen and immediately burst into laughter. Stephen was totally hammered, and in a weird way, it was actually sort of endearing. It was like the douchebag part of his brain was completely incapacitated by the alcohol and subsequently replaced with a pathetic drunk dork.

I reached into the fridge to grab a beer when I felt the weight of someone's shoulder roughly brush up against mine.

"Bitch," Kim said, without so much as glancing in my direction.

I nearly dropped my drink from the force of her "unintentional" shoulder bump. I rolled my eyes and watched Kim walk back towards the group of girls in the living room.

"This stupid rivalry is getting old," I mumbled.

"Maybe you should try talking to her? And Kate? Call for a truce?" Emma shrugged.

"And say what? *I'm sorry you guys invented a fake, completely idiotic feud, but you should know I really don't give a shit about either of you. Or Stephen. So, if you could just go away, that would be great. Thanks.*"

Emma laughed. "Yeah. I think that'll go over grrrreat."

Madeline peeled her body away from Colin's. The two of them had been intertwined in the corner of the kitchen, engaging in an intense display of very physical and very public affection. "One right hook to the face and this whole thing could be over." Madeline sort of swayed back and forth while Colin attempted (and failed) to hold her steady. She was almost as hammered as Stephen.

"I'm not going to fight them, Madeline."

"Fine. I'll do it!" She stumbled aimlessly towards Kim and her cronies.

"Don't be stupid." I placed my hand in front of her, turned her around, and guided her back towards Colin.

"Yeah, what she said. Let's make loooove not war." Colin pulled Madeline back into an affectionate embrace and proceeded to smother her with his lips.

"Don't get all high and mighty on me." Madeline popped up for a quick breath of air. "High school is like a prison. Survival of the fittest.

Shank or be shanked."

"Jesus. Madeline." I glanced towards the other side of the room. Kim and three other girls were throwing a smorgasbord of pissy glances in my direction. "Maybe we should just go."

"Alright." Emma shrugged. "This party's getting a little out of hand for me anyway. Everyone is seriously wasted." She was right. It was probably only a matter of time until one of Colin's neighbors called the cops.

"You coming, Madeline?" I asked.

She didn't answer. Her lips were basically super glued to Colin's face.

"Earth to Madeline." Emma rolled her eyes. "Come with us, and I'll buy you a burger or something. To soak up all the tequila."

That got her attention. "Fine. I guess I could eat."

"C'mon. Stay a little longer." Colin pulled her back into his arms.

"Colin, I think maybe you should pay a little less attention to Madeline and a little more attention to your guests." Emma pointed towards the living room; a couple of football players were tossing around some sort of ceramic statue.

"Oh shit." Colin's eyes widened. "Be right back."

"Have you seen my jacket?" I looked around. I'd definitely left it in the dining room with Stephen. "It was right here a second ago."

Emma looked to the left and right. No jacket. And, curiously, no Stephen.

I groaned. "You don't think Stephen took it, do you?"

"Maybe he grabbed it by mistake?"

"Mistake?" I rolled my eyes. "He was coddling it like a puppy."

Madeline swayed from side to side. "How much you want to bet one of Kim's minions stole it?"

"What? Why would they want my jacket?"

Madeline shrugged. "To make a little Dani voodoo doll, obvi."

I rolled my eyes. "I'm going to go look around. I'll be right back."

I checked the bathroom—nothing. I checked the master bedroom—still no sign of it. I was about to give up when I decided I'd check Colin's bedroom.

When I opened the door, I saw some guy face down on the bed with a girl underneath him. They were both fully clothed, but it was obvious I'd walked in on some type of intimate encounter.

"Fuck. Sorry," I said instinctively.

"Get out!" I heard a familiar voice say, and suddenly I recognized who, exactly, it was I was looking at: it was Dave—as in, Whitney's *boyfriend* Dave. And then my eyes landed on Kate, who poked her head out from underneath him. He was definitely cheating.

"The room's occupied—" Kate yelled with a shrill voice that made her sound just as trampy as she looked.

"Dani. Em found it. It was under the table—" I heard Madeline shout from behind me. I was silent; my eyes were totally and completely fixed on the scandalous scene in front of me. It was like one of those car crashes on the side of the road; you want to look away, but for some reason, you just can't.

"What. The. Literal. Fuck," Madeline snarled as she shoved me to the side, bounding into the room like a mother protecting her young. "What the fuck is going on here?" Madeline screamed at Dave.

"Nothing," Dave said as he stumbled off the bed, struggling to zip and button his pants back up.

"Yeah. Why don't you mind your own business?" Kate rolled her eyes and attempted to shove Madeline out of the room. Madeline pushed past her, making a beeline in Dave's direction.

"Jesus! Get out!" Dave screamed as he struggled with the top button of his jeans.

"Answer the question, Dave." Madeline shoved him back against the wall. He stumbled backward, slamming his head hard.

"Stop! Don't hit him," Kate yelped.

"Fine, I'll hit you." Madeline lunged at Kate, who scurried over the bed and used it as a sort of barricade to separate the two of them. Dave struggled to hold Madeline back, but that only caused her to refocus her energy back onto him. She flailed her arms, trying to get some sort of punch or slap into his chest.

"JESUS! Fuck. Calm down!"

"What the hell is wrong with you? It's not enough to put Whit through hell knocking her up? You go to go screw around on her with Kate the fucking skank?" Madeline finally broke free and slapped him in the chest.

"Whitney's pregnant?" Kate shrieked.

"Wait what?" Dave shouted.

Madeline ignored them completely. She shoved Dave in the chest hard. "Fuck you, Dave. Seriously."

"You're a goddamn hypocrite. You know that, right? You fuck around on Colin all the time," Dave shouted back.

"That's because we aren't in a fucking relationship!" Madeline shoved him again in the chest hard.

"Hit me again, and I swear to fucking God." Dave was fuming. His face was red, and his eyes were sort of bulgy.

"Fuck. You." Madeline pulled her fist back and slammed it into Dave's chin. His head ricocheted backward. Like clockwork, he pulled back his own fist and pummeled her across the cheek. Her body shot backward; she stumbled and hit the ground hard.

I don't know how to explain it exactly, but at that moment, something inside me snapped. Like a linebacker, I propelled my weight forward, thrusting myself into Dave's midsection. He flew back against the wall, and his head collided with the wooden panels lining the room. Our bodies sank into the brown carpet. He flailed his arms towards me, but the weight of my body on top of his kept him from doing any real damage. I threw blow after blow, until finally, I heard Emma from the other side of the room.

"Dani, stop!" My body froze, and I felt her hand on my shoulder, pulling me off the broken man in front of me. My eyes drifted to the corner of the room. Colin had literally picked Madeline up by her midsection in a half-assed attempt to thrust her up and off of Kate. He held Madeline for a moment like a claw machine holding a prize, and she flailed her arms back and forth as if trying to get one last blow into Kate's body.

"Get these psychos the fuck out," Dave finally screamed at Colin, as he covered his nose with his hands, attempting to stop the bleeding. Kate was curled up in the fetal position and crying hysterically.

Madeline spit at Dave as Emma and Colin dragged the two of us out of the room and out of the house. Colin slammed the door, and the three of us walked down an empty street alone.

"FUCK!" Madeline screamed as she kicked over a large trash can, pouring the contents onto the street.

24
WHAT'D YOU DO TO DAVE?

We missed breakfast the next morning and barely managed to get up in time for lunch. We sat at our regular table and mindlessly poked the food on our plates. Madeline and I looked like shit—our faces were both still bloody and bruised.

"Did you talk to Whitney yet?" Emma asked Madeline.

Madeline shook her head and poked a French fry on her plate. "She was asleep when I got back and was gone this morning by the time I woke up."

"What are you going to say?"

Madeline shrugged. "I don't know. That Dave's a lying piece of shit?"

Emma furrowed her brow. "Madeline."

"I'm kidding. I'll say something better than that."

"Uhm. Guys." I looked up and saw Whitney storming in our direction. "I think she already knows…"

"What the hell did you tell Dave?" Whitney barked when she reached our table. Her face was red, eyes narrow. She was beyond fuming.

"Wait. What?"

"You told him and Kate I was pregnant! It's all over the school. Everyone's talking about it!"

"That's not what—"

"Do you have any idea how mortifying that is for me? Like, did you stop for one second and even think—"

"Whit—"

"No. Fuck you. I spent the last two hours fighting with Dave, trying to convince him that *no*, I'm not pregnant. He made me get a freaking pee test. And then, once he finally calmed down, I spent the next hour icing his half-broken nose because YOU TWO beat the shit out of him. For no reason! What the hell is wrong with you? How could you—"

"Whitney. JESUS. FUCK. I don't know what the hell he told you, but that's not what happened."

"Did you or did you not say that I was pregnant?"

"I don't know what I said—I was kind of delusional after getting clocked in the face by that piece of shit. He's not the victim here."

"It was a misunderstanding. You completely overreacted!"

"Misunderstanding? Is that what he told you? Whitney, come on. You're not that dumb."

"Then what did happen? Because I've heard about three different versions of the story, and they all entail you drinking a pint of tequila, TELLING THE ENTIRE FUCKING SCHOOL I WAS PREGNANT, and then going completely and totally apeshit on my boyfriend."

"Boyfriend? You're serious? You aren't going to dump him?"

"For what? He didn't do anything!"

"Whitney, seriously. It was pretty clear what was going on." I said, trying to defend Madeline. "He was with another girl."

"I wasn't there. But it sounds bad," Emma said.

"SEE? HE. WAS. CHEATING. ON. YOU." Madeline was really starting to lose it.

"He drank too much and passed out on the bed next to her. They weren't fooling around." She crossed her arms. "You'd know that if you had asked him before you started wailing on him."

"Oh, so what then? You think I'm just some raging drunk lunatic?"

"I guess the apple doesn't exactly fall far from the tree, Madeline."

"And what the hell is that supposed to mean?"

"It means you're no different than your dad."

There was a long moment of silence. In all the time I've known Madeline, that had to be the first time I've ever seen her legitimately speechless. I looked at Emma for some type of clue as to what was going on, but she looked just as confused.

Madeline swallowed hard, stood up from her chair, and looked Whitney directly in the eye. "Fuck you, Whitney." Madeline picked up her tray and stormed off.

***

Sister Helen asked me to stay after class. I watched all the other kids file out of the classroom while I lingered back by my desk. Sister Helen pulled a chair up and took a seat beside me.

"That's quite the bruise under your eye."

"Uhm. Thanks for noticing."

"Care to tell me how you got it?"

"Tripped."

"You tripped? And what? A fist caught your fall?"

"No. I tripped, and the ground caught my fall." I rolled my eyes. "There's a cement square protruding out of the ground, uprooted by a tree or something. It's a real hazard. Someone should really do something about it."

"I'll pass your concerns along to the headmaster."

"Is that all, then?"

"No." She paused. "Madeline Gallagher showed up to my second-period religious studies class with a bruise just like yours. On her cheek. You girls are friends, so you've seen it, I assume?"

I shrugged. "Maybe."

"And low and behold, third-period rolls around, and I find Kate Hillier also has a large bruise just under her eye. And as far as I know, injuries like that aren't contagious. Any thoughts on how Ms. Gallagher and Ms. Hillier might have simultaneously developed those nasty marks?"

"You'll have to ask them."

"I intend to."

Silence.

"Unusual. Don't you think? A handful of my students show up to class with a set of matching bruises?"

"It would be unusual if they were *matching* because mine sort of looks like a taco. And the probability of us all developing food-shaped injuries, well, that's just—"

"A taco, Ms. Capello?"

"Yes, ma'am." I smirked.

"Do you think this is funny?"

"Of course not. Food-shaped injuries are no laughing matter."

"You don't really expect me to believe that this is all just some sort of quirky coincidence? Do you?"

I was silent.

"You want to know the funny thing about being an educator, Ms. Capello?"

I raised my eyebrow.

"The kids. The things they say when you're no more than a few feet away, it's astounding."

"Your point?"

"The point is, I hear things, Ms. Capello. Rumors travel fast around here, not just with the students, but with the faculty. And from what I've heard, there's more than enough reason to expel all three of you."

"I already told you. I tripped."

"Daniella, this is serious. I would strongly encourage you to cooperate."

"I am cooperating. You asked me what happened, and I gave you an answer. And I'm sorry if that answer doesn't fit with whatever rumor you heard from the oh-so-totally-reliable teenage girls of Willard Academy, but unless you have some sort of damning evidence that proves what I said isn't the truth, then I think we're at an impasse, Sister."

"This isn't a court of law, Daniella."

"Maybe not, but it's a religious institution. And the last I checked, your God forbade participating in gossip. So, punishing me based on the hearsay of my peers would make you a hypocrite. Is that really the lesson you want to send here? That we can pick and choose which commandments to ignore and which to honor based on mere convenience?"

Sister Helen raised an eyebrow, as if carefully calculating a response. "Is that all, Ms. Capello?"

"I could cite a few verses that emphasize my point if you'd like."

"That won't be necessary." Sister Helen looked at me for a long moment. "Detention. After school. Every day. With me. Indefinitely."

"WHAT? That's not fair."

"It's more than fair."

"But I told you. I didn't get into a fight with Madeline. Or Kate."

"I'm not punishing you for fighting. If I were, you'd be expelled."

"Then what exactly am I getting punished for?"

"For lying."

I was silent.

* * *

"Hey," I said as I entered my room. Emma was sitting at my desk studying. I let out an exhausted sigh, shut the door behind me, and clicked the lock shut. I flopped onto the mattress and stared at the ceiling. "How's Whitney?"

"Furious. Still." Emma shrugged and flopped onto the bed beside me. "She's spending the night in my room to avoid seeing Madeline altogether. You mind if I crash here tonight?"

"You know you don't have to ask, Em."

Emma sighed. "Thanks. I don't want to spend the night with Madeline. Whitney'll freak."

"So what, you're taking sides?"

"I'm not taking sides."

"Sort of sounds like you are. Madeline didn't even do anything…"

"She told Dave that Whitney was pregnant. That's a really, really big deal."

"Well, she's not pregnant now. Technically."

"Dani! It's a total violation of her privacy. She feels completely betrayed."

"Ok. I get it. But no one even believes the rumor. They think Madeline was just drunk and lying to get a rise out of Dave."

"Yeah, but only because I spent the last two days doing damage control." I shrugged.

"And when I was done dealing with the rumor mill, I spent the rest of my time trying—and failing—to calm Whitney down. She cried for nearly two hours today. She's really hurt, Dani."

"Ok, but being hurt doesn't give her an excuse. I mean, ignoring everything Madeline said? Refusing to believe what happened? It's completely ridiculous."

Emma was silent for a long moment. She took a deep breath and looked up at me.

"What?" I asked meekly, noticing the sudden change in her demeanor.

"It's just—" She sighed. "I don't know. Pounding Dave's face into the ground was kind of ridiculous, too."

"It was self-defense! I was helping Madeline. You saw the bruise under her eye."

"Yeah, ok. But I also saw Dave's busted nose. You're lucky he's not pressing charges."

"He totally wailed on her. What was I supposed to do?"

"I don't know. Exactly. But I do know that intervening in a bad situation doesn't mean you need to throw a punch. I'm just concerned. You've got a lot going on, between school, your cousin, this stupid feud with Kim and Kate..." she took a deep breath. "And you know, trying to figure us out. Keeping everything a secret. It's a lot."

I looked at Emma and slumped my shoulders, suddenly feeling like a jerk for getting defensive. Her eyes were red and puffy like she might burst into tears at any moment. I sighed. "I'm fine. Really."

"Dani, you were blinded by rage. I've never seen you like that before. Or anyone for that matter. And, I'm sorry, but seeing you like that—it doesn't exactly convince me that you're fine. It makes me think that you're letting things build up. That you're not dealing with anything. At least, not in a way that's healthy."

"I don't know what you want me to say."

"Neither do I, really. I'm just worried about you. You could have really gotten hurt."

"But I didn't."

"Not this time. But not everyone's going to be as cheap a shot as Dave."

"I'm a little offended you're crediting Dave's busted nose to a cheap shot instead of a killer right hook." I smiled lightly, trying to break the tension.

"This wasn't your first fight. Was it?"

I shrugged.

"That's kind of what I thought."

"Em, I grew up with four boys. In my house, it was punch or be punched."

"I get that, but—"

"But what?"

"But it's not really an excuse." Emma paused, thinking over her words carefully. "You're always so sweet with me. I guess it's just sort of weird to think there might be another side to you. One that I don't really know about."

"I'm sorry—really—I won't get into another fight. Especially not if it bothers you this much."

"Dani, don't make me a promise you're not prepared to keep."

"You have my word, Em."

"Ok."

I looked at her intently and sighed. "And I am sorry. Really."

"I know you are." Emma sighed. "And for the record, Whitney does too. She's not exactly upset with you."

"Really? Doesn't she know I did the bulk of the damage?"

"Yeah, but she also knows you didn't start the fight. Or spill her guts to the entire school."

I shrugged.

"And it probably helps that I made a strong case for you."

"Thanks. I guess."

"You should probably apologize, though. To her, I mean."

I shrugged. "I kind of don't want to."

"I know that." Emma leaned in close and kissed me. "But I want you to."

I laughed. "That was mean."

"Maybe a little." Emma smiled wide. "But I'm incredibly flattered that it worked."

"I didn't say I was going to do it."

"You didn't have to." She smiled. "You might be mysterious about some things, but every now and then, I can read you like a book, Capello."

25
WEDDING FITTING

I don't know what to say, except that dealing with feuding teenage girls is exhausting. Emma and I were basically functioning like the children of divorced parents. We'd reorganized our time and schedules to accommodate the fight, which by this point had been going on for about two weeks. I was spending my lunch period with Madeline at our regular table while Emma would sit with Whitney. At dinner, we'd alternate.

I think Emma and I foolishly believed the whole fight would work itself out by this point. After all, Madeline and Whitney were roommates, and it seemed implausible that they could actually go the remainder of the school year without speaking so much as a word to each other.

But we'd apparently underestimated their mutual stubbornness.

"I can't believe you're leaving me alone with Whitney and Madeline this weekend. It's going to be torture. Like, literal hell." Emma flopped onto my bed while I packed a weekend bag.

"I'm not happy about it either."

"I don't understand why you have to go all the way home for the fitting. You're not even in the wedding party. Couldn't you just, like, go to a shop around here?"

"I already suggested that."

"And?"

"And then my aunt proceeded to test me on the differences between coral and pink. For twenty minutes."

Emma laughed. "I take it you failed?"

"Yes. Because my aunt's a total control freak."

"To be fair, there *is* a difference between coral and pink, Dani." Emma laughed. "Couldn't you just tell her you have fashion-forward friends—me—who can help prevent any type of color-related wardrobe blunder?"

"No, because there isn't a difference. They're both pink. And also, I may have kind of lost the privilege of selecting my own clothes for formal occasions."

"What do you mean, you *lost privileges*?"

"I mean… once upon a time, I wore chucks and my black hoodie to an event that may have required cocktail attire."

"Oh my God. Dani." Emma playfully rolled her eyes. "I take it back. I'm starting to side with your aunt on this one."

"It was an act of rebellion."

"And how'd that work out for you?"

I smiled. "She shipped me off here. And I met you. So, great." I plopped down beside Emma and rested my head against the pillow.

She smiled and linked her arm in mine. "So, whose wedding is it again?"

"Gino. He's, like, a family friend, I guess. He works with my uncle."

"At the concrete store?"

"It's not a concrete *store*." I playfully whacked Emma across the chest with a pillow. "It's a manufacturing and distribution facility. They, like, work with the unions and stuff. On big construction projects."

"Same difference."

I laughed. "It's not. Really. And, no. Gino doesn't work at the *concrete store*. He owns a restaurant. And my uncle, like, I don't know, owns a share of it or something."

"That's cool."

I shrugged. "I guess."

"I'm actually a little jealous." Emma smiled wide. "I sort of love weddings."

I raised an eyebrow. "Why? They're terrible."

She gently slapped me on the arm. "They are not. They're nice. Everyone's all dressed up and doe-eyed and in love. It's sweet."

"And if by sweet you mean archaic and sexist, then sure."

"What? Dani, no. There's nothing sexist about a wedding."

"The garter toss? Wearing white to symbolize virginity? Giving away the bride to the groom?"

Emma rolled her eyes.

"And get this. Originally, best men were selected not for their friendship to the groom but based on their strength. The idea being that a strong best man could help fight off the bride and her family if she changed her mind and tried to escape."

"That can't be true."

"It is. And I'll spare you my thoughts on engagement rings."

"When did you get so cynical?"

"I'm not cynical. I'm a realist."

"So what? You never want to get married? Ever?"

"I don't know." I shrugged. "I guess it's just sort of hard to picture it."

"I get that." Emma grabbed my hand and squeezed it tightly. "But I still think it's nice. Even if the origin of the ceremony and the traditions maybe aren't so nice."

"I guess."

* * *

"I think you're going to like this one," my aunt said from the other side of the partition as she flopped the dress over the top of the dressing room door.

I took the garment and tossed it onto a small pile that I'd created on the floor.

I grabbed my phone and texted Emma. *I'm in literal hell.*

No, I'm in literal hell, she responded. *Madeline's trying to convince Erin to switch roommates.*

What did Erin say?

No, obviously. But Madeline won't let up. She's been pestering her all day.

Oh, God. Sorry. I'll try talking to her again when I get back…

I put my phone away. "Doesn't fit," I said without so much as picking up the dress from the floor. Olivia had been forcing me to try on dress after dress after dress, and I'd developed a system of passive resistance.

"Did you even try it on?"

"Of course, I tried it on."

"Well, that's the third dress I've given you that you claim doesn't fit."

"So?"

"So, they can't all not fit!"

I shrugged. "Maybe I'm getting fat."

"Oh, please, Daniella. I've given you three different sizes."

"Ok. I'm pregnant."

"For Pete's sake…"

"What? You know how it is, nothing fits the baby bump just right." I smirked. "Maybe we should try the maternity section…"

"Or maybe you're intentionally trying to drive me bonkers," my aunt said as she jiggled the handle of my dressing room door, letting herself in before I could protest.

"Oh, my God. Get out!"

"I knew it!"

I rolled my eyes as she pulled me up by the hand and borderline ripped my shirt off my body. "Here. Zip it up. I want to see it on you before you claim it doesn't fit," she said as she shoved the dress into my arms.

I held the garment against my chest, attempting to create some semblance of privacy. "Can't you just sit in the waiting area like a normal person?"

"I could if you would actually try on clothes like a normal person."

I sighed, knowing that resistance was futile.

"I just want you to find something you like."

"I'm not going to like any of them, so you might as well just pick whichever one *you* like."

"Or you could pick one we both like." She motioned for me to turn around, and I obliged. I rolled my eyes as she zipped me up. My aunt turned me around to face the mirror. "See?"

"See what?"

"This one's nice, right?"

"It's fine, Liv."

"There's another one out there I think you might like more. Let me have the clerk grab it for you."

"I've got a Chemistry test on Monday, you know."

"So?"

"So? I've got better things to do than spend my weekend trying on a million stupid dresses."

"You'll have plenty of time to study on the train ride home."

I rolled my eyes. "Nice to know you have your priorities straight."

***

"Pino Malta, President and CEO of Tecraid Industries, died in a fiery car crash Wednesday. Flames consumed the vehicle when Malta, 68, crashed into a divider on I-78."

"Hey turn it up!" I grabbed the remote from Luca and turned up the volume. My eyes were laser-focused on the television.

"Police confirmed that Malta's vehicle 'collided straight into the wall at a high rate of speed.' Malta was expected to turn himself in to the authorities at approximately 1:00 p.m. that afternoon, and local police are currently investigating the possibility of foul play."

"Holy shit." I stared with wide saucer eyes at the TV. "Pino's dead?"

"Don't you watch the fucking news? They've been covering the story nonstop for like three days." Drake rolled his eyes.

"You think someone offed him?" Luca asked.

"Course they did, he was turnin' himself in," Drake said matter-of-factly, like he was some kind of expert on the subject.

"So?"

"So? He was goin' to fuckin' snitch."

"Could have been a suicide." I shrugged. "Or a legitimate accident."

"No fucking way. Someone whacked him. For sure."

"We're here with Mario Signorelli, mafia historian and author. Thanks for coming out tonight, Mario."

"Thanks for having me."

"So, we all know Pino Malta was an alleged mob figure. The boss of bosses. How do you think his recent death is going to affect the status quo? Is this the end of organized crime as we know it?"

"It's definitely not the end of organized crime. As long as people have an appetite for the illicit—drugs, sex, gambling—someone will be there to fill that need. Whether it be the mob or some other organization."

"Interesting. So, what happens next?"

"Honestly, I expect we'll actually see a lot more public mob activity."

"How do you mean?"

"Hey!" Tony walked into the room and stood behind the couch. "What're you watchin'?"

"They're talkin' about Pino," Luca said, his eyes still glued to the tube.

"Ah, Christ. Not this shit again…"

"*Well, when something like this happens—a death of a major crime boss—you can expect a lot of confusion and instability within the organization. This leads to a struggle for power among the minor players, and struggles for power typically lead to public displays of violence. You know, the kind meant to send a message.*"

"*So, you're predicting we'll see some type of mob war?*"

Mario shrugged. "*It's hard to say, but it's not out of the realm of possibility.*"

"See! I told you he got whacked!" Drake said with a fat smile, pleased with his small victory.

"Ain't nobody whacked nobody, you understand? It's a tragic accident. And a real shame—Pino was a legitimate businessman. It's unconscionable, dragging his name through the dirt like that."

Drake rolled his eyes. "Whatever you say, Tony."

"What'd you say?"

"Nothin'."

* * *

My phone rang and without thinking I answered on instinct. "Hello?"

"Yo. Dani."

"Drake?" I rubbed my groggy eyes.

"You awake?"

"No," I groaned.

There was a long moment of silence. "Come get me."

I rolled my eyes. "Call an Uber."

"I—C—Can't."

"Why the fuck not?"

"Liv looks at—my—shit. She'll know—I snuck out."

"Fuck, Drake. It's two in the morning."

"Dani, please. I need—a—ride. C'mon." His speech was sort of slow and slurred.

"Fine," I grumbled, rolled out of bed, and slipped on my black hoodie. "Where are you?"

"A house."

"Drake, don't be an idiot. I need an address."

"I don—" his voice sort of trailed off into nothingness; like maybe he fell asleep.

"Drake! This isn't funny."

"Sooorreeee! Hold—hold on." He fumbled with the phone, and I overheard him ask someone for the address. After a few moments of muffled whispers, someone snatched the phone from Drake.

"Fifty-Seven and Lincoln. Brick building," said the voice of some guy I didn't recognize.

"Tell her to bring tacos," Drake shouted from somewhere off in the distance.

"Yeah. Tacos," the guy confirmed back into the phone. "I think fifty should do it."

"I'm not fucking bringing anyone tacos. Put Drake back on the phone."

"She says no tacos, bro." The random guy returned the phone to my brother.

There was another strange shuffle and exchange with the phone, and my brother reappeared on the line. "Daaaaani, we really need the tacos."

"Oh my God. We'll get food when I get there, ok?"

"But the guys!"

"What guys? Who're you with?"

"They need tacos, too."

"Oh my God, Drake. Enough with the tacos."

"But—Dani—I—"

Click.

He hung up the phone, but not intentionally. It was like the phone was pressed too closely against his cheek and it hung up by mistake.

I walked down the hall and grabbed my aunt's keys from a little ceramic bowl in the kitchen. I placed my hand on the handle of the glass door and took a deep breath, mentally preparing for the whole questionable escapade.

The door's metal frame dragged against the track and released what felt like a deafening screech, erupting vociferously in the silence of the night. Completely startled by my own raucous, I turned around suddenly, certain that I would be caught at any moment. My eyes scanned the darkened room. I took a deep breath and waited patiently for Olivia or Tony or anyone to barge down the stairs to investigate the noise. But no one came. So, I took another deep breath and pressed on.

I let myself into my aunt's Mercedes and started the engine. The car roared to life, and I gently backed out of the driveway.

It took nearly forty minutes to get to the address I'd been given, which was a run-down apartment just south of Hillside. I drove past the building, noticing the bars on the windows, chipped paint, and generally dilapidated appearance of the place. The whole neighborhood looked like I wouldn't make it much further than a block without getting mugged. I pulled into an empty spot down the road and texted Drake.

Drake. I'm here. Come outside.

I waited a few minutes, but he didn't respond. So, I dialed his number.

The phone rang. And rang. And rang and rang and rang and rang.

And still, no word from Drake.

I was starting to get worried, so I decided to go find him.

I got out of the car, walked across the street, and approached the building. There was a broken intercom in the front, which was mostly unnecessary because someone had duct-taped the lock on the door, preventing it from permanently closing. I let myself in and walked down a narrow hallway. The light was dim with an orangish tint, and the flooring was covered in this sort of dirty off-white linoleum that looked like it belonged in a gas station bathroom.

Music was booming from somewhere upstairs, so I followed the sound nervously. The steps creaked under my feet, and I eventually reached the apartment that was the source of the noise.

I knocked on the door.

"Hello?"

No one answered. I knocked louder this time. And then louder again.

"Drake. It's me. Open up!"

Still nothing. I sighed, placed my hand on the knob, and let myself in.

The little apartment was probably the filthiest place I'd ever seen in my life. There were beer cans and plastic cups and fast food and general garbage scattered everywhere. There were maybe twenty or thirty people crammed like sardines in the tiny two-bedroom apartment. I looked around for my brother. I was starting to think I might have let myself into the wrong party when I ran into Enzo, Carlo's son.

Enzo was dressed in his usual garb: a gold chain, a skin-tight, white V-neck, and a pair of black track pants.

"Hey! Daniel!" Enzo said as he slung his arm around me. "My favorite client!"

"It's Dani."

"That's what I said." Enzo rubbed his nose and took a sip of beer. "You want a drink? Or maybe some *crank*?" He winked and handed me his half-empty bottle, in a gesture that I'm sure he thought was generous, but I found totally repulsive.

"No. Thanks." I rolled my eyes and pushed the beer back in his direction.

"C'mon! It's a party!"

"I'm here for my brother. Where is he?"

Enzo shrugged.

"I'm not fucking around. It's late, and I need to get home. Where's Drake?"

"Christ. Don't get your panties in a twist. He's around here somewhere." He suddenly grabbed some random girl and shoved his tongue down her throat. The pair started making out, and I rolled my eyes and walked off in the other direction.

I eventually found my brother sprawled out, sleeping on a couch in one of the bedrooms. "Drake. C'mon. Get up." I shook him hard on the shoulder.

"What?" he barely managed to say as he looked up at me from the couch.

"C'mon, let's go."

"No." He collapsed back onto the pillow.

"Drake, this isn't funny. C'mon."

"What're you—" He closed his eyes for a moment then opened them, "—even doing here?"

"You called me. To come get you. Remember?"

He didn't respond. He just sort of closed his eyes and fell asleep.

"Drake, wake up!"

"What?"

"You fell asleep. In the middle of our conversation."

"No, I didn't."

"What's wrong with you?" I asked in desperation as he furrowed his brow and attempted to shoo me away. "You need to get up." I tried to sling Drake around my shoulder, but he was too heavy for me to carry myself. Seeing me struggle with my inebriated brother, Enzo swooped in.

"Here," he said as he slung Drake's arm around his shoulder. "Where to?"

I sighed. I didn't want Enzo's help, but I didn't have much of a choice. "My car's outside."

"C'mon, little buddy," Enzo said to my brother, and the two of them walk-hobbled out of the apartment building towards my aunt's car.

Enzo flopped my brother into the passenger seat and shut the door.

"I'd say thanks, but I have a feeling I wouldn't be in this particular situation if it wasn't for you."

"What's that supposed to mean?" Enzo narrowed his eyes.

"It means my brother's totally fucked up—on God knows what."

"Relax. He's just on the nod. He'll be all good tomorrow."

"Whatever." I walked over to the driver's side door and slammed it shut.

"Fuck you too, Daniel." Enzo flipped me the bird as he walked away from my car, back towards the party.

* * *

The next day, I wandered into Drake's bedroom. The afternoon sun was peeking in through the blinds. "How're you feeling?"

"Like shit." He buried his head under his pillow, attempting to shield himself from the light.

"You puked all over Liv's car last night."

"Fuck. You serious?" He lifted his head up from the pillow and looked at me with wide, panicked eyes.

"Just out the window. I hosed it off last night."

"She say anything?"

"No. I don't think she noticed."

"Good." He flopped his head back onto the pillow. "Thanks for picking me up. I owe you."

"You're welcome." I shrugged. "Who were those people?"

"Friends." He rolled over and pulled the sheets up over his body, cocooning his torso in the warmth of his comforter.

"Friends of yours? Or friends of E's?"

"What's that supposed to mean?"

"Were they *your* friends? Or Enzo's?"

"I don't know. Both."

"How'd you meet them?"

"Jesus, Dani. Will you quit it with the third degree? I'm trying to fucking sleep."

I rolled my eyes. "He said you were on the nod."

"Who?"

"E."

"So?"

"So… what does that even mean?"

"Means I took some fucking pills. Alright? Fuck." He shoved his head under his pillow in an attempt to silence me.

I looked at Drake for a long moment and sighed. "I think you should stay away from him."

"From who?"

"From E. The guy's bad news. Everybody knows that."

"Thanks for your opinion, Dr. Phil."

"Robert hated that guy."

"Robert's dead."

"Drake, I'm serious."

"Will you just fuck off, already?"

"Fine. Whatever," I said as I slammed the door behind me.

26

MADELINE

"Can we talk?" Whitney asked Madeline. Emma and I stared at one another, completely dumbfounded.

"Uh, sure." Madeline looked at me curiously, as if trying to gauge whether or not I knew anything about this. I shrugged. I really had no idea what was going on, but I secretly hoped Whitney had suddenly come to her senses and was planning on making peace.

"I just, uh, wanted to give you this." Whitney held out a small envelope.

"What is it?" Madeline raised a curious eyebrow and stared at the envelope, refusing to take it, like there might be something terrible lurking inside.

"It's your share of the deposit. You know, for the limo. For prom. I figured you'd probably want your money back so you can make other arrangements. I thought you, Em, and Dani might want to get a limo or something."

Madeline raised a skeptical brow. "So what then? You're not going to prom?"

"No. I'm still going." Whitney sighed. "I'm just getting a limo with some other people."

"Who?"

"It doesn't matter."

"If it doesn't matter, then tell me."

"Some girls from the tennis team."

"Girls from the tennis team? You mean Kate and Kim?"

"Amongst other people, yes."

Madeline did a slow clap. "Wow. Whitney. Just—fuckin'—wow."

"Look, I thought I was doing you a favor, ok? I figured you'd still want to go and—"

"Doing me a favor? By what? Bailing on me to pal around with Dave and the girl he cheated on you with? Some fuckin' favor, Whit."

"Look, I don't want this to be a thing, ok?" She shoved the envelope into Madeline's hands. "Just take your money."

"No."

"What do you mean, no? It's yours. Take it."

"I said, no." Madeline turned around, swiped her bag from the ground, and stormed away.

Whitney just stared blankly at me and Emma. "Will one of you guys give this to her? I can't keep it."

I sighed. "I'll take it." I grabbed the envelope and trailed after Madeline.

* * *

I climbed up the stairwell and eventually pushed open the large metal door. As I stepped out onto the roof of Gellar Hall, I spotted Madeline sitting in the corner.

"Hey," I said as I walked towards her. Madeline gave a reluctant nod of acknowledgment. "Mind if I smoke?"

"It's a free country." She shrugged.

I held out a box of Marlboros, offering her a light. Reluctantly, she slipped a cigarette from the box and placed it to her lips. I slouched down beside her and held a lighter under the tip. She took a deep breath and released the smoky air from her lungs.

"You alright?"

Madeline shot me a glare that unmistakably screamed: *How the hell do you think I'm doing?*

"Right. It was a shit move, giving you your money back so she can split a limo with Kate. But if it's any consolation, I don't think she was trying to be a jerk. I think she sincerely thought she was doing the right thing."

"I don't really care what she *thought* she was doing…"

"I get that but—"

"But nothing. Fuck her. Fuck prom. And fuck Kate Hillier." She took a deep breath, trying to calm her nerves as if the slightest glint of emotion would be the death of her. "I know what I saw. He was cheating on her.

But none of that matters because apparently, according to Whitney, I'm just some drunk hothead *just like my dad.*"

"What does that mean—just like your dad?"

"Nothing."

I raised a skeptical eyebrow. "No offense, but it doesn't sound like nothing."

Madeline took a long drag from her cigarette, then looked off in the distance. She swallowed hard and carefully contemplated her next words. "My dad just—I don't know—he drinks. Like, a lot."

"Oh…"

"It's mostly fine—he's got his shit together. You know? He's not like a deadbeat. But every now and then, I don't know, the stress of work really gets to him or something. And he just sort of… snaps."

"What do you mean, he snaps?"

Silence.

"Madeline?"

Madeline kicked a rock with her shoe. "When I was fourteen… he found my pregnancy test in the garbage… and well, he really fuckin' lost it."

"Oh." I swallowed hard. "Shit."

She shrugged. "He's not a terrible person or whatever. I just… dunno… really pissed him off, I guess. But my mom spiraled. She was so freaked out about the whole thing that she sent me to Willard. To protect me, I guess. She didn't want it to happen again."

"I didn't know that."

"Yeah, well, that's cuz I never told anyone… except Whit." Madeline shrugged. "I guess it was just sort of easier to let people think… I don't know… that I was the problem. The truth—that my mom was trying to protect me from my dad—I don't know. It just kind of… sucks."

"I'm sorry," I said stupidly. I really didn't know what else to say.

"It's fine. It doesn't matter."

There was a long moment of silence.

"Look, I know it hurts. Whitney should have believed you about Dave. And she shouldn't have thrown that thing with your dad in your face. But is this really what you want? To just leave Willard and never speak to each other again?"

Silence.

"I think you should talk to her."

"There's nothing to talk about. She chose Dave over me."

"I know that's how it feels… but I guess I just think that, given the circumstances, Whitney's probably not in the right mindset to make the right decision."

"What's that supposed to mean?"

I shrugged. "That people act irrationally when they're in love. And they act equally irrationally when they're depressed."

"What do you mean Whitney's depressed?"

I shrugged. "She's had a rough couple of months."

"What? You mean with the abortion?"

"Yeah, that and…" I sighed. "Em also kind of told me that Whitney got rejected from her top two schools last month."

"She never told me that…"

"Yeah, well… You were so amped on getting into NYU… when she found out she didn't get in, I dunno… I think she just didn't want to spoil it for you."

"Oh."

"I guess she's, like, really embarrassed and worried her dad is going to disown her or something. And you know how he is… even if she worked up the courage to tell him, she wouldn't be able to because he never takes her calls. So, I guess I just think, right now, she could probably use her best friend more than a lecture about her love life."

Madeline shrugged.

"This thing with Dave, while unpleasant at the moment, will work itself out on its own. Whitney's smart. When the dust settles, she'll see the same picture as the rest of us."

"Yeah, but what if she doesn't?"

"She will, Madeline." I sighed and took a long drag from my cigarette. "I know it sucks now. But it's better that we weather the storm. I don't want to find out what would happen if we let her crash and burn alone." I placed my arm around Madeline's shoulder.

"I'm still really mad."

"If you need to be mad, then be mad. Just figure out how to do it in the same room."

Madeline stared down at her feet and took a long drag from her cigarette.

"Talk to her. Ok?"

* * *

"So, I talked to Madeline." I swung open Emma's door and plopped into the swivel chair by her desk. I spun around and stared at the ceiling. "I think she's finally going to try to talk things out with Whitney. You know, make peace."

"Oh. Uh. Good." Emma's voice was sort of delicate and weak like she was barely able to get the words out.

I was startled by her lack of enthusiasm. I was expecting her to literally jump for joy at the news—given that we'd been trying to convince Madeline to apologize for nearly two weeks. And we were both sick of accommodating the feud.

I looked at Emma. Her eyes were red and swollen like she'd just wiped away a handful of tears moments before I barged into her room. I felt my stomach perform a guilt-induced somersault. I couldn't believe I hadn't noticed she'd been crying until just now. I got up from the chair and sat beside her on the bed. "Em, what's wrong?"

She looked up at me with a sort of surprised embarrassment. "Nothing," she said as she quickly wiped a tear from her cheek.

"Em, it's not nothing. You're crying." I gently wiped away a tear from her eye.

"Really. It's nothing. I'm just—I don't know. Being stupid." She blew her nose into a nearby tissue.

"It's not stupid. Not if you're upset."

She stared down at the floor. I sighed. I didn't want to pry, but I also wanted to help... but she wasn't giving me much to work with. "You want to get out of here? Go for a walk or something?"

"Sure." She shuffled clumsily up off the bed and walked towards the other end of the room. She grabbed her blue pea coat, slung her arms through the sleeves, and stood in the doorway, waiting for me to join her.

We left Gellar Hall, and I felt the cold air pierce my skin. The doors shut behind us, and I realized suddenly that I should have brought a thicker jacket. I stared at my shoes and kicked a small, round rock into the nearby grass. Light from the full moon poured down through the trees, reflecting delicately on the surface of a few small puddles that lined the walkway.

"You know ancient Christians thought that the man on the moon was some guy God banished for gathering wood on the Sabbath," I finally blurted out. I didn't know what to say.

"That's random," she half mumbled, and I watched her frosty breath dissipate into the air.

"Yeah." I took a deep breath and watched my own frosty air float into the night. "But it's actually just, like, solidified lava from some sort of moon volcano."

"You're totally geeking out," Emma said.

I couldn't tell if she was annoyed or teasing. "Sorry."

"No. It's ok. I just didn't know you were so interested in the moon." Emma let a half-smile creep between her cheeks, but there was still a touch of despondence in her voice.

We turned the corner and wandered back behind the church. I could hear the faint chatter of girls in the distance. "I just got curious about it once. Figured it might make me sound smart or something if anyone ever asked."

"Has anyone? Ever asked, I mean?" Emma teased.

I shook my head and stared at my feet. "No." There was a long moment of silence. "Look, I can walk all night. And I've got a few other tediously mundane facts about the moon I could bore you with." I slid my fingers into hers and held her hand tightly, not caring who saw us. "And I will if that's what you want. But if you wanted to talk about whatever's bothering you, we could do that too."

Emma squeezed my hand but said nothing. I shrugged. "Apparently, the moon has earthquakes like we do on Earth. Only they call them moonquakes. Which makes sense, if you think about it… but it sounds pretty stupid."

"Dani, my parents are getting a divorce," Emma suddenly interrupted.

"What?" I asked with wide eyes. I knew Emma's parents didn't get along, but the possibility of a divorce never occurred to me.

"I talked to my mom today. They signed the papers. It's official."

"I'm sorry, Em." I didn't know what else to say.

"Don't be. I don't even know why I'm surprised, really. They hated each other. I guess it's about time."

"I'm still sorry." I shrugged.

"Thanks."

I looked down at my feet and kicked another rock. "It's ok to be sad about it. Even if you think it's for the best."

Emma was silent for a long moment. We walked casually for a minute or two, then Emma suddenly stopped and looked up at me. "Dani?" she asked as she wiped her eyes.

"Yeah?" I waited for her to say something, anything at all, but the words didn't come. All at once, she buried her head into my chest and held me tightly. Tighter than I think anyone else has ever held me in my entire life. And she cried. Like, really cried. It was as if she hadn't shed a single tear in her entire life, and suddenly, they were all coming out at once in a tumultuous waterfall of emotion.

"Do you know any more stupid facts about the moon?" She barely managed to say the words. And I barely managed to understand them through the sound of sniffles and tears.

"When astronauts walk on the moon, they leave behind these footprints in the sand, and since there's, like, no wind or weather or whatever, the footprints stay there for over a million years." I wrapped my arms around her tightly and ran my hands through her hair. She laughed and cried all at the same time. She sniffed and looked up at me.

"I think I just blew snot on your jacket." She was still crying but managed to break a smile.

"It's ok. I never liked it anyway."

Emma laughed with a soft sniffle. "Liar." She rubbed a few stray tears from her eyes. "You wear it all the time."

"Em, would you maybe want to come home with me?"

"What?" she asked, confused.

"For Spring break? You know, instead of going to your parents' house? You'll have to come with me to the wedding." I smiled sheepishly. "It'll be kind of a drag... my family's insufferable... so if you didn't want to, I'd get it. But I thought maybe if you didn't want to deal with your parents and wanted a break or whatever—"

She looked up at me and smiled. "Yeah."

"Yeah?"

"I'd love that, Dani. Thanks."

I smiled. "C'mon. It's cold. I've got some tea back in my room. I'll even spike it. If you want."

"Thanks, Dani."

27
SPRING BREAK AT THE CAPELLOS'

"Holy shit, Dani," Emma said, looking around the entryway. Her eyes were fixed on the elaborate architecture. "You didn't tell me your family was loaded."

I laughed. "Emma, I met you at prep school. Everyone's family is loaded."

"Not like this." She smiled as we approached the large staircase in the foyer. Emma ran her fingers along the opulent wooden railing, then stopped suddenly. "Oh my God. Dani, is that a Renoir?" she asked, her eyes locked on the painting in front of her.

I smiled and grabbed her by the hand. "Come on. I'll show you the art collection later."

"What? Collection? There are more of these?" Her eyes drifted back to the painting as I pulled her up the stairs. I led her down the hallway to my bedroom. I pushed open the door, and Emma immediately burst into a fit of laughter.

"No. Fucking. Way." Her eyes widened as she threw her bag to the floor.

"Shut up," I groaned.

"Dani, it's *soooo* pink," Emma teased as she looked around my room, soaking in the decor. My aunt had painted the room a light shade of pink when I was a kid, and despite about a million arguments over the matter, I was never allowed to repaint it.

"I know. It's odious." I flopped onto the bed and glanced around the room, embarrassed by my aunt's absurdly feminine decor.

"No. It's amazing." She beamed. "Please give me permission to tell everyone we know about this."

I rolled my eyes playfully and smiled. "But, Emma, you'll ruin my carefully crafted reputation."

"Sorry, what was I thinking?" she teased. Her eyes fell on the porcelain doll fastened to a white display stand on my dresser.

"Oh, God. Dani. What is this thing?" She picked up the doll and held it in her hands.

"That was a present for my ninth birthday." I paused. "A present that, to this day, I'm not allowed to play with. The thing cost like three grand."

"You're joking."

I shook my head. "It's some sort of collectible, apparently." I gently took the doll from her and placed it back on the protective stand.

"It's sort of weird."

"I know. Who gives a nine-year-old a $3,000 doll?"

Emma laughed. "That's not what I meant, Dani." She flopped onto the bed beside me.

I smiled. "What's weird, Emma?"

"Seeing where you grew up."

"Weird good or weird bad?"

"Weird good."

* * *

The next day was Gino's wedding. I laid back comfortably on my bed and flipped the page of a tattered novel. Emma tapped on the door and entered my room.

"Dani," she said with obvious disapproval. "You aren't dressed yet?"

I wanted to make some sort of crack about how uptight she was, and how there was plenty of time, but I honestly couldn't because I was too distracted by the way she looked. She was wearing this pale green dress with little tiny straps that ran across her collarbones. Her hair was twisted up and pinned in the back with thin curls that danced down her cheeks. She was totally and completely stunning. "Wow." I sat up from my bed and tossed the book to my side.

"Thanks," she said as she unhooked the coral-not-pink dress from my closet and tossed it on the bed beside me. "But flattery will only get you so far. Come on. Sit up." She grabbed my hand and tugged me towards the edge of the bed.

"What're you doing?"

"Your makeup. And hair."

I scrunched up my face with repulsion. "C'mon, Em. No."

"The way I see it, you have two choices," she said with a cheeky grin. "You can let me do this, or you can take your chances with your aunt's makeup lady."

I rolled my eyes playfully. "Alright. You win."

She ran her hands through my hair and pulled it back and up into a clip. She went to work, and I tried my best to be a good sport about the whole thing. I tapped my shoes against the floor while Emma carefully separated my hair into sections. She meticulously wrapped bits of my hair around a hotter-than-hot curling wand and then finished each curl with an ungodly amount of hair spray.

I suddenly heard a soft voice from behind me. I turned around to find Katie, Gino's six-year-old daughter, bounding our way like an excited puppy. She was dressed in a little pink and white lace dress with shiny white dress shoes. I smiled as she jumped up on the bed beside me and leaned in for a hug.

"You're back," she said with a smile.

"So are you! I heard you were spending some time with your grandma in Maine?" Katie gave a shy nod of acknowledgment. "Did you have fun up there?"

She shook her head. "It was cold."

"Well, that stinks."

She nodded shyly, glanced over at Emma, then whispered into my ear, "Who's that?"

I smiled. "That's Emma. She's a friend of mine from school." I looked over at Emma. "Em, this is Katie."

"It's nice to meet you, Katie," Emma said, grinning from cheek to cheek. "Are you going to be in the wedding today?"

Katie nodded shyly. "I'm the flower girl."

"There you are!" Samantha, Gino's fiancé, stumbled into my bedroom and put her hand on her hip. Her hair was in curlers, and she was wearing one of those long, silky, white bathrobes with the word "Bride" written in pink cursive on the back. "I've been looking everywhere for you, kid!"

"I found Dani and some girl!" Katie said with a bright smile.

"I can see that." Samantha smiled. "Why don't you go on back to our room and finish getting ready, alright?"

"Ok!" Katie smiled wide and skipped out of the room.

"Well, that girl sure knows how to keep a lady busy."

I laughed. "Yeah, she's a handful."

"Sure is." Samantha laughed. "And she just thinks the world of you, Dani. She just about talked my ear off this morning. You should have heard her. It was so cute." Samantha smiled. "It's kind of a shame. I haven't gotten to know you that well, since you've been up at that fancy school. But I'm sure glad you were able to come down for the wedding. It means a lot to me and Katie. Gino too."

"Oh, yeah. Of course. Gino and Katie are like family. Which makes you family too." I smiled. It sounds corny to say, but I really did mean it.

"Aw, I appreciate that. Your whole family has been so good to us. Especially your aunt. I'm so grateful she was around to keep an eye out for Katie before I got into the picture."

"What do you mean?"

"Oh, you know, just coordinating everything with Katie's grandma. Makin' sure she got up to Maine alright. And Katie's grandma was so thrilled to have her. She was over the moon when your aunt suggested the whole thing."

"Wait. It was Olivia's idea? Sending Katie up to Maine?"

Samantha nodded. "Gino's drinking was making her nervous. Lord knows the man can throw em' back. And your aunt thought that maybe someone should keep a closer eye on her. So she suggested Katie go stay with her grandma until there was someone around who could really watch out for her. Make sure she's safe. You know, until Gino got himself in a better place."

"I, uh, didn't know she did that," I barely managed to say. I swallowed hard and mulled over the revelation.

"Oh, yeah. She's real thoughtful, that one. And things are just really good right now, you know? Gino's really cut back on his drinking. And I'm here to help out. Keep an eye on things. I just love that little girl, you know?"

I smiled. "Yeah, I can tell. I'm glad she has you around now."

"Me too." Samantha gently clapped her hand against her thighs. "Well, I'll let you girls get back to it. See ya at the wedding!"

"Yeah, uh, see ya," I said as I watched Samantha shimmy out of the room. I can't believe Olivia never mentioned that sending Katie to Maine was her idea...

* * *

After a short ceremony at the church, guests arrived at our house for the reception. My aunt had really gone all out. Our backyard was transformed into some sort of wonderland. There was a classy white tent with twinkle lights and sheer cloth draped around the edges. There was a dance floor, a DJ, and a string quartet. And the flowers—my God, you'd think we lived at a botanical garden or something.

There were seemingly hundreds of guests scattered about, some eating from the colossal buffet of food, others dancing under the elegant canopy, and others enjoying the open bar.

Gino and Samantha sat at a special table that was raised about a foot off the ground, giving them a prime view of the party.

Emma and I were assigned to a table with Drake and Luca out in the back corner of the yard. We took our seats, and Emma looked around curiously at the cohort of attendees wandering around the backyard. "So, what's the deal with the—err—guest list?"

"What do you mean?"

"This Gino guy? Is he like—" She paused, searching for the right words. "Some kind of Soprano or something?"

"His last name's Russo?" I said stupidly.

Emma rolled her eyes playfully. "You know what I mean. Half the people here look like they came straight from the pages of a Mario Puzo novel."

I rolled my eyes and laughed. "You know, some people might find that offensive."

"Not anyone with eyes." She smiled. "Like—look at that guy. What's his deal?" Emma pointed to Lou Collins, the haggard Man with the Marlboros I'd met at my aunt's fundraising party and subsequently re-met at Robert's memorial service. "He's sort of terrifying. I'm getting serious Luca Brasi vibes."

"He's a friend of my uncle's. They work together. I think."

"Work? Like at the concrete store?"

"I don't know exactly..." And that was the truth. I really didn't know...

but I had some ideas. "And for the record, his last name is Collins—which is English—so the Mario Puzo reference is a bit flawed."

"If an Irish Jew can grace the pages of the Godfather, then I don't think an Englishman is so far-fetched."

"Except, you're missing a key detail here, Emma."

"What?"

"The novel's a work of fiction." I smirked and poked her in the side.

"Yeah. Yeah. Yeah. Ok. I get it." Emma laughed and shooed my hands away. "But even so, that guy still looks sort of…" Emma stopped searching for the right words. "Criminal."

"That's because he is," Drake said with a wide grin as he and Luca plopped down beside us. "Heard he spent fifteen at Fairton."

"Fairton? What is that?"

"A prison." Luca smiled wide.

"Really? What'd he do?" Emma asked with wide saucer eyes.

"Cracked a dude's head open. With a pickaxe."

"Shut up, Drake."

"It's true. The guy's a total loon." Luca nodded eagerly.

"He is not." I looked over at Emma. "They're lying. There's no way that's true."

Drake scoffed. "Oh yeah? And how would you know?"

"Because every time I've talked to him, he's been… mostly normal."

"That's a load of shit."

"Yeah. No way you ever talked to Lou freakin' Collins," Luca scoffed.

I rolled my eyes. "He let me bum a cigarette… then freaked out when he found out I was underage. Which doesn't exactly sound like the reaction of an axe-wielding psychopath. Sounds more like the reaction of a law-abiding citizen."

"What do you think?" Drake looked at Emma.

She smiled wide. "I think you're trying to screw with me."

"Suit yourself."

Emma took a final sip from her soda. "My drink's out."

"Mine too, c'mon," I said as I grabbed her hand, eager to have an excuse to ditch my brother and Luca.

We walked towards the bar and waited behind a small crowd of people. Emma refused to drink around my family, so she got a club soda, and I got a ginger ale. I grabbed my drink from the bartender and turned around to walk back to our table. As I turned, my shoulder collided with Carlo Gatti, who had apparently been standing behind me. I hadn't seen Carlo since the fight at Olivia's fundraiser when I caught him with Katie and was subsequently sent away to Willard.

"Fuck," I said, surprised to see him standing there, and also surprised by how uncomfortably close he was to me. I swallowed hard.

"Hope I didn't scare you." He smiled a wide, bright, friendly grin.

I narrowed my eyes. "You didn't."

"Enjoying yourself?" He glanced down at my drink suspiciously, then placed his hand on my shoulder, squeezing my collarbone tightly.

I could feel the blood rush from my cheeks. I took a deep breath, attempting to calm my nerves. "It's soda," I said, relieved to be telling the truth.

"Right." He glanced over at Emma. "I don't think we've met before. I'm Carlo—a friend of Dani's uncle." He smiled wide and extended his hand. My stomach churned.

"Emma," she said as she shook his hand. "Dani and I go to school together."

"I've heard a lot of great things about that school—your aunt talks about it all the time. What was it called again?"

"Willard," Emma responded, her eyes switching uncomfortably between me and Carlo.

"We should go," I said suddenly, as I grabbed her hand and led her back towards our table.

"Uhm, nice meeting you," Emma said awkwardly as we dashed away.

We approached the table, and I was relieved to see that Drake and Luca had disappeared, at least for the moment.

"What was the deal with that guy?" Emma asked as we took a seat.

I rubbed my temple, trying to clear my mind—trying desperately to erase the uneasy sensation with nothing more than sheer willpower. I took a long sip from my soda. My face was tingling and hot. And my mouth was dry.

"Earth to Dani—" Emma said as she waved her hand in front of my face.

"Sorry." I blinked and forced a smile, trying my best to refocus my attention back onto Emma. "What'd you say?"

Emma raised an eyebrow. "I said, *what was the deal with that guy?*"

"Who? Carlo?" I took a deep breath.

"Yeah, you looked like a ghost when you saw him. And you're shaking."

I looked down at my hands. She was right. On instinct, I grabbed my wrist, attempting to calm the tremor.

"Well?"

It felt like a cotton ball was lodged in my throat. "I don't like him."

"I got that." She raised an eyebrow. "I'm just wondering why. Exactly."

I stared down at my drink and swirled the bubbly liquid around the plastic cup.

"Dani?"

I bit my lip and sighed. "He's kind of the reason I got sent to Willard."

"I thought you said your aunt sent you to Willard? Because you weren't getting along?"

"I did. We weren't. And that explanation was only half true."

"So, you half lied?" She smiled and kicked my shoe.

"I barely knew you when you asked."

"Fair." She thought for a moment. "So, what happened?"

"I don't know. It's just—like—I've known Carlo for a long time. Since my parents died. He's a friend of the family. He and my uncle work together. And we got into a fight. And—I don't know—my aunt freaked out. So here we are."

"What kind of fight?"

"The regular kind," I said with an exhausted sigh.

"Like, an argument or the kind that involves a right hook?"

"I didn't, like, punch him or whatever. I mean, not exactly."

"Oh my God, Dani." Emma's eyes widened. "That guy is like sixty years old. How could you get into a fist fight with an old man?"

"Look, I know how it sounds, ok? But trust me. The guy's a jerk."

"So what? You broke his hip?"

"No, but I might have sort of spit in his face. And then he kind of went ballistic."

Her jaw dropped, totally appalled. "Dani, why would you do something like that?"

"Because I apparently have some kind of drinking problem." I scoffed sarcastically. "At least, that's what he told my aunt."

"And the real reason?"

"He was alone with… Katie."

"What do you mean, *he was alone with Katie?*"

I wiped my sweaty palms against my dress. "I mean he was alone with Katie, and he's not the kind of guy who should be left alone with little kids…"

Emma's face scrunched up with repulsion as she began to understand the situation. "So, you mean—like—"

I nodded.

"Oh. God." She furrowed her brow and stared back in Carlo's direction. He was casually sipping a beer at the bar. "What a fuckin' creep."

I shrugged.

"Did you tell someone?"

I nodded.

"And?"

"And they sent me two hundred miles away. To Willard."

"Oh." Emma grabbed my hand and squeezed it tightly. "I'm sorry."

"Thanks." I sighed and stared down at my drink.

* * *

Late that evening, I found Olivia downstairs straightening up the kitchen. She sipped a glass of wine and unloaded the dishwasher, placing the clean dishes back into the empty cupboards. The room was dark. The glow of the moon shone through the back window, leaving a series of horizontal shadows against the wall.

"Hey," I said as I approached the fridge and filled a glass with water.

"Oh, Dani," my aunt half jumped. "You scared me."

"Sorry," I smiled meekly. "Just getting some water."

"Right," my aunt tossed a few plastic cups in the garbage and sighed. "This place is a mess."

"You don't have to worry about it. Tony said the cleaners were coming first thing tomorrow."

"I know. I guess… I just have a hard time… relaxing. You know, with the house like this."

"I know." I laughed. "It was nice of you, though. Throwing the whole thing together for Gino and Samantha. Letting a million guests trash the place."

She half smiled. "Well, they're family. I couldn't let them just run off and elope now could I? Wouldn't have been right."

"Yeah." There was a long pause. "Samantha seems nice."

"She and Gino are a good match. I've never seen him so happy."

"Me neither…" I rubbed my arm uncomfortably. "She uh, mentioned that you kind of coordinated Katie's trip to Maine? Sending her to stay with her grandmother?"

"Oh, uhm. Yeah. I had a little to do with it."

"You never mentioned that before…"

Olivia shrugged. "I guess I didn't think there was much to say."

"Why'd you do it?"

"What do you mean?"

"What made you send her away? Was it because of what I said about Carlo? At the party?"

Olivia closed the dishwasher, topped off her glass of wine, then sat down at the kitchen table. She took a long sip from the glass and signaled for me to take a seat beside her. So I did. She took a deep breath, as if carefully contemplating her next words.

"Dani, I know things haven't always been easy on you here. And I'm sorry for that."

I shrugged. "You don't have to apologize, Liv."

She sighed and ran her fingers across the rim of her glass. We sat in silence for a long moment.

"You're friend, Emma. She seems nice," Olivia finally said, breaking the silence. "I'm glad she was able to come visit."

"Me too."

"Must have been nice to have someone to pal around with at the wedding."

I nodded.

"So things are going alright? At Willard?"

"Yeah."

"Good. I'm glad." She placed her glass on the table. "I never meant it as a punishment. Sending you there. I just wanted what's best for you. And wasn't sure how else to do it."

I shrugged. "Yeah, I know that."

She tapped her fingers against the glass. She took a deep breath and looked up at me. "I love you, Dani. You know that right?"

"Yeah. I do."

"Good."

We sat there in silence for a long moment. I took a sip of water and stood up from the table. "I should… probably get to bed."

She nodded.

I placed my glass in the kitchen sink and walked towards the hall.

"Dani?"

"Yeah?" I stopped, turned around, and looked at my aunt.

"My mother told me once… 'a wolf in sheep's clothes is more dangerous if he knows you see him for what he truly is.'" She stood up from the table and walked towards me. She placed her hand on my shoulder and squeezed it gently. "Sometimes, in our world, when you know someone's a monster—it's best not to let them know, you know. At least not until the time is right. You can't protect the people you love if the wolf knows you're coming. You understand?"

"I think so."

"Right. Well. Goodnight."

"I love you, Dani."

"Love you too, Liv."

28

POUGHKEEPSIE

Tony and Olivia made their way to the front door with an oversized rolling suitcase, which seemed like overkill because they were only going to be gone for two nights. Samantha had arranged for Tony and Olivia to have a romantic weekend together in Poughkeepsie as a thank you for all their help with the wedding. It was a nice enough gesture, but I could tell my aunt wasn't looking forward to it.

"Is that everything?" Olivia studied the small pile of luggage by the front door.

"Yeah," Tony said with a slight eye roll. This was the third time she'd asked that question, and it was as if she expected the answer to change each time.

"I feel like we're forgetting something."

"God, go already," Drake groaned.

"The kid's right, Liv. We gotta hit the road."

"Fine." She sighed and left an extra hundred-dollar bill on the counter, presumably for food, supplies, and whatever else we might need while they were away. "Call if you need anything."

"We won't. Bye!" Luca said as he waved them out the door and shut it behind them with a loud thud.

"Finally." Drake flopped down onto the couch and popped open one of Tony's beers.

Later that night, there was a knock at the door. I flipped the latch and twisted the knob.

"What do you want?" I said with an eye roll when I saw Enzo on the other side.

"Here for the party," he said with a smirk as he casually held up a twenty-four-pack and a bottle of vodka.

"Thanks for the beer," I said as I took the beer and attempted to shut the door in his face.

"If I didn't know better, I'd say you were mad at me." He pushed open the door and let himself into our house.

"No shit." I rolled my eyes and followed behind.

He made a beeline for the kitchen and opened the fridge. "What? You aren't still pissed about the other night, are you?"

"You mean that night you fed my brother an ungodly number of pills and left me to clean up the mess? No, totally not pissed. Not at all," I scoffed in a sarcastic huff and stuffed the twenty-four-pack into the fridge.

Enzo popped the top of a beer and took a swig. "God. Chill. No one died."

"Look, I don't care what *you* do. Just keep that shit away from my brother, ok?"

He hopped up on the counter and leaned back casually. "Huh... that's interesting..."

"What?" I half rolled my eyes.

"Acting all high and mighty. You know, given *your* little habit."

"I don't have a habit," I retorted.

"You bought a half gram from me." Enzo laughed. "You think I'd forget about my favorite client?"

Silence.

"Hey. It's all good. I don't have a problem with it." Enzo smiled. "Your aunt might, though."

"Is that some kind of a threat?"

Enzo shook his head. "No threat. Just thinking out loud. It'd be a real shame if she found out."

I narrowed my eyes. "What do you want?"

"Nothing." He smiled. "Just want to make sure we're on the same page."

"Bro. Get in here. We got pizza," Drake suddenly shouted from the dining room. "And bring beer."

"How many?" Enzo shouted back as he ripped open the twenty-four-pack.

"Three!"

"Three?" He leaned over and peered through the door towards the dining room. Emma was eating with Drake and Lucca. "Who's the blonde?" He looked in my direction and smirked.

"A friend. From school."

"She's cute. Not a ten, but definitely an easy seven. Maybe an eight on a good day."

"Don't even think about it," I said as I grabbed two beers and walked into the dining room.

* * *

Apparently, Drake and Luca had informed a handful of people that we were having a party. It was still early in the evening, and things hadn't really gotten started, so Benny, Gino's man-child nephew, gathered everyone around the kitchen table and made us play some drinking game. The guys scattered a deck of cards around a glass cup in the middle of the table, and we each took turns drawing. Each card meant you had to do something—like take a drink, make someone else drink, answer a question, or do a goofy dance.

"Two." I furrowed my brow. "What does that mean, again?"

"You," Lucca groaned. "Meaning… *you* get to pick someone to drink."

"Fine. I pick you. You drink."

Luca rolled his eyes and took a swig from his beer.

"Alright, my turn." Drake smiled wide and drew a card. "Queen. Questions." He locked his eyes with Emma. "I pick you."

"Alright. Shoot." Emma leaned back in her chair, waiting for whatever question Drake was about to ask.

"Are the rumors about all-girls schools true?"

"What rumors?"

"You know, is it a giant les fest?" Drake smirked.

"Jesus, Drake." I rolled my eyes.

"What? It's a reasonable question."

"On what planet is that a reasonable question?"

"It's an all-girls school!"

"It's also a Catholic school…" Emma smiled.

"So?"

"Sooo, it's pretty dull on campus." Emma smirked. "Except on those occasional nights where we run around in our underwear and have pillow fights."

"Wait. Really?" Luca looked up like a curious puppy.

I rolled my eyes. "No, idiot. She's joking."

"Oh," Luca said as he took a sip of beer. He looked genuinely disappointed.

"Anyone else a little warm?" Emma asked.

"Yeah. Hang on. I'll turn up the A.C." I said as I got out of my seat and adjusted the thermostat.

Drake smirked and leaned over towards Emma. "Ya know, if you're hot, you could just take off your shirt instead," Drake smirked.

"Jesus, Drake. Stop," I said, flopping back down in my seat.

"Funny." Emma rolled her eyes. "I'm going to grab another drink. Anyone want something while I'm up?"

"Beer!" Benny, Luca, and Drake shouted simultaneously.

"Uh, ok. Four beers then?"

"You want some help?" Enzo asked casually as he got up and followed Emma into the kitchen.

I waited patiently for Emma and Enzo to leave the room. Once she was out of earshot, I punched Drake on the arm, hard.

"OW! What was that for?"

"For acting like an ass. Besides... should you really be making jokes about Emma when you've got a girlfriend?"

"What Becca doesn't know won't hurt her."

"And here I thought chivalry was dead."

"You don't need to be chivalrous to get laid." He smiled. "You just need a girl with low self-esteem."

"You're disgusting, Drake."

"I'd wager your friend thinks I'm charming."

"She thinks you're a tool. She's only being nice to you because you're my brother. You know that, right?"

"We'll see."

"What do you mean *we'll see?*"

I punched Drake on the arm again, hard.

"God. Calm down. I'm just fucking around." He rubbed his bicep.

"Whatever. Just fucking quit it, ok?"

* * *

By around ten o'clock, kids started arriving at our place by the dozens, carrying six-packs and handles of cheap booze. I wasn't surprised Luca and Drake had taken this opportunity to throw a house party—but I was surprised by the sheer volume of people that had come. I'm not even sure that Drake knew half the people that were there. The whole thing was stupid. We were definitely going to get caught.

Music boomed from the sound system in the living room. Some guys had pushed aside the sofa into the corner of the room, and a few girls were dancing and drinking and spilling their beer all around the house. Emma and I stood in the kitchen, watching the chaos unfold.

"Your aunt's going to flip," Emma said, watching in semi-horror as some random kid shot a beer bong in the living room, subsequently spilling nearly a liter of beer all over the floor.

"I know. I'm fucking dead."

Emma laughed. "No, your brother's dead. You're an innocent bystander."

"I guess," I said with an uneasy groan, knowing full well Drake was going to bring me down with him.

Suddenly, someone turned the music up. The bass thumped, and I could feel the music pulse through me. Emma leaned in close, struggling to be heard over the noise from the party. "I need to use the bathroom. Come with?"

I nodded, and she pulled me by the hand through the crowd; we swayed back and forth as people bumped into us from all sides. When we'd finally made it to the downstairs restroom, there was a line of about four girls outside the door.

"Use mine. Upstairs," I yelled into her ear. She nodded and headed off in the other direction. I followed behind her when suddenly, I heard something shatter from somewhere.

"Fuck," I said, looking towards the other side of the room, trying to decipher what was broken. "You go ahead... I think I need to go deal with that."

"You want help?" Emma asked.

"No, go ahead. I'll meet up with you in a minute."

She nodded and wandered off into the lifeblood of the party.

I went to find the source of the noise. After stumbling through a cohort of people, I found a ceramic vase nearby.

"Fuck," I said as I bent over and started picking up the broken shards.

29

EMMA AND ENZO

Emma switched off the bathroom light and closed the bathroom door behind her.

"Hey," a voice said from the other side of the room.

Emma let out a slight yelp when she looked up and saw Enzo standing in the doorway. "Jesus," she said, struggling to catch her breath. "You scared me."

"You scare easily," he said with a smirk as Emma walked towards the door.

"Uh, yeah. I guess." She stopped in front of him. "You come up here for the restroom too?"

"Something like that," Enzo said as he took a casual step into the bedroom, stopping by the dresser next to the door. Enzo picked up the porcelain doll from the dresser. "Damn, this is one ugly doll."

"Careful," Emma said with a friendly smile. "Dani said that thing costs like $3,000."

"This creepy thing?" Enzo said with a chuckle as he held the doll up on display.

Emma shrugged. "Apparently, it's some sort of antique."

"Huh." Enzo gently tossed the doll into the air. He caught it gracefully and placed it back onto the stand. "Guess I'd better be careful."

"Truth be told, I think she'd be glad if you busted it."

"Oh, yeah?"

"Yeah. But I have a sneaking suspicion that her aunt would have a meltdown."

Enzo laughed. "Right. The infamous Olivia Cappello."

Emma rubbed her forearm, uncomfortably, waiting for Enzo to move to the side. "So, are you just going to stand there all day? Or are you ever actually going to use the restroom?"

Enzo smiled and took a step closer to Emma. "I have a confession to make."

"Oh yeah?" Emma asked with a furrowed brow as she took a step back.

"I didn't actually come up here for the jon." He shut the bedroom door behind him, clicked the lock shut, and slowly inched his way towards Emma. Before she could respond, he pulled a small bag of white powder out of his pocket. "Didn't want to share. The guys down there are total fucks." He smiled. "You want a hit?" He carefully dumped the contents onto the dresser's flat surface.

"Thought you said you didn't want to share?" she said with a cheeky grin, trying to make light of the situation. She really wanted to leave the room, but she also didn't want to come off rude.

Enzo laughed. "I don't. But I'd make an exception. For you."

"Well, thanks," she said awkwardly. "But I'll pass."

"More for me," he said as he rolled up a small dollar bill, placed it over the white powder, and sucked a line through his right nostril. "Fuck!" he gasped, obviously pleased with the rush. "You sure you don't want in?"

"Really. I'm good." Emma eyed the door uncomfortably, searching for a tactful way to excuse herself from the unexpected encounter.

Before she could formulate the words, Enzo leaned back against the door casually, wiped his nose, and smiled a wide friendly grin. "Want to see something?"

"Uhm, sure. I guess."

"Come here." Enzo walked towards the bed and signaled for Emma to take a seat beside him. She reluctantly obliged.

Enzo removed his jacket, reached around his torso, and removed a gun that was holstered to his body. Emma let out a slight yelp as he displayed the weapon proudly.

"Nice, huh?" he asked as he gently traced the outline of the barrel with his fingers.

"I guess," she said with a twinge of panic in her voice. Being this close to a weapon made her wildly uncomfortable.

"You kidding? What do you mean, *you guess?*"

"I just—I don't know a lot about guns." Her heart was pounding. "I wouldn't know a nice one from a piece of shit." She forced an awkward smile between her cheeks.

Enzo laughed and handed her the gun. "Here."

"No, I couldn't." Her breath was shallow. She desperately wanted him to put the gun away, but she also didn't want to offend him.

"C'mon. Just touch it." He forced it into her hand and let her feel the weight of the instrument against her fingertips. The metallic barrel was nefarious and ugly, and holding it only increased Emma's discomfort with the object. "Browning Hi-Power. 9mm. Steel frame. One of the few pieces this size with hi-mag capacity."

"I don't really know what any of that means." She half smiled and handed it back to him. "But it's uh, nice."

"Fuck yeah, it's nice." He held up the gun and pointed it across the room, and closed one eye like he was aiming at a target. There was a long moment of silence. Enzo ran his hands along the edge of the gun, then looked up at Emma. "You mind if I ask you a question?"

"Uh, ok. What is it?"

"Me and the guys. We've been having a debate. And I was thinking maybe you could settle something for me."

"A debate?" Emma said with faux amusement. "Intrigue."

"See, Drake's been talking shit. Says that you and his sister are, *you know*—" Enzo emphasized the words *you know*, as if that was supposed to convey whatever it was he was trying to say.

"*You know*, what?"

"Involved," he said as he made a lewd gesture with the gun and his fingers. "Said he heard you guys the other night…"

Emma rolled her eyes and gently pushed Enzo's hand, making the gun point away from her. "Well, Drake's kind of an asshole."

"So, you're not?"

"Not what?"

"Some kind of a dyke."

"Look, I don't know what you're playing at, but—" Emma started to get up when Enzo grabbed her firmly by the wrist.

"Hey, hey. You don't need to get defensive. I wasn't the one talking shit," Enzo said with a smirk. "I told him there's no way a girl as pretty as you could be, you know, like that."

Emma rolled her eyes. "Is that some kind of line?"

"You want it to be?" He moved in close and pressed his body against hers.

"Look, I should probably get back—"

"Why?"

"I'm just—sort of uncomfortable."

"Because of this?" He held up the gun.

It wasn't just the gun, but that seemed as good an excuse as any. She nodded.

"You don't like guns?"

"Not really, no."

"Why not?"

"Because they're dangerous."

"Only in the wrong hands."

"I'd just feel a lot better if we went back to the party. Ok?"

He laughed. "What, you don't trust me?"

She didn't. But she didn't dare admit that. "No, it's just—"

"You don't need to worry. I'm not going to hurt you," he said as he cocked the weapon. It let out a loud springy click that made Emma jump. "But I might scare you a little." Enzo took the barrel of the gun and pressed it gently against Emma's neck and traced it down towards the thin black strap of her dress. He gently slid the barrel under the strap and tossed it to the side, exposing her bare shoulder. He ran the gun down her chest, across her breast, and smiled.

Her hands were shaking; her voice cracked. "Ok, very funny. But seriously. You can put it away now." She took a deep breath, sat up immediately, and slid the strap of her dress back onto her shoulder.

"Don't get bent out of shape. I'm just fucking around." Enzo followed Emma towards the door, placed the gun onto the dresser, and stepped in front of her.

"Well, it's not funny. You're really freaking me out." Emma attempted to brush past his abominable physique when, suddenly, he extended his forearm, blocking her path. "Can you seriously just, like, get out of the way?"

Enzo scoffed lightly under his breath, both amused and aroused by her resistance. "I don't want to," he said as he pressed his body against hers;

the stench of whiskey on his breath polluted the cold air surrounding them.

She shoved her hands against his chest and pushed with all her might, attempting to force herself past the two-hundred and twenty-pound human barricade. Unwilling to let her escape, he seized her harshly by the shoulder, turning her body towards him with a fierce jerk.

"Don't touch me." She forced the words out of her mouth with all the courage she could muster.

"Calm down," Enzo said with an annoyed groan as she struggled to break free. He strengthened his grip and leaned in close, whispering in her ear. "We're just having a little fun."

* * *

It had been a while since Emma had gone upstairs to use the restroom. I hadn't really seen Drake either, and I was getting worried that he was annoying the hell out of her somewhere, and I knew she'd be too polite to excuse herself. So, I wandered upstairs towards my room and found Drake standing outside my door.

"You can't go in there."

"It's my room. Why the hell not?"

"Occupado."

"Excuse me?"

"You dense? It's in use."

"By who?"

"Your friend. And E." Drake made a lewd gesture with his fingers, by which he intended to insinuate they were having sex.

"That's not funny, Drake." I tried to move past him, but he stepped in front of me.

"Who's joking?"

"Emma would never do that."

"I've never seen a girl turn him down. Ever."

"Well, there's a first time for everything."

"Doubtful."

"You're just trying to bug me."

"Why would it bug you?" Drake looked at me slyly, and something about the look in his eye said the question was rhetorical. He knew exactly why it would bug me.

"Because he's a creep. That's why."

"Grow up. It's just sex. He probably won't even cream on her face."

"FUCK. DRAKE." I punched him on the arm, hard.

He burst into laughter. "Oh, my God. You've totally got a hard-on for this chick."

I looked at my brother with wide eyes, then suddenly looked away, knowing my cheeks were starting to turn pink from embarrassment. "Jesus, Drake. No. Why would you say something like that?"

"Because you're totally freaked right now."

"I'm freaked because you're being a dick."

"Yeah, well. I've never seen you with a guy."

"Half the year I'm in another state. You hardly see me ever."

"I know Liv and Tony would flip, but you could totally tell me," Drake smirked. "Cuz I'm a huge supporter of girl-on-girl action."

"Fuck off, Drake."

"What?" He smiled. "We're twins. Who can you trust, if not your own flesh and blood?"

"Why do you have to be such an asshole all the time?"

"I'm not being an asshole. I'm just pointing out the facts. You get seriously fuckin' worked up every time I make a joke about her."

"Because she's my friend, and your jokes are gross."

"You think everything's gross."

"Yeah, when it's degrading and misogynistic."

"Get off your high-fucking-feminist horse."

"Screw you."

"Suck a dick..." He smiled. "Or clit, since that's more your thing."

I heard a muffled voice suddenly shriek from my bedroom.

"What was that?" I turned around. I don't know how to explain it exactly, but I had this sinking feeling in my gut, a wrenching ache that unmistakably said something isn't right.

"Probably just the sound of your friend... moaning in pleasure!" Drake thrust his hips forward like he was fucking an imaginary woman from behind.

"Get out of the way." I shoved my brother hard, and he stumbled to the side awkwardly. I banged on the door with all my might. "Em, you in there?" I jiggled the handle, but it was locked. "Em?"

* * *

"The fuck is going on?" I half-shouted as I barged into my bedroom. Enzo and Emma were standing in the corner. Enzo had pinned her up against the wall. At first glance, it looked like a romantic encounter, a couple intertwined in the heat of the moment. But one look at Emma's face was enough to tell the whole story—her eyes were wide like saucers, her body was shaking and consumed by fear; whatever was happening was anything but consensual.

"Get out! We're busy," Enzo shouted as I made a beeline towards the two of them. Drake followed after, trying, and failing, to hold me back.

"What the fuck is going on?" I shoved Enzo hard in the lower gut, right below his rib cage, knocking the wind out of him. He stumbled backward, tripped over a pair of shoes, and fell to the floor. Meanwhile, Emma scurried towards the door.

"FUCKING CHRIST. What's your problem?" Enzo peeled his body up off the ground.

"My problem is you, you piece of shit." Before he could fully recover, I stomped on his wrist. Hard.

"AH! FUCK!" Enzo winced in pain.

"Dani. Stop," Emma shouted from the corner of the room. "He's got a gun."

"Fuck." I turned around, and suddenly locked my eyes on the gun; it was sitting on the dresser, beside the porcelain doll.

Drake and I lunged for the weapon simultaneously. We both came up short on the dresser and bumped it hard, causing the gun and the porcelain doll to fall to the floor. The doll shattered into a million little pieces, decorating the floor in sharp shards.

Emma dropped to her knees, trying to swipe the gun up off the floor. To stop her, Enzo lunged to the ground and inadvertently elbowed her in the lip, causing her mouth to immediately swell and gush with blood. She wiped the crimson from her lips and passed the gun to me like she was a kid playing a game of hot potato.

I pointed the gun at Enzo, who was now standing on the other side of the room, reluctantly holding his hands up in surrender.

"Don't move," I ordered as I gently pushed Emma behind me, physically separating her from Enzo and my brother with my body and the loaded gun. The floorboards creaked with every step as we cautiously backed out of the room; the muffled sound of the party was still humming through the walls behind us.

"You're bluffing," Enzo said as he nursed his injured wrist. "Probably don't even know how to use the thing."

I removed the safety and cocked the weapon; the springy click echoed in the room. "You want to find out?"

Enzo took a step forward. "You wouldn't do it."

I took a deep breath and stared Enzo down.

Enzo took another step forward.

"Dani. Come on. Don't be stupid," Drake half pleaded.

My fingers were shaking violently against the trigger.

Enzo took another step forward. "Just hand me the gun."

"Not another move." I swallowed hard.

"Or else, what?" Enzo scoffed. "You're going to shoot me?" He took yet another step forward.

Suddenly, Emma reached into her bag and pulled out a small can of pepper spray. She lunged towards Enzo, smothering his face and eyes with the fumes.

"AH! FUCK!" he shrieked in pain and dropped to his knees.

"Holy shit," I muttered under my breath. My eyes widened as I removed my aim from Enzo.

"Dani. Let's go. Now," Emma demanded as she grabbed my hand and pulled me out of the room, down the hall, and towards the front door.

I grabbed a set of keys from a table in the foyer and slammed the front door as we left.

* * *

My hands forcefully gripped the steering wheel of my aunt's black Mercedes as we peeled out of the driveway; the tires screeched as I pressed my foot down firmly against the accelerator. My heart was racing, and my breath was turbulent. I glanced over at the passenger seat beside me; Emma sat curled up with her arms wrapped tightly around her own body. She gazed out the window at the road beneath us, her head pressed against the cool glass window. She breathed deeply, her body shaking from the combination of fear and adrenaline.

"Dani, stop the car," Emma said suddenly. I pulled off the highway immediately. The car slowed to a stop, and the tires gently crinkled against the wet gravel. Without wasting a moment, she clutched the door handle and swung it open. She leaned her torso towards the ground and immediately vomited.

"Emma—" I said weakly, my heart breaking at the sight of her distress. I felt totally and completely helpless. "Are you ok? Fuck. What am I saying? Of course, you're not ok. Your lip. Should I take you to a doctor? Shit. I'm sorry, Emma—I'm so sorry."

"Where's the gun?" she demanded, shutting the sedan door abruptly.

I tilted my head towards the back seat, motioning to the weapon resting on the cushy leather surface.

"Unload it."

"Ok." I turned around, grabbed the gun, then carefully removed the magazine. I held out the weapon, displaying its emptiness.

"How'd you know how to do that?"

"My uncle."

Emma locked her gaze with mine as if trying to discern whether or not I was telling the truth. "What kind of person teaches a kid to use a handgun?"

"He's really into—like—security." I paused. "He thinks everyone should know how to use a weapon."

"Security? So, like, what? For protection?"

I nodded.

"Why would your uncle need that kind of protection?"

I shrugged, knowing I'd never be able to provide a satisfactory answer.

Emma motioned for me to hand her the gun. I cautiously passed her the weapon, and she examined it thoroughly, running her hands along the side. "Dani, the serial number's been scratched off. That's incredibly illegal."

"I know."

"We need to get rid of it."

"Ok," I said as I rummaged through the dashboard, eventually finding a microfiber cloth used for cleaning sunglasses. I carefully wiped down the gun to remove our fingerprints. I stepped out of the vehicle, walked towards the thick woods that bordered the highway, and with all the strength I could muster, I tossed the gun into the darkness. I walked back to the car and shut the driver's side door behind me.

"I mean, this guy—Enzo—he's obviously some type of criminal," she suddenly said. "Why was he even there? How do you even know him?"

"He's a friend of the family."

"A friend of the family? What does that even mean?"

"His stepdad works with my uncle."

"And what does that mean... exactly?"

Silence.

"Dani, what does your uncle do for a living?"

Silence.

"Dani, answer the question."

Silence.

"For fuck's sake. Answer me," she demanded.

"I don't know. Entirely."

"What do you mean, you don't know?"

I swallowed hard.

Emma took my silence as a confirmation of what we both knew she was thinking. Her eyes widened like two big saucers. "Are we safe?"

"Emma, I won't let anything happen to you. I swear."

"That wasn't what I asked, Dani. You pulled a gun on some kind of thug." She looked at me. "Are you going to be safe?" Her eyes were puffy and swollen like she might burst into a grandiose display of emotion at any second. "Answer me."

Silence.

"Dani, answer the fucking question."

"I'll be ok."

The look in her eye unmistakably said she didn't believe me. "We can't go back to Willard tonight. There's no one there right now. We'd be totally alone."

"Where do you want to go?"

"—I don't know. A hotel. Or something. Anything. That guy knows we go to Willard, Dani. What if he tries to find us?"

"Em—"

"Dani, no. We need to get out of here."

276

"Ok."

I shifted the car into drive and merged back onto the highway. We drove two hours before finding a hotel.

* * *

I heard the shower knob squeal, and the water stopped. I tapped lightly on the door, and within seconds, Emma unlocked it, opening it no more than an inch or two.

"I got this for you," I said, facing my body in the other direction, attempting to give her every ounce of privacy I could. "It'll be more comfortable for you. I think." She reached out her hand, and I gave her the cheap, oversized, tourist shirt and sweatpants that I bought from the hotel lobby. "You can have my jacket too. If you're cold."

"I'm fine," she said with a weak voice, clicking the door shut once again.

"You sure?"

"Yeah. Thanks."

I walked over to the corner of the bed, took a seat, then leaned back. I stared at the ceiling, watching the wooden fan spin above me. Suddenly, I heard the door creak open, and I popped up immediately.

"I got you water. And ice," I said meekly as I stood up from the bed and shoved my hands into my jacket pockets. "And some alcohol swabs. You know, for the cut." Emma took a seat on the corner of the bed and looked up at me with a dim, broken stare. "Do you want me to clean it for you? Or would you rather do it yourself?"

Emma shrugged. "You can do it."

"Ok." I unwrapped one of the wipes; my hands shook as I carefully placed it against Emma's swollen lip. When I finished with the cut, I turned around and grabbed an ice pack from the pile of supplies.

"It's probably better if you hold it against your cheek yourself. I might press too hard or something. I don't want to hurt you or, you know, make it worse." She took the pack, placed it against her swollen cheek, and winced slightly as the cold ice brushed her skin. "Are you sure you don't want to go to a doctor?"

"Yes, Dani. I'm sure."

"Because there's a hospital about two miles away and—"

"Dani, they'll file a police report if I show up at the hospital like this. You know that."

"We can lie. I'll tell them we got mugged or something."

"Dani."

"Really. It's no trouble. You don't even have to say anything. I'll talk to them. I just want to make sure you're ok."

"Dani, no." Her voice was stern, so I dropped the subject immediately.

"Ok." I slouched my body into a nearby chair. "How's your head? You don't think he gave you a concussion, do you?"

"Wouldn't I have blacked out if I had a concussion?"

"Not necessarily. Do you hear—like—a ringing in your ear or anything?"

"No."

"You nauseous? Or disoriented?"

"No."

"How's your balance?"

She looked up at me with a warm, delicate stare. "Dani, really, I think it looks worse than it feels."

"Ok. But maybe you should wait a few hours. You know, before you sleep. Just in case."

"I will if you want me to."

"I don't know. Maybe. But if you're really tired, I don't want to keep you from sleeping either."

"I'm not that tired. We can watch TV or something."

"Ok. Good." I got up and grabbed the remote from the other side of the room. "And you can have the bed to yourself. I'll sleep on the floor. I don't mind."

"Dani—"

"Really, it's fine. I already called and asked for an extra set of sheets."

"Dani, I won't sleep at all if you're not beside me."

"Are you sure?"

"Yes. I'm sure." She sighed deeply and pulled me onto the bed next to her. "Relax," she said softly as she curled up beside me, resting her head on my shoulder. "Just having you here is enough."

"Ok," I said skeptically, unconvinced that there wasn't something more I should be doing.

"Thank you for taking care of me, Dani. Like right now. And, you know, earlier. I don't know what would have happened if—"

"Emma, listen—" I took a deep breath. "I know you're probably completely freaked out. If you need to take a break from this and, I don't know, rethink things, I'd understand."

"Dani—"

"No, Emma. I mean it." I sighed. "It's not fair to you. You shouldn't have to deal with this."

"Dani—"

"No. Really. I didn't see this coming. And I should have. Of all people, *I* should have known."

She locked her eyes on mine. "Dani, none of this is your fault."

"How can you say that? You never would have been in that situation if it wasn't for me. I never should have—"

"Dani!" she half shouted. "Will you just listen to me? I don't care. I don't care about any of that. That's *them*. It's not *you*. You're nothing like them."

"Em—"

"I'm not going anywhere. Not now. Not ever."

"But I want you to know that you could."

"Dani, stop."

"Really, Em. We could still be friends and everything. I'd understand. Completely." I paused, taking a deep breath. "You should be with someone normal."

"Dani, I don't want normal. I want you." She leaned in and planted a kiss on my lips. "Dani, I love you." She tilted my head up, forcing me to meet her gaze.

"I love you too, Em."

"Then there's nothing more to talk about."

30
WATER AND WEATHER

"Morning," I said as I handed Emma an oversized cappuccino.

She smiled and took a sip. "You brought me coffee?"

"Of course." I smiled. "I'd never be foolish enough to think you could start the day without your daily dose of caffeine."

"Thanks."

"You're welcome." I took a seat on the side of the bed. "So, where do you want to go?"

"We're going someplace?"

"Well, yeah. I mean, you said you didn't want to go back to Willard yet, and there's still a few days left of break. So, I figured we could at least make the best of it and do something fun—unless you'd rather take it easy and relax. We could just stay here. I think they have a pool and—"

Emma smiled. "No, that sounds great, Dani."

I smiled. "Good. So where do you want to go?"

"Honestly, I have no idea. I don't even know where we are."

"Good point." I grabbed my phone and opened up the GPS. "Let's see…"

"What's it say?"

I frowned and furrowed my brow. "It says we're in the middle of nowhere."

"Ha-ha." She smiled lightly and tapped me on the arm. "C'mon, let me see that."

Emma scanned the map on my phone, her fingers running delicately across the screen, tracing the potential routes in her mind's eye. "Scranton—"

"—gross."

"Williamsport."

"—no."

"Ithaca… Buffalo… Rochester…"

"Wait," I playfully grabbed the phone from Emma's grasp and studied the screen carefully. "I know where we're going. You're going to love it. But it's a bit of a drive…"

"I don't mind." She smiled. "So long as you let me stop every now and then, you know, to check out the weird roadside attractions."

"Deal."

* * *

I clutched the steering wheel as Emma held her hand out the window, letting the breeze flow through her fingertips.

As we neared our destination, a low rumble emanated from the landscape around us. With each passing moment, the bellowing moan of nature grew louder, transforming into a magnificent roar within a matter of minutes.

I parked the car, and Emma leaped out of the vehicle, eager to stretch her limbs after the four-and-a-half-hour drive.

"C'mon," she said as she grabbed my wrist, dragging me away from the car.

"Jesus. There must be, like, a million people here," I muttered under my breath as we sifted our way through a crowd, snaking in and out of tour groups and vacationing families.

"Well, it is one of the most famous waterfalls on the planet."

"I guess," I said with a shrug as we ambled towards Terrapin Point, one of the better-known American-side views of Niagara Falls.

I watched as Emma approached the railing, completely awestruck by the view.

I walked closer and suddenly felt the loud thunder of water gushing and plunging onto the rocks below. A dense mist floated up from the falls and dampened my hair and skin.

Emma turned around and locked her gaze with mine. She let out a slight laugh, just now realizing I was standing a full four feet behind her, keeping my distance from the railing. "What are you doing back there?" she said as she tilted her head and held out her hand. "Come here."

I shoved my hands inside my jacket pockets and took a step back, distancing myself even further from the edge. "I'm good. Thanks."

"You're serious?"

"Yeah. I can see it fine from here."

Emma furrowed her brow. "Oh, come on, you big baby. Stand next to me." She grabbed me by the sleeve and pulled me closer. I dragged my feet slightly, reluctantly obliging. I crept up beside her, peering over at the view from behind her shoulder. "See. That's not so bad. Is it?" she said, nudging me playfully in the side.

"I'm getting vertigo just from looking at it."

"You are not."

"—am too."

"Oh, come on. Admit it. It's kind of amazing," Emma said, pressing her body against the iron railing, leaning over to get a better view.

"Yeah, *amazingly* terrifying."

"I can't believe you sometimes," Emma said with a slight chuckle. "You're tough as nails when it comes to just about everything… but a little water and nature brings you to your knees."

"Well, I'm sure with the right emotional support, I could get through it." I smiled and wrapped my arms around her, slipping my fingers into hers, holding her hand tightly.

"Dani," Emma said as she turned back towards me, locking her unmistakably surprised gaze with mine.

"Yeah?"

"You're holding my hand."

"Oh, sorry," I said as my face turned a light shade of pink. "Would you rather I didn't?"

I pulled my hand away, and she stopped me, laughing as she wrapped her fingers back in between mine. "Of course, I want to hold your hand. You've just never—you know—done that before. In public. With *hundreds* of people around." She smiled, looking around at the bustling crowd around us.

I smiled and moved my body in close to hers. "I'd be willing to kiss you too, you know, if you'd let me."

Emma smiled. "You know you don't have to ask."

I slipped my hand behind her neck and pulled her in close, kissing her gently on the lips. "Shit. Sorry." I pulled away from her suddenly. "I forgot about the cut. I didn't hurt you, did I?"

"No." She smiled. "In fact, it was the best kiss I've ever had."

"Liar."

"It's the truth." She moved her hands up from my waist, wrapping them tightly around my neck. "I'd forgotten how nice the occasional public display of affection could be."

A wide smile emerged between my cheeks, my eyes relishing the twinkle in her baby blue stare.

"C'mon." I grabbed her hand.

"Where are we going?"

"Don't you want to go on one of those stupid boats that float right up to the edge or something?"

"Yeah. But I figured you wouldn't. You know, given that you're a scaredy-cat and all."

"I am. And I don't." I smiled. "But I will for you. You know, if you promise to catch me when I inevitably keel over from blind terror."

She smiled. "Deal."

* * *

"You feel any better?" Emma asked, struggling to hold back laughter.

"Don't you think it's a little mean to laugh at me? I don't think I've ever been so sick in my life." I smiled and sipped an oversized soda; the carbonation soothed the tumultuous knots inside my stomach.

"I'm not laughing at you. I swear," Emma said as she bit her lip, attempting to suppress yet another chuckle.

"Liar." I grinned and opened the car door for Emma. She slouched into the passenger's seat, and I walked around to the other side, plopping down into the driver's side of the vehicle.

"I'm sorry," she said as she shut the passenger door behind her. "I just sort of thought you were, you know, exaggerating the whole time. I didn't actually think you were going to get sick."

"Me neither, actually," I said as I put the key into the ignition and the lights inside the car illuminated all at once.

"Thanks for doing it, though."

"You're welcome. I'm actually sort of glad we did." I paused. "It was kind of *amazing*. You know, up until that last part when it was really *horrible*."

She smiled and placed her hand in mine as I steered the car down the long highway road.

"Have you heard from Madeline or Whitney yet?" Emma suddenly asked.

I pulled out my phone, only to discover it was dead. I held it up with a shrug as Emma reached into her purse, grabbed her own phone, and confirmed her battery was also completely drained.

"I wonder how long we've been off the grid?"

I shrugged. "We can stop and buy a charger if you want."

"No. That's ok."

The clock on the dashboard blinked 7:00 p.m., and I looked over at Emma.

"We've still got a few hours before it gets too late. If there's anything else you want to do."

Emma shrugged. "No. We should probably head back."

"You sure?"

"Yeah." She sighed. "They'll expect us back at Willard on Monday, and we're hours away. Plus, we'll need to get your aunt's car back before classes start."

I smiled. "Yeah. Something tells me she's going to lose her mind when she realizes I took it."

"Yeah." She smiled. "I hope you're not, like, grounded for a lifetime."

"Me too. I'll drop you off at Willard first, you know, so you don't have to come back with me."

"Dani, I wouldn't let you go alone."

"Emma, I'd feel better if you were at Willard. Whitney and Madeline should be there by now. You can just hang around with them until I get back. I won't have to worry that way."

"But then I'll have to worry. About you."

"Really, Em. I'll be fine. My uncle should be home by now. You've got nothing to worry about."

"Dani, no. I'm coming with you," she said sternly.

"Ok," I said reluctantly as she pulled my hand up to her lips and planted a kiss on my fingertips.

"I'm sort of sorry this has to end. You know, being here. A hundred miles away from everyone," Emma said with a doleful expression.

"If you want, we can knock off a liquor store after you graduate. That way, we'll have another excuse to go out on the lam."

"Could we? Please?" Emma let a slight laugh escape her lips just as her expression transformed into something more serious. She sighed deeply. "It was just sort of nice, you know, *being* with you, like, without worrying what anyone was going to think about it. It felt so—"

"—normal?"

"—incredible."

I smiled. "You know, Em, I was sort of thinking—" I took a deep breath, "—if you still wanted to tell Madeline and Whitney, you know—about us—I wouldn't object."

Emma smiled wide, her blue eyes glistening as she locked her gaze with mine. "Wow, Dani. I don't know what to say."

"It's not a big deal."

"Yes, Dani. It is."

I shrugged.

"And you're sure? I don't want you to feel pressured like you have to."

"Yeah, Em, I'm sure. I mean, unless you've changed your mind."

"I haven't."

"Ok. Good."

"But I do have one condition," Emma said as a loving smile emerged between her cheeks.

"Yeah?"

"That we tell them together."

"Deal."

Emma smiled wide and raised her eyebrows playfully. "Dani, pull over."

I obliged, steering the vehicle off the highway and into the parking lot of an empty rest stop. The parking lot was dark, illuminated only by the tungsten glow of a single streetlight. A small cloud of dust emerged around the sedan as I pulled the car to a stop.

"What? Did you need to use the restroom or something?" I asked as Emma opened the passenger door and hopped out of the car. "Em?" My eyes watched her curiously as she climbed into the backseat and shut the door behind her.

She cozied her body into the plush leather fabric and leaned forward, smiling flirtatiously. "Come here," she said with a grin as I suddenly felt her hands grab each corner of my jacket. She kissed me and pulled me up and over the seat, into the back of the car beside her.

She climbed on top of me and wrapped her arms around my shoulders, pressing the weight of her body against my own. She tenderly bit my lip and slid my body down onto the back seat, smothering me in the warm, welcomed weight of her own flesh.

* * *

Darkness surrounded the vehicle, and condensation filled the windows. We sat curled up in the backseat, my jacket thrown over our partially clothed bodies like a blanket. I relaxed my head against Emma's chest, our limbs intertwined as I listened to her heartbeat.

"So, Emma, I've got a serious question for you."

"What is it, Dani?" she asked and looked at me curiously.

"How do you feel about, you know, turning me into some kind of cliché?"

She raised an eyebrow skeptically. "What do you mean I turned you into a cliché?"

I grinned wide. "Well, now I'm just another sixteen-year-old girl that got seduced by a good-looking senior in the backseat of a flashy car."

Emma tapped me playfully on the arm. "Stop that."

"What?" I smirked. "It's technically the truth."

"Well, I hope you don't feel cheap and used." She playfully poked me in the side.

"I don't. You bought me a soda and a burger before I put out, so I know you really care and I'm not just another notch on your belt."

"It's amazing how you always manage to crack a joke in the most sentimental of moments," she said with a furrowed brow and playfully disapproving tone.

"C'mon. You thought it was funny."

"You think?"

"Kind of, yes."

"Dani—"

"Yeah?"

"I love you."

"I love you, too, Em."

"You aren't going to make another joke, are you?"

"No." I smiled. "There's nothing funny about that. You mean the world to me, Emma."

Emma pulled me close and ran her fingers gently through my hair. I felt my eyes grow heavy, and eventually, I drifted to sleep.

* * *

"Dani. Wake up," Emma said just above a whisper as she gently shook my body.

"What?" I asked as I rubbed my sleepy eyes, looking up at Emma. Her gaze shifted towards the window, and she tilted her head in the same direction, motioning for me to turn around.

"Fuck," I said under my breath as I twisted my body, locking eyes with the police officer standing at the passenger window as the harsh red and blue glow of trooper lights poured through the back of our car.

Emma grabbed her shirt and held it against her chest, attempting to cover her partially clothed body. I scrambled to slip my arms through my jacket and wrapped the edges around my chest, covering my bra. The officer motioned for me to hurry up, and I leaned over, rolling down the window.

"License and registration."

"Right." I sighed and rolled my eyes. "It's in the front glove compartment. Can I step out of the vehicle and grab it?"

The officer nodded and motioned with the flashlight for me to get out of the car. My hands shook as I fumbled through the glovebox, eventually finding the necessary documents. I handed the paperwork to the officer and slumped my body back into the sedan.

The officer let out a weak grunt of acknowledgment and walked back to his sedan. Within moments, the officer returned.

"I'm going to need you both to step out of the vehicle," the officer said with a stern voice.

"Uh, ok, sir," I said, as Emma and I slid our bodies across the back seat, stepping out of the car. "Can I ask why?"

"You're under arrest."

"Excuse me?" Emma said, completely dumbfounded. "What did we do?"

"You're in possession of a stolen vehicle."

I rolled my eyes, realizing that my aunt had reported the car stolen. "The car belongs to my aunt. I'm sure if we could just call her and explain. You don't need to arrest us, sir."

"—you have the right to remain silent."

I placed my hands behind my back, allowing the officer to cuff my wrists with ease. I stood with my face pressed against the vehicle as he did the same to Emma.

* * *

My aunt wasn't pressing charges, so the police released Emma almost immediately. Since she was eighteen, she didn't need a parent or guardian to pick her up, so she called Madeline and Whitney to come get her. Since I was a minor, I could only be released into the custody of a guardian.

Sometime in the afternoon, Sofi arrived at the station. I was relieved to see her instead of my aunt, and she gave me a sort of half-assed hug as we walked out of the little building into the parking lot.

We drove back home in silence mostly. I stared out the window and pulled my jacket around my torso, cocooning my body in its warmth.

We drove in silence for miles and miles until eventually, we arrived back home. Sofi clicked the little garage door opener, and I started to get out of the car when suddenly, Sofi grabbed me by the hand.

"Daniella, wait."

That was odd. Sofi never called me by my full name.

"Tony's inside."

"Ok," I said as I studied her facial expression, trying to decode what exactly she was playing at. We spent nearly three silent hours alone in the car together—why would she choose this particular moment to strike up a conversation?

"He's really—"

"Pissed?"

"Yeah." She swallowed hard. "So is your aunt."

I shrugged. I wasn't surprised. I knew I was dead from the moment

I took my aunt's car. It was just a matter of time before the inevitable retribution.

"It's just—" She took a deep breath and looked me in the eye. "We need to talk. Before you go in there."

"About what?"

She fidgeted with her fingers and opened her mouth to say something, then stopped herself suddenly.

"Well?" I pressed on.

"It's just that—" She paused for another excruciatingly long moment as if searching for just the right words. "Your brother told them. About you and your friend."

"What's that supposed to mean?"

Sofi furrowed her brow. "Dani, I think you know what it means."

Silence.

"I just—" Sofi paused as if trying to formulate the right words. "I thought you should know that. So you aren't caught off guard."

"I don't know what you're talking about," I snapped as I let myself out of the car. But we both knew I did.

* * *

"Upstairs. Now," Tony barked as soon as I walked into the house. I didn't argue. I could tell he was furious.

To say I was in trouble would be a gross understatement. I was grounded indefinitely—and wouldn't be returning to Willard until my aunt and uncle figured out the appropriate solution to my "problem." I kept trying to convince myself that once the initial shock of it all had worn off, things would go back to normal. Once they had some time to adjust, everything would be ok. But the sinking feeling in my gut was an ever-present reminder of the truth; things were never going to go back to normal… whatever the hell normal even meant.

I spent most of that evening sitting perched on top of the stairs, listening to Olivia and Tony argue. Olivia kept throwing around these euphemisms…

Confused.

Misguided.

Experimentation.

"This little *thing*" was all "just a phase." With a little time, I would apparently "grow out of it."

Tony's anger was palpable, and his words harsher. Less sedated. More direct. He didn't beat around the bush. And he yelled. A lot. It was hard to believe he was talking about me. It sounded like he was talking about someone else. Someone horrible.

Sick.

Disgusting.

Wrong.

It went on like that for a few hours at least. I sat curled up on the top of the stairs, leaning against the wooden banister, wondering what would happen.

I thought about denying it. Running downstairs and saying it wasn't true. That Drake had lied. That I wasn't like *that*. That I was normal. Just like everybody else. That it was all just some misunderstanding.

But I couldn't do it.

I didn't want to lie anymore.

I didn't want to pretend I was someone that I wasn't.

I pressed my fingers against my tear ducts, attempting to suppress the emotional swell rising within me. Then, suddenly, I heard a noise from down the hall. I turned around slowly and narrowed my eyes. Drake was standing in the shadows, watching me.

I locked my eyes with his, studying his expression. His lips were dry and cracked, and his hair was greasy and unkempt. His brown eyes were cold, lifeless, not showing the slightest glint of emotion. "You told them," I finally said.

Silence.

"You told them," I said again, firmly.

Silence.

"That's it? You aren't even going to say anything?"

"What do you want me to say?" he snapped.

"I don't know, Drake. How about an apology?"

"I'm not apologizing. I didn't do shit."

"Are you kidding? You totally fucked me over. You. Told. Them."

"Is that all you care about? Your little gay ass secret? Because in case you forgot, you pulled a gun on Enzo fuckin' Gatti. You remember that? You got any idea how much shit I've got to deal with because of you?"

"Oh, please, Drake. You're not the victim here."

"And you are?"

"Drake, you're my brother. We're family. You're supposed to have my back. I thought I could trust you."

Drake scoffed. "If it didn't come from me, it was going to come from Enzo. He was tellin' fucking everybody. Everyone knows. Ton' was going to find out eventually."

"So?"

"So, you should be thanking me. I did you a fuckin' favor. Did you want him to find out from someone else? From some fuckin' douche bag on the street talking shit? You got any idea how fucked you'd be if Ton' found out from a stranger? If he was just Shanghaied with no warning?"

Silence.

"This is your own damn fault. You know that, right? It's fucked up. It's embarrassing. *You're* embarrassing."

I suddenly stopped and turned around. "You done?"

He rolled his eyes.

Silence.

"Good. Because so are we." And I meant it. I wanted Drake out of my life. For good.

31

DANI AND ENZO

I brushed past Drake and made a beeline for my room. By now, it was nearly midnight. I furiously slammed my door and went to work packing my things. My mind was racing. I didn't have a plan exactly; I just knew I needed to get the hell out of here. Away from my brother. Away from my aunt and uncle. Away from everything.

I started strategizing my next moves. Madeline's dad was a lawyer. Maybe I could file for emancipation. My grades were good enough for a scholarship. I could stay at Willard or transfer to a different school; room and board would be covered, so long as I stayed in the boarding school system.

I could do this.

I could figure it out.

I didn't need *them*.

I grabbed my phone and tried to call Em, but it went straight to voicemail. Her cell was still dead, apparently.

"Em. Call me when you get this." I hung up and stashed the phone in my back pocket.

I hurled my bag over my shoulder, walked out onto the balcony, and slipped my leg over the railing. I looked back at my bedroom. My eyes scanned the pink walls, my frilly white sheets, the empty spot on my dresser where the porcelain doll used to sit.

I took a deep breath and waited patiently for Olivia to barge through my bedroom door, for someone to stop me—for someone to give a shit. But no one came. I could still hear their muffled voices from the living room, fighting about what to do with me.

I took another deep breath and pressed on.

I hurled my body onto the limb of the tree and shimmied down the trunk. I fell with a thud, and my shoes squished against the moist grass. The cold air brushed my cheeks as I made my way out of the backyard, into the neighborhood streets.

The gravel crackled against the thick soles of my boots, and I mumbled under my breath, fully immersed in my plan. I'd go to the bus station and get the first ticket to Willard.

And then I heard something.

I stopped suddenly, turning slowly, looking curiously behind me. I held my breath and listened again.

Silence.

I tightened my grip on my bag and walked a little faster, assuming whatever I had heard must have been a small nocturnal animal. Something unsuspicious, unalarming.

I looked around at the road in front of me, the trees beside me, the dark shadowy buildings that surrounded me. Spooky orange patches of light leaked from the streetlamps across the asphalt; the tungsten glow drizzled softly into the shadows.

Everything looked different at night.

Empty.

Hopeless.

Hollow.

I stopped again.

I could have sworn I heard the sound of crunching leaves.

Silence.

I swallowed hard and quickened my pace.

I felt the pain of a blister forming on the sole of my left foot. I stopped under the glow of a tungsten streetlight to adjust my shoe. Suddenly, a beam of light shone through the crisp foggy air. I turned my head and spotted a sedan about a half-mile down the road. The headlights shone in my direction, half blinding me with their heavy gleam.

The car whirled past me, kicking up some dirt and gravel as it raced down the road.

"Asshole," I murmured under my breath as I slipped my shoe back on and tightened the laces.

Almost instantly, the car screeched to a stop.

"Fuck," I said with a sinking feeling in my gut.

"Holy, shit. It's her!" I heard a voice say as the car shifted into reverse and plowed back in my direction. My blood boiled when I saw who, specifically, was exiting the vehicle. It was Enzo, his roommate Tits, and a third guy I'd never met before.

They slammed their car doors shut, and I dropped my bag, immediately sprinting in the opposite direction.

"GET HER!" I heard Enzo shout at the top of his lungs.

I bolted back down the main street; my feet crashed against the asphalt with hard heavy steps. I looked behind me. I had a hundred yards on them easily. Tits was lagging behind, I could outrun him no problem, but Enzo and the other guy—they were bigger, faster, and gaining on me with every passing moment.

I pressed forward, quickening my pace. The rubber soles of my boots resonated through the empty streets, echoing against the cement and asphalt with every step.

My heart was racing.

My breath was shallow.

Inhale.

Exhale.

Inhale.

Exhale.

A sharp pain suddenly gnawed at my side; I felt sick. My adrenaline couldn't sustain me much longer. My legs felt like lead—hollow and insufficient to outrun the men.

I took a sharp turn into a park. It was dark. My heart thumped in my chest as I dashed behind a tall, round tree, hiding my body against the trunk. I held my breath.

"Where'd she go?" Tits shouted as he caught up to Enzo and the other guy.

Silence.

I held my breath.

Suddenly, my phone went off. It was Emma, calling me back.

"Fuck." I fumbled with the phone and tossed it into the grass, sprinting as fast as I could in the opposite direction.

"Over there!"

My feet sprang against the muddy ground, propelling my body forward with all the strength I could muster. Suddenly, I tripped and came crashing down into the mud face first.

"Got her." The guy I didn't recognize grabbed me by the back of the neck. I winced in pain.

"Don't touch me." I kicked and struggled with all my might; it was no use. This guy was easily twice my size.

"Well, I'll be damned." Enzo grinned wide. "It's my lucky day."

"Let me go." I shrieked and kicked some more.

"Calm down. I just want to talk. You know, come to an understanding." He wiped the corner of his nose with his sleeve. His eyes were red and foggy.

"Sorry—but I'm not in a very kumbaya sort of mood."

"Me neither." Enzo spit, struggling to catch his breath. "I want my gun back."

"I don't have it."

"Then we'll go get it. Together."

"Can't."

He laughed a long, slow sort of chuckle. "And why the fuck not?"

"Because it's somewhere off the side of Highway 87."

"That better be some kind of a fuckin' joke." He grabbed me by the collar and leaned in close to my face, like an angry drill sergeant berating a new recruit.

I stared back, totally deadpan. "I'm not afraid of you, Enzo." I tried to yank my body away from his firm grasp.

"Maybe not. But you should be."

I spit in his face.

"CUNT." He pulled back his fist, and I felt his knuckles collide with my cheek; my entire body numbed as the heavy, overpowering shock knocked me to the ground with a hard thud. He grunted and kicked me in the abdomen. A thick, hollow pain echoed through my insides. I gasped for air but couldn't get enough, like my lungs were constricted.

"Bro, she's a girl. C'mon," Tits suddenly pleaded, visibly uncomfortable with the sudden escalation of violence.

"She's not a girl. She's a fuckin' dyke." He kicked me again. I winced in pain and gasped for air. My insides burned and spasmed like a bolt of electricity had ignited my core.

"Get up," he commanded as he pulled back his leg back to kick me again, but before he could get another whack into my side, Tits grabbed Enzo's shoulder firmly.

"Christ, man, it's Tony's kid. Let it go."

"Yeah, c'mon. You made your point. Let's go," the third guy pleaded.

"You got a problem, you two can get the fuck out of here," Enzo snapped back at the two guys, who just sort of stared back dumbfounded.

"Go!" Enzo shouted.

The guys backed away slowly.

"I said *go*, you fucks!" Enzo shouted, and the guys immediately ran off in the other direction.

I coughed heavily, dry heaving while holding my midsection, attempting to protect myself from another blow.

"Get up," Enzo demanded.

I didn't move.

"I said, *get up*." He forcefully grabbed my hoodie and tugged me up off the ground, holding me tightly in his grasp. "You scared yet?"

Silence.

He plucked a switchblade out of his pocket and ran his fingers along the sharp tip. He moved in close, strengthened his grip on my arm, and ran the blade of the knife against my chest. He pressed his body against mine and whispered in my ear. "You ever been with a man?"

I spit on the ground. My lip was bleeding.

He smiled and moved the blade up from my chest, pressing it firmly against my neck. He placed his free hand behind my neck, using his thumb to gently part my lips.

I took a deep breath as he traced the outline of my lips with his fingertips, the knife still pressed rigidly against my flesh.

The silence was deafening; the only audible sound was the steady pulse of my breath.

Inhale.

Exhale.

Inhale.

Exhale.

He traced the knife down from my neck, across my chest, and released a low, breathy chuckle.

It was now or never.

I lifted my leg and kicked with all the force I could muster. As my boot collided with his testicles, he screamed, dropped the knife, and fell instantly to his knees, completely incapacitated.

"BITCH!" he shouted as he stumbled and staggered back up to his feet. I ran in the other direction. Enzo trailed close behind.

He reached forward and grabbed a fist full of my hair, pulling me back towards him. Surprised by the force, I tripped and fell, landing on my wrist, sending blinding pain through my entire body.

He pinned me down on the ground with the weight of his body. I winced as his firm grasp pierced my skin, his nails digging into my flesh.

"Don't touch me," I screamed as he climbed on top of me.

"I'll do whatever the fuck I want," Enzo said with an annoyed groan as I struggled to break free. He strengthened his grip and leaned in close, whispering in my ear. "The more you struggle, the worse it's going to be."

"Let me go." My voice was brittle and weak.

He grabbed me by the jaw and forced his mouth onto mine.

I bit him.

"Cunt!" He grabbed me firmly by the hair and shoved his palm firmly against my cheeks, pushing my skull into the cold, grassy dirt while he used his free hand to undo his belt. I froze; my body was completely consumed by fear as he tore at the button and zipper on my jeans. I stared up at the dark sky, watching the trees rattle in the wind, accepting my fate with complete and utter helplessness.

CLICK.

I heard the unmistakable sound of a cocked weapon. My body froze. I didn't dare move a muscle.

"Lay another hand on her, and I'll end you," I heard a scratchy voice say with the indomitable presence of a soldier. My gaze fell from the dark sky and rested finally on the scene in front of me. I was both relieved and horrified at the sight of Lou Collins, the mysterious man with the Marlboros, coming to my defense.

He pressed the matte black handgun firmly against Enzo's skull. His hand was steady, his nerves unflappable, the calm in his voice unnerving.

Enzo took a deep breath, immediately recognizing the springy click of a cocked weapon. "Go away, old man," he scoffed, though his body was completely frozen. "This doesn't concern you."

"It's loaded." Lou shoved the gun deeper into his skull. "And I won't lose an ounce of sleep over pulling the trigger. Get off."

Enzo lifted his body up and off of mine and turned to face Lou. "Do you have any idea who the fuck I am?"

"I know who you are."

"Then you know you're a fucking dead man." Enzo wiped his mouth.

"Go. Now. I'm not going to tell you again."

Enzo spit on the ground. He narrowed his eyes and swallowed hard, focusing all of his attention on Lou. He licked his lip and smirked a wide cocky grin. And then, suddenly, without warning, Enzo lunged towards Lou. I watched as Enzo propelled his body forward, like a linebacker ready to take down his opponent. Enzo landed the tackle, dipping his shoulder hard into Lou's chest.

Lou released a loud breathy grunt but miraculously, he didn't falter. He firmly stood his ground. Enzo scratched and pawed at the weapon, trying to release the gun from Lou's grasp.

And then I heard it.

The deafening, horrible, hollow sound.

Lou fired the gun three times.

Instinctively, I cowered and curled my body, covering my head for protection from any stray fire.

And then everything was silent.

Inhale.

Exhale.

Inhale.

Exhale.

The wind rustled against the trees. I swallowed hard and uncovered my head, unsure if I was actually safe. I looked up and saw Enzo. His eyes were wide, filled with shock. He teetered back away from Lou as crimson blood slowly soaked his shirt. He staggered for a few moments, and then suddenly, his limp body collapsed onto the ground.

Lou's eyes were cold, steady, unwavering. "Stupid fuckin' kid." Lou holstered his gun back to his belt and gently tipped Enzo's body with the sole of his shoe as if ensuring his victim was actually dead.

"Holy shit," I muttered in a breathy whisper as I stared wide-eyed at the scene in front of me. Enzo's eyes were open, staring straight ahead with a stiff, dazed sort of expression. His body was cold and lifeless. It was strange to think that only a few minutes before, the corpse in front of me had been so incredibly full of life.

"You ok, kid?" Lou asked as he walked towards me.

I nodded.

"Good," he said as he picked himself up off the ground. He pulled a flask out of his back pocket and took a long swig.

"How'd you know I was here?" I asked suddenly.

"I didn't." Lou wiped his brow.

"But you saved me—you must have—"

"Coincidence."

"I don't—I don't get it."

"Look, it's not personal 'er anything. That kid's been on contract for months—been followin' him. Waitin' for the right moment."

"Someone put a hit on Enzo? Why?"

Lou was silent for a moment... then shrugged, suddenly, as if there wasn't much point to concealing the truth. "The stupid fuck killed yer cousin."

"Wait. You mean—Enzo did it? Enzo killed Robert?"

Lou nodded. "It was supposed to be a cleaner job. No witnesses. But given the circumstances—I expect you'll keep yer mouth shut?"

I nodded.

* * *

It was nearly 3:00 a.m. by the time we got home. I carefully opened the front door. The house was dark and lifeless; Olivia had gone to bed. My uncle was still up. I could see a light from his office down the hall.

My stomach churned as I hobbled towards the light. Lou followed me inside, like a shepherd steering me on course.

I knocked lightly on Tony's office door.

"What?" my uncle barked as the door slowly creaked open.

"Ton'." I barely managed to say. He was reading and didn't even bother to look up at me.

"Yer grounded. Get back in yer room."

"We need to talk."

"I got nothin' to say," he said, refusing to look up at me.

"You, eh, might want to hear her out," Lou said, suddenly entering the room from behind me.

My uncle finally looked up from his desk, locking his eyes on Lou and then me, suddenly registering my injuries.

"What's going on?" He looked at me with wide eyes as I stepped aside and Lou entered the room behind me. My uncle stepped away from his desk and studied my bruised eye, my bloodied lip, my limp stance. The anger in him instantly disintegrated, transforming into sincere concern. "Who did this?"

"I need your help," I said, suddenly releasing a swell of emotion. Tears streamed down my cheeks uncontrollably. I was battered. Bruised. Terrified.

It was only a matter of time before Carlo found out what had happened to his son. That he was dead. And it wouldn't be long before Tits and the other guy pieced it all together—that I was the last person who had seen Enzo alive.

Tony listened carefully. He nodded and waited for me to finish. After a short discussion, the decision was made. Tony would take care of everything on my behalf, so long as I agreed to his terms. Which I did. No contest. And as much as it tore me apart, I knew I didn't have a choice—it was the only way I could guarantee that we'd both be safe.

32

ARE YOU IN TROUBLE?

I took a deep breath and knocked on Emma's door.

"Come in," I heard a voice say from behind the wooden barricade. I sighed, twisted the knob, and let myself in.

"Dani!" Emma half flew out of her chair, ran towards the door, and threw her arms around me, pulling me into a tight, unequivocally loving embrace. "Jesus. Is everything ok? I thought you'd be back sooner. I tried calling but didn't get through. Was your aunt livid? Sorry. Stupid question. Of course, she was. Are you grounded?" she asked then stopped suddenly as if she had just woken from a trance. "Dani." Her voice suddenly grew weak as she pulled her arms away from mine and gently placed her hand against my cheek, examining the fresh bruise under my eye. I winced and pulled away.

"Holy shit. What happened to your face?" Madeline asked with surprisingly sincere concern as she got up from the other side of the room and approached the two of us.

"You didn't get into another fight, did you?" Whitney asked as she put down a magazine; her brow was furrowed, like she was worried but also not entirely surprised.

"No." I rolled my eyes.

Emma was silent. I felt her piercing blue stare study the shiner under my eye, attempting to decode any ounce of truth from my body language.

"So? What the hell happened?" Madeline pressed.

"Nothing."

"Nothing? Your uncle didn't—you know—do that? Did he?" Madeline asked, gesturing to my bruised face.

"I don't want to talk about it. Ok?"

"Sorry. I'm not trying to be a bitch. It's just—" Madeline raised an eyebrow. "That's one hell of a fucking bruise..."

"She's got a point, Dani." Whitney raised a curious eyebrow.

"Guys," Emma said firmly. "Why don't we talk about something else?" Madeline and Whitney shrugged and slouched back onto Emma's bed.

"Em, can we talk?" I looked at Madeline and Whitney. "Alone."

"Uh. Yeah. Sure, Dani." Emma turned to Whitney and Madeline. "We'll be right back, guys."

They watched us curiously as we left the room.

Emma shut the door, and we walked down the hall in silence, eventually wandering outside. I kicked a small rock against the pavement and sighed.

"Dani, what actually happened to your eye?" Emma suddenly broke the silence. "It looks like your cheekbone might be broken. Have you seen a doctor?"

"No."

"I can call my dad. We can send him a picture or something. He'll write a prescription if you need antibiotics or painkillers."

"Emma, no. It's fine. Really."

"It doesn't look fine, Dani."

I was silent.

"Dani. Tell me the truth. Was it that guy? Enzo?"

"Emma. Stop."

"It was him, wasn't it?"

"Emma. Really. I don't want to talk about it."

"Is it bad? Are you in trouble? Like real trouble? Because Madeline's dad's a lawyer. We could, I don't know, file a police report or restraining order against Enzo. Whatever it takes."

"Em. Just wait a minute, ok? We need to talk." I paused, barely able to formulate the words. "I need to tell you something."

"Ok, Dani." She grabbed my hand and ran her thumb gently across the tips of my fingers. "What do you want to talk about?"

"They're transferring me out of Willard. I just came back to get my things. You know, from my room. There's a car waiting for me in the lot. I don't really have much time."

"I don't understand; there are barely two months left of school."

"I know."

"Well, that seems like pretty inconvenient timing. You can't start a new school this late in the semester."

I shrugged.

"Dani, talk to me. What's going on?"

"I'm leaving. That's what's going on."

"Dani—"

I was silent.

"Where are you going? Back home? To your old school?"

"Torbay."

"Dani, that's in the UK."

"Yeah. I know."

"Is this because of the car? Because I can talk to your aunt. I'll tell her what happened. I don't mind. Really. I'm sure she'll cool off if we just—"

"Emma, it doesn't matter."

"Of course, it matters, Dani. How can you be so nonchalant about this?"

"I'm leaving tomorrow. The ticket's booked."

"What about the shiner under your eye? Does that have something to do with this?"

"I don't want to talk about that."

"Dani, I'm sorry. I just—I love you. And I'm concerned. That's all."

"I know."

Emma leaned in and kissed me softly. She pressed her forehead against my own as our lips slowly separated. There were only centimeters between us. "It'll be ok," she said softly. "I graduate in a little over a month. I'll go with you. We already talked about this. I'll get a job. We'll travel on the weekends. It's not really a change of plans. We'll only be apart for a little while. A month, two tops. And that's not so long."

"Em—"

"Yeah?"

I shut my eyes, took a deep breath, and reluctantly pulled my body away from the velvety touch of her skin, away from the warm breath against the side of my neck, away from the pleasant scent of lavender perfume. "You can't come with me."

"What?"

"I think you should go to Brown next year."

"Don't say that."

"It's the right thing to do. It's the smart thing." I paused. "And if you really want to travel, you can always study abroad or go in the summer. Going to school won't stop you from doing that. It doesn't have to anyway, not if you don't let it."

"Where is this coming from?"

"It's coming from me."

"Don't be smart, Dani."

"We both know it's the right thing for you."

"You don't mean that."

"Yes, Emma. I do."

There was a long moment of silence. "So, what happens to us?"

"What do you mean, what happens to us?"

"Don't answer my question with another question, Dani. You know what I mean."

I was silent. My eyes were locked on the ground.

"You're breaking up with me?"

"Emma—"

"I asked you a question. Answer it."

"That's not what I said."

"Well, then, what are you saying, Dani? Because you're telling me you're leaving—to another country, I might add—and now you're telling me to go to Brown. A million miles away from you. It sounds an awful lot like you're breaking up with me."

Silence.

"The least you could do is own up to it. You can lie to yourself, but I'm not going to let you lie to me."

Silence.

"I know you, Dani. I know you better than anyone. This isn't you. This isn't what you want."

Silence.

"Two days ago, you told me you loved me. More than anything. You said you were all in, Dani. You said I meant the world to you. And now, you're doing a complete one-eighty. You can't honestly tell me nothing happened. That something hasn't changed."

Silence.

"Dani, say something—"

"Emma, I don't know what to say."

"Are you still in love with me?"

"Yes."

"Then don't shut me out. We can figure this out. Together."

"There's nothing to figure out, Emma. Go to Brown." I sighed. "I want you to be safe."

"Safe? What the hell is that supposed to mean?"

Silence.

"I don't care about any of it, Dani. Your family. Enzo. Whatever. We can figure it out."

"No, Emma, we can't."

"And so what? I walk away from you, right here, right now, and we never speak to each other again?"

Silence.

"I need to hear it, Dani. I need to hear you say it. Tell me this is what you want. Tell me that you don't want to be with me."

My gaze inadvertently drifted to the ground.

"Look at me, Dani."

I obliged, locked my eyes with hers, and took a deep breath. "This is what I want, Emma."

"You know, I really hate that about you."

"What?"

"That I always know when you're lying. It would be so much easier to walk away if I believed you."

I watched her eyes well into a sea of frustrated tears. I placed my hand on hers, and she pulled it away. "I don't know what to say, Emma."

"Say that I'm wrong. Say it's the truth. Say that you don't love me. Say anything to make this feeling go away. Because the truth, Dani, it's killing me. I hate it. I hate that when I look at you, I feel like I know you better than you know yourself. I hate that I know this isn't what you want. I hate that I know you're upset and confused. And I hate that I know you're scared of fighting for this. You're scared of what that would mean."

"Em—"

"And I hate that I know that while I'm sitting here with my heart broken, you're probably taking it twice as hard. I hate that I know that it's killing you to watch me cry." She wiped a stray tear from her eye. "It makes it a lot harder to hate *you*. It makes it impossible to hate you."

She took a deep breath and regained her composure. "But mostly, Dani, I hate that knowing how you feel means nothing if you can't own up to it yourself. Because at a certain point, prying the truth out of you at every turn, struggling to keep your head in this relationship, it's not romantic, Dani. It's pathetic. I shouldn't have to work this hard. I shouldn't have to beg you to open up to me. And I shouldn't have to convince you that this is worth fighting for. So, I guess you're right, Dani. If that's what being in this relationship means, then maybe we shouldn't be together."

"Emma. I'm so sorry."

"Me too, Dani."

She wiped the tears from her eyes as she got up from the bench and shoved her hands into the pockets of her jacket. "Good luck in Torbay. I'll send Madeline and Whitney over to help you pack. I know they'll both want to say goodbye."

"Em—wait."

"Yeah, Dani?"

"I love you."

"I know you do." She whipped a stray tear from under her eye. "Goodbye, Dani."

33

GRADUATION

"Here!" Madeline said with a wide smile as she shoved a silver cell phone into Emma's palm.

"Who is it?" Emma asked with slight hesitation.

"Dani."

Emma's stomach churned. They hadn't spoken in over a month. She rolled her eyes, furious with Madeline; how could she spring this on her without so much as a warning? Of all the cruel, insensitive things to do to a person… but then her anger suddenly dissipated, and she remembered that Madeline was completely oblivious to everything that had transpired between her and Dani. And Whitney, of course, was equally oblivious.

Emma took a deep breath and pressed her fingers against her tear ducts, using every ounce of strength she had to suppress the urge to cry. She didn't want to make this any more difficult than necessary.

"Uh, hi, Dani." Her voice trembled as the words barely escaped her lips. She took a few small steps away from Madeline and Whitney, attempting to gain some semblance of privacy.

"Hey, Em." Dani's voice was weak. Tired. Like she hadn't seen a full night's rest in weeks. But also nervous. It was obvious she didn't know what to say or how to act. There was a long, awkward moment of silence. "So, the speech went well?"

"I guess." Emma's voice was curt, but unintentionally so. She simply had no idea what to say. Her mind was racing. Her heart was pounding.

"Madeline said you killed it."

Emma smiled nervously. "Honestly, Madeline and Whitney were so baked, I doubt they even know what I said."

"Sounds like Madeline… But toking up at graduation seems a little out of Whitney's wheelhouse."

"She's turned over a new leaf… you know, ever since she broke up with Dave."

"Right," Dani said with a sigh. "Well, I'm sorry I missed it."

"Me too, Dani."

"Can I read it?"

"What? My speech?"

"Yeah. I mean, if that's ok?"

"Of course, it's ok, Dani. I'll email you a copy." Emma took a deep breath, her nerves finally beginning to calm. "How's Torbay?"

"You know, the same as Willard… except the school's co-ed, doesn't belong to the Catholic church, and everybody talks funny."

Emma couldn't help but laugh. "I think they call that an accent, Dani."

"Well, it feels like I'm trapped in a Harry Potter novel."

"It's hard to sympathize with you when that kind of sounds amazing."

"No, it's terrible. Trust me." Dani smiled.

"What time is it there?"

"Almost nine-thirty."

Suddenly, Emma heard a voice on the other end of the phone.

"Dani, you coming?" the voice barked.

"Give me a minute. I'm on the phone," Dani shouted back.

"Who was that?" Emma asked.

"My roommate. Jess."

"Oh, right." Emma's stomach churned at the name: *Jess*. Someone she hadn't met before, didn't know, and probably never would meet. Emma obviously knew that life would move on, that Dani would make new friends and meet new people; but that didn't make it any easier to digest. "What's she like?"

Dani shrugged. "A lot like Madeline, actually."

"So, she's a neurotic minx?"

"That's actually a surprisingly accurate description."

"Dani—which one? The red or the blue?" Emma heard Jess yell through the garbled lines of the long-distance call.

"Red," Dani shouted back at her roommate. Her voice was gruff; she was obviously annoyed by the incessant interruptions.

"I didn't just hear you give that girl fashion advice, did I?"

"Sadly, yes." Dani laughed.

"Wow, Dani, Europe really has changed you," Emma teased. "You aren't wearing a little black dress and heels, are you? Because if so, I expect pictures."

Dani laughed. "No, Em. I'm wearing faded jeans and combat boots. Per usual."

"Well, it's nice to know some things never change." Emma faked a friendly laugh, attempting to conceal her real feelings, hoping Dani wouldn't sense a twinge of dejection in her voice. "You guys going out tonight or something?"

"Yeah, there's a pub down the street. And the drinking age here is like—you know—as soon as you can walk. So—"

"Right. Europeans." Emma sighed. "Sounds like a good time, Dani."

"It's ok."

"Thomás and the guys already left. Let's go!" the muffled voice of Dani's roommate rang through the speaker again.

"Sounds like you'd better go. You wouldn't want to keep *Thomás and the guys* waiting," Emma said with a lilt of bitter sarcasm. It was hard not to let her mind wander. And it was even harder not to feel the sharp pang of jealousy. Who was Thomás? And who were these guys waiting on them?

"Yeah. I'm sorry, Em."

"It's ok. I get it."

"Well, uh, congratulations. On everything. The speech. Graduating." Dani paused and took a deep breath. "Brown."

"Thanks, Dani."

"You're welcome." Dani sighed and contemplated her next words for a long moment. "Maybe I'll call you next week or something? We can catch up?"

"Yeah. Maybe. I mean, yes. That'd be good, Dani." Emma sighed. Even if they couldn't be together, she wanted to stay friends—regardless of how hard it might be.

"Ok, well, uh. Bye then. For now. I guess."

"Bye." Emma took a deep breath.

"Em. Wait."

"Yeah, Dani?"
"I miss you."

ABOUT
M.S. IZBICKI

M.S. Izbicki studied the craft of storytelling at Chapman University, where she received a BFA in film production. After a three-year stint playing the role of "starving artist," she decided money and health insurance had more value than she initially anticipated. Thus, she returned to school and received a boring, parent-approved MBA.

When she's not writing books, she's pretending to be a rock star. You can catch her singing lead vocals in her alt. punk band, Cigarette Juliet, and her country band, Myles and Ash.

Izbicki's other hobbies include drinking gallons of boxed wine, accidentally killing plants, spending time with her two insanely mischievous dogs, and watching endless hours of animal documentaries.

YOU CAN VISIT HER ONLINE AT:
www.melissaizbicki.com
www.cigarettejuliet.com
www.mylesandash.com

FOLLOW HER ON:
Instagram, Twitter, and TikTok @melissaizbicki

CPSIA information can be obtained
at www.ICGtesting.com
Printed in the USA
BVHW080241131022
649110BV00002B/15